I0592408

Raimundo Cabrera

Cuba and the Cubans

Raimundo Cabrera

Cuba and the Cubans

ISBN/EAN: 9783337379254

Printed in Europe, USA, Canada, Australia, Japan

Cover: Foto ©Andreas Hilbeck / pixelio.de

More available books at **www.hansebooks.com**

CUBA AND THE CUBANS

BY

RAIMUNDO CABRERA

AUTHOR OF "MIS BUENOS TIEMPOS," "LOS ESTADOS UNIDOS,"
"IMPRESIONES DE VIAJE," ETC., ETC. MEMBER OF THE BAR
OF CUBA. PROVINCIAL EX-DEPUTY. MEMBER OF THE
EXECUTIVE COMMITTEE OF THE CUBAN AUTONO-
MIST PARTY, ETC.

TRANSLATED FROM THE EIGHTH SPANISH EDITION OF
"CUBA Y SUS JUECES"
BY LAURA GUITERAS

REVISED AND EDITED BY

LOUIS EDWARD LEVY

AND COMPLETED WITH

A SUPPLEMENTARY APPENDIX BY THE EDITOR

ILLUSTRATED WITH 124 ENGRAVINGS AND A MAP

PHILADELPHIA
THE LEVYTYPE COMPANY
1896

TO

THE MEMORY OF HER BELOVED UNCLE

EUSEBIO GUITÉRAS

THIS TRANSLATION IS DEDICATED

BY HIS NIECE

LAURA GUITÉRAS

EDITOR'S PREFACE.

—

At a time when the condition of Cuba and its people has been forced upon the attention of the civilized world by another sanguinary contest between Spain and its Great Antillan colony, there is no need of an apology for the appearance of the present work.

The American people, especially, have an abiding interest in Cuba, not alone as a matter of sentiment, but by reason of extensive commercial relations with the island and of the important economic facts resulting from those relations; the condition of Cuba and the Cubans largely concerns us, and a disturbance of those conditions affects our material interests in many ways. Since the beginning of 1895 the prolonged contention between the Cuban colonists and the mother country, which in the past has resulted in numerous insurrections and in a devastating civil war of ten years' duration, has again been taken out of the domain of parliamentary discussion by a resort to force. The political agitation for administrative reforms and a due measure of self government which has constantly and persistently been maintained by the progressive parties among the Cuban people, especially since the failure of the Spanish government to develope the reforms agreed upon by the Compromise of 1878, has again been replaced by an insurrectionary movement that has spread over the greater part of the island of Cuba. Again the Cuban question, turgid with the wrongs of centuries, distorted by social misconceptions and by political chicanery, an anachronism at the close of the 19th century, is illuminated by the torch of war.

But the gleam of battle fire illuminates an historic subject in but a garish and imperfect light. Its various phases are brought out in gross relief against a sombre background and such presentations are necessarily misleading in their nature. In the midst of the confusion and turmoil incident to a clash of arms, statements of fact, discussions of opinion and contentions of argument inevitably partake of the heat of the conflict and are apt to be over-colored by passion or prejudice. Affected by these conditions, the press and the tribune are alike prone to give ex- pression to the rancors of the conflict, rather than the calmly ascertained causes which underlie and have produced it ; the real import of those causes is apt to be obscured by the bitterness of partisanship and the far-reaching significance of their effects hidden in the smoke of battle.

To afford a true light under such circumstances there is need of a competent and acknowledged authority, whose position is conceded and whose standpoint is fully recognized; an authority unaffected by the rancors of the moment, actuated by logical and well-determined motives and influenced by considerations apart from present exigencies. Such a light is afforded by the volume before us.

It renders accessible to English readers Raimundo Cabrera's *Cuba y sus jueces.* That work, as will be found noted in its admirable prologue by Rafael Montoro, attracted universal attention throughout the Spanish-speaking world at the time of its first publication in 1887. Since then it has gone through eight editions in the Spanish, and has been accepted as a faithful reflex of public opinion among the liberal thinkers not only of Cuba, but of the mother country as well. The work affords the most comprehensive and thorough statement of the Cuban question that has thus far emanated from the press; it has stood the test of criticism and review by all parties in Cuba and in Spain, and remains an unquestioned and unimpeached authority on the subject of Cuba and the Cubans.

The idea of presenting this work to the English speaking public had been conceived by the present editor some years ago, when, as publisher of the seventh Spanish edition, he became minutely conversant with its contents. The author's permission to translate the work was then obtained with that

end in view, and now, with the growing interest
of the American people in the struggle between
Spain and its rebellious colonists, an English
translation of this standard work will especially
commend itself. In view of the existing situation
of affairs, the editor has deemed it proper to confine
the translation to the text as it was published in the
Spanish edition of 1891, which was the seventh of
the series and the last which received the revision
of the author, he having then augmented his previous work with numerous notes and supplemented
it with appendices and illustrations. A brief summary of descriptive and historical data, which the
author, writing for a Spanish and particularly a
Cuban public, naturally regarded as unnecessary,
has been added to this translation by the editor, and
the illustrations of the original work have been increased by a number of photographic views and a
map of the island and its surroundings.

Señor Cabrera has dealt with his subject-matter
from the vantage ground of an acknowledged leadership of the Autonomist party cf Cuba. His statements may therefore be regarded as an expression
of that element of the Cuban people whose hopes
of the future of their country have been based on
the belief that their aspirations could be realized
through an effective system of Autonomy, and who
looked forward to achieving their political aims by

constitutional agitation, rather than by the possibly
shorter but immeasurably more costly method of a
resort to arms. The earnest and thoughtful leaders
of the Autonomists based their contention for a
peaceful propaganda of the reform movement upon
the fact that socio-political problems which, a generation ago, seemed impossible of determination except by force, were now open for solution by appeals
to justice and to reason; that the intelligence and
education upon which they relied were being rapidly
disseminated by the spread of commerce and of industry; that the spirit of the times was making
strongly for their cause and that the progress of
modern thought and enlightenment, slow though it
was in making an impress on Spanish policy, might
still with confidence be left to work its way in Cuba,
as it had worked and was yet working throughout
the civilized world. Cabrera's book indeed, as voic-
ing the demands of the Cuban people for reforms
which Spain has constantly postponed or absolutely
refused, has commanded the recognition and respect
of the advanced rank of Spanish statesmen.

The original publication of this work in the
Spanish, as already noted, marked an era in the agitation for Cuban Home Rule. It was put forth,
as is indicated by Montoro in his Prologue, and by
the author in his introductory chapter, as a refutation of statements by a Peninsular writer, published

in a book entitled "*Cuba y su gente*" (Cuba and its People), and hence proceeds upon a plan of dissertation which Cabrera found forced upon him. But the latter's work is much more than a polemic; it takes a wider sweep and presents a broad and philosophic statement of its subject. With scholarly insight and thorough analysis, Cabrera traces the existing social, political, and economic condition of Cuba and the Cubans with a facile pen, in brief but comprehensive outlines and in a lucid and trenchant style. He elucidates the needs and aspirations of the Cuban people as evinced by that portion of the community of which Cabrera himself is a typical representative, the thoughtful, conservative and substantial elements of society, which form the true basis of the social structure. It was these elements that composed the Autonomist party of Cuba, which sought, through every possible peaceful effort, to move the Home Government to a recognition of the needs of the times, of the demands of justice, and of the dictates of an enlightened self-interest, and it is these elements which must form in Cuba, as in all civilized societies, the foundation whereon the lasting reconstruction of the community must eventually be based.

LOUIS EDWARD LEVY.

Philadelphia, February, 1896.

TABLE OF CONTENTS.

VIII.

IX.

X.

XI.

XV.

APPENDIX I.

APPENDIX II.

EDITOR'S SUPPLEMENT.

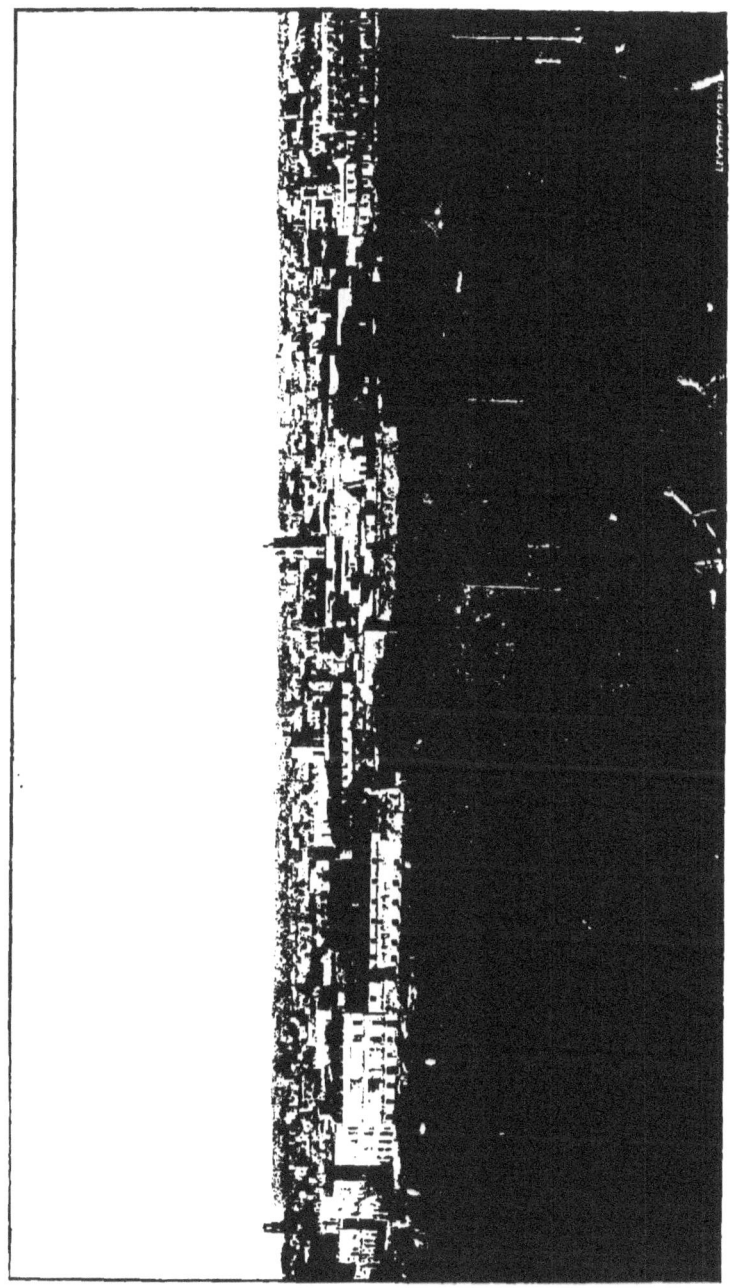

General View of Havana, from the Cabanas Fortress.

NO. 1. RAIMUNDO CABRERA.

PROLOGUE.

The extraordinary success attained by the first edition of "Cuba y Sus Jueces" (Cuba and its Critics) has afforded ample proof of the great merit of the work and of its eminent opportuneness. As regards the former, it is fully attested by the warm eulogies accorded the work by the entire liberal Press of Cuba, by the evident alarm manifested in the reactionary organs and by the unusual gladness with which the good people of Cuba, laying aside for the time their various concerns, have sought, almost unanimously, a grateful solace in the pages of this fascinating and patriotic book. On the other hand, no more thorough demonstration of its fitness for the occasion could be possible than the fact that this book, for some days after its appearance, completely monopolized the attention of the public, the discussion of its contents replacing all other topics of current interest, not only in newspaper polemics but also in the conversation and spontaneous comments of the people.

The present prologue cannot, therefore, be like ordinary compositions of this class. Its object

17

cannot be the presentation to the public of a work already celebrated, nor the introduction of an author already so distinguished ; but it appears to me desirable, for various reasons, to record with reference to the latter a few circumstances which enhance our estimate of the originality as well of the noble purpose of his work.

It will be well, however, that we speak with reserve, inasmuch as it is in the nature of things political that the generous plaudits of a fair and impartial public are counteracted, or more properly speaking, are sought to be counteracted, by the coarse attacks of disappointed adversaries. These attacks attest the merits of the book, and afford sufficient proof even were there no other evidence.

No one attains to moral or intellectual authority, least of all, certainly, in the domain of politics, without incurring many a secret hate and lasting antipathy, errors which are gradually corrected or chimerical ambitions which are finally overcome in the path of the victor.

Looking forward, then, as one may, to this inevitable fate of all who are worthy and more especially of all who struggle, I would remark that Señor Cabrera affords in the story of his own life the best commentary on his work. A son of the soil, he owes to his own efforts, notwithstanding his youth, all that he has acquired, position, wealth and fame. To those

who persist in accusing the Cuban of being indolent
or apathetic, of lacking enterprise, activity or perseverance, Cabrera's life affords an answer more eloquent even than his interesting book. Well may so
creditable a production receive the testimony of the
author of this prologue, united as he is with Cabrera
by the ties of an old friendship, dating back to the
sweet years of childhood and the ineffaceable memories of school. Cabrera is one of the class of self-
made men, the true warrant of the culture and the
progress of all new countries, where the individual
has all the task of accomplishing results, and has
the impulse to their accomplishment. The first,
because a new social organism precludes the existence of classes privileged by law or custom, and of
traditional institutions which, in communities of
an extended history, appear as an expression of
that history, and partake with the individual, in
priority even to the latter, in the work of social
development. The second, the impulse to action,,
inasmuch as it is the characteristic of immigrants
and their immediate descendants in new communities, to which they are drawn by a spirit of adven-
ture and by a yearning for liberty and an eagerness
for fortune, to repel all social ingredients and all
constraints of government which remind them of
their circumstances in the old country, where the
feeling of restraint and ill-condition had finally

brought them to dare all the risks of a new life, in a distant land and under unknown circumstances.

The true cause of the relative backwardness of Spanish America and of the enormous difficulties with which it had to contend in establishing on a solid basis its political and economic organization, cannot, in the opinion of the highest authorities, be other than the error committed by our ancestors in disregarding the supreme necessity, felt by every colony and by every colonist, of individual and social expansion, a principle which, on the contrary has been fully recognized in Anglo-Saxon America, where such admirable progress has been attained.

Gervinus has compared in the classic pages of his famous introduction to *the History of the Nineteenth Century*, the different spirit to which the policies of the British and Spanish colonizations have respectively responded, proving how far superior in this respect was always the former over the latter. The English colonist, upon his departure for new territories, leaves behind him the the historic institutions, social complications and the rigid prescriptions and limitations which are the product of former centuries. The Spaniard, on the other hand, enamoured of an impossible uniformity, has striven to reproduce in newly discovered territories, with all its characteristic elements, the same organization as that which the stormy march of events had created in

the mother country. He has tried to establish, as
Leroy Beaulieu points out, "old societies in new
countries," without spontaneity or life of their own;
an evil which Merivale found to be the root of all
the misfortunes that afflict Spanish America, as also
of the turbulent uprisings that finally culminated
in its separation from the common nationality.

This erroneous idea of assimilation still holds
sway and one of its most natural and lamentable
results is the deplorable antagonism that never
ceases in Spanish colonies to divide into hostile camps
the Europeans and the Americans. Under the shadow
of a suspicious and jealous tutelage which condemns
as calamitous and criminal every idea of expansion, always so necessary in new societies, the proud
and dominating spirit of those who assert themselves as the true representatives of the national interest, violently bursts forth, stirring up among the
settlers of metropolitan origin the most cruel enmity
against the natives of the country in which they
live.

Thus becomes developed that psychological condition, described in so masterly a manner by John
Stuart Mill in the suggestive lines which serve as
fitting epigram to this work, and which if ever,
in a restricted sense, applicable to English colonization, could, unfortunately, always be applied with
more or less positiveness to the Spanish colonial

system.   It was logical that such a disposition in the
dominant element should give rise to corresponding
protests and reproaches from the humiliated and
oppressed colonists.   Hence the antagonism of which
I speak, with all its odious and deadly fierceness,
followed by a procession of horrors, violence and
public calamities which constitute one of the saddest
episodes of modern history! . . . . . In continental America these are now passing, with the
sad memory of their origin.   An eloquent lesson,
indeed, and one that is not appreciated.

   In Cuba and Porto Rico, with the continuance of
its causes, that antagonism still persists, engendering
nearly all the dangers and difficulties which those
countries encounter in the rough pathway of their
civilizing evolution.   And if this antagonism be the
greatest evil which they suffer it is well that all
true lovers of the public weal should battle to correct
the errors which false prejudices or absurd animosities are constantly fomenting.

   A free-lance pamphlet into which the insolent
pen of an unjust foreigner packed all kinds of errors
and insults against this unfortunate country, serving thus as the mouthpiece of those who to-day
symbolize the spirit of domination among us, has
afforded the motive for this judicious and striking
reply of Mr. Cabrera.   We wish it were read by
both elements of the community with absolute cool-

ness of judgment. The dominating classes might comprehend their injustice and thoughtlessness; the others would see that right upholds them, and that good discipline, union and perseverance constitute the most efficacious remedy for the evils they suffer.

The mature reflection to which these pages invite will indicate primarily that there exists in Cuba a people endowed with all the qualities and elements necessary to attain a high degree of civilization and prosperity, if it can only overcome the fearful crisis which now agitates it.

In a profound and notably just criticism of this book, Mr. Enrique José Varona has pointed out, with his usual mastery, this principal factor of the Cuban problem.

"The culminating subject of this book," says this distinguished thinker, "because it is developed from the reality of things, is that the old European race which conquered and repeopled Cuba, has here produced an ethnological variety well adapted for its new physical conditions, and capable of a well ordered and progressive social life; for it has been fruitful and has demonstrated a high degree of mental aptitude, exceptional activity and a persistent spirit of enterprise. But as though living under the weight of the inexorable fatality conceived by the ancients, whatever has been due to its historical antecedents, whatever of political ties and institutions it brought from the old European soil, seems to have arisen in its pathway as an insurmountable obstacle, or bound up its limbs with unyielding bonds. Favored by nature on every side, it has gathered only a harvest of evils from its social and political organization."—*Revista Cubana*, September, 1887.

The first part of Mr. Verona's observation is exceedingly important, as it establishes, in our judgment, the just title of the Cuban people to consider themselves as a people, with perfect right to colonial autonomy. It furthermore solves one of the most interesting of the problems which press upon the colonists to-day, viz.: that of the adaptability and capacity for indefinite reproduction of the white race in the torrid zone, which, up to the present time, have been considered negatively by most writers, with discouraging and pessimistic conclusions, forgetting possibly that races may change according to their environment. The isothermic lines so precisely traced by I. Guyot in the map which accompanies his remarkable *Lettres sur la Politique Coloniale*, appeared to be definitive only a short time ago. It is true that in the works of Rochard, Bordier and of Guyot himself, an exception is noted in favor of the Spaniards and Portuguese, as more apt in establishing themselves and multiplying in our zone. True it is also that the physical conditions of our beautiful island, and its topographical peculiarities, render it manifestly better adapted than any other tropical country for the acclimatization of the South-European. The observation of Verona is above all decisive as regards the complete tracing out of the problem, indicating as it does the possibility of ethnological varieties, whose adaptability will in Cuba exceed all our hopes, if not disturbed in their development by monstrous political conditions, for whose reform we must resolutely struggle.

We need not deprecate these hopes as being exaggerated, if we consider how vast is the field which presents itself, even in our uninhabited domain, not alone for the development of the existing population, but to increasing numbers of new immigrants and their descendants. According to the highest estimates there are in Cuba but 12.84 inhabitants to the square kilometre. Calculate now the time and the effort necessary for our community to reach even a medium density of population, such as is considered in other countries as but a partial occupancy of the soil. Development, it is maintained, can follow only upon our regeneration, and this is impossible so long as the conditions to which we are subjected are not essentially reformed.

But, can these conditions possibly be reformed?

Is it permissible to hope for better days when, to quote the phrase of a Spanish statesman, "the reign of justice in Cuba shall begin?" This is the crucial point of the question. It is certainly not necessary for the author of this prologue to state that he does not figure among the pessimists. He may permit himself to believe, without being accused of lack of modesty, that this fact is well known by all who are acquainted with the political affairs of the country. It is not to be denied, however, that the difficulties are most grave. But whatever solution the course of time may afford this fateful problem, we may feel sure of this, that we cannot obtain peace of mind nor lasting tranquillity, neither prosperity nor true civilization, so long as we do not put an end to the enmity between the two elements of our white population. On harmony depends our welfare as surely as that discord breeds all our evils and dangers. Certain it is that this happy union will not be accomplished until the day when a full measure of self-government, founded on liberty and justice, render impossible at once the daring imposition of the powers that be and the just resentment of the oppressed victims. Then, and then only, will Cuba be saved for herself and for Spain.

RAFAEL MONTORO.

September 10, 1887.

" If there be a fact to which all experience testi-
fies, it is that when a country holds another in
subjection, the individuals of the ruling people
who resort to the foreign country to make their
fortunes, are of all others those who most need
to be held under powerful restraint. They are
always one of the chief difficulties of the government. Armed with the prestige and filled with the
scornful overbearingness of the conquering nation,
they have the feelings inspired by absolute power,
without its sense of responsibility * * * * The
utmost efforts of the public authorities are not
enough for the effectual protection of the weak
against the strong, and of all the strong, the European settlers are the strongest. * * * * They
think the people of the country mere dirt under
their feet; it seems to them monstrous that any
rights of the natives should stand in the way of
their smallest pretensions ; the simplest act of
protection to the inhabitants against any act of
power on their part which they may consider
useful to their commercial objects, they denounce,
and sincerely regard as an injury. * * * *
The Government, itself free from this spirit, is
never able sufficiently to keep it down in the young
and raw even of its own civil and military officers, over whom it has so much more control than
over the independent residents."

JOHN STUART MILL.

(On "Representative Government," Chapter XVIII.)

CUBA AND THE CUBANS.

I.

No. 3. MORRO CASTLE. ENTRANCE TO THE PORT OF HAVANA.

EXPLANATORY INTRODUCTION—THE PORT OF HAVANA—THE HARBOR
OFFICIALS—CUSTOM HOUSE EXAMINATIONS—STREETS OF THE CITY
—ARCHITECTURAL PECULIARITIES—CHARACTERISTICS OF THE CITY
CROWDS—THE NEGROES AND THE CHINESE—THE "SECTION OF
HYGIENE"—OTHER FEATURES.

An easy-going writer, signing himself F. Moreno,
who was born in the neighborhood, probably, of
the Sierra Morena or of Albarracin, and who
came to Cuba evidently in search of gold coins,
found, in their stead, alas! only torn and filthy
banknotes, difficult, at best, to get hold of or to cash
in the Banco de España. He escaped the dreaded
"Yellow Jack," and quite likely landed in Havana at
the wharf of San Francisco; he doubtless sauntered
through the streets of La Muralla, O'Reilly, and
San Miguel; met in the evenings some congenial

spirits, his countrymen, at the "Louvre"; frequented the Cervantes Theatre; lived on the public revenue; visited a few odd families of the few stray natives of his Province, and so obtained from the Island which bore the burden of his personality only such impressions as can be derived from such centres and such places. He discussed public affairs only in the company of small office clerks and their boon companions, and at last, becoming weary of his surroundings, or, perchance, disappointed at not reaping a harvest of gold pieces or banknotes in the unhappy land of the sugar-cane, he thought it best to return whence he came—to Madrid, centre of culture, focus of office-seekers, metropolis where art, literature, talent and the court ministers are gathered together. This writer, who according to the announcement of the publishers appears to have written of other things, has dedicated to you, Paco, a work entitled "Cuba and its People," which I have read with interest, which has made me laugh at times and incensed me at others, and which, altogether, has but served to strengthen my long established opinion of the little love which our Peninsular brothers bear us, and of that ungracious spirit of our race, which, while very proud and haughty, is constantly boasting a capacity for doing great things—an ever certain sign of the small results it actually accomplishes—for example, the Colonies.

And it is for the purpose of informing you, friend Paco, not only of the doings of Señor Moreno and his congeners, but also of the true causes which make the "most beautiful land which human eyes ever saw" a theatre of all the "horrors of the moral world;" it is for this purpose I take the liberty of writing you the present and succeeding letters.

Follow then, my narrative and my comments, and if you have the ardent blood of the good Castilians in your veins, and wholesome ideas of patriotism in your brain, prepare to agree with me that all the evil it possesses—which is no small matter, this much calumniated Cuban people—is the result of its Spanish colonization; and that the little or almost nothing which it has of good, is what it assimilates spontaneously from the American atmosphere.

Let us enter Paco, Cuba, by the same route that F. Moreno took—whether by steamer or sailing vessel—through the mouth of the Morro; on either side are the ancient castles and fortresses which have cost and still cost much hard earned cash to maintain, and which guard in their moats the bloody memories of political convulsions to which we will not refer, but which would make the least sensitive reluctant to, recall. Pray do not scrutinize too closely the waters of the port. The filth which is deposited in thick crusts at the bottom makes the

waves muddy, and its emanations, if we are to believe
the doctors of the country—reputed for their knowledge and scientific attainments—constitute the
principal cause of yellow fever.   It is quite true that
while there is an abundance of filth, there is also a
yearly collection of large sums by a Board of Port
Wardens, whose numerous members are composed of
Spaniards that came to Cuba by the same route as
Señor Moreno, and who will surely busy themselves
in perceiving defects and in criticising the country,
but not in cleaning the port.

Do not investigate, either, the other services connected with the port; that of the police for example.
Be very careful of your baggage and of your person
among the boatmen, who are all old tars of the
Spanish Navy, and proceed to make your landing on
terra firma.   You must quickly open your baggage
and show your belongings, but do not alarm yourself.   If you have it about you, give a dollar to the
officer—who is, indeed, not a Cuban—and you will
find this ordeal not at all a trying one.   If you
have occasion to deal with the Custom House you
will discover that this matter of having your baggage searched or left unmolested is insignificant in
comparison with examining the manifest of a valuable cargo.

We are now in the city; the streets are in truth
narrow and dirty; they reveal at once the fact that

NO. 2. JOSÉ DE LA LUZ CABALLERO.

the city was planned by the first settlers—natives of an European country. Some streets are indeed paved with Belgian blocks; this novelty dates from 1862 and its introduction was celebrated with great festivities, but most of them are not so paved, for the Belgian blocks are imported from abroad and the City Fathers have not been able to afford the heavy duty imposed by the tariff.

There is a drainage system, but so bad is it that it serves only as a receptacle for filth, and there is not enough water for cleaning purposes, here, where springs abound. Public improvements have certainly not pre-occupied the Colonial Government, which, while appropriating eight millions one hundred and sixty-five thousand dollars for the maintenance of the army, allows one million two hundred and thirty-eight thousand for public works, and this almost entirely expended on the personnel.

The buildings are for the most part low, like those in the towns of Andalusia. The first architects were the Spanish settlers, and their plans and models have been preserved, thus giving to our cities a peculiar and characteristic stamp. Even the famous convents of San Juan de Dios, of Santo Domingo and others, built by the monks who flocked to Cuba from the earliest times, and which have been regarded as model edifices, were, and are yet, in the worst possible taste.

2

In the streets you will come upon what is certainly a motley crowd. The negroes, by their numbers and their depth of color, will attract your atttention ; slavery will be recalled to your mind, transplanted by Europe to American soil. The historian will no doubt remember that Spain received from England in 1817 four hundred thousand pounds sterling to abolish the slave trade, and that Emancipation, first gradual (Moret law of 1870), afterwards absolute (Cortes of 1886), and never indemnified, is owing to the generous efforts of the Reformists, to the Revolutionists, and finally to the Cuban Autonomists.

You will also see the Chinamen; a type which brings to memory another importation, that of the the coolie contract laborer, not to say slave; a system against which the civilized world has at last cried out, while Spanish statesmen are cherishing the philanthropic idea of contracting for 400,000 more Chinamen, notwithstanding the treaty of Pekin, for employment in the agricultural work of Cuba. And it must not surprise you, Paco, that this degraded race has brought along its vices to Cuba; but what may truly astonish you is that this is but a new means of exploitation at the expense of public morals, and that through the gambling dens, etc., of the Chinese, many functionaries of the police, and other public employes, become enriched.

You will also see in the heart of the city, in the most thickly populated streets, a spectacle of never ceasing scandal and demoralization, but if you should mention this to one of those discontented members of society who abound in this country, or to some conscientious paterfamilias who is anxious for the moral education of his children, and who, by the way, Senor Moreno did not meet, he will tell you that there is in the Civil Government, never by chance entrusted to a Cuban,* a department called Section of Hygiene, whose duty is supposed to be the punishment and prevention of immorality, but which, disgraceful as it may seem, makes this but another source of revenue to the officers. And like this Section of Hygiene which, by the way, is not a small detail of the administration of our Spanish Colony, you will see many other things which Moreno has not pointed out to you, and which I will proceed to indicate in other letters.

---

* Since the first publication of this book, Don Carlos Rodriguez Batista, a Cuban by birth, has held the office of Civil Governor of Havana. Although educated in Spain and identified with its policy his origin must have greatly contributed to forming his good intentions for the improvement of the moral condition of affairs, but the many difficulties and obstacles inherent in the general system of government of the island are such that he was unable to execute them. Señor Batista is, however, one of those rare governors who have left a pleasant memory in Cuba.

P. S.— You will likewise find in the heart of
Havana (just as Moreno tells you) that the laundries,
and particularly the undertakers' establishments,
instead of transacting their business quietly with pen,
ink and paper, make a great sidewalk show of palls,
candelabra and other trappings which are commonly
used on funeral occasions. But you must not ignore
the fact that there are municipal laws which forbid
all this, yet ward officials who consent to it, City
Councilors who are blind because they will not see,
Governors whom this state of affairs does not concern, and a country that suffers it with patience.

II.

No. 5.—CALLE DEL PRADO, HAVANA.

HAVANA INNS AND HOSTELRIES—LOW COST OF LIVING—THE ROYAL
LOTTERY—THE COUNTRY MONOPOLIZED AND EXPLOITED—CUBAN
SACRIFICES DURING THE SEPARATIST WARS.

Permit me to tell you, Paco (whom I have not
the distinguished honor of knowing), that your
friend Don F. Moreno has not given you, as he pretends, a good or even an indifferent idea of the
capital of the Great Antilles.

Of what he has given abundant proof is his utter
ignorance concerning it; and that he knows as
little of Havana as all the genteel employes and
bureaucrats that travel to and fro between Cuba
and Madrid, by the National Steamship Line, and

who study in the island only the most expeditious manner of accumulating money in order to
spend it in Fornos and other like centres of Madrid.
He pomposely entitles his book " *Cuba y su gente* "
" Cuba and its People," but far from describing
Cuba, its political, social and economic conditions,
he entertains you chatting about the streets of
Havana and the manner of paving them, of a dozen
or so of individuals, of some third rate hotels and
lodging houses and of all sorts of low places and
their habitués.

If these were the only resorts and social circles
which he frequented it is not to be wondered that
so select a writer speaks evil and calumny of
woman, of the family life and of the youth of Cuba
to whose homes he was never admitted, and contact
with which was repugnant to him, as is the
atmosphere of virtue to the vicious man.

As Moreno did not show you our hostelries,
permit me to do so. It would not be strange if in
Havana there were no comfortable hotels. The
proprietors of these, like those in nearly all the
other industries, hail from those famous Spanish
provinces where Alexander Dumas and his traveling companions sought in vain for a place where
they might find relief from hunger and fatigue, and
found in their extremity only a thimbleful of chocolate for each person.

I should inform you, and can prove to you, my dearest Paco, that in Havana you can find innumerable restaurants and inns where all, whether rich or poor, can satisfy their appetite with much or little money. Fortunately the land is naturally fertile, and offers in abundance many edible products.

For fifty cents in paper, equivalent to twenty-five in silver, you can get an excellent breakfast at which bread, fresh meat and vegetables will not be wanting. For correspondingly more money you will find tables served with a luxury and good taste unsurpassed in Paris. Modest and cheap inns are everywhere to be found, and are a source of never ending comfort to the laboring classes. Do not doubt this, though Moreno assures you to the contrary. The Cuban table is one of the most abundant, cheap and varied in existence; that is precisely why the Cuban does not emigrate (and God knows he might well do so) and it is precisely on this account that Señor Moreno came to Cuba and will return only when expedient; and for this same reason his countrymen have followed and will continue to follow in his wake.

The hotels, some of them yet conducted in primitive Spanish style, are improving, especially since the facilities of communication with the United States and the low rates of fare permit Americans

to come and winter among us and teach us how to
install and direct these undertakings. Some of the
hotels are now sumptuous establishments, where
electric lights, reading rooms, elevators, and other
comforts of American origin have been introduced,

No. 6.—GRAND HOTEL, INGLATERRA.

and where, quietly and without ado—admiring
and praising the natural beauty of this unhappy
land—have resided such noted travellers as Froude,
Plant, Archbishop Corrigan, United States Senator
John Sherman, and others of equal station.

Inquire of these eminent persons, Paco, and not
of the bull fighter Mazzantini, as your friend ad-
vises, if it is not true that they have published in
their respective countries, criticisms and impres-

sions of this island much more favorable and gratifying to our national pride than those which appear
in the book of a Spaniard so ultra-Spanish as Señor
Moreno.

It matters but little to foreigners whether our
ports are open to admit immigrants. It is true that
if foreigners did emigrate to Cuba, they would not
find employment in the selling of Royal Lottery
tickets. That industry is reserved for the Canary
Islanders, retired army officers, and for others who
are not Cubans, nor even negroes; for all these,
or the greater part of them, devote themselves to
mechanical or agricultural pursuits, and not even
in these occupations enjoy the comforts or privileges
which the government in its various departments
offers in all shapes, combinations and sinecures to
our peninsular brethren.

What? Is this indeed a Spanish province without a
domestic tariff and without contributing of its blood?

By no means; this is a country monopolized and
exploited; the domestic tariff is the aspiration towards supreme monopoly. And as for contributions of blood, these are made when required.
During the Separatist Wars the Cubans were en-
listed, recruited and transported to the field without
distinction of classes; the only exceptions were
those who paid to General Concha or his successor
a thousand dollars as redemption fee.

More than thirty thousand Cubans died defending the national flag. The companies of discip-
lined militia, composed of Cubans organized for the
defense of rural districts, were marshaled and compelled to go from one department to another. They
suffered hard campaigns; most of them perished;
and the survivors at the end of the war returned
to their homes without recompense, without discharge, without pay, without honor; without other
honor than seeing themselves insulted by Señor
Moreno and his kind.

A contribution of blood? The people pay it now,
but with the sweat of their brows and the fruit
of their labors, for the Cuban people are the miserable tenants of a heartless landlord called the Department of Public Works.

III.

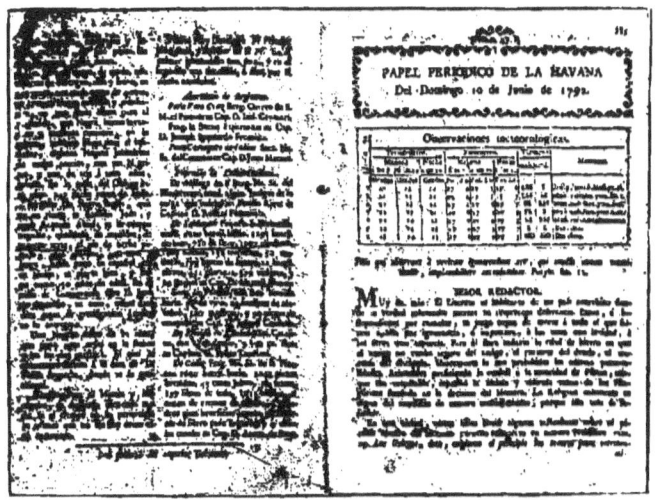

No. 8.—First Periodical Publication in Cuba. "Papel Periodico."

THE PRESS OF CUBA—ITS GENESIS—THE TWO CLASSES OF THE COM-
MUNITY—THEIR RESPECTIVE AIMS AND IDEALS—THE TWO CLASSES
OF JOURNALS—HISTORY OF CUBAN JOURNALISM—ITS PAINS, PENAL-
TIES AND REWARDS—THE PRESS LAWS—SCIENTIFIC AND OTHER
PERIODICALS.

In considering the newspaper press of the Island
of Cuba, as also all other manifestations of this
peculiar social organism, you have always to distinguish not only the political factions, but also their
various antecedents.

In order that you may well understand what I
mean, unknown Paco, and that you may be able to
refute the assertions of your *cicerone*, Señor Moreno,
you must know once for all, that in Cuba, as in

ancient Rome, there exist two distinct social classes, the patricians and the plebeians. One of them is the dominating or governing class, composed of all the Spaniards who have come and are still coming to reap the fortune not in prospect in their own country, and some of whom engage in commerce and the trades; of the officials who live at the expense of the government a certain length of time, then either return or remain in the colony according to which way the wind is blowing; of the ex-army officers who live at ease as civil government employés; of the army officers themselves, and finally, of all the adventurers of the home country who form the personnel of the colonial organization, but who, in general, are not conspicuous for their culture. This class has one all-absorbing interest in common, namely, bleeding the country; and this interest is veiled behind a pretense of sentiment—love for the nation which gives them her unlimited protection. And both these impulses, sentiment and interest, combine to assert themselves with overwhelming force.

The other class is composed (and in this I include the negroes now free) of the Cubans, natives of the country, those dominated over, the permanent element of this social body, who till the land, practice the arts, the trades and the professions; but who are, nevertheless, systematically excluded from all government positions, and who do not enjoy privileges of any description; who pay, suffer and endure the injustice of their exploiters.

These are also closely united by one sentiment, one aspiration, the love of a liberty which they do not enjoy, and the yearning for the justice of which they stand in such sad need; but, unfortunately, they are not protected nor shielded by a supreme authority that enforces equity and justice and which gives to every man his due, or at least endeavors to do so; on the contrary, they are constantly cast off, persecuted and treated with suspicion and mistrust.

Between these two classes one may formulate logical subdivisions which I shall not stop to point out. It is requisite only that I advert to the fact that in the former class there are but few men of good faith, sound judgment and conscientious spirit, who look upon this, their adopted home, as part of their common country, and on its people as their veritable brothers; who ask and wish for Cuba and the Cubans the same guarantees and privileges which the Spaniard enjoys in the home country, and who reprobate and condemn the rule maintained here for so many years, and which produces only the sad result of a class division, unending discord, impoverishment and misery.

The classification thus made, for the exactness of

which I can vouch, and in proof of which I can
cite reputed writers, will enable you to clearly understand what I stated at the beginning of this letter: *In considering the newspaper press of Cuba you
must distinguish not only the political factions, but also
their various antecedents.*

Two primary types predominate among our periodicals; one class legitimately represents the interests
of the dominant order, its supremacy, its aspirations,
its prejudices; and inasmuch as the only eagerness
of this class of journals is to drain the country of all
that it has to offer, it naturally follows that the
distinctive characteristic of these periodicals is mercantile and reactionary.

The second type represents the earnest longings
and generous purposes of a cultured but oppressed
people, who, conscious of their rights, maintain, in
the narrow channel left them, their struggle for the
franchises and prerogatives of citizens of civilized
nations. Their character is such as naturally results
from the necessity of combating with self-denial
and tenacity against arbitrariness and injustice; it is
virile and enlightened. While the first class angrily
upholds and supports the impositions and exactions
of the power secured to the favored class, the second,
with ardent patriotism, discusses and defends the
principles of government which affect the present
and future of the Cuban community.

It is easy to infer from this, esteemed Paco, that it is not the journalists of the second class who are ahead in the arduous campaign against adversaries so formidable, and for whom journalism is a means of enrichment. Certainly not; for the former there have been reserved its persecutions, its pains and penalties; for the latter, its favors, recompenses, honors, and wealth.

The history of Cuban journalism is short; notice the following dates which your correspondent Moreno, in his eagerness to tell of Cuba and her people, has overlooked, and you will find what I say confirmed.

In 1790, that is, three centuries after the discovery of America—at the same period when the spirit of humanity was marking its progress in the French Revolution—this European colony had its doors still closed to the commerce of the world, and had not yet given that sign of culture which the publication of a newspaper reveals.

In 1792, under the government of Las Casas, a weekly newspaper first saw the light, and was published gratuitously by Don José Agustín Caballero, Tomés Romay, Manuel Zequeira and other distinguished Cubans, who devoted its profits to the maintenance of a public school.

In 1793 the Sociedad Patriótica took charge of the enterprise and made it a semi-weekly. In 1805 it became a tri-weekly, and it was not until September 1, 1810 (in this nineteenth century!) that it became a daily paper, devoting its profits to the founding of a library. The dimensions of this miniature newspaper were those of a sheet of foolscap, folded in two leaves. The printer tried in vain to improve the edition, but could find no new types in the Havana market. And this was the state of affairs in the fairest gem of the Castilian crown, which already had over 400,000 inhabitants. Later on, this paper flourished under the titles of "*Papel Periodico*," and "*Aviso y Diario de la Habana*," and subsequently was converted into the "*Gaceta Oficial*," which still exists under the immediate supervision of the Government, with unheard-of privileges and monopolies, and which serves to enrich its managers and augment their influence.

Thus, the first newspaper published in the history of Cuba, the result of the patriotic and disinterested efforts of some of her children, became a money-making concern for the favored class; and if I were to penetrate into historic annals, how many sad pages would not this official newspaper reveal, founded and supported gratuitously, as it was, by generous Cubans who have lived to see it devoted to the printing of the laws and the decrees intended to stifle the intellectual movement of the country.

In 1818, through the initiative of an illustrious

THE CABANAS FORTRESS, FROM OPPOSITE SIDE OF HARBOR ENTRANCE.

No. 4.—FRANCISCO ARANGO Y PARRENO.

and deserving Cuban (Don Francisco Arango y Parreño) the ports of Cuba were opened to free commerce, the currents of civilization penetrated with vigorous impulse from North America and other countries, and it can be said that intellectual life among us dates from that time. Thenceforward we had a press and books. . . . . The Press, which is a stronger power, more efficient and more certain in its effects than any that despotism can ever hope to exercise.

But since the time of the "*Papel Periodico*" Cuban journalism, properly so called, has always retained the noble characteristics with which it was marked by its generous founders. It has always been a labor of love and patriotism; and accordingly, it has been the faithful, although stifled organ of the liberal aspirations of an oppressed people.

NO. 9.—D. GASPAR BETANCOURT CISNEROS.

Such were the "*Faro Industrial*," "*El Siglo*," and "*El Pais*," which, constantly battling in defense of their cherished ideals, gave expression from 1847 to 1868 (the period of the Revolution) to the sentiments of the Cuban people. They contended for social

4

and political reforms, and an administration supported and maintained through patriotic enterprises by men of experience and of wealth; they sought in their publications neither enrichment nor glory, but willingly sacrificed their means, their leisure, their individual safety and that of their families, for the welfare of their unhappy country. To this galaxy of illustrious worthies belong José de J. Quintiliano García, Cristóbal Madan, José Quintín Suzarte, Eduardo Machado, the memorable Gaspar Betancourt Cisneros, Juan B. Sagarra, Francisco Javier Balmaseda, José María de Cárdenas, José Frías, and above all the venerable Count de Pozos Dulces, a patrician whose name, since it is not wrought in bronze, should be engraved with inextinguishable gratitude in the hearts of the Cubans.

NO. 10.—D. JOSÉ QUINTÍN SUZARTE.

All these were either men of fortune or were living at ease in the practice of the learned professions; they belonged either to the aristocracy of blood or to that of letters, and they were all capable of withstanding with dignity and uprightness the allurements of power and of resisting the perils of persecution, practising journalism gratuitously without other hope of recompense than the benefit which the country might receive.

Side by side with these distinguished men, there arose the beginning of the first of the social classes which I have described, with all the patronage and all the privileges which the Government and its branches could offer. Their organs were "*El Noticioso y Lucero*," "*La Prensa*," and "*El Diario de la Marina*." Founded and carried on as commercial enterprises, they have had the satisfaction of seeing their stocks quoted as marketable securities, and their standard of politics has always been determined by the Government which sustains them, and by the stockholders who pocket the dividends. For the journalists of this class, who, against all reason and without scruple, have upheld the mismanagement of the Colonial Government, and who have assumed to dignify themselves as "Ministers of all the Ministries," there have been plenty of crosses of honor, titles, pensions and other rewards which a country prodigal in riches, governed and administered for the benefit of the minority, naturally has to offer.

We have scarcely to refer to the journalism of Cuba during the period of the Revolution. From 1869, whence dated a liberty of the press conceded off-hand and which served only to give vent to repressed animosities, until 1878, there was in Cuba no other than the official press. The political situation conspired during this decade more than at any other time to serve as a foothold for Spanish journalists, convinced as they were that their own advancement depended on an exaggerated defense of Government interests, and on flattering the political sentiments and fanning the animosities of their countrymen. The voice of the Cuban was not heard during this period.

When peace was established and it appeared that new horizons were presenting themselves to the Cubans, our press reappeared in a paper called "*El Triunfo*," founded by a deserving and generous Spaniard, Pérez de Molina, but edited gratuitously and with patriotic disinterestedness by Cuban writers, who from the beginning gave it their support in the defense of liberal movements and reforms, ideals always cherished and never realized.

No. 11.
D. RICARDO DELMONTE.

To-day, unknown Paco, our newspaper press boasts the same characteristics as those to which I have drawn your attention in this extended letter. The two typical journals are the "*Diario de la Marina*," long the organ of the bureaucracy, of restriction, of abuses of power and of monopolies, and "*El Pais*," defender of the aspirations of a cultured, liberal, but oppressed and badly governed people. The former continues to enjoy all the favors and privileges which have afforded it sustenance from the beginning, and the latter continues to battle against all the opposition which have assailed it from the first.

Yonder are the rich and the rewarded, here the poor in power and influence; there, those who barter in journalism, here, those who, though busily employed in the professions, gladly devote what time they can spare to the cause of their country. Among these writers is An-

tonio Govin, a lawyer who is an honor to our literature and to our forum; who at an early age had gathered brilliant laurels, more because of his great talent and profound erudition than even his well known uprightness of character and acknowledged patriotism; Rafael Montoro, landed proprietor,

NO. 12.—D. FRANCISCO A. CONTE.

jurist, philosopher and deputy to the Cortez at thirty-four years of age, attaining in parliament a place among the foremost orators; Francisco A. Conte, a Spanish publicist who devotes his pen to the advocacy of our reforms; Ricardo Delmonte (editor of *El Pais*), a cultured literateur whose reputation as an honorable and discreet journalist was gained in the columns of *El Siglo*; Federico García Ramis, a lawyer, whose early journalistic efforts already indicate him as a conscientious writer; Leopoldo Cancio, attorney and landed proprietor; Bernabé Maidagán, Fabio Freire, Eduardo Dolz, Pablo Desvernine, and Antonio Zambrana, members of the bar; Francisco de Zayas, M. D.; León Broch, lawyer, and many more who with infinite self-denial have indefatigably labored in the defense of Cuban interests, without other reward than the hope, not yet realized, of one day seeing the unfortunate land of their birth free, prosperous and happy.

In this slight historical review, unknown Paco, I have made no mention of the other newspapers which your correspondent Moreno quotes, nor of the press and censorship laws which have weighed so heavily upon our journalism in various ways.

Of the former there is but little to say: the two periodicals described are types of the rest.

Cuban journalism in Havana, as in the other cities of the Island, is an undertaking that requires perseverance, disinterestedness, and patriotism. "Conservative" (Spanish) journalism is an industrial enterprise thriving on the barter of patriotism.

And as regards the press laws? aye, Señor don

Francisco! If in Spain you have heard in its time of the "red pencil," please remember that in Cuba until 1879 it was dipped in blood, to drown Cuban thought and to give strength to their adversaries!*

Later on . . . . a law which permitted General Fajardo to carry to the Tribunal of the Press through the medium of his satraps, all autonomistic newspapers, so as to cause their suspension and ruin. . . . .

And to-day there exists a law which kindly permits the editor to discuss all subjects which are not prohibited, which exiles or imprisons him for infringing it, and which upholds the immunity that government abuses possess by converting a censure of administrative actions into a crime against the authorities.

Of course all these restrictions concern Cuban journalism alone . . . but as for the other . . . . !

But this letter waxes long and it behooves us to study other matters besides the Press laws of this blessed Spanish colony.

*A Royal order of November 19th, 1853, prohibited the circulation in the Island of Cuba of Spanish newspapers and books which had been printed in foreign countries, confirming a previous order of 1837.

Another Royal order of April 25th, 1851, prohibited the circulation of even the "*Revista de España*" in Cuba.

P. S.—Before closing I wish to say that your friend F. Moreno, in his eagerness to acquaint you in his book with "Cuba and her People," and with many people who are not of Cuba, has also enumerated various newspapers which are published in Havana, and likewise their editorial personnel, most of them, however, more or less obscure.

But I do not know whether it is with the best intentions that he omits mentioning the many literary and scientific publications sustained and edited by Cuban associations and by intelligent Cubans throughout the country, who thus show the degree of culture this people has attained, notwithstanding the obstacles by which it has been surrounded, thanks alone to its geographical position, its territorial extension, its daily contact with other communities, and to the vivid tropical imagination that

easily assimilates modern knowledge and ideas.

Among these publications I recommend to you :

"La Revista de Cuba," rewarded at the Amsterdam Exposition; founded by the late José A. Cortina, a man of fortune who employed his wealth in works of this kind.

NO. 13.—D. JOSÉ ANTONIO CORTINA.

"La Revista Cubana," managed by Enrique J. Varona, a talented philologist and profound thinker.

" Memorias de la Real Sociedad Económica."

" Los Anales de la Academia de Ciencia."

" La Revista de Derecho y Administración."

" Memorias del Círculo de Abogados."

" Revista de Agricultura."

" El Eco de Cuba—Revista Enciclopédica."

" La Revista de Derecho."

" Anales de la Sociedad Odontológica."

" La Crónica Médico-Quirúrgica."

" La Enciclopedia—Boletín Fotográfico."

" Boletín de la Sociedad Protectora de Animales y Plantas," and many other publications which I assure you are worth more—much more—than the obscure papers which your not-too-veracious correspondent has offered to you as samples of Cuban journalism.

IV.

It is manifest that Don F. Moreno was at a loss how to begin his fourth letter, and yet there being no lack of material, it was not an *embarras de richesse* that deterred him.

No. 15.—JUNTA DE FOMENTO.
Estación del Ferrocarril de la Habana.

It may be proper, however, to mention that this same superabundance of poor material, for which Moreno so strongly censures us, is Spanish and wholly Spanish.

It is true that Cuba has changed considerably since Columbus discovered it. My last letter demonstrates that with regard to journalism, during a period of ninety years, the people of this country have not been outstripped, notwithstanding the fact that in 1774 the National Government opposed the establishment of printing presses in its colonies, and that in 1790 only that of the Captain-General existed in Havana.

We had the great good fortune to have the Americans export to us the railway in 1836, long before

its introduction in Spain, and later on to teach
us to make use of the telegraph; these advances
directed us on the paths of civilization, and
helped us to overcome the obstacles which beset our
progress; worthy of record is the fact that these
notable improvements were the results of the private
enterprise of these same Cubans who are accused of
indolence, and who, at the memorable Council of
Fomento showed themselves most active in this and
other undertakings not less progressive. And by the
way, this work was greatly retarded and interrupted,
to its no small detriment, by the authorities, who ob-
jected to the tracks infringing upon the military
confines of the castles Príncipe and Atraés (!).

It is true that money seems to be a thing of the
past. But pray, why has this financial crisis come
to pass, which causes Spanish statesmen to appre-
hend a national catastrophe? Is it, perchance, the
imputed indolence and prodigality of the people of
this soil, or is it that in Cuba has been graphically
enacted the story of the goose that laid the golden
eggs? It is because that emporium of riches to
which the scions of Peninsular families ran in
shoals, dreaming a repetition of the Golden Fleece,
which they sometimes realized, has been converted
into a sterile land, where misery has fastened her
iron clutches and where no ray of hope can be discerned.

On these points, Paco, I do not intend to speak; I withdraw in favor of a young Cuban writer and lawyer, as remarkable for his modesty as for his vast erudition and talent; he is a distinguished journalist who edits one of the many newspapers published in Cuba out of sheer patriotism and love of science without a thought or hope of gain, and which treat with discretion and sound sense local questions of far more interest than those of which Moreno and his confrères—because of total ignorance—have not even given approximate ideas in those mockeries of journalism and mercenary sheets known under the names of *La Verdad, El León Español, La Polémica, El Rayo,* and other like concoctions of impossible nonsense.

The talented writer to whom I refer is Don Leopoldo Cancio, ex-member of the Cortes; the paper to which he contributes is *"La Unión de Güines,"* and the article which comes most *à propos* is the following:

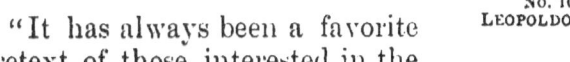

No. 16.
LEOPOLDO CANCIO.

"It has always been a favorite pretext of those interested in the slavery of the Negro and the servitude of the Chinese that the Caucasian race is not adapted for agricultural work in the heat of the tropics, and to justify their claim they have insisted with extraordinary tenacity on the theory that the Creoles (natives of the white race) have degenerated from their progenitors, whom they do not equal in either persistence or activity at work. With this assertion and a similar one to the effect that the negro does not work in the field except under the constraint of slavery, they have had at hand a host of arguments with which to defend African slavery and the Asiatic contract law.

The idea of the indolence of the native whites has been propagated and maintained here with extraordinary success, thanks to the political assumptions of the ruling Spaniards, who have found it an easy and pleasing task to attribute and take to themselves all the virtues, and to place the Cubans on the level of an enervated and lazy people, slow in agricultural work, and disturbers of the country's peace and of its lords. In their polemics with the Cuban press their most authoritative official organs affirm with an unperturbable self-complacency that it is they who represent the classes that work and pay, in contrast to the others, who, it would appear, by a special dispensation of Providence, are able to live regardless of what we were under the impression was the common precept—that man must earn his bread by the sweat of his brow.

Nevertheless, the observation and study of our political economy in comparison with that of Spain and of the Spanish American republics, proves that no man of the Spanish race is more laborious than the Cuban. In spite of the drawbacks attached to the immense accumulations of landed property, and

the debasing effects on labor due especially to
slavery, and notwithstanding that Cuba is an
exploited colony whose tariff laws and system of
taxation have not been calculated to encourage
production, but on the contrary, the special object of
which has been to fill the royal coffers, no matter to
what extent the island might be drained; in spite
of all this, the people of the country have worked
with a faith and perseverance perhaps excessive,
revealing a spirit of industry not excelled in Spain
nor in any of its former American colonies.

It was owing to the superhuman efforts of Cuban
planters, such as Poey, Diago, and Arrieta, that the
great inventions of European engineers for the
manufacture of sugar were introduced, and almost
entirely owing to the Cuban planters is the development and renown which this industry afterwards
attained. It was they who, foreseeing coming
events, established centralized plants of machinery
to cope with the effects of the abolition of slavery,
thus sowing the seed which was afterwards to
germinate and bear fruit.

Battling against the antiquated civil laws, and
subjected to the rigor of a monstrous military
regimen, a system of government altogether unique,
they promoted the establishment of the majority of
the sugar plantations which to-day give Cuba a
prominent place among countries producing that
article.

The *mayorales* (overseers), and the rest of the
inferior employes who are familiar to us under the
name of *operarios* (laborers), under whose immediate
management the cultivation and fabrication of the

sugar is effected, have, in spite of all that may be
said of our industrial developments, comparing it
with that of other nations standing in the front of
civilization, been the efficient agents of an industry
which has produced from eighty to ninety millions
of dollars a year.   .

Who has ploughed and cultivated the fields of
Vuelta Abajo, producing the best tobacco in the
world? There also the natives of the country have
been in the great majority among the *regueros*
(tobacco workers), maintaining the production in
spite of all the obstacles set against it by the law
and by the usurers.

This district of more than 6000 square miles
has not a single port qualified for foreign commerce. The producer has been obliged to succumb
before the tavern keeper, the necessary middle man
between himself and a market located at a distance
of 150 miles over well-nigh impassable roads, thus
forcing him to maintain a continuous chain of
parasites until he reaches Havana, the first port
after Cape San Antonio. In this unfortunate
province there seem to have gathered with especial
rapacity the monopolies and privileges which have
flourished in Cuba to such an extent as even to allow
the Company of Fomento y Navegación del Sur the
exclusive use of the sea coast for steam navigation
from Batabanó to the extreme east of the island.
Here the Spaniards with very few exceptions, have
done nothing but carry on the retail trade and that
of usury, waiting in the pleasant-shade of their
taverns until the *reguero* toilsomely gathers his
precious harvest, and then starts out, suffering for

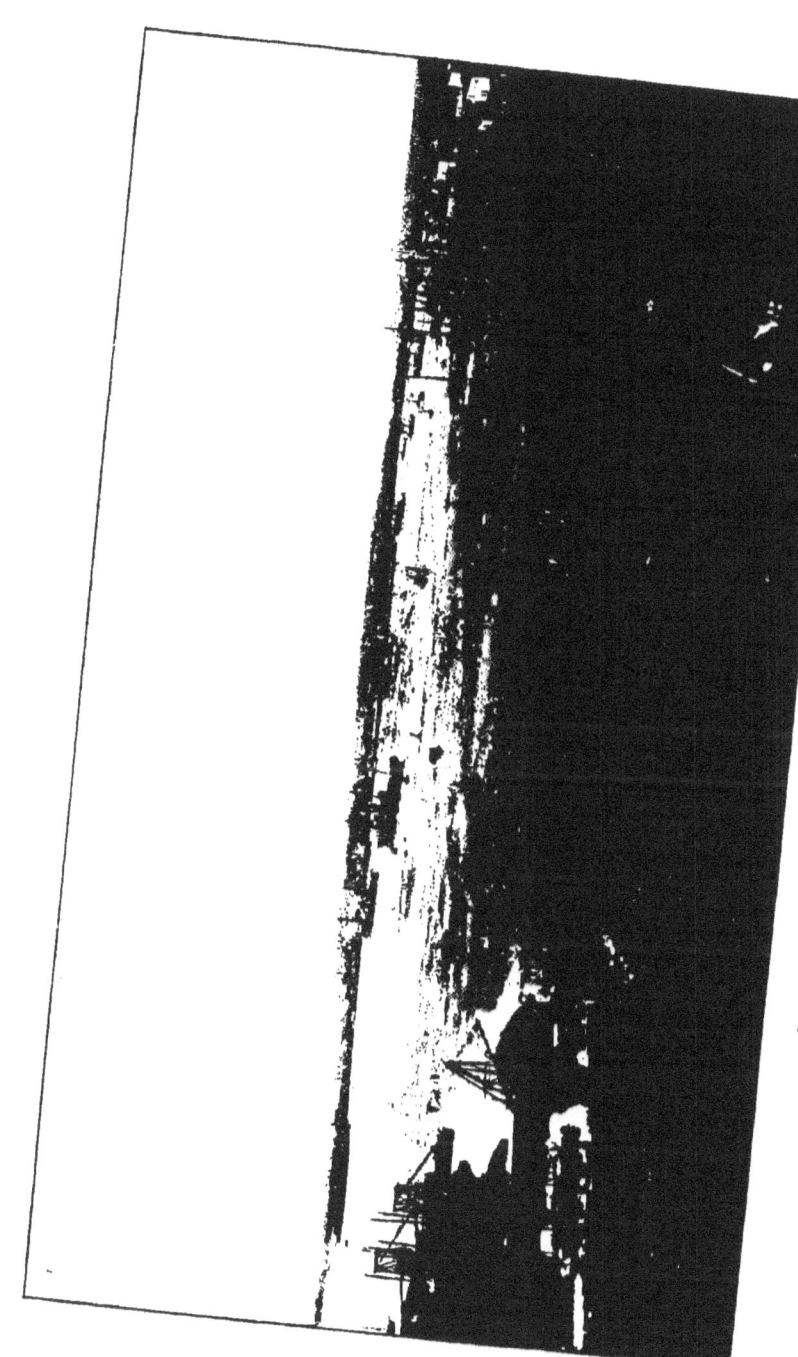

INNER HARBOR OF HAVANA, FROM CABAÑAS FORTRESS.

NO. 7. CONDE DE POZOS DULCES.

some days the burning rays of the tropical sun, in search of money with which to repay his advances together with all of the fabulous usury imposed on him. The minor productions, and also the pork industry, have always been in the hands of native Cubans in the same proportion as in the other agricultural pursuits, that is, almost entirely. Worthy of mention is the considerable progress made in Puerto Príncipe and Las Villas in cattle raising through the efforts of Cuban landowners, who by means of selection or crossing with the best foreign breeds, have perfected the native cattle so that in few years most excellent results have been obtained. Mola, Betancourt, Cisneros, Monteverde, Arteaga and Borrero in Puerto Príncipe; Castillo, Luna, Legón, Castro and García, in Sancti Spíritus were the promoters of this progress, and they were all native Cubans.

The magnificent farms of these districts were for the most part the work of free labor. It was the white peasantry that cleared the wilds and produced the extensive Guinea-herb pasture lands, which are still the finest in Cuba.

If we had the official statistics of approximately all the agricultural products of the island, we would have no difficulty in proving that at least half is the work of white creoles, and if we include, as is proper, the colored people, then only fifteen or twenty per cent. at most would relate to inhabitants of other origin, Canary Islanders, Spaniards and Chinese. In the absence of statistical figures the reader can easily prove within the range of his own observation the exactness of our statements.

5

"But what more eloquent proof of their industry
than the astounding fact that the abolition of slavery, effected without compensation or indemnity,
has in no way lessened agricultural production?
Contrary in fact to expectation and to the law
established by those who have studied the transition from slavery to liberty, and have marked as
consequent a diminution of products, we have seen
our sugar and tobacco crops increase during a financial depression and our pork industry rise again
after a nearly total extinction during the Ten Years'
War (1868-78). Our rural middle class came to the
rescue of the old sugar plantations with their fortunes and labor, and while giving them new life
saw buried forever, alas! the better part of their
resources, their faith, and their hopes.

"Eagerness to produce, without stopping to reflect
to what end and for what purpose, has dragged
many to irretrievable ruin, or to an existence full
of anxiety, uncertainty and privation.

"Nearly all the Spaniards here devote themselves
to the retail business, the wholesale trade having
always been in the hands of foreigners and of a few
Cubans. Although many economists have questioned whether this branch of activity is or is not
to be regarded as production, no one has ever
yet doubted that agricultural labor is the root and
foundation of all others. But in commerce also the
Cubans in our cities have occupied positions as
clerks, bookkeepers, brokers, etc., without counting
those who like Mariátegui, Drake, Castillo, Illos
and others, have been bankers and merchants on a
large scale. It seems scarcely necessary to speak of

the professions and many of the trades. The physicians, lawyers, pharmacists, engineers, musicians, tobacconists are Cubans in proportion of one hundred to one, for though it be true that in Havana one sees many Spanish tobacconists, the number of Cubans is much greater; and besides, Santiago de las Vegas, Bejucal, San Antonio, Guanajay and other towns of the Island make good my assertions.

" The offices of Government seem to be the exclusive property and privilege of the Spaniards; their aversion to labor is manifested in the recent regulation issued by the Marquis of Mendez Nunez, Secretary to the Governor General, to the effect that business would be transacted in his offices from 6 A. M. to 12 M. only; and this in a city where activity begins at 8 A. M. and where everybody is breakfasting from ten to eleven. Furthermore is the notorious fact that the business hours in the Government offices are but too short at best, as the unfortunate victim who has had occasion to visit them can well testify. In return, the natives of the Island work from sunrise to sunset, and from New Year's Day to Christmas Eve.

"It is obvious that the Cubans, being the more cultured and wealthy class, and not living for gain alone, both produce and consume more than the Spaniards, the majority of whom are poor, and who, by dint only of much saving and scraping, are enabled to raise the meagre sum which they came in search of, in order to realize their cherished dream of possessing a bit of land in their native town, that is, if they do not fail in the effort. Those among them who succeed in making and consolidating a competence are, of course, very few, and their mode of life is practically the same as that of the native Cubans, whom they decried before having themselves ascended the social scale.

"In the United States, Santo Domingo and the Antilles, more than thirty thousand Cubans have gained an honorable livelihood by their personal efforts during long years of exile, enriching Santo Domingo with the sugar industry, and Key West with that of tobacco. Nowhere have they offered such a spectacle as the French nobles, for example, afforded Europe at the end of the last century, when they were driven from their castles by the torrent of the Revolution.

"It seems incredible that it should be necessary to discuss so trivial a subject, but in Cuba every statement of the facts is questioned, even the evidence of one's own senses, thinking in this way to mitigate to some extent the system of exploitation and schemes of monopoly which have ruined the country. It is necessary to rectify these false assertions if we would have the light of truth penetrate everywhere and dissipate the darkness which despotism requires in order to exist and thrive.

"Catalonia has for centuries enjoyed a legislation calculated to assure to it the Peninsular and Colonial markets; Cuba has never participated in these favors of power. Nevertheless the Catalonian industries have not made greater progress than those of Cuba; and yet the industrial spirit of the Catalonians is praised to exaggeration while the Cuban character is belittled and maligned. No woman of

our race surpasses those of Cuba; they know how
to enjoy the fruits of prosperity as well as to battle
against adversity; and still there are not wanting
creatures to deny them virtues which only the blind
or evil-minded do not see.

"Let these prejudices cease; let justice be done to
Cuba, and then the bands of social solidarity will
reappear, so that this country may continue to be
what it is in truth—one of the most vigorous and
healthy offshoots of the Spanish race."

In my undertaking to refute one by one the mis-
statements of which your correspondent has been
guilty in regard to this poor Island of Cuba—so
little known and so harshly judged—I find myself
compelled to submit to his incoherencies and want
of sequence and of unity, revealing an absolute lack
of critical ability (not wishing to employ a stronger
term), which denotes the imperfect writer, just as
his ideas denote the passionate, enraged enemy of
Cuban society, and at the same time the uncon-
scious defamer of his own country, which is responsible before history and humanity at large for all
the horrors that are perpetrated in a land colonized
and governed by Spain.

· According to F. Moreno, the prostrated condition
of Cuba is owing first to the Spaniards who impro-
vise fortunes by perpetrating swindles and by rob-

bing the treasury; and second, to the Cubans who
squander in orgies the inheritance of their Spanish
fathers, acquired through privation and toil. It
therefore, follows that by confiscating the goods of
the spendthrift Cubans, and imprisoning those who
rob and swindle, the causes would be radically ex-
tirpated, and we could ever after live in peace and
glory.

But, do you understand these vaticinations, friend
Paco? Can you grasp what is meant by inheri-
tances obtained *through privation and toil* by means
of wretched swindling and defalcation? And that
this is what constitutes the ruin of a country so
richly gifted by nature? . . . .

Oh! no! Let Spaniards come to Cuba to till and
promote by means of honest labor this land of extraordinary fertility; let them and the natives enjoy
the same rights and guarantees which the Spaniard
does in the metropolis; let division and class privilege vanish; establish order and equity; let the
country take part in the administration of common
interests, or rather, let it govern its own interests;
let the Colony cease to be a great field of exploitation where gather a multitude of office seekers that
like an ineradicable plague pollutes the corridors of
the ministry; let, in fine, the old regime of Spanish
colonization disappear; let the mother country follow the example of England. .   .   and

Cuba will regenerate from her ashes and rise anew from her ruins. A good system of government will dispel demoralization by its natural and logical consequences; Home Rule will make the existence of defaulting officials all but impossible; and there will be no prodigal sons when the industrious fathers give the edifying example of ever-faithful morality.

Under the influence of this new departure, which will transform the diverse elements of this society into a compactly solid body, there will surely not arise a Moreno to assert that the robberies and embezzlements perpetrated in the cities are committed in the name of *Cuba Libre*, thus requiring a Cuban like myself, jealous of his country's honor, to assure you that the revolutionary cry of 1868 was never dishonored by the depredations of brigandage; that that generous impulse of a cultured people may have been mistaken in its purpose, but it was not the work of bandits and marauders, far rather was it an effort of self-sacrifice and patriotism in which a whole generation of valiant and heroic men sacrificed their fortunes and shed their blood.

No; it is not true that the thefts and embezzlements are the work of the "Separatist" islanders. Separatism does not exist to-day, or at least has no military power: highway robbery is not the occupation of the islanders. Pray look up, friend Paco, the criminal statistics of these provinces, investigate the nativity of the delinquents, and through the official testimony of the Regents of our Courts find out from whence the bandits hail. I fear it will cause you sadness to learn that the lesser number, considerably the fewest of those tried and convicted, were born beneath this tropical sky, and that by far the greater number are natives of Spain, and foreigners. In case you should experience a feeling of bitterness over this result, it may comfort you to hear that in order to avoid giving rise to murmuring the following expedient has been adopted :—that in the publication of the criminal statistics the nativity of those sentenced shall be omitted. Surely this is an advantage !   .

Nevertheless, the statistics of 1884 remained printed, and as it is opportune and may interest you, I copy them from a paper at hand*.

.*Subsequently, the statistics of 1886 were published, and since the first edition of this work, have been reproduced in the periodical "*La Semana*;" but its figures, with but slight differences, show results identical with those noted above.

CRIMINAL POPULATION OF CUBA.

Statistics published by the distinguished editor of "Los Sucesos," José de J. Márques, Havana, November 18th, 1885.

" From the quarterly synopsis of the penal statistics of the Island of Cuba during the year 1884, published in the *Gaceta* of Madrid, it appears that 1415 individuals are suffering terms of imprisonment. Of these 508 are Negroes, 108 Chinese, 586 European Spaniards, 180 Cubans (White Natives), 19 Canary Islanders, and 14 foreigners. The colored race is represented by something more than one-third, and adding the Chinese, these two elements compose something less than one-half of the number of prisoners.

" The statistics of population are divided as follows : Negroes, 460,000 ; White Natives, 860,000 : White Europeans, including the Canary Islanders, 140,000 ; Chinese, 30,000 : Foreigners, 10,000 : a total of 1,500,000. Taking this as a basis it follows that the convicts are in proportion of 1.06 for every 1,000 inhabitants.

" In relation to the several subdivisions the ratios are respectively as follows :

NATIVE WHITES : Population, 860,000 ; Convicts, 180 ; 1 for every 4,777 inhabitants.

NEGROES : Population, 460,000. Convicts, 508. Proportion, 1 for every 905 inhabitants.

FOREIGNERS : Popoulation, 10,000. Convicts, 14. Proportion, 1 for every 714 inhabitants.

CHINESE : Population, 30,000. Convicts, 108. Proportion, 1 for every 277 inhabitants.

EUROPEAN SPANIARDS, including Canary Islanders: Popoulation, 140,000. Convicts, 605. Proportion, 1 for every 231 inhabitants.

"It follows that there are imprisoned : 1.10 for every 1000 colored inhabitants, 1.40 foreigners, 3.61 Chinese, 4.32 Europeans, and only 0.20 of native whites."

And now let me drop my badly cut pen to treat later another subject. Comment on the above is unnecessary.

V.

No. 18.—SALA SORRIN.
Library of the Sociedad Económica.

LITERARY ACTIVITY IN CUBA—PUBLIC AND PRIVATE LIBRARIES—
SPREAD OF INTELLIGENCE—CUBAN AS DISTINGUISHED FROM
SPANISH LITERATURE—CUBAN AUTHORS AND THEIR WORKS.

I find on examining Moreno's fifth letter, in which he makes known to you the *principal* Cuban writings published in latter days, that I am enabled to save much ink, much paper, and no little effort in the preparation of these epistles, for he pretends to picture *Cuba and its People*, and I assure you he has not met the *people* of Cuba, nor is he acquainted with Cuba itself, his citation of the writings and publications which he mentions serving but to confirm my statement.

All of these are the work of foreigners. understanding as such those who are not natives of the country in which they reside, so that if his intention has been to have you think ill of Cubans who cultivate the profession of letters, and in this way belittle our literature, let me at once state that the productions which he has brought to your notice are not the work of Cubans.

But I will more fully present this subject to you, Paco, so that you may realize what distorted accounts your guide and instructor has submitted to you.

Before beginning the task allow me to make a counter-statement. In Cuba there are many persons who spend money in the purchase of literature, but it does not transpire that cultured people buy such pamphlets as "Cuba and its People," nor do they subscribe to papers like *La Verdad* (Moreno's) or *El Rayo* (Rivero's), nor do they read the almanacs and novels which are printed by shoals in Madrid and Barcelona. Inasmuch as the Government here has not founded nor does it support libraries, the only public library being that of the Sociedad Economica, oganized and enriched by donations from its members, who are Cubans, it naturally follows that the citizens have their private libraries where their means permit.*

*To the commendable zeal, labor and enthusiasm of Don Juan Bautista Armenteros, treasurer of the Sociedad Economica, are due many important reforms in the public library,

In any professional man's office you will find at least a thousand volumes of scientific and literary works by authors of universal repute. In Havana, with a population of 250,000 souls (from which deduct the negroes, the Chinese, the Europeans, and native whites who do not know how to read), there are more than fifty book-stores which are surely not maintained for mere pleasure or caprice on the part of their proprietors. If they are not all registered, and if the printing offices and lithographic establishment do not appear in the census, where I have sought them in vain,—for in this, as in all other matters our statistics are incomplete—it is because the means resorted to by the trades-people in order to avoid paying the exorbitant taxes are regulated

which was almost wholly abandoned from 1868 to 1878. Jorrin Hall and Chaple Hall were added to the galleries while he was in commission; 3775 volumes, 44 collections of newspapers, 2691 brochures, 1042 pamphlets, and 322 loose sheets or prints were added to the library; 1430 volumes of works, 138 collections of newspapers, and 5 of prints were bound.

At the close of his term the library numbered 21,078 volumes, comprising

NO. 19.
D. JUAN B. ARMENTEROS.

21,430 books, which go to form 10,551 works, in place of 17,303 volumes which it formerly counted; 217 complete collections of newspapers in lieu of 184; also a number of incomplete ones; 5 large portfolio cases, containing maps, designs, draw-

according to the much or little favor dispensed them by the employés of the tax office. I can assure you of the truth of my assertions. On Obispo street alone there are ten bookstores and four subscription centres. The knowledge of languages is no unusual thing, and while these may not have been learned in the official institutes, whose methods are founded on the principle that everything should be studied and nothing learned, nevertheless the cultured classes of the country, which are numerous, study foreign languages, and teach them to their children. Daily communication with the United States, and above all, the emigration to that country during the Revolution, has taught us English and continues to do so, and our litterateurs are familiar with Corneille, Victor Hugo, Byron, and Shakespeare, as well as with Moratin and Cervantes.

NO. 20.—CARLOS NA- VARRETE Y ROMAY.

ings, etc. He and his friends made valuable donations, such as Froud's History of the "Æcumenical Council" (costing, unbound, 3000 francs), "Treasury of English Art," by Vernon, and Montaner's edition of "Don Quixote."

Senor Armenteros also collected seven volumes of manuscripts and autographs, and the six numerical and alphabetical catalogues relating respectively to the Robredo, Jorrin and Chaple Halls. The library has recently had an increase of nearly 1000 volumes.

In the twelve months of 1886, according to the report of the committee, more than 5600 persons visited the library.

But let us return to our literary productions. In perusing the passages quoted by Moreno from various sources, we make another discovery, namely, that the writers are not only foreigners, but are furthermore members of that privileged class of society which is full of prejudice and bitterness against the country, and which I have described in a previous letter.

Am I to concern myself with the vaticinations of Don Fernando Casanova Gil, a personage entirely unknown in the political and literary circles of Havana, and whose name I here see for the first time in print? Who, according to Moreno, has published a number of pamphlets in which he designates the Cubans as parricides, and exhorts the Catalonians to "awaken" against

NO. 21.—ENRIQUE PIÑEYRO.

them; in which he wounds deeply the public sentiment of our country by defaming and desecrating the ever-venerated memory of that learned Cuban, Don José de la Luz Caballero? It would be descending too low to place myself on a level with those who, like Señor Moreno, regard as truth what appears in such publications.

Neither shall we stop to consider the other writ-

ings and writers whom he quotes; there is not a
Cuban author among them.   It is this that I would
insist upon.

NO. 22.
JOSÉ IGNACIO RODRIGUEZ.

If you desire, inquiring
Paco, to acquaint yourself
with our works in this domain, and to form a true
and correct judgment con-
cerning the efforts of Cuban
publicists, whether in the
sphere of politics, economics or sociology, through
which fruitful· means of
agitation and persuasion
they have striven for im-
provement, for progress, and for the reform of old
and obstinate evils, pray read, consult, study, or
at least look over the numerous treatises which
I shall name for you, and whose authors, by their
learning, their talents, their reputation and their
works, suffice to prove the culture of the community
in the midst of which they have lived, oppressed,
but persevering in their ideals.

It is they, and those whom they represent, that
really constitute the *people of Cuba*, whose worth
and merit it is most important should be known in
Madrid, in order that it may there be realized that
it is not a semi-civilized country which is to be

THE PUNTA BATTERY AND MORRO CASTLE AT THE ENTRANCE TO THE PORT OF HAVANA.

NO. 14. JOSÉ ANTONIO SAGO.

governed, but a cultured, progressive, intelligent community, fully capable of governing itself.

First of all, procure and read carefully the innumerable treaties and essays which have gained for Don José Antonio Saco, native of Bayamo, a universal reputation as a publicist. These essays, embracing the various subjects of Political Economy, Statistics, Colonization, Public Instruction, Hygiene and Colonial History, together with many pertaining to local interests, you will find compiled in several volumes, published in New York, Paris and Havana.

No. 23 —JUAN G. GÓMEZ.

Read the dissertations of the Count of Pozes Dulces, which will enlighten you upon the most important branches of agriculture and colonial administration. Read *Dos Banderas*, a pamphlet for which we are indebted to the pen of Don José Ramon Betancourt, an illustrious Cuban who, for political reasons, withheld his name. This essay will inform you of the true causes of the revolutionary movement of '68.

Read the two memoirs, *Indicacion* and *Reforma Politica*, by the venerable patriot, Don Calixto Bernal, friend of Saco. He died in Madrid in 1868,

6

and, like the latter, was a republican of European reputation. Read the famous *Folleto de Ginebra*, a  work, which of itself, justifies the reputation of the author, whose name (no longer a secret), is Don José Silverio Jorrin.

Read the works of Enrique Piñeyro, of José de Armas y Cespedes, and of Antonio Zambrana, upon the events of the revolution. The fine historical studies of Don José Ignacio Rodriguez; the works upon slavery by Francisco de Armas; *La Cuestion de Cuba*, by Juan Gualberto Gómez; the dissertations upon *La Cuestion Economica de Cuba*, by José Quintín Suzarte; *La Reforma Politica*, a work by the editors of El Triunfo; *Las Leyes Especiales*, due to the masterly pen of Don Antonio Govin; *Les Oradores de Cuba*, by the noted and elegant writer, Dou Manuel Sanguili; *El 27 de Noviembre de 1871*, by Fermín V. Dominguez; *El Espinar Cubano*, by Don Rafael M. Merchán, an eminent Cuban, who, during his voluntary expatriation has devoted his studies to the defence and honor of his country. Read *Cuba Autonómica*, by Don Alfredo Zayas.

But, pray read no more; for you might be exhausted by such a gigantic effort. These selected models are presented as sufficient to show you that

No. 24.—D. RAFAEL M. MERCHÁN.

in Cuba, notwithstanding its demoralization and bad government, there are literary, scientific and talented men, who study, learn, think, and work.

1 will yet have occasion to prove this to you, but must proceed now on the path of rectification which has been traced for me by the detractor of *Cuba and its People.*

VI.

No. 26.—PRINCIPAL PERIODICALS OF HAVANA.

CUBAN LITERATURE—ITS BEGINNINGS AND DEVELOPMENT—CUBAN
POETS AND HISTORIANS—ACTIVITY IN THE FIELDS OF SCIENCE,
ART AND GENERAL LITERATURE—CUBAN PAINTERS AND COM-
POSERS.

Let us now treat of Cuban literature which,
although still in its infancy, holds no small nor
unimportant place in our Parnassus.

Were you to judge it, however, by the report of
your officious informant and the models which he
brings to your notice, you would surely be con-
strained to believe that Spain has here founded and
governs such an incapable colony that the inhabitants have not even preserved the language of their
progenitors.

Fortunately this is not the case : the children of this ardent soil have a superabundance of imagination and talent, and to these natural gifts, above all, is due their intelligent progress.

How little flattering it were to the Spanish nation if in the last quarter of the nineteenth century the literature of her chief American colony offered as *morceaux choisis* only the patched up, pedantic program-advertisement of a negro ball, or some of the sonnets and romantic effusions that appear in the "Personal" columns of newspapers the world over!

But perhaps Moreno was so engrossed with his official duties that he found no opportunity to study our literary movement, nor to examine our bibliography, nor the occasion to meet and know our litterateurs; or, if he had time—and being a Government employé, that goes without saying—he lacked good faith and a desire to interest himself in these things ; he did not lack, however, the evil intent of describing in Madrid Cuba as he imagined it, or as he found it in the narrow, noxious circle where he, bird of passage, and confined to the lobbies of the bureaucracy, alone breathed freely and felt at home.

The three young writers, Bobadilla, Valdivia and Hermida, whom Moreno quotes, satirizes, and presents as a literary trinity, are not representatives of Cuban literature, nor is Don José Fornaris the classical poet of Cuba. The three first, considering their youth—particularly Señor Bobadilla. give promise of a brilliant future if they will know how to cultivate their faculties by observation and study. Fornaris is not a classic, but he is an estimable poet, and among the many things he has written and published are some lyrical compositions of real and distinguished merit.*

Nor are Don Francisco de Armas, Don Rafael Villa, or Señor Perez prominent as writers or poets. Señor Moreno critizes them and others with unpardonable levity, and as if the condition and character of our literature were to be estimated by their works alone.

Undoubtedly these young men may some day

---

* The true merit of Señor Fornaris consists of his having been, during a period of absolute oppression, one of the most laborious and zealous men of letters. All his works may not be of especial excellence, but in them he taught, as best he could, love of Cuba, her liberty and her cherished ideals, concealing his doctrines from the tyranny of the censor in allegories and Indian tales. To those who write to-day under the aegis of the liberty of the press, the songs of " *Siboney* " and others, have no meaning. But for those who lived in that reign of terror, or who have studied it, these songs echo the lamentations in which the people who memorized them gave expression to their woes, and through which they became kindled with the realization of their political misfortunes. To Fornaris, Luaces, Nápoles, Fajarda and others, belongs the glory of having figured among the most popular minstrells of an enslaved people.

honor the country in which they begin with praise-
worthy enthusiasm the rough and thorny career of
the public writer, but at present they do not afford
a true reflex of the advance of Cuba in the matter
of letters.

I propose, patient Paco, to give you more exact
information, following always the plan which I
have formed of tracing these letters so that you and
all your Madrid people may have a correct, however scant idea of *Cuba and its People*.

You have already been informed that until 1790
the Cubans did not know the printing press at all.
Now let me tell you that until 1800 no private
printing press existed anywhere in Cuba!

Our first minstrels could reproduce their inspirations only in manuscript, and but few of these have
been preserved. These few have been discovered

as historic relics by some of our
well-known bibliophiles (Saco,
Bachiller y Morales, Mendiver,
etc.), and reveal the state of a
country where schools were
sparse in number and established
with difficulty.

Every nation has had this
dark epoch in its history. The
first steps are as uncertain as

NO. 27.—D. ANTONIO BA-
CHILLER Y MORALES.

those of a child learning to walk. But what is truly

remarkable and strange is that it should be a Spanish colony, founded in 1492, that should find itself in darkness and in intellectual infancy at the beginning of the nineteenth century.

Our Juan de Mena* was chronologically the poet Rubalcaba. He and Don Manuel de Zequeira are the pioneers of a literature which, in less than ninety years, offers a long list of illustrious men, some of whom already figure among the great Spanish poets of the present century. Rubalcaba, who studied the classics, especially Virgil, and who successfully imitated the latter, had no opportunity to publish his compositions. He consequently lacked (in a country where the printing press was a rarity when not entirely prohibited), the incentive that publicity offers to polish his productions.

Zequeira, who possessed solid learning, and who excelled Rubalcaba in feeling and in correctness of of style, was also unable to' publish his works. The first edition of his poems was printed by his friends in New York (1828) five years after the intellectual death of the poet. In his own country he did not obtain this glory,—always so dear to those who cultivate the muses.

Homers of a people without traditions, without a history, almost without culture, what more could

---

*The Spanish Chaucer.

these minstrels do than offer the first fruits of their
imagination in a limited number of lyrical compositions ?

But after these there sprang forth that extraordinary genius—José Maria Heredia.
He appeared as the elaborated outcome of the new schools established in Havana, focussing the
modern philosophic ideas, which
were studied and taught by
talented men in the recently
established professional chairs,
and combined in his works all the
progress made in but few years by
the Cuban youth of that period.

No. 28.—D. JOSÉ MARÍA
HEREDIA.

He was a poet at
ten years of age, linguist and litterateur at fifteen,
lawyer and journalist at twenty, judge in Mexico at
twenty-five, historian, professor, publicist and an
exile from his beloved country at thirty-five, the
time of his early death.

He, too, had to publish his works in a foreign
land. The first collection of his poems, printed in
New York (1825) and reprinted in Toluca, Mexico,
(1832), gained for him in both Europe and America
the merited title of a great poet.

He also published an *Historia Universal* (1832),
Sila de Jouy, Abufar de Ducis, Atreo Tiestes, a tragedy,
and various memoirs, translations, and other works.

He left unpublished some tragedies and descriptions of travels.

It is not for me, Paco, to commend to you the greatness of this fruitful genius, who rivals Quintana. You might think with Moreno that I am actuated by a provincial Cuban sentiment.

Read rather what Don Alberto Lista, who calls him a great poet, writes of him; read Gallego and Martinez de la Rosa; and if you have a knowledge of languages, read Kennidi's *Conversations Lexikon;* read Ampère, Mazade and Villemain, who have made Heredia known respectively in Germany, England and France.

I will only add that the venerated remains of that illustrious Cuban—an exile from his country— have been lost in a foreign land. And since Moreno has given you as samples of our literature a series of selections which I consider as the juvenile expressions of an immature poet, let me invite you to read the following ode of our classic poet. It is the sublime conception of a surpassing genius who dictates therein a touching remembrance to his unhapy country.

EL NIAGARA.*

Templad mi lira, dádmela, que siento
En mi alma estremecida y agitada
Arder la inspiración.   ¡ Oh! ¡ cuánto tiempo
En tinieblas pasó, sin que mi frente
Brillase con su luz . . . . ¡ Niágara undoso,
Tu sublime terror solo podría
Tornarme el don divino, que ensañada
Me robó del dolor la mano impía.

Torrente prodigioso, calma, calla
Tu trueno aterrador: disipa un tanto

---

*NIAGARA.

Translated from the Spanish of José María Heredia
by William Cullen Bryant.

My lyre ! Give me my lyre ! My bosom feels
The glow of inspiration ; O, how long
Have I been left in darkness, since this light
Last visited my brow ! Niagara !
Thou with thy rushing waters dost restore
The heavenly gift which sorrow took away.

Tremendous torrent ! for an instant hush
The terror of thy voice, and cast aside
These wide involving shadows that my eyes

Las tinieblas que en torno te circundan;
Déjame contemplar tu faz serena
Y de entusiasmo ardiente mi alma llena.
Yo digno soy de contemplarte: siempre
Lo común y mezquino desdeñando,
Ansié por lo terrífico y sublime.
Al despeñarse el huracán furioso,
Al retumbar sobre mi frente el rayo,
Palpitando gocé: ví al Oceano
Azotado por austro proceloso
Combatir mi bajel y ante mis plantas
Vórtice hirviente abrir, y amé el peligro.
Más del mar la fiereza
En mi alma no produjo
La profunda impresión que tu grandeza.

Sereno corres, majestuoso, y luego
En ásperos peñascos quebrantado,

May see the fearful beauty of thy face.
I am not all unworthy of thy sight;
For, from my boyhood, have I loved—
Shunning the meaner paths of common minds—
To look on Nature in her loftier moods.
At the fierce rushing of the hurricane,
At the near bursting of the thunderbolt,
I have been touched with joy; and when the sea
Lashed by the winds, hath rocked my bark, and showed
Its yawning caves beneath me, I have loved
Its dangers and the wrath of elements.
But never yet the madness of the sea
Hath moved me as thy grandeur moves me now.

Te abalanzas violento, arrebatado,
Como el destino irresistible y ciego.
¿Qué voz humana describir podría
De la Sirte rugiente
La aterradora faz?   El alma mía
En vago pensamiento se confunde
Al mirar esa férvida corriente
Que en vano quiere la turbada vista
En su vuelo seguir al borde oscuro
Del precipicio altísimo: mil olas,
Cual pensamientos rápidas pasando,
Chocan y se enfurecen,
Y otras mil y otras mil ya las alcanzan,
Y entre espuma y fragor desaparecen.

Ved! llegan, saltan!   El abismo horrendo
Devora los torrentes despeñados:
Crúzanse en él mil iris, y asordados

Thou flowest on in quiet, till thy waves
Grow broken midst the rocks ; thy current then
Shoots onward like the irresistible course
Of Destiny. Ah ! terrible thy rage—
Thy hoarse and rapid whirlpools there ! My brain
Grows wild, my senses wander, as I gaze
Upon the hurrying waters and my sight
Vainly would follow, as toward the verge
Sweeps the wide torrent : waves innumerable
Urge on and overtake the waves before,
And disappear in thunder and in foam.
They reach—they leap the barrier : the abyss
Swallows insatiable the sinking waves.
A thousand rainbows arch them, and the woods

Vuelven los bosques el fragor tremendo.
En las rígidas peñas
Rómpese el agua: vaporosa nube
Con elástica fuerza
Llena el abismo en torbellino, sube,
Gira en torno, y al éter
Luminosa pirámide levanta,
Y por sobre los montes que le cercan
Al solitario cazador espanta.

Más ¿qué en tí busca mi anhelante vista
Con inútil afán! ¿Por qué no miro
Al rededor de tu caverna inmensa
Las palmas ¡ay! las palmas deliciosas,
Que en las llanuras de mi ardiente patria
Nacen del sol á la sonrisa, y crecen,
Y al soplo de las brisas del Oceano,
Bajo un cielo purísimo se mecen?

Are deafened with the roar. The violent shock
Shatters to vapours the descending sheets :
A cloudy whirlwind fills the gulf, and heaves
The mighty pyramid of circling mist
To heaven. The solitary hunter near,
Pauses with terror in the forest shades.

What seeks my restless eye? Why are not here
About the jaws of the abyss, the palms,—
Ah, the delicious palms,—that on the plains
Of my own native Cuba spring and spread
Their thickly foliaged summits to the sun,
And, in the breathings of the ocean air,
Wave soft beneath the heaven's unspotted blue?

Este recuerdo á mi pesar me viene . . . .
Nada ¡ oh Niágara ! falta á tu destino,
Ni otra corona que el agreste pino
A tu terrible majestad conviene.
La palma y mirto y delicada rosa,
Muelle placer inspiren y ocio blando
En frívolo jardín: á tí la suerte
Guardó más digno objeto, más sublime.
El alma libre, generosa, fuerte,
Viene, te vé, se asombra,
El mezquino deleite menosprecia,
Y aun se siente elevar cuando te nombra.

Omnipotente Dios ! En otros climas
Ví monstruos execrables
Blasfemando tu nombre sacrosanto,
Sembrar error y fanatismo impíos,
Los campos inundar con sangre y llanto,

But no, Niagara.—thy forest pines
Are fitter coronal for thee. The palms,
The effeminate myrtle, the frail rose, may grow
In gardens, and give out their fragrance there,
Unmanning him who breathes it. Thine it is
To do a nobler office. Generous minds
Behold thee, and are moved, and learn to rise
Above earth's frivolous pleasures ; they partake
Thy grandeur at the utterance of thy name.

God of all truth ! In other lands I've seen
Lying philosophers, blaspheming men,
Questioners of thy mysteries, that draw
Their fellows deep into impiety ;

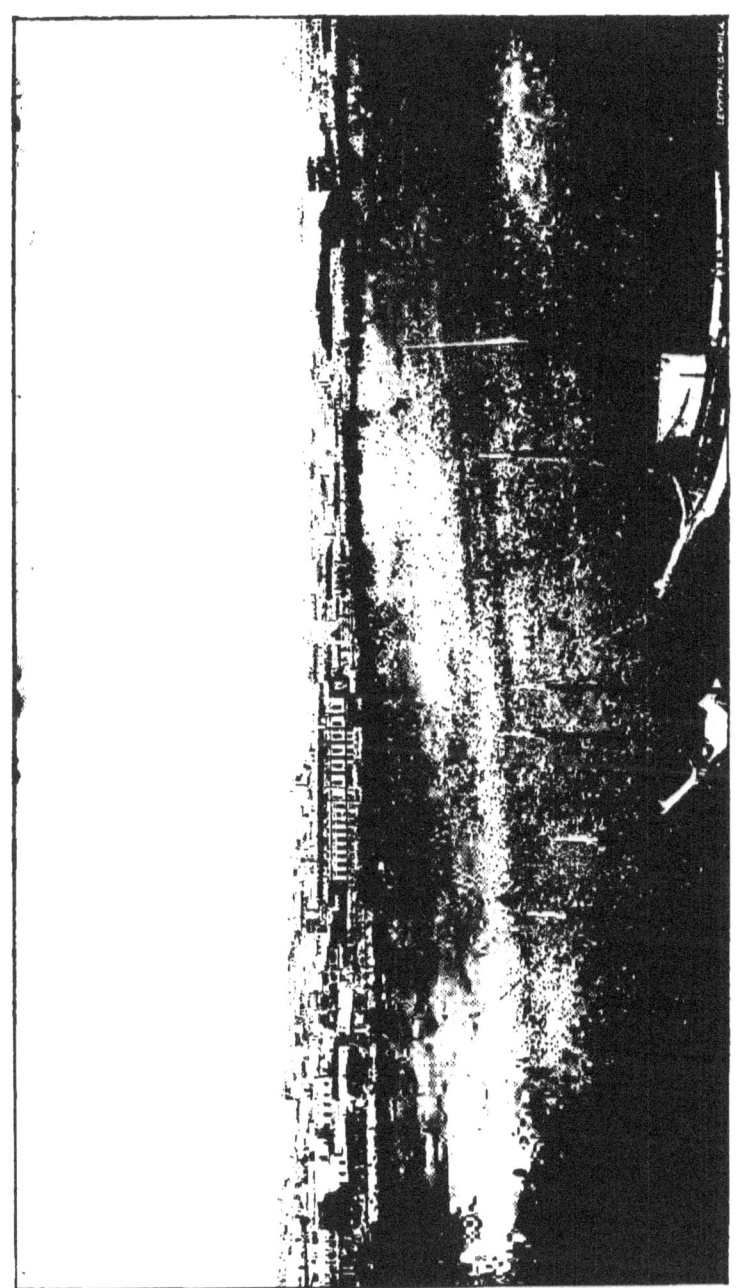

HAVANA FROM CABANAS FORTRESS, LOOKING TOWARDS THE PUNTA BATTERY AT ENTRANCE TO THE PORT.

NO. 17. JOSÉ SILVERIO JORRÍN.

De hermanos atizar la infanda guerra,
Y desolar frenéticos la tierra.
Vilos, y el pecho se inflamó á su vista
En grave indignación.   Por otra parte
Ví mentidos filósofos, que osaban
Escrutar tus misterios, ultrajarte,
Y de impiedad al lamentable abismo
A los míseros hombres arrastraban.
Por eso te buscó mi débil mente,
En la sublime soledad: ahora
Entera se abre á ti; tu mano siente
En esta inmensidad que me circunda:
Y tu profunda voz hiere mi seno
De este raudal en el eterno trueno.

    Asombroso torrente !.
  ¡Cómo tu vista el ánimo enajena
  Y de terror y admiración me llena !

And therefore doth my spirit seek thy face
In earth's majestic solitudes. Even here
My heart doth open all itself to thee;
In this immensity of loneliness
I feel thy hand upon me. To my ear
The eternal thunder of the cataract brings
Thy voice, and I am humbled as I hear.

  Dread torrent ! that with wonder and with fear
Dost overwhelm the soul of him that looks
Upon thee, and dost bear it from itself,
Whence hast thou thy beginning? Who supplies
Age after age thy inexhausted springs?
  7

¿ Dó tu origen está?   ¿ Quién fertiliza
Por tantos siglos tu inexhausta fuente?
¿ Qué poderosa mano
Hace que al recibirte
No rebose en la tierra el Oceano?

Abrió el Señor su mano omnipotente;
Cubrió tu faz de nubes agitadas,
Dió su voz á tus aguas despeñadas
Y ornó con su arco tu terrible frente.
Ciego, profundo, infatigable corres,
Como el torrente oscuro de los siglos
En insondable eternidad . . . . !   Al hombre
Huyen así las ilusiones gratas,
Los florecientes días,
Y despierta al dolor . . . . . !   ¡ Ay ! agostada
Yace mi juventud; mi faz, marchita;
Y la profunda pena que me agita
Ruga mi frente de dolor nublada.

What power hath ordered, that when all thy weight
Descends into the deep, the swollen waves
Rise not and roll to overwhelm the earth?

The Lord hath opened his omnipotent hand
Covered thy face with clouds and given his voice
To thy down-rushing waters: He, that girt
Thy terrible forehead with his radiant bow.
I see thy never-resting waters run,
And I bethink me how the tide of time
Sweeps to eternity. So days of man
Pass, like a noon-day dream—the blossoming days,—
And he awakes to sorrow.

Nunca tanto sentí como este día
Mi soledad y mísero abandono
Y lamentable desamor . . . . ¿ Podría
En edad borrascosa
Sin amor ser feliz?   ¡ Oh ! ¡ Si una hermosa
Mi cariño fijase,
Y de este abismo al borde turbulento
Mi vago pensamiento
Y ardiente admiración acompañase !
¡ Cómo gozara, viéndola cubrirse
De leve palidez, y ser más bella
En su dulce terror, y sonreirse
Al sostenerla mis amantes brazos . . . .
Delirios de virtud . . . . ¡ Ay ! Desterrado,
Sin patria, sin amores,
Sólo miro ante mí llanto y dolores !

    Niágara poderoso !
    Adios ! Adios!   Dentro de pocos años

Never have I so deeply felt as now
The hopeless solitude, the abandonment,
The anguish of a loveless life. Alas !
How can the impassioned, the unfrozen heart
Be happy without love? I would that one,
Beautiful, worthy to be loved, and joined
In love with me, now shared my lonely walk
On this tremendous brink. T'were sweet to see
Her dear face touched with paleness, and become
More beatiful from fear, and overspread
With a faint smile while clinging to my side.
Dreams—dreams ! I am an exile, and for me
There is no country and there is no love.

Ya devorado habrá la tumba fría
A tu débil cantor.   Duren mis versos
Cual tu gloria inmortal !   Pueda piadoso
Viéndote algún viajero,
Dar un suspiro á la memoria mía !
Y al abismarse Febo en occidente,
Feliz yo vuele do el Señor me llama,
Y al escuchar los ecos de mi fama,
Alce en las nubes la radiosa frente.

(Junio 1824.)

Hear ! dread Niagara ! this my latest verse.
Yet a few years, and the cold earth shall close
Over the bones of him who sings thee now
Thus feelingly.   Would that this, my humble verse,
Might be, like thou, immortal—I, meanwhile,
Cheerfully passing to the appointed rest,
Might raise my radiant forehead in the clouds
To listen to the echoes of my fame.

June, 1824.

AFTER Heredia—a star of the first magnitude—there shine as poets of considerable merit, Don Ramon Velez Herrera, the first who had the honor of publishing a collectien of poems in Cuba (1830) and of whom Salas y Quiroga speaks in high praise. Don Domingo del Monte, a most learned man of letters, who endeavored to form in his admirable *Romances Cubanos* a literature peculiar to the country, was the mentor of the young writers

NO. 29.
D. CIRILO VILLAVERDE.

of the time and a critic of whom Antonio Cánovas del Castillo makes honorable mention, as also of Don

NO. 30.
D. JOSÉ JACINTO MILANÉS.

Félix Tanco, who devoted but too short a time to the inspiration of his muse. Eminent above these was Placido, the humble mulatto, Gabriel de la Concepcion Valdés, who began his checkered career in a foundling's cradle and ended it on a scaffold. He would have equalled Heredia, if instead of spending his childhood and youth in a workshop he had received some stimulus from a protecting government or if a less prejudiced social order had opened for him a pathway to the fame and laurels

everywhere reserved for genius. A poverty-stricken descendant of an abject race of slaves—an humble laborer, without education, without incentive, he yet possessed in a superlative degree the poetic spirit. This has been recognized by critics, both at home and abroad, and accords him a title to immortality. On his native soil his lot was but misery, insult and death.

NO. 31.—D JOAQUÍN LO-
RENZO LUACES.

Some of his sonnets, romances and other compositions would not be disdained by the classic Spaniards. If you desire, Paco, to know something more of our literature, I pray you, instead of reading the doggerel rhymes of a negro ball program, which Moreno quotes for your benefit, read with tears in your eyes and anguish in your heart, the beautiful, touching prayer which Placido wrote in his last days. It was recited by that unhappy member of the negro race as he was conducted to the scaffold, and remains an undying glory of Cuban letters. Placido was condemned to death for having sung in his works the liberty of his country and of his race.

PLEGARIA A DIOS.*

Ser de inmensa bondad, Dios poderoso,
A vos acudo en mi dolor vehemente;
Extended vuestro brazo omnipotente,
Rasgad de la calumnia el velo odioso,
Y arrancad este sello ignominioso
Con que el mundo manchar quiere mi frente.

Rey de los reyes, Dios de mis abuelos,
Vos solo sois mi defensor, Dios mío:
Todo lo puede quien al mar sombrío
Olas y peces dió, luz á los cielos,
Fuego al sol, giro al aire, al Norte heilos,
Vida á las plantas, movimiento al rio.

---

* A PRAYER.

Translated from the Spanish of Placido by the Editor.

Being of boundless good ! Almighty God !
To Thee I turn in my most poignant grief;
Extend thy hand omnipotent to hold
This odious veil of calumny from me,
And tear away the ignominious seal
With which the world would harshly brand my brow.

King of Kings ! Thou God of my forefathers !
Thou art my sole defender, oh my God !
All may He do who to the sombre sea
Its waves and fishes gave, to heaven its light,
Fire to the sun, and to the North its ice,
Life to the plants, and movement to the rills.

Todo lo podéis vos, todo fenece
O se reanima á vuestra voz sagrada:
Fuera de vos, Señor, el todo es nada,
Que en la insondable eternidad perece;
Y aun esa misma nada os obedece
Pues de ella fué la humanidad creada.

Yo no os puedo engañar, Dios de clemencia,
Y pues vuestra eternal Sabiduría
Vé al través de mi cuerpo el alma mía
Cual del aire á la clara trasparencia,
Estorbad que humillada la inocencia
Bata sus palmas la calumnia impia.

Mas si cuadra á tu suma omnipotencia
Que yo perezca cual malvado impío,

All things canst Thou accomplish ; all things die
And live again but through thy holy word.
Apart from Thee, oh Lord, all things are naught
And lost in fathomless eternity ;
Yet doth obey Thee this same nothingness,
For thereof didst Thou humankind create.

I cannot Thee deceive, thou God of Truth,
And since it is that thy omniscient eye
Doth through my body see this soul of mine
As through the clear transparency of air,
Do Thou prevent that innocence be crushed
And wicked slander triumph undisturbed.

But if in thy omnipotence Thou wouldst
That I shall perish like a godless wretch,

Y que los hombres mi cadáver frío
Ultrajen con maligna complacencia,
Suene tu voz y acabe mi existencia . . . .
Cúmplase en mí tu voluntad, Dios mío !

And that men may my cold and lifeless corse
Abase and outrage with malignant joy,
Then let thy voice be heard and end my life,
And let thy will, oh Lord, be done in me !

Do not weary, Paco, if over-solicitous in this task, I continue to quote Cuban writers and poets whose works deserve to be read and recommended : such are Don Ramon de Palma remarkable for the purity of his diction, and for his journalistic efforts : also, Orgaz, Foxá, Blanchie, Briñas, Roldán, Leopoldo Turla, Tolón, Quintero, Andrés Días, N. Fajardo, Ramón Piña, Santacilia, V. Aguirre, the slave Manzano—the merit of whose facile and simple prose exceeds even that of his poems—Luisa Perez, Anselmo Suárez, L. V. Betancourt, Villaverde, the Carrillo brothers, Toroella, del Monte, the Countess de Merlin, Zambrana, N. Azcárate, José I. Armas, Navarrete y Romay, and Fornaris. There are yet

NO. 32.
D. ANTONIO GUITERAS.

others whom I omit, or whom I do not recall, that
manifested in the period from 1830 to 1868 by their

various literary works and in
their unceasing journalistic
efforts, the zeal and enthusiasm with which literature has
been cultivated among us.
Notable among them all is
José Jacinto Milanes, the most
popular, the sweetest, and
simplest of our poets; he is
polished and correct in language, and has distinguished
himself in dramatic as well
as in lyric poetry.   Gertrudis

NO. 33.
D. JUAN CLEMENTE ZENEA.

Gómez de Avallaneda, who was the wonder and
admiration of Quintana, and whose
distinction was recognized by Lista
and Gallego ; she was a poet, a
novelist, and a journalist of acknowledged rank, while as dramatist she initiated a renaissance
of classic tragedy in her " Alfonso Munio."   Rafael María de
Mendive, the chaste, gentle, and
inspired poet,—highly regarded
by the Spanish critic Cañete ;

NO. 34.
D. JOSÉ FORNARIS.

Joaquín Lorenzo Luaces, our Tirtensis, author of

"Aristodemo," who has given expression in his odes to the elevated epic flight of the early classics, and finally, Juan Clemente Zenea, the sweet singer of "Fidelia" and author of *Diario de un Mártir*, wherein are expressed the last sublime inspirations of a Cuban poet, written with the blood of his viens in the dark dungeon of a Spanish fortress. They are the outpourings of a tortured soul during eight months of martyrdom ; the tender farewell of a father and patriot to his family and to his country, as he was preparing to find on the scaffold the end of his inexpressible sorrow.

Read now one of his exquisite lyrics; read it, Paco, for its gentleness and sweetness will efface from your mind the unpleasant impression produced by the selections of your friend Moreno.

A UNA GOLONDRINA.*

Mensajera peregrina
Que al pie de mi bartolina
Revolando alegre estás,
¿De dó vienes golondrina?
Golondrina, ¿á dónde vas?

Has venido á esta región
En pos de flores y espumas,
Y yo clamo en mi prisión
Por las nieves y las brumas
Del cielo del Septentrión.

Bien quisiera contemplar
Lo que tú dejar quisiste;

---

* TO A SWALLOW.

Translated from the Spanish of Juan Clemente Zenea, by the Editor.

Thou messenger, for wandering,
Who 'neath my cell art fluttering
And round and round me gayly fly,
Whence, oh swallow, art thou winging?
And whither, swallow, dost thou hie?

To this south country thou hast flown
In quest of flowers and Zephyr's breath,
While I within my prison moan
And clamor in my dungeon lone
For wintry skies and snowy heath.

With longing heart I yearn to see
That which thou'st lightly left behind;

Quisiera hallarme en el mar,
Ver de nuevo el Norte triste,
Ser golondrina y volar!

Quisiera á mi hogar volver
Y allí, según mi costumbre,
Sin desdichas que temer,
Verme al amor de la lumbre
Con mi niña y mi mujer.

Si el dulce bien que perdí
Contigo manda un mensaje
Cuando tornes por aquí,
Golondrina, sigue el viaje
Y no te acuerdes de mí.

Que si buscas, peregrina,
Dó su frente un sáuce inclina

I long to fly beyond the sea,
To feel anew the northern wind,
To be a swallow and to flee.

I long to find again my nest
And there, as was my wont of old,
Without a fear to mar my rest,
Repose in midst of Love's sweet fold,
With wife and child to make me blest.

And if my dear ones, lost to me,
Should ask that thou a message bring
When thou again wilt cross the sea,
Pursue thy flight, thou bird of Spring,
Be not detained by thought of me.

For if thou, wanderer, seekest there
To find a drooping willow where

Sobre el polvo del que fué,
Golondrina, golondrina,
No lo habrá donde yo esté.

No busques, volando inquieta,
Mi tumba oscura y secreta,
Golondrina, ¿no lo ves?
En la tumba del poeta
No hay un sáuce ni un ciprés!

It shades the dust of him that's free,
Thou swallow fair! thou swallow fair!
Thou'lt seek in vain where I will be.

So seek not thou with restless flight,
To find my dark and hidden grave,
For know'st thou not? thou winged dace?
O'er poet's tomb no willows wave,
No cypress marks his resting place.

But do not imagine, Paco, that the majority of the Cuban people live by writing poetry bemoaning their sorrows, which are many, and making merry over their joys, which are só exceedingly few.

The men of letters whom I have quoted were not alone minstrels, poets or writers who cultivated the muses, fiction, and general literature. Many of them were at the same time distinguished lawyers, physicians, chemists, publicists, learned professors, men of knowledge or of recognized social standing, who in the various branches of art and of science did honor to their country. Literature, as you may have observed, does not serve in Cuba as a means

of enrichment; it has only served to obtain imprisonment, exile and other misfortunes.

Continue reading, with patience, if you are weary, or with pleasure if you are interested, and you will see that the number of Cubans distinguished by their labors in the fields of knowledge and of art apart from poetry is not less notable and numerous.

No. 35.—D. FRANCISCO BALMASEDA.

Bear in mind that until the very end of the last century Cuba was deprived of all those means of enlightenment and intelligence which indicate in a country the progress of civilization.

Among historians we count Ambrosio de Zayas Bazán, whose manuscript works,—the first bearing upon the early history of Cuba,—were sent to the mother country and unfortunately lost: José Martin Felix

NO 36.—D. FRANCISCO CALCAGNO.

de Arrate, Ignacio de Urrutia, and Antonio José Valdés, who accomplished difficult and valuable work and made most important investigations regarding the early events of the Island; these data were collected and transmitted to us as a precious treasure by the Sociedad Economica. Saco, the indefatigable publicist, who did not neglect any subject relating to the life and improvement of the country ; and finally the industrious José M. de la Torre. The errudite and celebrated Pichardo, geographer and historian, Santacilia, Pedro Guitéras, Manuel Sanguili, author of select historical and fine-art studies; Francisco Calcagno, who has published a Cuban biographical dictionary, being the first work of the kind among us, and Dr. Antonio Bachiller y Morales, an untiring bibliophile, member and correspondent of several foreign historical societies and of the Archæological Academy of Madrid. He was born at the beginning of this century, and being one of the teachers and educators of our youth, has had the satisfaction of witnessing and sharing in their triumphs.

No. 38.
D. NICOLÁS GUTIÉRREZ.

In Medicine we have as conspicuous figures Tomás Romay, who, apart from his vast knowledge and scientific labors, and if only as having been the means of introducing vaccine, deserves that his name

VIEW ON THE CALLE DEL PRADO, HAVANA.

No. 25.—ENRIQUE JOSÉ VARONA

be commemorated in marble. A. Cowley, an eminent professor; Francisco Zayas, founder of the first chair of Histology in the Spanish dominions; Nicolas Gutiérrez, corresponding member of several foreign academic bodies, and founder and President of our Academy of Sciences; he has just been named Vice-President of the Pan-American Medical Congress to meet at Washington, a recognition accorded by a foreign country to the valuable services of a learned Cuban;

NO. 39.
D. PEDRO GUITERAS.

G. Lebredor, prize-winner in the Academy of Medicine of Madrid; Antonio Mestre, founder and President of the Society for Clinical Studies; Càrlos Desvernine, who in the last Medical Congress held in the capital of the United States (1887) obtained the applause of the notable men there assembled, thus winning, in spite of his youth, laurels and renown for his country; Albarrán, and so many others, who in scientific reviews, in the laboratory, and in the pro-

No 40.—D. NÉSTOR PONCE DE LEON.

8

fessor's chair have done honor, and continue to do honor to us in the broad field of the science of Hippocrates.

NO. 41.
D. ANICETO MENOCAL.

Distinguished as rhetoricians, educators and grammarians are Vidal, Andrés Dueñas, and Pedro, Antonio, and Eusebio Guitéres; Luís F. Mantilla, the illustrious professor of languages; José María Zayas, author of Spanish Grammar and other works, Néstor Ponce de León, author of an important technical Spanish and English dictionary; Enrique J. Varona, a profound thinker and able philologist, although he has not yet attained his fortieth year, nor been a student at any public institute of learning.

There have excelled in Mathematics and Engineering, Ménendez, Sotolongo, and Truvejos; Aniceto Menocal is distinguishing himself as an engineer in the United States Navy; D. I. M. de Varona, is author of a remarkable project for the Brooklyn aqueduct

NO 42.—D. FRANCISCO ALBEAR Y LARA.

recently accepted; Francisco Albear y Lara, whose plans and execution of the Vento Aqueduct of Havana are the admiration of foreigners and who received a gold medal at the Paris Exposition.

In Jurisprudence are distinguished the names of

NO. 43
D. ALVARO REINOSO.

Urrutia, González, Armas, Govantes, Escovedo, and Bermudez ; at the present moment Antonio Govín, author of several works on law and administration, is making a name for himself ; also Pedro G. Llorente, José Bruzón, and Leopoldo Berriel ; the merits of the latter secured for him the recognition of the College of Advocates (*Illustre Colegio de Abogados*), and his subsequent appointment as Dean.

In Philosophy, the reverend prelate and earnest thinker Félix F. Varela is the author of several notable works on logic, metaphysics, and politics ; he was exiled from his country, to which as an educator he had devoted his services, and his revered remains are preserved with sacred care by the diocesans of St. Augustine, Florida ; Zacarías and Manuel Gonzalez del Valle ; the latter

NO. 44.—D. FELIPE POEY.

celebrated for his philosophical contest with José de la Luz Caballero, the wise Mentor whose erudition was the admiration of Sir Walter Scott and other notabilities of Europe. De la Luz initiated his disciples in the study of modern philosophy; his character was full of virility and gentleness, and he is venerated and loved by his compatriots as a Messiah of new ideas, but he will always be calumniated by men, who like Moreno, cannot even reach within sight of the pedestal of his greatness.

As statisticians and philanthropists, I will name for you Françisco Arango, Peñalver y Cárdenas, O'Reilly, and Caspar Betancourt Cisneros, known as the *Lugareño*.

No. 45.—D. NICOLAS RUÍZ ESPADERO.

In the Natural Sciences, Tranquilino Sandalio de Noda, a modest student who acquired his vast erudition in the retirement of the country and in the solitude of his library. Alvaro Reinoso, an eminent chemist to whom the members of the French Institute gave evidence of the esteem in which they held his merits in Europe; he is an agriculturist of universal reputation; Barnet, who obtained the chair of Chemistry in Madrid in spite of opposition; he was an early victim to his love of the science of Lavcisier.

And finally, Felipe Poey, the nonogenarian naturalist, the unquestionable glory of our country. His work upon Cuban Ichthyology received an award at the Amsterdam Exposition and is now laid on the shelf by the Colonial Ministry, which acquired it for three thousand dollars.   Shame on the Spanish nation if it be not published in a worthy manner !

NO. 46.—D. JOSÉ WHITE.

As forensic orators I will cite Escobedo, Carbonell, Cintra, Bermúdez ; as pulpit orators Cernada, Tristán Medina, who gained admiration in Europe, Miguel D. Santos and Arteaga.

In the Arts may be cited Baez, engraver; Escobar, *genre* painter and Chartrand, a notable landscape painter.   In music, White, Cervantes, Díaz Albertini, Jiménez, distinguished alumni and winners of first prizes at the Conservatory of Paris, artists whose genius has been admired in Viena, London, Paris and other great centres of Europe and in America ; some of the former, like the mulatto, White, are exiled from their native soil ; he is the head of the Conservatory of Music of Brazil.   Diaz Albertini,

notwithstanding his youth, was judge in the examinations at the Paris Conservatory.

As most distinguished composers we count Gaspar

Villate, author of *Zilia*, Espadero, who wrote the famous *Canto
del Esclavo ;* he was the favorite
friend of Gottschalk.

As professors, orators, writers,
and artists, as zealous friends of
the sciences, I could cite a whole
phalanx of contemporaries, both
old and young, lawyers, physicians and artists, whose modesty
I do not wish to wound ; they
are doing honor to the coun-

No 47.—D. RAFAE. DÍAZ
ALBERTINI.

tries in which they at present reside, study, work
and shine. But let me conclude this task, for I
divine that you feel your heart beating with patriotic
enthusiasm, through being convinced, after having
read all that this letter contains, that Cuba is a civilized Colony which does honor to the mother country.
I am sure you will be the first to maintain hereafter
that a people who offer so telling a picture of their
civilization and culture, are worthy not only of
respect, but of governing themselves and of being
free.

VII.

No. 49.—STATUE AND FOUNTAIN OF WEST INDIA.

POLITICAL CONDITIONS.—THE OPPOSING PARTIES AND THEIR HIS-
TORY.—PERIOD OF CONSPIRACIES.—FUTILE HOPES OF REFORM.—
THE TEN YEARS STRUGGLE.—THE COMPROMISE AT ZANJON.—
THE AUTONOMIST PARTY.—ITS PLATFORM.—THE CONSERVATIVE
OR SPANISH PARTY.—BROKEN PROMISES OF THE GOVERNMENT.

From what you have already read you will have
divined that we Cubans have not been nor are we
yet a happy people. You must also have perceived
that if there existed in this much-to-be-pitied Island
a cultured and intelligent element it must have had
to battle, still battles, and has yet to battle for the
obtainment of that well-being which is the ideal of
mankind and the supreme object of all oppressed
people.

As regards political matters I go on with real pleasure, Paco, quite contrary to Moreno, to chat with you,
being desirous to tell you everything that he has
withheld either intentionally or through ignorance.
With your permission I will begin, according to my
custom, with a little historical sketch.

In Cuba there have always existed two parties;
that of the dominators, and that of the dominated:
the one which exploits and enjoys privileges, and
the other which is exploited and oppressed. I repeat at this juncture the points contained in my
third letter concerning our two social classes. The
former have always had the support of the Government, with which they have a well-defined connection; the latter have been perpetually harassed by
suspicion, prejudice and mistrust. The one has
assumed the pompous name of " Spanish Party" (*Partido Español*); the other has not been, nor is it now,
ashamed to be known as the " Cuban Party " (*Partido
Cubano*). But between the two parties the observer
perceives a dividing line, illogical and discouraging,
not drawn according to the unity of aspirations and
sentiments of nationality, nor even of race; it is a
generator of evil; but it exists, and it becomes necessary for me to consider it.

From the earliest dates of the Colony these two
tendencies have manifested themselves, although for
a time after the beginning of the present century, from

about 1820 down even to 1837 (date of the expulsion
of the Cuban Deputies from the Spanish Parliament),
they did not evince such marked and visible characteristics. Until the latter date, at least, there prevailed a system of political identity, and the Cubans
shared the same constitutional rights that the Spaniards enjoyed from 1812, with some modifications.
The logical consequences of this system must be, as
indeed they were, that the natural ties were strengthened, and that the mutual relations of friendship
and common interests, which common customs and
traditions and an equal standing necessarily create
in the members of a community, were fostered.
The settlers and their descendants were alike Spaniards.

Eloquent proofs of the truth of this proposition
were afforded by our ancestors : their support of the
mother country at critical moments was given and
recognized. Jácome Milanés and Pepe Antonio are
glorious examples.

Subsequently, however, through the culpable lack
of foresight of such purblind politicians as Arguelles
and Sancho, the Cubans were excluded from participation in social life. Since the government and administration of this rich territory were left in the
despotic charge and at the absolute discretion of
Captain Generals, invested with the power of dispensing desirable offices *ad libitum*, it is not to be won-

dered that class rivalry and hatred were fomented. The ties of affection which the common interests and relations of a civilized people produce were severed, gradually at first, and afterwards completely.

Then was initiated that feverish period of political conspiracy directed to do away with an order of

things so contrary to human dignity and self-respect, and to the well-being of the Colony. At this epoch our history is full of sad and bloody pages. But even then the public indignation was restrained by the voice of reason. Authoritative men, like José Antonio Saco, arose to combat the revolutionary tendency, and to demonstrate

No. 50.—D. RAMÓN PINTÓ.

that a system of reforms and of liberal government would preserve its dominion to the Nation and assure prosperity and happiness to the Colony.

But, deaf to the subdued clamors of a people devoid of a free press, of the right of assembly and of the security of law, repeating frequently the proscriptions of Sila; blind to the signs of the times and puffed with pride, the Government failed to heed the lessons of its history even after the conclusion of the American Civil War and the complete downfall of European domination on this continent. It could not realize that a radical change was necessary in the politics and administration of Cuba.

That change was what the country confidently hoped for when the Committee of Inquiry on reforms in Cuba and Porto Rico was appointed, but only too soon a new and more painful undeception came to fill its cup of bitterness. That Committee was convened by a Government that had founded and ruled the colony with the idea, it appears, of discovering its necessities by interrogating the commissioners, as if the Government did know these necessities but too well. That Committee, in which the Cubans joined with all sincerity and with legitimate expectations, was adjourned after a number of secret sessions. Its proceedings would have remained unknown but for their publication in foreign lands, thanks to the patriotism of some of the commissioners. The Committee dissolved without result, without other result than the imposition on Cuba of a new and heavier direct

No. 51.—D. CARLOS MANUEL DE CÉSPEDES.

No. 52—D. JULIÁN GÁSSIE.

tax. The disastrous administration of General Lersundi came into power, established Military Commissions, enforced an arbitrary despotism, inaugurated a reign of terror, and raised a permanent scaffold in the Plaza.

Little wonder is it that in 1868 the revolutionary cry of Yara should have gone forth. I shall draw a veil, Paco, over this historic period of ten years, which in the beginning was a mere frolic and pastime for Lersundi, but in the end, according to Jovellar, cost the Spanish nation two hundred thousand men and seven hundred millions of money.

That struggle, upon which contemporaries cannot pass judgment, terminated in a compromise. Forgetfulness of the past was proclaimed. The government promised an administration of liberty and an era of concord, and the country, wearied and impoverished, again took heart in the hope of a brighter future.

The Autonomist Party was then organized. On the 9th of August, 1878, a Committee of Organization was appointed. It was the first liberal political body created in Cuba under the protection of the law. Its creed and aspirations were proclaimed in the following :—

PLATFORM OF THE LIBERAL PARTY OF THE ISLAND OF CUBA.

THE SOCIAL QUESTION.

Exact fulfillment of the 1st clause of Article 21 of the Moret Law, which declares: "The Government will present to the Cortes, when the Cuban Deputies are admitted therein, the project of a law for the indemnified emancipation of those that have remained in servitude since the enactment of said law, the regulation at the same time, of free negro labor, and the moral and intellectual education of those emancipated.

Exclusively *white* immigration, giving preference to families; and the removal of all the obstacles put in the way of Peninsular and foreign immigration individually undertaken.

THE POLITICAL QUESTION.

Necessary Liberties.—The full concession of the several rights guaranteed in Article I of the Constitution, namely: Liberty of the press, the right of assembly and of association and the right of petition. Furthermore, liberty of worship and of instruction, both as regards methods and books.

The admission of Cubans on the same basis as other Spaniards to all offices and public trusts, in accordance with Article XV of the Constitution.

The full application of the Municipal, Provincial, Electoral, and all the other organic laws of Spain to the Islands of Cuba and Porto Rico, without other modification than those which local conditions necessitate, in conformity with the *spirit* of the Zanjon convention.

Fulfillment of Article LXXXIX of the Constitution, having in view a system of special laws defining the fullest possible decentralization consistent with national unity.

Separation and independence of the Civil and Military powers. Application to the Island of Cuba of the Penal Code of the Law of Criminal Procedure, of the Mortgage Law, of that concerning Judicial Powers, of the most recent Code of Commerce, and other legislative reforms, with the modifications required by local interests.

The National Economic Questions.

Abolition of export duty on all products of the Island.

Reform of the Cuban Tariff in such a manner that the import duties be solely for revenue; abolition of all differential duties, whether specific or relating to the flag.

Reduction of the duties imposed in the Custom Houses of the Home Country on Cuban sugar and molasses, until they be reduced to a revenue basis.

Commercial treaties between Spain and foreign nations, particularly the United States, upon the basis of the most complete possible reciprocity between these and Cuba; giving in the Custom Houses and ports of the Island the same immunity and privileges to the products of foreign countries which these grant to our productions.

Havana, August 1st, 1876.

This important document was signed by José María Gálvez, Joan Espoturno, Carlos Saladrigas, Francisco P. Gay, Miguel Bravo y Sentís, Ricardo del Monte, Juan Bruno Zayas, José Eugenio Bernal Joaquín G. Lebredo, Pedro Armenteros, Emilio L. Luaces, Antonio Govín, and Manuel P. de Molina, editor of *El Triunfo*.*

It would not have been surprising if the country,

---

* The General Committee of the Liberal party at a meeting on April 1st, 1882, amplified the above Platform by a precise definition of its principles in the following Declarations:

" The General Committee, considering that the convictions and aspirations of the Liberal Party are constantly subjected in this and in the home country to the most gratuitous imputations, deems it proper to sum up the aims and purposes of the party in the following affirmations:

"1st. Identity of civil and political rights for Spaniards of both hemispheres, thus making the Constitution of the State apply in this island without restrictions or limitations. Complete expression of the unity and integrity of a common country. These constitute the fundamental principles of the Liberal Party.

" 2nd. The immediate and absolute emancipation of all colonial subjects.

" 3d. Colonial Autonomy, with regard to all local questions and in accordance with the reiterated declarations of the Central Committee, that is to say, under the sovereignship and authority of the Cortes, together with the head of the nation.

"These declarations are solemnly and deliberately approved by the Central Committee and contain the essential features of the system of Autonomy to the realization of which the Liberal Party is steadfastly devoted."

still suffering from the stupor and depression consequent upon the late conflict, had been deaf to the

NO. 53.
D. CARLOS SALADRIGAS.

call of the patriots who organized that movement. But it
was not so. The Cubans from
one extreme of the island to
the other responded unanimously, affiliating themselves
with the party which, under
the protection of the law, and
by means of peaceful agitation,
endeavored to raise the standard of liberty and to promote
the reforms which had so long
been claimed and had at last been promised.

Then it was that we came to know Montoro,
Govín, Varona, Cancio, Lamar, Márquez, García,
Montes, Mesa, Cortina, Oruz, Borrero, Vilanova,
Viondi, Muxó, Oritz, (Carlos and Alberto) Pellón,
Portillo, Giberga, Dorbercker, Pascual, Gássie, Montalvo, Font y Sterling, C. García Ramis and Gabriel Zendegui. A numerous phalanx of generous
and eloquent youths, until then unknown. They
were full of enthusiasm, of patriotism and of wisdom gathered in the solitude of their studies during
the days of great affliction, or in the isolation of
ostracism; they sprang forth as by enchantment,
and like apostles or militants of the new idea, they

NO. 37.   EUSEBIO GUITÉRAS.

NO. 48. JOSÉ MARÍA GÁLVEZ.

came to offer the invaluable aid of their oratory, of their energy and of their efforts, to the pioneers of the party which proclaimed that colonial liberty was compatible with national unity.

Brilliant and impressive was the spectacle now offered the country which had lived so long a time under menace and oppression. It had just emerged from the ten years' suffering of a rude conflict and of the most galling rigors of a military regimen, and now it was agitated by a spontaneous movement and gave itself up, with a confiding trust in the good faith of its rulers, to the promotion and attainment of its political ideals.

The country was not even deterred in its new path by the thought that of the few reforms hastily introduced in the administration, some, the political ones, were left to the discretion and temper of the Governor General, while others, like the municipal and provincial laws, took on the character of *temporary* enactments, which they still retain. But the intelligent spirit of Cuban patriotism which so eloquently manifested itself in the spontaneous and energetic organization of the Liberal Party very soon discerned the awakening of the old, retrogressive and intolerant party, which was fearful lest the new order of things undermine the stronghold of its interests.

9 .

There was then organized a party under the name of "The Constitutional Union" (*Unión Constitucional*), which promulgated the program that Moreno has made known to you. It is an artful paraphrase of the platform of the Liberal Party, and while it seemed to respond to the necessities of the times, it but veiled in reality the intolerances, evasions and dissimulations calculated for the protection and the benefit of ٫ne class, for the slavery of the negro and the unlimited power of the white man. Both parties labored to attain their ends; the one strove for liberty, for decentralization, for autonomy; the other, for the maintenance of its old privileges and monopolies.*

---

*The promulgation of the Autonomist platform elicited an impassioned protest from the Conservatives of Cuba, who, as usual, feigned to believe that the national integrity was in danger. At Santiago de Cuba a man was arrested and tried because he cheered for autonomy at a political gathering. The newspaper, *El Triunfo*, was denounced by the Censor of the Press, and public opinion was greatly excited; but finally the court rendered the following decision, which the Attorney of the Supreme Court accepted, waiving the recourse of appeal which the Inferior Court had established:

" In the City of Havana, the 31st day of May, 1881, in the suit instituted between parties, the party of the first part being the Censor (*Fiscal*) of the Press, through his denunciation of the article entitled "*Nuestra Doctrina,*" (Our Doctrine), published in number one hundred and twenty, of the fourth year of the daily periodical named *El Triunfo*, the party of the second part being the Chief Editor of the said periodical, Ricardo del Monte.

Very soon, friend Paco, the spirit of harmony and conciliation which, after the close of the war, preceded the first moments of the organization of the parties, and which for a time was sustained only through the personal influence of a Governor, gave place to the old jealousies and to the re-establishment of the old dividing line, with all favors and

---

Whereas, on the twenty-third of the present month of May, the said denunciation was presented in this Court, accompanied by a copy of the periodical, the Censor believing that the article referred to falls within the provisions of Case 4, Article XVI, of the Press Law now in force, and offering to make in the trial of the case such further applications as he may deem requisite.

Whereas, on the said twenty-third above named, the presentation of the said denunciation was acknowledged, the trial of the case was fixed for the thirtieth, the parties were duly summoned, and the notification of the trial was made to the said Chief Editor of the paper.

Whereas, on the twenty-fifth of the present month, another denunciation was presented by the Censor of the Press, relative to the article published in the periodical *Diario de Matanzas*, number one hundred and seventeen, fourth year, issued in the city of that name, entitled "*Nuestro Programa*," reproducing that of *El Triunfo*, "*Nuestra Doctrina.*"

Whereas, on the twenty-seventh of said month, the presentation of this latter denunciation was acknowledged, and it was ordered that notice be given the proprietor of the *Diario de Matanzas* that the trial of the denunciation of *El Triunfo*, from which its article was reproduced, had been set down for the thirtieth, and that whatever the sentence may be, shall be equal in its effects for one and the

offices for the Conservatives, i. e., the Spanish party,
to the total exclusion of the Liberals, i. e., the Cuban
element.

Need I continue, my dearest Paco, the narration
of like injustices? Must I remind you of the
actions of General Blanco, who exiled three journalists without trial? of General Prendergast,

---

other periodical, and that he may appoint attorney and
counsellor for the trial and be present and give evidence in
the proceedings of the trial; to which end a communication
was addressed to the senior Judge of the Inferior Court of
the City of Matanzas, for notification to the said proprietor
of the *Diario de Matanzas.*

Whereas, at the public trial on the day, hour and place
appointed, and in successive order, spoke the Censor of the
Press and the counsellor of the editor and proprietor of the
newspaper, *El Triunfo,* the former setting forth the
following conclusions: First, that the defense and advocacy
of an Autonomic regime for the Island of Cuba tends to
undermine the principle of national unity, attacking it
indirectly at least; second, that in view thereof, *El
Triunfo,* which in its article *"Nuestra Doctrina,"* makes
such advocacy and defense, commits thereby the offence
provided in Article XVI, Paragraph 4 of the Press
Law; and third, that for the reasons above set forth
it must be condemned to a thirty days' suspension, and the
payment of the costs of the trial.

The counsellor of the editor of the *El Triunfo* set forth
the following: That a defense of the Autonomic regime
such as presented in the article of *El Triunfo,* entitled
"Nuestra Doctrina," does not attack, either directly or
indirectly, the national unity, nor the integrity of its territory, and therefore, the said defense is perfectly legitimate,

who confined in the Morro and then drove from the country Don Francisco Cespeda without even a hearing, merely to meet the exigencies and pander to the prejudices of the Conservative party whom this journalist, although a Spaniard, had dared to oppose? Likewise the unprincipled appointment of two officers of the Permanent Conservative Com-

and praying that *El Triunfo* shall be acquitted without cost, there having been no one present to represent the *Diario de Matanzas.*

Considering that the Autonomist policy, as developed in the article of the periodical, *El Triunfo*, referred to in the present denunciation, does not, as an expression of a doctrine, constitute any attack whatsoever upon the national dignity, the said periodical limiting itself to the petitioning for the Island of Cuba of special laws in the sense of the greatest decentralization possible within the national unity, notwithstanding that the clearest and most concrete form of this decentralization is the Autonomic system developed in the said article:

Considering that no attack is indirectly made on that principle of the fundamental law of the State by reason of the ideas and considerations expressed in the defense of the said doctrine:

Considering that through the contents of the article in the periodical *El Triunfo*, entitled "*Nuestra Doctrina*," the offense of an indirect attack upon the national unity, and to which the Censor's accusation refers as comprised in Case 4 of Article XVI of the Press Law now in force, has not been committed:

Now, therefore, it is our judgment that we must declare and we do hereby declare, that the newspaper, *El Triunfo*, in its article *Nuestra Doctrina*, has not committed the

mission to preside over provincial deputations of an acknowleged liberal majority and the scandalous overthrow of Liberal mayors and magistrates to suit the

No. 54.
D. MANUEL SANGUILÍ.

pleasure of the preferred class and to make room for their favorites. The whole electoral machinery was worked so as to give over to the Conservatives the government of even the last precinct of this unhappy land, an artifice openly confessed in full Congress by the Count of Tajeda Valdosera, Minister of the Colonies. Is it necessary to point out the significant fact that from out of the Conservative Party there has gone forth a mighty arrry of counts, magistrates and other

---

offense of attacking the national unity; and that we must acquit, and do hereby acquit, without costs, the said periodical from the Censor's denunciation imputing to it the commission of the said offense; and whereas, the periodical, *Diario de Matanzas,* has been equally denounced for the article " *Nuestro Programa,*" in which that of *El Triunfo,* "*Nuestra Doctrina*" is reproduced, and in view of Article LIV of the said Press Law, we order that this decision shall also have equal effect in regard to the said periodical, *Diario de Matanzas,* which decision we pronounce, order and sign.

JOSÉ M. GARELLY,
SEBASTIÁN DE CUBAS,
GREGORIO GUITÉRREZ.

grandees with glistening coats of arms about which still lingers the odor of varnish, and who strut proudly about in this essentially democratic country?

No; my purpose of refuting the errors into which you have been led by your informant is sufficiently served by the foregoing brief history of our political parties.

Thus organized, and constituted as you have here observed, the Liberal Party has fought and is fighting its bitter contest. It will never relinquish its purposes; for in them is bound up the future of Cuban society, and of the Cuban home. This party is the permanent and durable element here, and it will withstand future evils, as it resists the present ones, until it reaches the goal of its aspirations. Its constancy and abnegation have already been proven by the severest tests. It *must* conquer and it *will* conquer.*

---

*The managing Board of the Autonomist Party is composed of the following gentlemen :

Juan B. Armenteros, Pedro Armenteros y del Castillo, Luis Armenteros, José Bruzón, Raimundo Cabrera, Leopoldo Cancio, Francisco A. Conte, José Cárdenas y Gassie, Miguel Figueroa, Rafael Fernández de Castro, Fernando Freyre de Andrade, José García Montes, Joaquín Güell y Renté, José Hernández Abreu, Manuel Francisco Lamar, José Luna y Parra, Herminio C. Leyva, Rafael Montoro, Antonio Mesa y Domínguez, José Rafael Montalvo, Ricardo del Monte, Alberto Ortíz, José Manuel Pascual, Ramón Pérez Trujillo, Demetrio Pérez de la Riva,

And be assured, Paco, once for all, that the people
who have the resolution to conspire for their liberties through thirty years, and the courage to sus-
tain a fierce and bloody struggle during a whole
decade, do not need to hide their aspirations under
a mask. The sons of Cuba would display equal
valor to-day, the same heroic courage, were they not
persuaded,—and that by the most enlightened
minds, that in Colonial Autonomy lies the salvation
of Cuba for the Cubans, for the mother country and
for civilization.

Emilio Terry, Juan Ignacio Zuazo, José María Carbonell,
Carlos Zaldo, Antonio Zambrana, Pedro Estéban y González Larrinaga, José F. Pellón.

VIII.

No. 56.—THE CHARITY THEATRE AT SANTA CLARA.

CUBA, ITS POLITICAL, ECCLESIASTICAL AND JURIDICAL DIVISIONS.
—THE MORAL STATUS OF THE PEOPLE.—THE SOCIAL EVIL.—ITS
EXPLOITATION BY THE GOVERNMENT.—PURITY OF THE CUBAN
PEOPLE.—THE STATUS OF EDUCATION.—HISTORICAL REVIEW OF
THE SYSTEM OF INSTRUCTION.—GOVERNMENT NEGLECT OF EDU-
CATION.—FREE SCHOOLS, SEMINARIES AND COLLEGES PRIVATELY
INSTITUTED AND CONDUCTED.

The Island of Cuba, Paco, has an area of 43,319
square miles; the adjacent Island of Pines, (*Isla de
Pinos*) 1215 square miles, and the smaller islands
along the coast contain 1350 square miles, a total of
45,884. It is divided into six provinces, which
bear the names of their respective capitals, namely,
Havana, Matanzas, Pinar del Río, Santa Clara,
Puerto Príncipe, and Cuba, and contains a total of

about 1,500,000 inhabitants. The island is divided into two territorial jurisdictions, (*Audiencias territoriales*) namely, Havana and Puerto Príncipe; the former constitutes an episcopate with 144 parishes and the latter an archepiscopate with 55 parishes. The jurisdiction of Havana is furthermore divided into twenty-seven judicial districts, and that of of Puerto Príncipe into ten such divisions, altogether embracing twenty-one "cities," sixteen "towns," and numerous villages and settlements.

I give you this information because I presume, (and pray do not be offended) that you are ignorant of our physical and political geography, considering that even our colonial ministers are unacquainted with it. This is one of the many studies they take up on assuming office. A *statesman* once referred in open Congress to the inland town of Victoria de las Tunas as a seaport, and I furthermore recall that in Spain the erroneous impression is very general that Havana is Cuba. And finally I give you this information because I find that Moreno, either intentionally or through unpardonable ignorance, speaks of Cuban customs and of its immorality from what he has seen in certain centers of Havana—as though the country was so contracted that the whole of it was necessarily represented in the sinks of vice which he frequented, and of which he proves himself so well informed.

Havana is simply the capital of this *pearl in the mire*, and inasmuch as it contains the great offices of administration, is our best situated and best equipped seaport and our great mercantile focus, it consequently is the Babylon of this tottering empire, where are collected and accumulated the wickedness and the misery that constitute the scum and the dregs of society.

The general customs of a people, however, are not to be judged by those signs of corruption which great and populous centres everywhere afford. The family—the real foundation of morality—is never to be found in dens of vice and iniquity ; these are the rotten and isolated members of the social structure. Their greater or lesser numbers indicate a corresponding degree of laxity in the morals of the people and it is this that we have carefully to study.

The Cuban family does not frequent such places as Capellanes and the Chorrera, known only through the "personal" columns of certain newspapers, or through books like that of Señor Moreno. These foci of foulness have their analogy in every metropolis; they are places of resort for the soldiers and bureaucrats who live in the country without family or ties of affection, for the permanent denizens of the lodging houses, for the frequenters of the public cafés, for that floating population that daily pours into a large city in search of diversions and pleasures, and for the prodigals and spendthrifts of all ages and conditions who compose the retinue of vice everywhere.

But not there is to be found the laborer, who rests from the day's fatigue in the hours when vices thrive; not there the professional man, who, in the tranquility of home, and in the bosom of his family lives far removed from such repellant centres of corruption; not there the peasant who has fertilized the fields with his labor and his sweat, and these, friend Paco, make up by far the greater number of our people.

Search the towns of the interior, in the heart of the country, and you will find none of those establishments of vice and immorality with which Moreno has had the leisure to become so well acquainted in the metropolis. They are there repelled and driven out by public opinion. And even in Havana, where vice has such a hold and is subjected to an impost for the support, as we are to believe, of a Hygienic Hospital, you may make some very curious studies. I do not invite you to look up the statistics of this subject, for as happens in all the other branches of Spanish administration, there are no statistics. If some imperfect data should exist, you may be sure that they will not afford you access to it at the office of the Department. The writer speaks from experience. However, this defect may be supplied by a little diligence.

Four years ago (in 1885) there were in Havana two hundred registered houses of prostitution, of various official classifications, and the total number of the inmates noted in the lists as being under " regulation" was 516, besides 135 not so included, and who by so much defrauded the tax office in the exercise of their calling. Ninety per cent. of these numbers was composed partly of women of the colored class, but chiefly of foreigners; that is, of Peninsulars, Canary Islanders and others of extraneous origin, and only the remaining ten per cent. comprised white women, native to the country. The proportion now existing, according to data easily comparable, is yet more significant, and speaks much in favor of the moral status of our native population. In 1886 there were admitted in the Hygienic Hospital 281 patients; the number of the native-born among them was insignificant, almost all having been foreigners or Peninsulars. The individuals of native origin "regularly " treated comprise from a fourth to a sixth of the total number, and constantly in about these same proportions.

The war caused the dispersion, the ruin of the family. Corruption was its sequel. Immorality ceased to be rare, but even so the natives of the

country figure in the great minority in the statistics
of the social evil. These are indeed wretchedly

imperfect, despite the dispropor-
tionate pains taken in the matter
by our government, for whom it
is a question of dollars and cents.*

The customs of the country are
austere and simple. The Cuban
youth does not consume in vice
the vigor and strength necessary
to raise itself, as it has raised itself,
from debasement and ignorance.

This is, to be sure, the country
of which a certain Governor General, O'Donnell, said with insulting
flippancy, that it could be governed with a fiddle
and fighting cock (*con un violin y un gallo*). This

NO. 57.—D. FRANCISCO
VICENTE AGUILERA.

* The " Regulation of Public Hygiene" promulgated July
17, 1877, and still in force, notwithstanding the fact that
many of its provisions are unconstitutional, affords a curious
study.

Neither health nor public morals is the objective point of
its provisions. It is a revenue inspiration, it creates high
duties; it organizes expensive offices; it imposes *redeemable*
penalties, it establishes a secret hygienic police, and constitutes, on the whole, and in all the details of the artfulness
with which it is combined, not a regulation, but a combination of methods to exploit the social evil. It is a law deeply
demoralizing, and what there is of usefulness in it is never
obeyed as far as the municipal police is concerned.

The votaries of immorality are required to be inscribed in

is the land where the authorities, in consideration
of certain fees, consent to the conducting throughout the year of obscene public balls in the most
thickly populated quarters of the city, villainous
and nauseating haunts where mingle all the races;
where, dancing and contorting in giddy confusion, are the lowest types of the social scale,—the
prostitute, the drunkard, and the criminal. This
is the city where it is permitted to the courtesan to
select the precinct, the street and the house in
which she is to carry on her miserable traffic; this
is the land where no regard whatever is paid to the
dignity of the family, to honor, and to decency;
where a Spanish general and his staff scandalized
the community by their lecherous conduct in

the Registry (Art. 1). Its clandestine traffic is prohibited,
and a woman above fifteen years of age (Art. 3) wishing to
practice it has only to notify the Section of the fact, pay the
impost and be inscribed.

A woman of seventeen years, according to our law
requires the paternal consent to get married; to appear in
court on trial she requires a guardian until she is twenty-
five years of age; but to become a prostitute it is enough for
her to pay a few dollars to the Administration. The card
certificate of inscription must bear the likeness of the
inscribed (Art. 4). She who repents or reforms cannot obtain
her rehabilitation if the reasons are not satisfactory to the
members of the Section; this law does not profess the for-
bearance of Christianity; Magdalens do not pay.

Unfortunate country! It is fairly covered with corroding
sores.

camp; the colony where the game of "monte," and others no less illicit and scandalous have been actually established in the streets and public squares as a means of collecting funds to build churches, where gambling has always been a source of revenue; this is the unhappy country where everything is made an object of underhanded speculation and of corruption. But notwithstanding all this, Paco, Cuban society, properly so called, rises superior to all these impurities, and its superiority is due to its own efforts; it resists with courage and intelligence the allurements of officially protected vice.

It is true that the causes of demoralization have been many and serious. Slavery alone—introduced and maintained by our paternal government —was through its contingent of vicious habits, sufficient to degrade and corrupt the people; then the military regimen, the despotic rule to which we have always been subjected, and whose pernicious influence gradually depraves and debases those whom it dominates; and then the incursions—that is, the constant migration of officials without means, without families, and without regard for the country; dwelling in our cities temporarily, their sole stimulus and ambition being to acquire a fortune in the most expeditious manner, and leaving no trace behind them but the baleful influence of their vices and the remembrance of their bad faith; but above

TACON THEATRE, HOTEL INGLATERRA AND PARK, HAVANA.

NO. 55.   MARTA ABREU DE ESTÉVEZ.

all, Paco, the lack of schools—the absolute, deliberate, criminal neglect with which public instruction
has always been treated.

I repeat, that the Cubans have withstood all these
evils; not through incessant feasting and by means
of lewd dances have they made the progress in
science, art and literature which has gained for them
a place among the cultured peoples of the world,
and which my previous communications have
pointed out.

Notwithstanding that the Cubans enjoyed the
iniquitous profits of slavery, they were yet the first
to demand its abolition, and they obtained it in
the Spanish Cortes of 1887 only after untiring
efforts. Although living in a colony where public
instruction was looked upon with suspicion and
distrust, and never protected, it was they who spontaneously and liberally established schools and disseminated intelligence. These, my dear Paco, are
the true indications of morality and purity in the
customs of a country. That you may be better able
to judge them, follow my investigations, for I make
no statement that may not easily be confirmed by
the facts of our history.

Cuba, a Spanish colony, has had an existence of
four hundred years. During the 16th and 17th
centuries schools were unknown; there were none.

10

Until the last century was far advanced, the 18th,
recollect, the Cubans had not a single institution
where they could have their children taught to read
and write. The first school was that of the Beth-
lehamite fathers in Havana, and was established
through the generosity of Don Juan F. Carballo;
he was, according to some authorities, a native of
Seville, and according to others, of the Canary
Islands; he repaid thus generously the debt of
gratitude he owed the country where he had acquired his wealth. Already in the 16th century
a philanthropist of Santiaga de Cuba, Francisco
Paradas, had afforded a like good example by bequeathing a large estate for the purpose of teaching
Latin linguistics and Christian morals. The legacy
was eventually made of avail by the Dominican
Friars, who administered it; but when the convents
were abolished it was swallowed by the Royal Treasury, and thus the beneficent intentions of the founder
were frustrated to the permanent damage of this
unfortunate country.

Only these two institutions, due entirely to individual initiative, are recorded in our scholastic
annals during the three first centuries of the colony;
the scent and thirst for gold reigned supreme. What
other seed than that of demoralization could be sown
on such a soil? Fortunately, its advantageous geographical position, its contact with other civilized

communities, notably the United States, whose increasing prosperity was perhaps due to the attention given to public instruction, saved the Island from utter ruin. The sons of wealthy families, in the absence of places of learning at home, sought schools and colleges in foreign parts; on their return, with the patriotic zeal natural to cultured men, they endeavored to better the intellectual condition of their compatriots. This enforced emigration of Cubans in quest of learning was fought against by our government. The children of Cuban families were forbidden to be educated in foreign countries. This despotic measure was adopted without any honest effort being made to establish schools for instructing the children of a population already numbering nearly 500,000 souls.

The Sociedad Economica was founded in 1793, during the term of Las Casas,—whose name has always been venerated among Cubans. Then, as now, the members of this association were the most talented men of the country, and their best efforts were directed towards promoting public instruction. To this worthy institution, essentially a Cuban body, are due the first advances made in this branch of administration; it was this association that gave the impulse and organization to the school system in Cuba; it established inspections, collected statistics, and founded a newspaper to promote instruction and devoted its profits to this cause; it raised funds, and labored with such zeal and enthusiasm that it finally secured the assistance of the Colonial Government and obtained an appropriation, though but of a small amount, for the benefit of popular instruction.

In 1793 there were only seven schools for boys in the capital of Cuba, in which 408 white and 144 free colored children could be educated. From this privilege the slaves were debarred and, in sooth, their masters enjoyed it but seldom. The seven schools referred to, besides a number of seminaries for girls, afforded a means of livelihood for a number of free mulattoes, and some whites; the schools were private undertakings, paid for by the parents. Only one, that of the Reverend Father Zenón, of Havana, was a free school.

Reading, writing, and arithmetic were taught in these schools. Lorenzo Lendez, a mulatto of Havana, was the only one who taught Spanish grammar. The poor of the free classes were on a par with the slaves.

When this was the state of things in the metropolis, with its 400,000 inhabitants, what must have been the degree of culture in the rest of the island? It is certain, friend Paco, that the seeds of refinement were not there being sown.

The Sociedad Economica founded two free schools,

one for each sex, and was authorized by the Government to negotiate with the Bishop of Havana, as to the best means of raising funds for educational purposes. It is with repugnance that I here write the name of Bishop Felix José de Tres Palacios. In his blind and stupid opposition he nullified the laudable efforts of the country's wellwishers by maintaining that it was unnecessary to establish more schools.

However, this group of distinguished Cubans continued their efforts, although from 1793 to 1816 they were unable to accomplish even a part of their noble purpose: it was found impossible to obtain an official sanction of popular education. During this period the increase of schools and of the number of pupils was relatively small. In the rest of the island—note carefully, Paco—in as many as nineteen districts, there existed in 1817 ninety schools; all, or nearly all, founded by private individuals, as was the case in the capital.

The number of philanthropic persons who thus founded and supported free schools affords a clear proof of the patriotism of the Cubans and not of their demoralization. Besides the originators of the Sociedad Economica, Don Francisco y Parreño should also be mentioned; he donated to the district of Güines a building for the support of a free school; (the author recalls with pride and gratitude that he there received his elementary education in 1863); Don Juan Conyedo in San Juan de los Remedios, and Mariano Acosta in Bayamo, were also generous educators of destitute youth.

In 1816 the Section of Education of the Sociedad Economica was established. It afforded a powerful impulse to the cause of education, thanks to the influential support of the Governor, Don Alejandro Ramirez, a man as worthy of our gratitude as General Las Casas. Governors of their rare good qualities have been very scarce in Cuba.

The schools improved, the boys and girls, both white and black, were taught separately; literary contests were opened; annual public examinations were made obligatory; prizes were distributed and a powerful incentive was created among all classes for the cause of education. Men like Don Desiderio Herrera offered to teach a certain number of poor children, and to supply them with .the necessary materials. Herrera afterwards received a pension from the patriotic association.

But though this institution, under the fostering influence of Ramirez, obtained certain concessions of municipal aid for gratuitous instruction, these concessions were soon revoked (*Royal Order of February,* 1824). Public instruction, friend Paco, was totally neglected by our government, but the patriotism of the Cubans overcame this neglect.

Do not fail to notice these dates, that you may understand our customs and our intellectual status. In 1826 there were only 140 schools on the island, and of these but sixteen were free. The Sociedad Economica after repeated petitions, obtained from the municipality of Havana in 1824 *one hundred dollars* for the schools outside the city walls and that *only as a loan*. Such were the meagre resources with which the future civilization of Cuba was to be prepared!

The schools established in the convents to make good this paucity proved by their results the poor success of the monks in the education of youth. In 1827 the Socieded Economica succeeded in obtaining from the Treasury an appropriation of 8000 dollars per annum for the establishment and maintenance of new schools. Thus the Colonial Government, which here reaped such fabulous wealth to aggrandize the Crown, eventually yielded to the repeated supplications of a patriotic social organization, and relinquished that miserly sum for this noble purpose.

During the same period the citizens of Matanzas, through the initiative of Don Juan José Aranguren, maintained two free schools by subscription. Thus the country struggled to regenerate itself in the absence of official stimulus or protection; the cause of public instruction was sustained only through private efforts; it was thus, friend Paco, that we reached the middle of the present century, presenting throughout all the towns of the island the spectacle which in these brief lines I have endeavored to sketch.

In 1836, according to statistics collected by the "Society of Friends of the Country" (*Sociedad Amigos del País*) and which, by the way, were forbidden publication during Tacón's term of office, only 9082 children were receiving elementary instruction on the whole island. This included both sexes and the two races and included also the schools supported by annuities, by subscription and by individuals.

If such was the case with regard to elementary education, so indispensable for the enlightenment of the masses, what could have been the status of higher education?

The two seminaries (that of Havana and that of Cuba), constituting the "Pontifical University," were almost entirely devoted to the study of theology, and did not have in view an advanced course of study. Fortunately Cuba had philanthropists and educators like the Reverend Fathers Caballero and Varela, Don Nicolas de Cárdenas y Manzano, Chaple, and José de la Luz Caballero. The latter was the founder of a great college; under his scholarly and patriotic direction other teachers were trained, and the Cuban youth received the treasures of science and of learning, so sadly needed to free them from the dominion of ignorance to which they had been subjected. For this reason it is, that among the *crimes* of which Moreno accuses de la Luz is that of having taught the Cubans without restricting himself to the text books and system of the Government.

Text books? System? The scanty portions that were given us of these were those of the monks, who imported absolutism.

Until 1841—until yesterday we might say—the giving of a primary education to the poor classes was not recognized in Cuba as obligatory on the State, but the opposition and neglect of our government was overcome by the perseverance of the Cubans whom I have quoted, by the efforts of the patriotic societies, by the spirit of the age, and above all by the weight of public opinion which manifested itself in various ways in the foreign and local press. A Board of Education and Committees of Public Instruction, general and local, were organized, and the maintenance of free schools was imposed on the district governments.

But— do not cry victory yet, unknown Paco; notwithstanding that in 1860 the number of schools on the island supported by the municipalities was 283 for the white, and two for the colored children, yet the number of pupils attending them was, in view of the increased population since 1836, relatively smaller than at that date. The schools had not increased in proportion to the requirements of the people. In the country districts and in many of the towns there were none at all.

Alas! we were subjected to a military government. The cities were presided over and ruled by the Deputies of the Governors. Public instruction was always neglected or despised by those potentates. Besides, the State, which raised in Cuba through the tariff on imports twenty-five millions of dollars, had not devoted one single cent of it to popular instruction, while we Cubans had to defray the cost of maintaining Fernando Po as a penal colony for political exiles; we had also that same year to contribute 3,495,700 dollars to the Spanish coffers. We were furthermore taxed 2,333,210 dollars to cover the cost of re-incorporating San Domingo, and another 2,500,000 for the senseless Mexican expedition. We were not taught to read, Paco, but we were made to pay heavily all the same.

In just this way has the refinement of our people been undertaken ; thus have our schools been managed. The wretched condition of the schools was made even worse by the "*reformed course of studies*" of 1863, which was one of the most disastrous measures of General Concha's administration up to 1871. Must I speak of the famous scheme hatched in that year by Ramon de Araístegui, secretary to the Governor General ? It was a neo-catholic conception aggravated by political animus; and its preamble clearly reveals the fact that its object was to kill

education as the fountain head of liberal views and the cause of the revolutionary movement.

Shall I remind you that these documents declared with unblushing effrontery that in order to *iberianize* us, to keep us Spanish, it was necessary to maintain us in

NO. 58.
D. SALVADOR ZAPATA.

the grossest ignorance? Shall I picture to you the present state of our ruined University? Shall I refer to the appointment of professors, favoring certain predetermined personages in a manner contrary to the law in force? Must I say that if the primary schools have increased in number it is due to the growth of municipalities, but that it is a notorious fact that public school teachers are not paid their salaries, and that everything here speaks forcibly of the culpable neglect with which public instruction has been treated?*

*In 1883, the primary schools of Cuba aggregated as follows:

PROVINCES.	PUBLIC.	PRIVATE.	VACANT.
Havana (Entire Province)	173	101	8
" (City)	33	83	
Matanzas	95	22	13
Pinar del Rio	82	18	25
Santa Clara	103	18	3
Puerto Principe	24	4	3
Santiago de Cuba	58	21	15
	568	267	67

Total (exclusive of vacancies), 768 schools.

No; let this pass. What I may yet take time to remind you is that the country whose profound demoralization has been denounced on such meagre knowledge by your informant, Moreno, has produced many notable examples of generous and disinterested philanthropists. Not the least among them have some broad-minded and intelligent Spaniards like Salvador Zepata, who left a considerable estate to the Sociedad Economica for the support of free

NO. 59.—D. JOSÉ ALONSO Y DELGADO.

schools : his legacy has been zealously guarded by that patriotic body and sustains five schools for children and adults, of both colors and both sexes.*

*This institution has from its foundation comprised in its membership the most earnest men of the community, and at its head have figured such men as Ramírez, Peñalvar y Cárdenas, O'Fárell, Herrera, Romay, Saco, and Luz Caballero.

At present the Governing Council of the Society is composed as follows :

Director (presiding),	José Maria Gálvez.
Vice President,	José Bruzon.
Second Vice President,	Carlos Saladrigas.
General Secretary,	Rafael Cowley.
Second General Secretary,	Rafael Montoro.
Librarian,	Carlos Naravetta y Romay.
Treasurer,	Pedro E. G. Larrinaga.
Actuary,	Alvaro Carrizosa.

Board of Trustees : Hilario Cizneros, José de Cárdenas y Gassié, José Hernández Abreu, Juan B. Armenteros, Manuel F. Lamar, and Raimundo Cabrera.

President of the Section of Education : Antonio A. Ecay.

Don Francisco de Hoyos, also a Spaniard, founded by another legacy a free institution of learning, at

present in charge of the distinguished Cuban, Prof. Manuel V. Rodríguez; and Doña Susana Benítez ensured through the income of a rich patrimony the maintenance of a college for poor boys and girls. A philanthropist, Doctor Bruno Zayas, maintains two free schools out of his

NO. 60.—D. JUAN BRUNO DE ZAYAS.

private means; Don José Alonzo y Delgado affords free education to over fifty poor children in his intermediate academy "San Francisco de Asís;" another woman, Doña Marte Abreu de Estévez, has given $120,000 for the erection of a theatre whose income is devoted to the maintenance of free schools. Don José E. Moré, a wealthy planter, has founded and endowed with adequate means a school of Agriculture; Doña Josefa Santa Cruz de Oviedo bequeathed a fortune for

NO. 61.
D. JOSÉ EUGENIO MORÉ.

the construction of a Charity Hospital. The heirs of Don Tomas Terry devoted $115,000 to the

erection of a theatre in Cienfuegos, the income of
which is applied to the promotion of primary education. Doña Antonia, widow of Alfonso Madan,
maintains a free school in the country. There are
innumerable other benevolent private institutions
in this country maintained by private charity.
Numerous associations for the promotion of education, like the societies " La Caridad," " El Pro-
greso," " El Pilar," " La Divina Caridad," maintain numbers of free schools, from all of which it
may well be concluded that a people among whom
such a spirit is manifest is not a people abandoned
to vice and immorality.*

---

* As further indicating the degree of earnestness with
which the Cubans endeavor to make good the wretched
neglect of education by the Colonial Government there may
yet be cited a number of the more conspicuous examples of
this spirit.

Don Miguel Delmonte y Aldama left $10,000 for the pur-
pose of affording an European education to five pupils in
agricultural science. Francisco Biszarrón bequeathed $2000
to the free schools of Güines. Antonio L. Caraballo donated $1000 for the same object. Belisario Galcerán main-
tains, out of his own means, the free school of Caunao.
Miguel Delgado gave $1000 towards the school of Macagua.
Miguel Matienzo furnishes the means for the maintenance
of a school of Guanajay. Silvestre Alfonzo left an endowment for the school at Sabinilla which he founded. The
Count of Mompox did likewise for those of Palos; Rev. Ignacio
O'Farrell lef. a demesne for the school of Tapaste. Francisco
Giraldo maintained the school of Sabanicú until the muni-

cipality took charge of it; Juan Suárez left $4000 for the school at Santiago. Rev. Antonio Hurtado established a free school at Villaclara, erected the building and donated $1000 towards its endowment. He maintained it during his lifetime. Rafael Rodríguez Torices may well be mentioned in this connection. He was a Spaniard whose beneficence gave full evidence of his appreciation of the country in which he had acquired family and fortune.

In numberless cases throughout the country school houses were erected by individuals or by public subscriptions and donated to the district authorities on condition that free schools be maintained in them. This one fact alone suffices to indicate to what a degree private initiative has had to make good the neglect of public instruction by the government.

See " *Guía del Profesorado Cubano*," by Mariano Dumas Chancel, a Spaniard, and one of our laborious and ill-rewarded teachers.

No. 62.—BISHOP ESPADA.

IX.

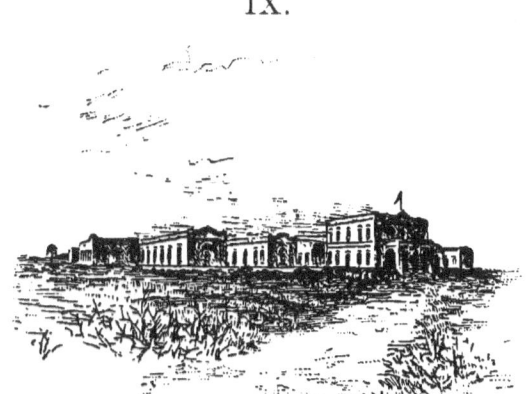

HOSPITAL OF OUR LADY OF MERCIES, HAVANA.

THE PUBLIC OFFICES.—CHAOTIC CONDITIONS OF THE ADMINISTRA-
TIVE SYSTEM.—EVIL EFFECTS OF CENTRALIZATION.—DISHONEST
OFFICIALS.—OFFICIAL SALARIES IN CUBA.

The author of "*Cuba y Su gente*" had inevitably
to write something that I am not compelled to contro-
vert. He has declared that public administration on
this Island "is a perfect chaos" and that it "discredits
the honor and good repute of the mother country."
But he who has not hesitated to besmirch Cuban
society with insults, experiences a *profound regret*
in treating of these affairs "superficially, without
penetrating into the dark corners of each department, of each office."

Nor shall I dive into them either, not indeed for
11

the like reason, friend Paco—for the truth should
be told, though the heavens fall—but because I am
unaccustomed to delving in our beaurocratic centres;
and I would do it with repugnance, though they
present to the observer the most curious spectacle
which this community has to offer.

A visit to any of the government offices in this
country is a source of displeasure and mortification.
The citizen is there treated with deliberate scorn and
disrespect and not as a taxpayer who has a right to
be heard and served. From the pompous porter who
remains sitting when he is addressed, or refuses to
admit you, up to the high functionary who turns
his back upon you without deigning to acquaint
himself with your request, they all affect the superiority of masters and assume a tone and manner
calculated to humiliate the applicant. In every
grade of the official scale they appear to have the
consciousness of the joint dominion which they exercise by virtue of their hierarchy. The taxpayers
are the vassals; they, the feudal lords.

General Martinez Campos, recognizing this state
of things, which creates no small amount of ill feeling, attempted during his term of office to effect an
improvement, and the enthusiasm for peace and
the efforts towards adjustment did not die out until
after he had given up his task. Since then we have
fallen back into the old rut.

For this reason, unknown Paco, we will touch on this subject only *from the outside*. I shall not trouble myself with the individuals of the immense personnel of our administrative system, whom your informant in his book names and classifies, with ingenuity, indeed. They are not Cubans; they are totally unknown; their names (which I trust are respectable) and their functions (which I ignore) do not concern the object of my letters. What I seek to study, analyse, and bring to your cognizance so that you may join me in condemning it, is the *system*, that system which is the fountain head, the generating vice of all the vices.

The system of centralization, the utter absurdity of directing from Madrid the administrative machinery of a country situated nearly 7,000 miles away ! The gross error of entrusting the management of this governmental machine to a minister who ignores the requirements, the customs and mode of existence, the peculiarities of a people so distant. To such an extent does he ignore them that the apparent mission of a Spanish politician during his transitory reign as Minister, appears to be the study of said requirements; studies which are made through that retinue of officials that every ministerial change brings with it; the changes merely satiating the ambition of Spanish political leaders and their followers with Cuban spoils. It is this and nothing else that produces the profound demoralization, the irremediable chaos of the administration.

The evil is antiquated; it has been studied and denounced by many patriots—but the rulers in Madrid have put no check on it. The many offices of the Colonial administration have been invented for the purpose of affording snug berths to politicians, and they are reproduced and multiplied within the intricate administrative machine to serve as gifts from bosses to their henchmen. It were an old story to tell of the many offices which have been given with the understanding and on condition that the patron is to receive from the protegé a monthly stipend or annuity in return for the favor shown. Is it remarkable then, that under the existing order of things, the office holder usually comes to Cuba, risking the dangers of the climate, not to render patriotic and distinguished service to the state, while gaining an honest living, but to accumulate, at all hazards, money which is thereafter to be enjoyed at the Court or in his native town? Is it surprising, under the circumstances, that at each step are encountered scandals, such as the falsification of the accounts of the Public Debt Commission or the loss, some fine spring morning, of great quantities of Government-stamped paper and revenue stamps; or the selling of duplicate-numbered tickets of the National Lottery, calling for a prize of

200,000 dollars; or the clogging of the wheels of justice with unfinished cases of defalcations, embezzlements, stealings, and of public malfeasances of every name and nature, known to those initiated in the ingenious bureaucratic slang as "chocolates," "manganillas," and "filtrations?"

These evils have one decisive and efficacious remedy, for which the country, which is being lacerated by so much corruption, is constantly clamoring, AUTONOMY: the administration of the country by the country itself; the guardianship of their own interests by those who feel and know their own necessities—the collecting, the appropriating, the disbursing and controlling to be done by those who do the contributing and paying.

Let Cuba cease to be the feeding place for the hungry adventurers who cross the Atlantic to obtain, quickly and easily, a fortune through their official stations. Let the Cubans organize their own administration and all, that according to Moreno, lowers the dignity and besmirches the good name of the country, will vanish in the glory of the nation and the well-being of its people.

The authorities recognize the evil, they see it, feel it and deplore it; but they deny the country the right to complain. The protest of the Cuban is always regarded as subversive; the remedies he proposes are supposed to tend to separation, and the deep rooted evil continues to spread, while Spain apparently does not know how, or does not desire, to extirpate it.

Not I, who might be suspected of partiality, but a Spanish economist speaks, who treats of these things in a book which serves me in my refutations, and who like myself, strives in vain to conceal certain factors of the problem. In plainly visible characters these loom up before him in the following

CUBAN SALARIES.*

Governor-General	$50,000.00
General Manager of the Treasury	18,500.00
The Archbishop of Cuba	18,000.00
The Bishop of Havana	13,000.00
The Chief of the Arsenals and Dock Yards	18,000.00
The President of the Court	15,000.00
The Lieutenant General	15,000.00
The Governor of Havana	8,000.00
The First Secretary of the Governor General	8,000.00
A Field Marshal	7,500.00
A Brigadier	4,500.00
A Colonel	3,450.00
A Lieutenant-Colonel	2,700.00
The Brigadiers have besides an allowance of	500.00
The Staff Officers, an allowance of	375.00
In the navy a Captain in command of a ship receives	6,360.00

* The reductions which these salaries have suffered, or the discounts to which they are subjected according to the law on the subject lessen but little the value of these lucrative assignments.

The Captain of a frigate	4,560.00
A Lieutenant in command of a first-class ship . .	3,370.00
" " " of a second-class ship	2,280.00
A Chief of Bureau, (first class)	5,000.00
" " " (second class)	4,000.00
" " " (third class)	3,000.00
A Collector of Customs	4,000.00
A Postmaster	5,000.00
Governor of the Lottery	4,000.00

And in each department, furthermore, the director, the heads of sections, the various grades of officials, the clerks, the porters—an infinite array with infinite emoluments.

Item: By the provisions of Article 21 of the Tariff Law the right of quarters and the cost of a substitute is accorded to many of the employees of the Customs.

Item: The Minister of the Colonies and his supplies, $96,800.00.

At the moment while I write these lines the cable announces a reform by the.reduction of the salaries in the new estimates to the half of the quota paid heretofore. Futile hope! the same cable announces also the speedy adjournment of the Cortes and the continuance of the existing salaries.

But, if the former system was bad when the employés were well paid what would be the consequence if they receive less? What we must do is to simplify the administration, do away with superfluous offices, lessen the number of public employes, and above all, let them not be appointed by the Colonial Ministry, and let not the natives of the country be excluded from public functions. That is all.

X.

STATUE OF COLUMBUS AT CARDENAS.

The author of *Cuba y Su gentes* has devoted only three short paragraphs to the administration of justice. He has not wished to "reveal the gangrene which corrupts this body." He has, however, abundantly expatiated on the minor magistrates and court o ffi c i a l s who are generally natives of the country and whose object he would have us believe is to sow the seeds of dissension and demoralization in the public offices. He greatly fears that in a little while "the courts will be in the hands of the masked separatists."

But this subject, which he treats with such scruple, required more care and all the temerity that he displayed in treating of the pretended vices of Cuban society and youth.

I, Paco, have neither those fears nor those scruples, and since I have undertaken the thankless task of refuting the senseless reports and statements of our affairs which Moreno has published in such a prejudiced spirit, I will not rest until I have accomplished my purpose.

I affirm that as we have in Cuba a demoralized civil government, so we have through like causes a vicious administration of justice. It is not that we are lacking in laws;—no; from the Charter of Rights to the latest Recompilation; from the Ordinances of Castile and Arragon to the Royal Decrees and Rescripts and Compilations and new Codifications, we enjoy in Cuba the same tremendous conglomeration of laws as in Spain. With all the Commissions of Codification—which we pay for in great part—it has not been possible to unify and straighten out these laws. What we very sadly need are Judges; judges in the true sense of the word we have very few indeed.

In countries governed like England and the United States written laws are mostly general. Considered scientifically, they are even deficient or imperfect. But bad judges are rare; they are soon denounced and done away with by the force of public opinion. In this country, on the contrary, the rare instance is the *good judge*. When by some strange coincidence an upright man, of a just and impartial character is found among the Judiciary, who does not yield to political or party influence, or to considerations of wealth or station, who proves himself conscious and worthy of his high mission, the fact is bruited on every tongue and the people everywhere proclaim his exceptional incorruptibility.

Sometimes, however, these conditions are not altogether convenient for certain exalted interests; the mode of existence of this administrative organism is at variance with good, and there have been cases where special judges have been appointed when the energetic zeal and rectitude of some functionary might become troublesome.

Here, where a privileged class dominates, everything succumbs to the influence of the rulers. The tenure of office is at the caprice of the powerful and influential. The functionaries of justice who cross the sea to make a living by the exercise of their vocation are soon convinced that their personal comfort depends entirely upon the managers and bosses. Political partisanship has undermined even the highest altar of justice, and our judges, with the exception of a few good Spaniards, have yielded and manifestly continue to give way to this pernicious influence.

The system of government which exists in Cuba, and in which there prevails no other principle than that of exclusiveness and favoritism, is opposed to the existence of justice. There is perfect solidarity and communion among all the functionaries. The poison which affects one branch must necessarily and by a logical sequence spread to the others. There is no severance in their continuity.

Let there be no fears then that the Courts will fall into the hands of the native Cubans, or that the immorality of the latter undermine the powers of the State. The Cubans are excluded from holding the office of judge as from the other offices of the administration.*

The number of those who have figured as such is very small. This assertion may be proved by a simple arithmetical exercise; add those of the respective places of nativity and subtract the one from the other; the difference will be noticeable. Not one Cuban has obtained a position of importance.

---

* The defense of the poor and of insolvent criminals is made incumbent on the lawyers, solicitors, notaries, etc., as a public charge, without any compensation whatever. The diverse and arduous duties which these gratuitous services entail oblige the unfortunate notaries to incur the expense of assistants, clerks, offices, etc., without any recompense by the State. Since the publication of this work, the Tribunals of Correction and Courts of Criminal Arraignment have been established, but the innovations have all the shortcomings of the old system—the service is poorly endowed and cannot otherwise than fail in a country condemned to be exploited and to pay in every possible way.

The Presiding Judges, Magistrates, Justices, District-Attorneys and Councillors are appointed by the Ministry of the Colonies,—even the solicitors and clerks. There remain the constables and porters, but these must be veterans of the military service, and here there is no "military" service.

Just as Araístegui's plan attempted to "hispanicize" public instruction, just so is the forum being "hispanicized" to-day; the expression is not mine—it is official.

NO. 66.—D. GUILLERMO BERNAL.

The offices of notaries public and of official attorneys are retained for the Spaniards; the birthplace invariably decides the question; so that jurisprudence becomes rather a one sided affair.

This monopoly accounts for the fact that a convict could serve as notary public during a number of years and take affidavits in a prominent court of justice.

·The municipal judgeships are solicited and given as recompense for electoral services rendered to the "Constitutional Union" party.*

---

*The municipal courts are deservedly discredited in the public mind. But all the blame must not be laid upon the personnel of these offices. Our government, while making its reforms, has sown the evil, together with all its conse-

There have been heads of important judicial districts who left the tavern to don the ermine (learned and experienced men being put aside for ignorant, uncouth Spaniards) and it has been observed that though the tavern did not appear to make large profits between the sessions of the Court, yet the novel judge prospered visibly.

A law suit of any kind is the cause of great alarm to families and invariably means ruin. Both parties, the right and the wrong, seek rather influential recommendation than a good counsellor. We frequently see here the case of an insignificant tradesman coming suddenly and most unexpectedly

---

quences. For instance, there has been imposed on these Courts, without compensation, the hearing of criminal cases. They have charge of the Civil Register, which by virtue of its organization alone requires a numerous personnel, who receive no remuneration. The State does not even allow them official quarters, neither for their offices nor for the Civil Register, the business and importance of which requires a proper location.

What results must such conditions produce? The same or like conditions could be mentioned in regard to the Registry of Deeds established by the new Mortgage law of 1880; a most useful reform, but which has only served to increase the troubles and murmurings of an impoverished country; all because the State has not known how to avoid and prevent the illegal and scandalous exactions which public opinion has denounced. These offices should be supported by the State in the same manner as the civil, judicial and military administration.

into possession of valuable plantations, which have been fraudulently adjudicated at figures far below their value. Who has not seen here the administration of large estates placed by legal procedure, without surety, in the hands of men who were actually insolvent?

Alas! the long, interminable series of injustices which I could reveal to you. Do not tell me of judicial responsibility; the principle of equity is not judicially recognized here; the solidarity of those who exploit this vicious system condones the faults of individuals.

It is certain that there is a profound immorality in our jurisprudence, but it germinates, spreads, and is propagated from the top to the bottom; from the superiors to the inferiors and not inversely. It cannot be otherwise; the blood circulates from the heart to the extremities.

Let there be good government and there will be upright, impartial and zealous judges. Let the courts cease to be unipersonal. Let the judicature cease to be exercised exclusively by Spanish patricians; put an end to summary processes of law;*

---

* Since the publication of the sixth (Spanish) edition of this work public oral hearings have been instituted in Cuba, but with such meagre recourses and such deficiencies in both form and matter that, as stated in a preceding note, the reform is a miserable experiment. Each jurisdiction comprises a vast

corect the evils pointed out in this chapter and the
disgrace with which the administration of justice is
branded will cease to exist.†

Innocent men will not then languish in their
cells, while villainous wretches stalk abroad,
insolent in their security. Nor will a high functionary in the pride of his exalted station keep thousands of criminal suits back year after year, to the
detriment of those under indictment — because, for-
sooth, he cannot entrust them to his assistants; nor
will the prosecutions for embezzlements be super-
seded for lack of evidence, nor will the documents
filed against certain functionaries be mislaid and
never found, nor will the decision of the Supreme
Court against magnates of the land be altered for
their benefit—and so on to the end.

But, my dear Paco, in a country where the

---

extent of territory; besides civil matters, the judges of the
courts of first instance have the hearing of criminal suits
also; the difficulty of communication, the lack of sufficient
appropriation for the expenses of the tribunal, everything
tends to maintain disorder, injustice and chaos.

† The courts in the metropolis (Madrid), as in other
civilized countries, enjoy a vacation through the heated summer term. Those of Cuba have emulated the former, not
indeed, out of humanity nor in the cause of hygiene; but the
sessions are furthermore frequently interrupted by vacations
capriciously declared without any reason on many occasions
throughout the year, to the prejudice of justice and the great
annoyance of the parties concerned.

VIEW OF THE CALLE DE LA REINA, HAVANA.

NO. 61. PBRO. FÉLIX VARELA.

administration of justice is not a charge of the state, but a source of income for the state; in a colony where the budget shows the receipt of $750,000 for stamped paper, and only $475,061.20 for the administration of justice, there is obtained for the treasury a profit of $274,938.80; what other use is there for a judicial system, either big or little, high or low, in toto or in detail, than money! money! money!

12

XI.

CITY HALL, HAVANA.

LOCAL GOVERNMENT IN CUBA.—ITS PAST AND PRESENT.—THE MU-
NICIPALITIES AND THEIR ORGANIZATION.—AUTOCRATIC ADMIN-
ISTRATION.—THE LOCAL GOVERNMENT LAW OF 1859.—THE RE-
STRICTED FRANCHISE.—RESTRICTED POWERS OF THE LOCAL
COUNCILS.—THE LAW OF 1879.—A SEMBLANCE OF REFORM.—A
REALITY OF CENTRALIZATION.

I shall not attempt the defense of the municipal
government of Havana nor that of other cities of
the island. There is not a wheel in our administrative machinery which runs smoothly.

The municipalities but reflect the administration
of the State. The latter is the basis on which the
former are planned, the mould in which all are cast.

If chaos prevails in the State, the municipalities
may be regarded as dark caverns where no light
penetrates.

The evil, the profound evil, which afflicts this
social body in all its aspects is invariably due to the

same causes—misgovernment, favoritism, centralization.

It is against these causes, and against these evils
that the country has protested and still cries out in
anguish, but its voice has always been heard with
displeasure and disdain, when not peremptorily
stifled.

Do you wish me to prove this, Paco? Do you
wish me to demonstrate how even in the municipal
sphere the Cuban has been systematically excluded
from the management of the affairs of the country,
of his town, and even of his own home? If ever he
cherished the hope of reaching the distinction of
taking part in that management, it was but an idle
dream born of an unfulfilled promise. Do you
want to know why our municipalities are ruined;
why they are overwhelmed with debt and scandalized with defalcations; why their officials are in-
subordinate; why the public accounts have never
been in order? Do you want to know why there
is no sanitation, why we have no paved streets, no
adequate sewerage, insufficient water, wretched
lights, no sidewalks nor bridges, no parks, and
no suburbs, no hospitals nor police service, no
schools, no libraries, nor anything which by right
belongs to a people who pay more taxes per capita
than any other in Spain, or anywhere else in the
wide world? Then read again the letters which I

have already written you, for in them, as far as the general government of this land is concerned, the greater part has already been explained. As for the rest, continue reading, for although with so copious and varied a subject I might fill a book, I will drive my pen so that a comparatively few paragraphs will suffice to point out the remainder.

Their Catholic Majesties and their descendants, Charles I, Philip II, and Philip IV, wished to give Cuba—as to their other American colonies—the same form of government which the Spanish monarchy enjoyed. So it was declared in the Law 2nd, Title 8th, Book 4, of the Summary of the Laws of the Indies; or, as Humboldt observed, they endeavored to give a new society the structure of an old nation.

Of course we had in Cuba the municipal organization of the ancient régime, pompously rigged out with a Board of Regents composed of a perpetual membership of royal appointment, with a lot of higher councilmen (*Alguaciles mayores*) all under the exalted direction of a Burgomaster. The executive administration was simply a delegation of the central power and a privilege of blood, of family, of class, and of fortune.

Let us not speak of the benefits which the community at large could reap from such a system. Remember, ·Paco, that under this order of things the municipality of Havana in 1824 had not founded a single school, and *as a loan*, afforded the Sociedad Patriótica *one hundred dollars* to assist the latter in maintaining those which it had established under difficulties.

Until the year 1859 the electoral system did not prevail in our municipalities. But do not smile with satisfaction in the belief that Mother Spain then showed her liberality to these cities. Nothing of the kind. The election, if you could call it an election, was made exclusively by the richer tax payers. The list of these was made up by the Lieutenant-Governor. To have the privilege of taking some part in the local administration it was necessary to pay a high contributing quota, and so the councilmen and other relics of absolutism, with the acquired privileges of the old régime, remained unmolested. The people were always excluded from all participation in public affairs.

Add to this as a finishing touch, as a crowning finial to this rickety political edifice, the fact that those who presided over and governed the municipalities so constituted, the lieutenants of the governors, were ignorant, despotic, military chieftains, who exercised absolute power in our towns.

Under this system of irresponsibility, which lasted until Jan. 1st, 1879, and which was overthrown only by a bloody revolution, the municipal system of Cuba had its origin; thus it took root, flourished and ripened its harvest of confusion, disorder and immorality. The capricious will of the governor ruled in each locality, the sword was all-powerful; there were no associations of the people ; instead of these there were juntas of rich vassals controlled by a feudal despotism.

A lasting example of this abominable autocratic government, a system which the Municipal law of 1869 did not radically modify, was General Tacon in Havana. He is highly praised for his promotion of public works, for which money was raised without stint by imposing taxes on the people, and the work carried on by forcing to excessive labor the unfortunate soldiery and political offenders from the Peninsula. He enriched various individuals and contractors through his favoritism, and gratified his excessive pride and vanity by putting his execrable name on the works which—like a new Pharao— he accomplished with no arbiter but his own pleasure, and no limitations but those which he himself imposed. ·

Similar proceedings were repeated in all the jurisdictional centres of the island, under the aegis of the law and of an absurd system of administration, by those lilliputian viceroys whom Cuba supported under the title of Lieutenant-Governors; odious dictators of the local administration, demoralized and irresponsible.

· Like General Tacon, they had a vainglorious longing to leave their names written or engraved as lasting memorials of themselves in the places over which they ruled. What Cuban town does not possess an unattractive plaza, a wretched market place, a defective aqueduct, a miserable fountain, or at least some street or tower bearing the name of the military governor who ordained its construction, who made the appropriation, determined its approval, imposed charges on the people and thereby began, or increased, or multiplied an hundred fold the deficit in the municipal administration?

NO. 69.
D. NICOLÁS ESCOBEDO.

On the other hand, there is not to be found, in Havana for example, a single public square or even a commonplace street which boasts the name of Luz Caballero, of Arango, Cárdenes Manzano, or Escobodo; of Saco, Bernal, Heredia, Placido, or of any of the many great sons of Cuba, of its litterateurs, philanthropists or educators.

The Municipalities Law of 1859 is alone sufficient to condemn our Colonial system. In each governmental department we were given a corporation consisting of one Mayor (*alcalde*), one magistrate,

and six aldermen if the population reached the
number of 5,000 souls; two deputy mayors and ten
aldermen, if it counted 10,000; with the exception
of Havana, which was privileged to have seven
deputy mayors, four magistrates or syndics and sixteen aldermen. But if the life-aldermen appertain-
ing to the municipalities covered these respective
numbers then they alone governed. Remember we
are dealing with corporate officers, alienated from
the Crown, with their several and corresponding
emoluments, honors and perquisites.

The minor councilmen were elective, but do not
imagine that the people had a right to nominate
the men considered worthy of their trust; no,
indeed; the election was made by a number of the
biggest tax-payers. These electors numbered twice
as many as the councilmen to be elected, or thrice
as many if the population exceeded 10,000 souls.
Three to elect one! four to elect two! How nice!
But wait a moment; that was not the final election.
The electors simply nominated their candidates to
the Governor-General, who was entirely free to
accept or refuse the nominees. In this manner,
amiable Paco, the solicitous and paternal eye of our
government penetrated to the utmost corner of this
ungrateful land, placing its seal on the simplest and
most primitive acts of public life. But the mechanism did not end here, nor must you believe that

those bigger taxpayers were electors of themselves or by their own right. No; the lists were formed by the Governors or Lieutenant-Governors, together with three aldermen and three major contributors. As you know what a Lieutenant-Governor was, you can easily imagine that he appointed, as he pleased, such men as he felt sure would not undertake to resist his authority, supposing such a thing to have been possible under those lords of the manor. To cap the climax we find that all protests regarding such appointments were passed upon by himself alone, without regard to his associates. Do not suppose, however, that the electoral process guaranteed a free vote even to the major contributors ; consider that the ceremony was presided over by the Lieutenant-Governor in person, and that the vote had to be certified through papers made out by himself.

Woe to the rebel who did not approve the official candidate !

It naturally followed that each locality had such municipal officials as suited the purposes of the governor. Each corporation was, in point of fact, like an obedient flock of sheep.

I forgot to mention, and it is no unimportant historical detail, that only *reputable whites*, and those who were not under the surveillance of the authorities (who were by no means few) were eligible for office.

You see, most esteemed Paco, that the Cubans had goodly reason to fairly burst with gratitude for the zeal which the government displayed in freeing them from all annoyances and care, from all concern and trouble, in the organization of their municipal corporations.

Everything was cut and dried for them ; but the most satisfactory and gratifying circumstance of all was the easy obligations of these administrative bodies.   What art, what solicitous care in the concoction of the law, and how light the labors of the municipal councillors !

They were to appoint those officers only whose salaries did not exceed $25 per month ; those paid more than that sum must be submitted to the Governor.   In this way the blessed aldermen had one worry less and the poor governors one care more. The latter were thus forced to consider petitions and listen to office seekers and to decide, as was their invariable custom, in favor of some nephew, godson, relative, friend or recommended individual from his province—or from the " Provinces ;" for at that time this word had not yet been fully adjusted in the colonial geography.

The councilmen might also attend to the material improvements which the town required, if the cost did not exceed $200 ; but anything over and above that sum was supposed to be too deep an

arithmetical problem for the fortunate Cuban aldermen, whose comfort and repose was sought at all
hazards by the kind, paternal government, which,
with unheard-of abnegation, takes all those hard-
ships upon itself.

But even decisions concerning works not ex-
ceeding $200 were subject to the approval of the
Lieutenant Governor and to the sanction of the
Captain-General.

The system was truly delightful; the "natural
indolence" of the Cubans was thus respected and
guarded. How could they learn to work under a
government which spoiled them to such an extent
and freed them with such tender solicitude from the
necessity of any effort?

Nevertheless, the government had in mind some
day to take advantage of their slight abilities. In
order that they might slowly and gently learn to
deal with public affairs, it graciously permitted the
councils and corporations to *deliberate;* but only to
deliberate, on the formulation of ordinances, on works
of utility, on public improvements, on the laying
out of new streets and other matters; but if the
Governor of the department took it into his head to
ignore these deliberations, then the councillors had
only wasted their time.

And all of this, dear Paco, came to pass in Cuba,
not in the last century, nor prior to the invention

of railroads; not before the discovery of the telegraph, nor before the revolution of '68, which the
Spaniards term "the glorious" and in which the
rights of the people were so loudly proclaimed.

No, my sympathetic friend, this went on until the
first of January, 1879. Now you can see whether
the Cubans have been happy, whether they have
had a chance to receive a civic education and acquire
the habits of public life, or if they have had examples of administrative morality.

You smile? Well, listen : The municipal councils could not deliberate on any other matters than
those determined by law; they could not proceed of
their own initiative ; *could not even adopt resolutions*,
nor express an opinion on problems of general
administration ; much less could they publish their
views without permission from their superiors.

And how they had to beware of expostulating !
On the other hand the military governors, victims of
their self-denial, were burdened with duties, or rather
with powers. They presided over and directed the
municipal corporations, decided the elections, convoked the councils, called to account those who were
derelict, granted leaves of absence, carried on the correspondence, commanded in the offices as elsewhere ;
in short, it was their *prerogative* to execute decisions,
make payments, sign the treasury bills (this was
most interesting), regulate the polls, make appro-

priations, and so forth. I do not mention (for it
would be too lengthy) that calamitous invention,
which, known as "extra assessments" (*Derramas*),
would suddenly be precipitated on our taxpayers.
Felicitous resource for the vicious intermeddlers in
this system of government. It was under such a
system of law that municipal life in Cuba had its
inception.

But in spite of these drawbacks the virile and
patriotic character of the Cubans manifested itself
constantly in battling against the impositions of the
central power. The natives of the country were at
that time the wealthy class, the owners of real estate,
and of the sugar plantations ; in their hands were
the landed estates, and they were consequently the
larger taxpayers on whom the municipal charges
fell.

Although their power was limited and held in
check, it was to their zealous intervention that the
increase and improvement of the schools and the
establishment of other public services was due. I
examine at this moment the royal decree of December 29th, 1865, authorizing the foundation of sixteen
schools solely by the municipality of Colon.

But the Cuban aldermen were obliged to deal
with the Lieutenant-Governors, strongly and systematically supported by the Captain-General ; their
generous efforts were balked by the artful combina-

tion of an all-pervading despotic system and the solidarity of its ministers. Over and over again those struggles in behalf of municipal interests were the real causes of cruel political persecutions against many patriots who gave expression to their public spirit, and who manifested their enthusiasm for the progress of the country in the council deliberations.

In view of the centralization of the municipal administration, and with the bare semblance of municipal organization which I have cursorily sketched above, is it strange that in 1879 on putting the new law in force, and on inaugurating the newly organized councils, all, absolutely all, of the old Lieutenant-Governors presented empty treasuries and overcharged accounts. Deficits, debts, neglected services, frauds, starving employés and demoralization everywhere.

Oh, in those days of transition, hailed so joyfully by the people, we saw as in an illusory mirage, the so-called popular Alcaldes take charge of the local governments ; the proud Lieutenant-Governors give up the city halls—converted into palaces—where they had enjoyed at the expense of the municipalities luxurious furniture, golden plate, rich stuffs of a character the most extravagant and least necessary for existence. With what faith we believed that a new life, full and expansive, had begun for the Cuban municipalities!

Sad hallucinations of deceptive hope! the new law, promulgated as a *provisional enactment*, brought with it the original evil, the very germ and primary cause of demoralization. A few fetters loosened; duties somewhat more divided, the immediate influence of the military on the corporations suppressed, and the number of municipalities increased; something was certainly gained, but there still remained and still remains the centralization of power, the tutelage and the prerogative of an almost absolute Governor to override all initiative.

Furthermore, an electoral mechanism which was soon to exclude, as it has since done, the natives of the country in order to confer the local management on the favored Spaniards.

Not true?——Here you have the list of the present members of the Havana Board of Aldermen.*

Francisco F. Ibáñez, Laureno Pequeño, Luis G. Corujedo, Ricardo Ricardo Calderón, Idelfonso A. de la Massa, Juan A. Castillo, Rafael Joglar,

---

*The City of Güines, for example counts 13,000 inhabitants; of these 500 are Spaniards and Canary Islanders. Notwithstanding this discrepancy, there is not a single Cuban in the board of Aldermen, and in the electoral registry there appear only 32 Cuban as against 400 Spanish electors!

NO. 67. ANTONIO GOVÍN Y TORRES.

Juan D. Orduña, Pablo Tapia, Bernardo Alvarez, Pedro A. Estanillo, Juan Pedro, Serafin Sabucedo, Nicolás Serráno, Peregrín G. Martínez, Manuel H. Ochoa, Juan B. Ablanedo, Jenaro de la Vega, Francisco Salaya, Prudencio Rabell, José M. Galán, Antonio Arenas, Fidel Villasuso, José Rafecas, Ezequiel Aldecoa, José A. Tabares, Manuel P. Melgares, Enrique L. Villalonga.

There are 28 in all. Of these one is a Cuban and 27 are Spaniards. The Cubans figure in scarce numbers in the so-called Spanish party; if they hold any office it is through favor or recompense, thanks to their abjuration of patriotism and to their having approved and supported the policies of the enemies of our liberties. This same condition is repeated in nearly all the towns and corporations of the island.*

---

*The Provincial Deputation of Havana is composed of 20 deputies, who at the present time are the following: Antonio C. Tellería, President. Leopoldo Carvajal, Antonio Corzo, Celso Golmayo, Amilio A. Prida, Fernando de Castro, Fernando S. Reinoso, Narcisso Galats, Serapio Arteaga, Julián Chavarri, Jorge Ferrán, Joaquín Ginerés, Miguel Ochoa, Mariano de la Torre, Manuel Carrascosa, Rafael Vallanueva, Antonio Govín, Gabriel Casuso, Gabriel del Cristo, Raimundo Cabrera. (a.) The first 16 belong to the Conser-

(a.) Since the publication of this work, through the new elections under the exclusive system in force, the liberal Cuban deputies in the department of Havana have diminished in number. To-day there remain only Antonio Govin, Gabriel Casuso and Antonio Messa.

13

I can prove to you by figures, and by means of scrupulously exact statistics, that less than twenty-five per cent. of the Mayors of the Island are Cubans, the rest being Spaniards. Are they not appointed by the Captain General? The same thing may be said of the Councils, and if you keep in mind that the census shows 850,000 white natives, and 140,000 Spaniards and Canary Islanders, it must be obvious that a system of monopoly and

---

vative party, which has given majorities to only three Cubans ; the rest are Spaniards. The last four are Autonomists and Cubans. This party succeeded in 1882 in holding the majority of this deputation, but the official element soon robbed them of this advantage ; the former went to the extreme carrying by bribery the election in one district and usurping the seat of the Deputy elected for Alquizar (Don Ricardo del Monte). These proceedings went without reparation.

It is proper to state that our provincial deputations, without means or proper resources, without a sphere of action, and without power of initiative, have been, and are still among the unfulfilled promises of reform made since the peace of Zanjon. The deputations are but useless wheels in our administrative machinery, created only to give employment, or rather salary, to the numerous idle officials whom the law imposes upon our impoverished municipalities.

The deputation of Havana, for example, has an expense budget of $100,000; it was formerly much greater, having reached $200,000, but was reduced through the impossibility of putting it into practice. The deputation occupies a palace, sustains three very costly offices, and allows for "expenses of representation " $2,500 !

favoritism exists, and that the Cubans are not responsible for the corruption of our municipalities.

These assertions are not dictated by a blind love for Cuba. After the peace of Zanjon, in the days when warm words of concord were written in the official documents, when in many places the conservative element relaxed its hold on the electoral machinery, it was possible to obtain *true* representations. The Cubans by right of contribution appeared in the registries and obtained legitimate representation in many towns.

But when the spasmodic reconciliation was over, the monopoly began anew; the Government in all its branches neither neglected nor did it hide its design. Cuban Alcaldes were deposed, the councillors put down, the electors excluded from the registry, nor have their formal protests elicited justice anywhere. The Government has gone even to the length of showing such hatred and injustice as to grant universal suffrage without distinction of age to the Spaniards, while the Cubans were little less than prohibited from voting.

This, friend Paco, is our past and our present. What can be expected of the Cuban municipalities? What can be their future promise in a country where the State drains all the vital forces of the people, and the municipality does not offer advantages even to the favored ones who exercise the council duties?

It leaves them only the vanity of being the overseers in a system which works everything for the
master ; neither have they the satisfaction of eleva-
ting and purifying their homes in the midst of a
people whom they do not govern, but of whose exploitation they become accomplices.

XII.

No. 71. THE TEMPLE MONUMENT (EL TEMPLETE), HAVANA.

NATIONAL CUBAN REPRESENTATION.—HISTORICAL SKETCH OF THE
INSTITUTION.— ANTAGONISM OF THE GENERAL GOVERNMENT.—
MILITARY DESPOTISM INTENSIFIED.—MOVEMENT FOR REFORM.—
COMMISSION OF INQUIRY APPOINTED.—FAILURE OF THE COMMIS-
SION.—THE INSURRECTION OF 1868.—THE COMPROMISE OF ZANJON
IN 1878. — CONCESSIONS BY THE GOVERNMENT. — NEW BASIS OF
REPRESENTATION.—THE ELECTIONS.—GERRYMANDERING BY THE
GOVERNMENT. — MISREPRESENTATION AND REPRESSION OF THE
CUBAN ELEMENT.—THE NECESSITY OF AUTONOMY.

As I will now proceed to consider the Representation of Cuba in the Cortes, let us pause a moment,
Paco, to cast a retrospective glance on the political
constitution of Cuba. Moreno has given us occasion for slight sketches of our history, such as the
character of these letters renders possible; these
sketches may serve to prevent your being led astray by
his notations and also to instruct our countrymen.
You must be aware that we Cubans have at times

absolutely, and at others partially, been excluded
from the Spanish Parliament—and continue so to be.

This is an assertion which I shall endeavor to
explain so that you may better understand it.

Until 1837 Cuba enjoyed legislative rights and
accordingly participated in legislative functions,
but never in the manner and to the extent due the
country. From 1837 to 1879 we were absolutely
deprived of representation in the General Legislature. Since 1879, although it may appear that our
right of representation in the Cortes is recognized,
and although there are Cuban representatives in
both Congress and Senate, nevertheless Cuba is not
in reality represented there, nor are the few who
ostensibly represent the Island listened to. The
absurd system of monopoly which has crushed us
down was maintained by surreptitious political
means, by electoral combinations, and by such
schemes as have always characterized the Madrid
Colonial Administration. Among these, the policy
of parliamentary obstruction, of which the Government gave unpleasant proofs in the last legislature,
is the most striking.

After you have learned something of these matters, even though but passingly, it will not be necessary to tell you that the Cuban deputies,—that is to
say, those of them who have really endeavored to
care for the interests of Cuba in the General Legisla-

ture, have never at any period gone to Madrid to obtain or solicit appointments and favors ; they have gone to seek some way of redeeming their oppressed country. If they obtained anything, it was, occasionally, persecution and exile, as happened to Varela and Saco, or again, contemptuous treatment, like that which befell the commissioners of 1865. The one fact, of which they always became convinced, was that while the Spanish politicians may understand their colonies, while they perhaps study them — which I doubt—they trouble themselves neither with the present nor the future interests of their charges.

* *
*

In the 17th century, during the prevalence of the assimilating tendencies which continued until 1808, and which are manifested in the " Laws of the Indies," Cuba had a semblance of representation in the shape of *Juntas de Procuradores*, appointed by the people to deal with the affairs of the Island.

The Junta of Notables which met in Seville in 1808, during the calamitous troubles of the country, proclaimed unity of rights for the Spaniards of both hemispheres.

The Royal Decree of Feb. 14th, 1810, issued on the Island of Leon through the Council of Regency in the name of Ferdinand VII, " considering the

grave and urgent necessity of having the Spanish
dominions in America and Asia represented in the
extraordinary sessions of the Cortes," convoked the
Cubans to the National Congress.

One deputy was to be elected for each district
capital. Havana and Santiago de Cuba had each
one representative. The elections were to be made
by the City Councils " choosing first *three natives of
the country* who must be honest, intelligent, educated
and free from all stain," afterwards choosing one of
these by lot; "the one first drawn to be Deputy
to the Cortes." Pay strict attention, Paco, to these
words of the law. The first deputies were *required*
to be *natives* of the country ; a requisite not necessary now. The law at present is such as to permit
the deputies to represent anything and everything
conceivable except Cuba.

In those first elections by the City Council of
Havana, August 6th, 1810, distinguished men like
Francisco Arango y Parreño, Andrés de Jáuregui,
and Pedro Regalado Pedroso were chosen, the lot
falling to the second. He and Juan Bernardo
O'Gavan, elected by Santiago de Cuba, took part
in the drafting of the constitution of the year
1812, in which no apparent distinction is made
between the European and American Spaniards.
The Marquis of San Felipe y Santiago, and Joaquin
de Santa Cruz had previously acted as substitutes.

During that brief period of constitutional government Cuba enjoyed its advantages; a division of
civil and military powers was effected; provincial
deputations and constitutional municipal councils
were established; liberty of the press was accorded;
educated judges were appointed, and the fetters of
centralization were materially relaxed.

In 1813 Francisco Arango y Parreño was elected
Deputy. Through his determined efforts were
effected the important economic reforms which
raised the commercial interests of Cuba from the
prostrated condition in which they were languish-
ing. The continental war in South America undoubtedly inclined the government to a policy of
attraction towards Cuba, but it was mainly owing to
the constant solicitude and powerful influence of this
able man that when the absolute system of Government was re-established by the decree of May 4th,
1814, Cuba suffered less than the other parts of the
monarchy by reason of the restored despotism. In
consequence of the restoration of this régime the Deputies elected March 14th, 1814, by the Municipality
of Havana, Messrs. Juan J. D. de Espada, Juan
Bautista Armenteros and Count Montalvo were not
permitted to take their seats in the Cortes.

After the revolution headed by Riego the Cubans
again participated in the benefits of a constitutional
government.

On August 22, 1820, Havana elected as Cuban Deputies Lieutenant-General José de Zayas, Magistrate José Benitez, and Antonio Modesto del Valle. Santiago de Cuba elected Juan O'Gavan.[1]

In 1822 the election fell to the Rev. Felix Varela, of blessed memory, Leonardo Santos Suarez, both Cubans, and Tomas Gener, a Spaniard whose name is cherished by Cubans among those of her benefactors. To this epoch may be traced the beginning of the class distinction between Cubans and Spaniards, a distinction which was brought about by the monopolizing intruders.

NO. 72.
D. TOMÁS GENER.

Again the liberal institutions of Spain fell, this time through intervention of the French armies, and until the promulgation of the Royal Statute we ceased to have a representation in the Cortes. That Statute was promulgated in Havana June 5th, 1834; but although, with much official bluster they had a brillliant illumination, erected arches and celebrated fêtes, the country saw with profound discontent that so far as Cuba was concerned there

---

[1] The election of the last two was declared null and void because colored persons had taken part in the election and on account of other defects in the electoral lists.

was little or nothing to be expected from it. It discriminated against the Colonies as regards the electoral laws and freedom of the press, and the right to organize a militia was denied. The Military Commissions, and the unlimited powers of the Captain-General remained in force.

Thus was marked out the dividing line which separated into classes the subjects of one government, the people of a common country. The life councillors appointed the following six Procurators for Cuba, who took their places in the representative body (*Estamento*): Andrés A r a n g o, Juan Montalvo y Castillo, Prudencio Echavarría, José Serapio Mojarrieta, Sebastián Kindelán.

NO 73.—D. FRANCISCO DE ARMAS Y CARMONA.

The Queen appointed as members of the upper house (*proceres*) Miguel Tacon, the Counts of Villanueva, Fernandia, and O'Reilly, and the Marquis of Candeleria de Yarayabo.

In 1836 the constitution of the year '12 was again promulgated in Spain. General Tacon was governing in Cuba with unlimited powers. In his unbridled despotism he ignored the laws and the very constitution, suppressing its proclamation in Santiago de Cuba by General Lorenzo. He was truly the well chosen instrument of the oppressive policy which had begun its effects in 1820, which, in 1836, had already resulted in the independence of the other Spanish-American countries, and now had become developed in all its horrors.

Amid the contradictory proposals which were propounded at that period regarding the participation of the Antilles in the Cortes, a measure which accorded that right was accepted, but with restrictions.

In the Peninsula one deputy was to be elected for each 50,000 inhabitants. In Cuba it was decided that only four should be elected, when according to the number of the white population *nine* was due to it.

In the meantime the despot Tacon sent with a great flourish a military expedition to Santiago and there imprisoned, exiled and persecuted all those who had joined General Lorenzo in proclaiming the constitution of 1812, which was already in force in the Peninsula. Three successive elections took place, and the following were chosen to represent Cuba in the Constituent Assembly:

José Antonio Saco, Francisco de Armas, Juan Montalvo y Castillo, Nicolás Escobedo.

The fatal policy of Tacon and his dictatorial actions were approved in the metropolis, despite the strenuous efforts of Don Porfirio Valiente, commissioner from Santiago de Cuba and of General Lorenzo as well.

We now reach, my dear friend, that period of our history in which the very furies were let loose; in which all scruple was set aside; in which was manifested all the rancor and hatred with which our rulers have ever regarded the liberties of Spaniards born in the colonies.*

Until now, Cuba had either lacked importance, or had been something like a general barracks for the armies engaged in suppressing revolutions on the Continent. The relative degree of freedom which Cuba enjoyed was rather tolerated than granted, with the view to securing the fidelity of the inhabitants and at the same time to utilize it as a blandishment for the rebellious American countries: but never because of a sincere conviction that political liberty was at all desirable in the Colonies.

It is not I who say so, Paco; Sr. Sancho revealed all this in open Parliament, in the Constituent Assembly of April 2, 1837: "The government has NEVER held the opinion that deputies should be sent from America; it has been considered as an evil which it was necessary to cut short. .

---

*It was even considered as dangerous, (and prohibited by Royal Order of the Madrid government) to deport to Cuba the liberal Spanish political prisoners. The propaganda of their doctrines in the enslaved Colony would be undesirable.

Their advent was a calamity." . . . "Since 1812 it has been proposed that the Constitution should not there be operative" . . . . "and it was resolved that the smallest possible number of Deputies should come from those countries." . . .

The Spanish historian Zaragosa—whom you will surely not regard as partial—has fully recognized these facts. See his work on *Cuban Insurrections*, page 413.

In the session of February, 1836, the Cortes accepted the report of a select commission inspired by its leaders, Argüelles, Sancho and Heros, by which it was resolved to no longer admit the Deputies from the Colonies.

The energetic protest of the Cuban deputies, drafted by Saco, served only to show to advantage the patriotic energy of our representatives. The unjust despoliation was ratified. To the adoption of this measure the rabid reports of Tacon contributed not a little.

From this date on, the political constitution of Cuba became established in accordance with the decree which I submit for your analysis below. This decree together with the unlimited powers of the Captain Generals—"Governors of cities in a state of siege"—was to delight a people who had been sarcastically termed the "ever faithful."

" The Secretary of the Department of the Navy, Commerce, and the Government of the Colonies conveyed to this office on the 22nd inst., the communication following : To the governing Captain-Generals of the Islands of Cuba and Porto Rico I herewith communicate the following Royal Order : Her Majesty the Queen Regent has deemed it proper to resolve that, in the remission to your Excellency of the accompanying Royal order of the 19th inst., in which you are instructed to make public the disposition of the Cortes, to the effect that the Provinces of America and Asia be governed and administered under laws especially adapted to their respective locations and circumstances and proper for the promotion of their welfare, in consequence whereof the said Provinces will cease to be represented by Deputies in the Cortes, your Excellency be advised as follows : 1st: Her Majesty having in mind the opinions and desires of the majority of the inhabitants of those provinces, manifested on all occasions, and very particularly through the multitude of petitions made in consequence of the events in Santiago de Cuba, cannot doubt but that the adoption of the aforesaid measure will be applauded and satisfactory ; but as it may *also be distasteful to the wicked, who under the semblance of desiring a liberty which they do not understand,* aspire to some other object, damnable and prejudicial to their own safety and interests, her Majesty desires that your Excellency for these reasons redouble your vigilance to such end as may best suit the tranquility and safety of the country, acting with as much discretion as energy, and always in accordance with the

laws, so that should the malcontents take steps of
a nature such as might disturb the public peace,
they may be subject to the judgment of the competent Tribunals. 2nd: That inasmuch as in consequence of the said resolutions of the Cortes it
naturally follows that these provinces shall continue to be governed by the laws of the Indies, by
the ordinances and Royal orders issued for their
observance, and by such as may in the future be
considered as conducive to the prosperity of the
country ; your Excellency will see that those laws
be rigidly enforced, and that no measures adopted
in the Peninsula be promulgated in the Colonies un-
less communicated to your Excellency by the proper
Minister with the express purpose that it be executed
and fulfilled on the Island under your charge. 3d :
That as the Colonies should be ruled and admin-
istrated by special laws, conformable to their conditions and *calculated to ensure their happiness*, the
higher authorities should assist the government of her
Majesty by adopting in their respective departments
such measures as they may conceive will obtain this
important object. And 4th : That considering
that the liberty of the press shall not be permitted
in that country, your Excellency will take great
care that the censure be exercised with the greatest
discretion and in such manner that it does not prevent the publication of writings which serve to
instruct the public, nor permits those which in any
way endanger the tranquility and safety of the
country, the honor of the Spanish Government, and
the just national cause ; this same vigilance should
extend to the introduction and circulation of

The Ingenio de Santa Rosa. A Typical Cuban Sugar Plantation.

NO. 70. RAFAEL MARÍA DE LABRA.

pamphlets, newspapers and writings, printed in other countries. Her Majesty relies on the well-known zeal of your Excellency for the good use you will make of these advices, communicated by Royal order.

"All of which is herewith transmitted to your Excellency for your information, etc.

"God keep your Excellency many years."

Madrid, April 25th, 1837.

Facundo Infante.

What followed upon this Royal order I have already sketched for you in my references to our political parties.

The military system in Cuba gave rise to excesses of every kind, not the least being the infamous contraband slave trade carried on and tolerated in violation of existing treaties. So rigorous did this despotic military rule become that it gave rise to spasmodic agitations and frequently repeated struggles of the suffering people, who sought their salvation through conspiracies and insurrections.[1]

---

[1] In 1823 was discovered the vast conspiracy known as *Los Soles de Bolivar*, whose object was to establish the Cuban Republic, and in 1830 that of the *Black Eagle* with the same object.

In 1850 were made the attempts of Narciso López. His object was to assist the revolt of the Separatists. The second and last attempt had been aided in the central districts by Joaquin de Agüero, and in Las Villas by Isidoro Armente-

14

Verela and Saco, the favorite Deputies under the
old *régime* obtained the laurels of proscription ; for
others, less fortunate, were re-
served the dungeon and the
scaffold. As Saco observes :
" Talent, learning, probity, and
patriotism, qualities so prized
in other countries, were in
Cuba considered unpardonable
crimes."

Even the Spaniards residing
in Cuba raised their voices in
righteous indignation against
that intolerable system. Emi-
nent men in Madrid clamored in the tribune and
in the press against such outrageous injustice and
corruption. Among these men I will mention
Olózaga, who in the Constituent Assembly of
1854 pleaded for justice for the Cubans ; Araujo
de Lira, Julián de Zulueta and other merchants

NO. 74.
GENERAL NARCISO LOPEZ.

---

ros, who were executed together with other Cubans, Agüero in Puerto Príncipe and Armenteros in Trinidad. General López suffered death by the garotte in Havana.

In 1855 the conspiracy known as that of Pintó was discovered. He also was garotted in Havana and many others
were punished. . Several Separatist, Abolitionist and Annex-
ationist revolts of lesser importance followed. See Chapters
7 to 12 of Vol. I and Chapter 2 of Vol. II of Don Justo Zara-
goza's work, *Las insurreciones de Cuba.*

established in Havana sent in an earnest memorial praying for the restitution of the political representation of Cuba in Parliament. Also Dionisio A. Galiano, who in a pamphlet wherein he could not altogether shake off the common prejudices of all who belonged to the Spanish party, proposed decentralizing reforms; Ramón Just, who with greater impartiality and a higher criterion, formulated a brochure entitled the "Aspirations of Cuba" (*Las aspiraciones de Cuba*); Félix de Bona, Eduardo Asquerino, editor of *La América*, and others to whom I, as a Cuban, do not begrudge the gratitude due to them. They honestly sought to better the condition of the country, though perhaps not to the full extent that its necessities demanded.

NO. 75.
GENERAL FRANCISCO SERRANO.

A similar debt of gratitude will ever be due by Cuba to Captain Generals Francisco Serrano and Domingo Dulce, who ruled successively from 1860 to 1865. The tolerance, the marked degree of interest, which our misfortune awoke in them, contrasted strongly with the monstrous dictatorship begun by Tacon and maintained since his time. Under their command the oppressed people

felt the halter loosen. But with all this their rule
had always one essential defect ; the same defect
which that of Martinez Campos had later on, and

NO. 76.
GENERAL DOMINGO DULCE.

that was, that the system itself was not modified and that
the very mildness of the rule
was arbitrary in its nature.

It having become possible
to hold a political banquet in
Havana, such a demonstra-
tion was organized as a com-
pliment to the editor of *La
América*, as representative of
the press of Madrid. On this
occasion 20,000 Cubans signed
a letter addressed to General Serrano as a testimonial
of gratitude for his efforts in behalf of Cuba in the
Senate, and a memorial to the Queen requesting
the greatly desired reforms.

The reactionaries, misnamed "The Spanish Party,"
could no longer remain impassive in the face of
these eloquent demonstrations. The iron rule of
Tacon suited them better than the advance of liberty. Their newspapers—*El Diario de la Marina*
taking the lead—combated the reforms; the party
formulated a counter petition to the throne and sent
commissioners to Madrid to carry out their purpose.

These various efforts, the retreat from Santo Domingo, the Spanish war in the Pacific, the general progress of the Colony, and above all, the termination of the civil war in the United States, rendering the continuation of the slave trade impossible, brought about the Royal Decree of November 25, 1865. This authorized the Minister of the Colonies to institute a formal inquiry on the social, economic and political reforms necessary for the government of Cuba and Porto Rico. This Decree was received with rejoicing throughout the land, although

NO. 71.
D. JOSÉ MORALES LEMUS.

its limitations and tendencies revealed a want of political sincerity, and the intention to retain the special laws; at the same time it clearly showed the real or affected ignorance of the Government concerning the requirements of a country which its predecessors had founded and which it now administered.

This want of sincerity manifested itself from the first moment. The election of Commissioners, according to the royal decree, was to take place in the mode and manner prescribed for that of the municipal councilmen; that is, by the higher tax-payers classified into three groups of equal numbers; 1st, landed property; 2nd, commerce and industry, and 3rd, the professions. This classifica-

tion was modified by a decree of the Captain General, organizing four electoral groups, equal in number: 1st, urban and rural real estate; 2nd, industries; 3rd, commerce; 4th, professions. The new combination had the obvious purpose of diminishing the majority of native voters and re-

NO. 78.
D. NICOLÁS AZCÁRATE.

formers, who controlled the landed estate and professional vote, by doubling the number of the electors arrayed against the reforms, that is, the Spaniards, in whose hands commerce and the urban industries had always been.

This duplicity was made the subject of a demonstration by the councils of Havana and of Cardenas; the former was supported by the Count of Pozos Dulces, José Silverio Jorrin, and José Bruzón, Sr., who placed themselves in opposition to Señores, Rato, Ibáñez and Ochoa.

NO. 79.
D. CALIXTO BERNAL.

In Cardenas the opposition was supported by Carrerá. But the highest authority of the island and the Supreme Court severely reprimanded these councils and warned them to refrain in the future from adopting any resolutions, or formulating and giving circulation to opinions regarding matters of government and administration. Such was their law.

Is it not true, esteemed Paco, that all this, of itself, afforded a sufficient assurance of the little or nothing which the people of Cuba were to expect from their rulers at this juncture?

In spite of these measures, and of the official partiality, the Cuban element triumphed at the elections; and this notwithstanding that the censors stifled the voice of reform expressed through the columns of the famous periodical, "*El Siglo*" (The

NO. 80.
D. RAFAEL FER-
NÁNDEZ DE CASTRO.

Century), edited by the acknowledged chief of the Reformists, the beloved Count of Pozos Dulces. We could not then speak of parties. Party organization was not permitted by the government.

The following were appointed as Commissioners :

Havana.—Manuel de Armas and Antonio X. de San Martín.[1]

---

[1] This candidate was opposed by the Count of Pozos Dulces, who was defeated by a vote of 50 against 47.

Matanzas.—José L. Alfonzo, Marquis of Montelo; he resigned and José M. Angulo y Heredia was elected.

Cuba.—José Antonio Saco.

Colón.—José Antonio Echeverría.

Pinar del Río.—Manuel Ortega.

Puerto Príncipe.—Calixto Bernal.

Cienfuegos.—Tomás Terry.

Villa Clara.—Antonio F. Bramosio, who was also elected by Cardenas and chose the latter mandate. The Count of Pozos Dulces was appointed in his place.

Holguin.—Juan Munné.

Sagua.—The Count of Vallellano.

Cardenas.—Antonio F. Bramosio.

Remedios—José Morales Lemus.

Guines.—Nicolás Azcárate.

Sancti-Spíritus.—Augustín Camejo.

Guanajay.—Antonio R. Ojea.

At the same time the government appointed as members of the Commission persons who were notoriously opposed to the reforms, and this in equal numbers to those elected by the aldermanic boards. Continue, Paco, to analyze these measures, for I limit myself to facts and make no comments. These facts are very eloquent, and are of themselves an effective criticism of our Colonial administration and of the injustice of our authorities.

The president of the Commission (*Junta*) was also appointed by the government so that the deliberations should be directed according to his discretion. The commissioners were to respond to the questions formulated by the government and—the sessions were to be secret. Full of doubts, though flattered with honeyed words of governmental assurance, the undaunted sons of Cuba crossed the water, leaving family, country and interests, to battle against numberless deceptions and annoyances. They fulfilled. their mission, answering with truth, loyalty, and thorough scientific learning the questions formulated by the Supreme Government. Their work made a proud record for Cuba, and furnishes a brilliant testimonial of the patriotism and culture of its people.

NO. 81.
BERNARDO PORTUONDO.

NO. 82.
D. GABRIEL MILLET.

Of what followed this investigation, Paco, I have already informed you in a previous letter.

Far from obtaining a remedy for its deep rooted evils, Cuba only obtained an increase of taxation

NO. 83.
D. JOSÉ GUELL Y
RENTÉ.

and the government of General Lersundi, a disciple of Tacón, who wished again to drown in blood the liberal and generous spirit of an American people. And then came Yara and the War; the spontaneous revulsion of a people weary unto death of the vampires of exploitation, overwrought with suffering and stung with taunts—ten years of ruin and of tears—and then, in 1878, the Peace of Zanjon. The conferences which brought the war to a close resulted in an agreement as follows:

THE COMPROMISE OF ZANJON.

"Article 1. Concession to the Island of Cuba of the same political, organic and administrative privileges accorded to the Island of Porto Rico.

"Article 2. Forgetfulness of the past as regards political offences committed from 1868 to the present, and the amnesty of all at present under sentence for such offenses within or away from the Island. Full pardon to deserters from the Spanish army, irrespective of nationality; including all who had taken part directly or indirectly in the revolutionary movements.

"Article 3. Freedom to the Asiatic coolies and the slaves who are now in the revolutionary ranks.

"Article 4. No one who by virtue of this convention recognizes and remains under protection of the Spanish government, shall be compelled to render any military service until peace be established throughout the land.

"Article 5. All persons affected by these provisions who desire to leave the Island without stopping in any town, shall receive the aid of the Spanish government to that end.

NO. 84.
D. JOSÉ MARÍA CARBONELL.

"Article 6. The capitulation of the forces shall take place in the open field, where preferably the arms and other implements of war shall be relinquished.

"Article 7. The General-in-Chief of the Spanish army, in order to facilitate the disposition of the several sections of the Cuban army, will place at their disposal the rail and steamship facilities at his command.

"Article 8. This agreement with the Central Committee is to be considered general and without special restrictions, extending to all the departments of the island accepting these conditions.

Camp of San Augustin, February 10, 1878.

E. L. LUACES.

RAFAEL RODRIGUEZ, Secretary.

Following this was promulgated provisionally, for Deputies to the Cortes, the electoral law of July 20th, 1877, and subsequently that of January 28th, 1879.

In accordance with these laws Cuba has political

representation, and as in the Peninsula, one deputy
is appointed for every 50,000 souls; only that here
the elections are made by districts or provinces, a
form which assures the majority to the Spanish
tradespeople and merchants in the capitals and
mercantile centres. Thus Cuba is represented by
8 Deputies for Havana; 3 for Pinar del Río; 3
for Matanzas; 5 for Santa Clara; 1 for Puerto
Príncipe; 4 for Santiago de Cuba: Total, 24.

But do you suppose, Paco, that it was the realization of terrible mistakes, a sentiment of justice, or a
purpose of giving the people desired satisfaction,—
do you think it was these considerations that prevailed to restore Cuban representation in the Cortes?

No! The reforms which followed the Peace of
Zanjon had the same lack of sincerity which has
always characterized our administration.

The electoral machinery, perfectly calculated to
assure the triumph of the bureaucratic and Peninsular elements has maintained and continues to
effect the exclusion of the country from national
representation.

But why stop to explain these and the other
legal and official machinations which were brought
into play in the concoction of the registry? It is
sufficient for you to know that more than one
million Cubans have only eight deputies in the
Cortes; two of these, thanks to the disinterestedness

with which four "Conservative" deputies have given up their seats to accept more lucrative positions; that 140,000 Spaniards and Canary Islanders have 16 so-called "Cuban" representatives; and that in the populated provinces like Pinar del Río, Matanzas, and even in that of Havana, the Cuban element has sometimes no representation whatever!

While the general tax of $25 is exacted as a franchise qualification in lieu of the tax on real estate, the hordes of employés enjoy the·franchise without taxation, and the same privilege applies to those who are recognized as being members of any mercantile company. These artifices I have pointed out in my letter on municipal affairs, and I will avoid a repetition. If you should ever find a Cuban, to whom the Spaniards have given their votes, you may be sure that he has afforded adequate proof of having forgotten his origin, and even this meagre concession has notoriously fallen into disuse.

Behold the evidence in the following exhibits of the results of several successive elections of members of the Cortes:

GENERAL ELECTION OF 1879.—DEPUTIES TO THE CORTES.

	Spanish Conservatives	Cuban Conservatives	Cuban Autonomists
Habana	Mamerto Pulido Francisco de los Santos Guzmán Manuel Armiñán	Ramon de Armas Francisco de Armas Frederico Giraud	Rafael Montoro Rafael María de Labra
Pinar del Rio.	Miguel Suárez Vigil Martín Golzáles del Valle José de Argumosa		
Matanzas . . .	Miguel M. Campos Francisco Gumá Antonio F. Chorot		
Santa Clara .	Mariano Díaz	Julio Apezteguía Vicente Hernández	Leopoldo Cancio Calixto Bernal
Puerto Príncipe.			José Ramón Betancourt
Stgo. de Cuba.	Antonio Dabán Santiago Vinent		Bernardo Portuondo José Antonio Saco

TOTALS.—7 Cuban Liberals, 17 enemies of Cuban liberty, 5 of the latter Cubans and 12 Spaniards.

GENERAL ELECTION OF 1879.—SENATORS.

	Spanish Conservatives	Cuban Conservatives	Cuban Autonomists
Habana		José Eugenio Moré (*Venezuelan Conserv.*) José P. y Cárdenas Marquis of Aguas Claras	Marquis of O'Gaban D. José Güell y Renté
Sociedades Económicas. Universidad Literaria.			
Matanzas.	Augusto Amblard Leon Crespo		
Santa Clara	Francisco Loriga Manuel F. de Castro		
Pinar del Río.	Vincente Galarza Manuel S. Bustamente		
Pto. Príncipe.		Felipe Lima y Reate	José Silverio Jorrín
Stgo. de Cuba.	Luis Prendergast José Bueno José M. de Herrera		

TOTALS.—3 Cuban Autonomists, 13 enemies of Cuban liberty, 3 of them Cubans, 9 Spaniards and 1 Venezuelan.

GENERAL ELECTION 1881.—DEPUTIES TO THE CORTES.

	Spanish Conservatives	Cuban Conservatives	Cuban Autonomists
Habana	Gabriel de Cubas Miguel Villanueva Mamerto Pulido Francisco de los Santos Guzmán Manuel Armiñán	Francisco Duquesne Ramón de Armas	Bernardo Portuondo
Pinar del Rio	Antonio Batanero Miguel Suárez Vigil José Argumosa		
Matanzas	Francisco Gumá Jovino G. Tuñón Camilo F. Sotomayor		
Santa Clara	Mariano Díaz	Felipe Malpica Julio Apezteguía	Calixto Bernal Gabriel Millet
Pto. Príncipe	Manuel Longoria		
Sgo. de Cuba	Manuel C. Quintana Antonio Dabán José Ferratges		José R. Betancourt

TOTALS.—4 Cuban Autonomists, 20 opponents of liberal reforms and of complete abolition of slavery, 4 of them Cubans and 16 Spaniards.

VIEW AT SANTIAGO DE CUBA, SHOWING HARBOR AND COBRE MOUNTAINS IN THE DISTANCE.

NO. 91. JOSÉ BRUZÓN.

GENERAL ELECTION OF 1881.—SENATORS.

	Spanish Conservatives	Cuban Conservatives	Cuban Autonomists
Habana . . .	Juan Soler Count of Ibáñez	José E. Moré (*Venezuelan Conserv.*)	
Universidad Literaria. .			José Güell y Renté
Sociedades Económicas. .			Rafael María de Labra
Pinar del Río.	Vicente Galarza Manuel S. Bustamente		
Matanzas . .	León Crespo	Marquis of San Carlos	
Santa Clara. .	Rafael R. Arias Manuel F. de Castro		José Silverio Jorrín
Pto. Príncipe..	José R. Leal (*Spanish Liberal*)		
Stgo. de Cuba...	Manuel de la Torre Santiago Vinent		

TOTALS.—3 Cuban Autonomists, 1 Liberal Spanish apostate, 11 enemies of our liberty, one of them a Cuban, one a Venezuelan, and 9 Spaniards.

15

GENERAL ELECTION OF 1884.—DEPUTIES TO THE CORTES.

	Spanish Conservatives	Cuban Conservatives	Cuban Autonomists
Habana . . .	F. de los Santos Guzmán Mamerto Pulido Miguel Villanueva Manuel Armiñán Antonio Batanero Gonzalo Pelligero Víctor Balaguer Ernesto Zulueta		Rafael M. de Labra Bernardo Portuondo
Matanzas . . .	Manuel Bea Jovino García Tuñón Fermín Calvetón		
Pinar del Rio..	Miguel Suárez Vigil Manuel R. San Pedro José Perogordo		
Santa Clara. .	Martín Zozaya José Granda	Julio Apezteguía	
Pto. Príncipe..			Enrique J. Varona
Stgo. de Cuba..	Manuel Longoria Manuel C. Quintana F. Durán y Cuervo		Fermín Rosillo (Cuban Liberal)

TOTALS.—3 Cuban Autonomists, 1 Cuban Liberal, 20 enemies of Cuban liberty, one of them a Cuban, and 19 Spaniards.　The figures are significant; exclusion becomes accentuated.

GENERAL ELECTION OF 1884.—SENATORS.

	Spanish Conservatives	Cuban Conservatives	Cuban Autonomists
Habana	D. José E. Moré (Venezuelan Conserv.) Marquis of Balboa Manuel Cardenal		
Sociedad Económica . . .			José R. Betancourt
Universidad Literaria .			José Silverio Jorrín
Matanzas. . . .	Angel Barroeta	Count of Peñalver	
Pinar del Rio .	Count Galarza[1] Pedro A. Alarcón		
Santa Clara. . .	Manuel E. de Castro Emilio Calleja		
Pto. Príncipe..	Francisco Loriga Antonio V. Queipo		
Stgo. de Cuba..	José Bueno Manuel de la Torre		

TOTALS.—2 Cuban Autonomists, 13 opponents of Cuban liberty, one of them a Cuban, one Venezuelan, and 11 Spaniards.

[1] This Senator, constantly re-elected by his party, in common with Señor Moré and others, has never occupied his seat in the Senate.

GENERAL ELECTION OF 1886.—DEPUTIES TO THE CORTES.

	Spanish Conservatives	Cuban Conservatives	Cuban Autonomists
Habana	Miguel Villanueva F. de los Santos Guzmán Antonio Batanero Antonio V. Queipo Salvador Albacete Manuel Armiñán Victor Balaguer		Bernardo Portuondo
Matanzas	Fermín Calvetón	Enrique Crespo	Alberto Ortiz
Pinar del Rio	Crescente G. San Miguel Faustino R. San Pedro Luis María Pando		
Santa Clara	José F. Vérgez Martín Zozaya	Julio Apeztegía	Rafael F. de Castro Miguel Figueroa
Pto. Príncipe			Rafael Montoro
Stgo. de Cuba	Manuel C. Quintana Manuel G. Longoria Luis M. Pando		Bernardo Portuondo

TOTALS.—5 Cuban Autonomists, 18 opponents of Cuban liberty, two of them Cubans and 16 Spaniards.

GENERAL ELECTION OF 1886.—SENATORS.

	Spanish Conservatives	Cuban Conservatives	Cuban Autonomists
Habana	Count of Moré (Venezuelan Conserv.) Marquis of Balboa	Marquis of San Carlos	José S. Jorrín
Sociedades Económicas..			José M. Carbonell
Universidad Literaria . .	Count Galarza Pedro A. Alarcón[1]		
Pinar del Río.	Jovino G. Tuñón Manuel Bea		
Matanzas. . .	Manuel Casola Manuel F. de Castro		
Santa Clara..			
Pto. Príncipe..	Manuel G. de la Cámara		José R. Betancourt
Stgo. de Cuba..	Manuel de la Torre Angel Barroeta		

TOTALS.—3 Cuban Autonomists, 12 opponents of Autonomy; of the latter, 1 a Cuban, 1 a Venezuelan and 10 Spaniards.

[1] This representative of Cuba, like Señores Albacete, F. R. San Pedro and others, has never been in Cuba. Whom, accordingly, do these men represent?

In February of the year 1881, a
partial election took place in Havana, and Ramón de Armas was
re-elected ; he was the Cuban Conservative who had accepted the
under secretaryship of the ministry of the Colonies.   José Cortina
was elected by the autonomists ;
he was a distinguished Cuban
whose untimely death occurred
shortly thereafter.

NO. 85.
D. EMILIO TERRY.

In the year 1884, in a partial election, there
were chosen in Havana, Miguel Villanueva (Spanish Conservative, re-elected), and Emilio Terry
(Cuban Autonomist).   In another election, Antonio
Zambrana, Cuban Autonomist, and Pascual Goico-
chea, Cuban Conservative, were
chosen.   In Matanzas Eliseo Giberga, Cuban Autonomist and
Basilio Díaz del Villar, Spanish
Conservative, were elected.

NO. 86.—D. JOSÉ RAMÓN
BETANCOURT.

Thus distorted, falsified and restrained, political representation
has been conceded to Cuba since
the peace of Zanjon.   But, if our
representatives have been inferior
in numbers they have not been so in capacity.

NO. 87.
D. ANTONIO.ZAMBRANA.

The most eloquent proof that liberal sentiment and opinion predominates in the land—though stifled—is the oft-repeated fact that institutions of culture like the University and the various *Sociedades Económicas*, in which the Spaniards figure in a small minority, have invariably elected autonomist representatives.

As to the political course of our deputies, suffice it to say that not one of them has ever solicited, obtained or accepted secretaryships, commissions, titles or honors in return for consenting to the imposition of a crushing tax on an impoverished country or to the suppression of its liberties.

Publicists and eminent statesmen like Bernal, Saco and Jorrín; distinguished writers and jurists like Betancourt, Güell and Carbonell; sincere and earnest patriots like Millet and Ortiz; preeminent orators like Portuondo, Montoro, Figueroa, and Fernán-

NO. 88.
MIGUEL FIGUEROA.

dez de Castro; men of learning, experience and patriotism, under the indefatigable leader of the Antillan representatives, Labra, whose popu-

NO. 89.
D. ALBERTO ORTIZ.

larity has been proved by twenty years of stainless services; these men, though opposed by thirty antagonistic and suspicious deputies, have at all times known how to maintain the standard of Autonomy with a firm and undaunted spirit. Tempting offers of gifts and of power have never shaken them; calumny has not deterred nor have bitter deceptions unnerved them; they have not been swerved by the fatuousness of rulers who declared to the world that Cuban freedom was incompatible with the national idea, nor by the duplicity of those who, with artful promises have endeavored to prevent an exposure of the wrongs of an unfortunate people,[1] and I repeat, they have steadfastly held aloft the standard of Autonomy as the symbol of the liberty and the constant hope of a colonial community which, of all those founded by Europeans on American soil, is the most unhappy and the most oppressed.

NO. 90.
D. ELISEO GIBERGA.

---

[1] On the 29th of March, 1887, the Cuban Deputy, Señor Portuondo, opened a debate on the economic condition of

Cuba, which the Minister of State cut short pending the arrival of other Autonomist deputies from Havana. These arrived, but the postponement was continued. On May 9th the question was again taken up for discussion, but on the following day the President of the Chamber interrupted Señor Portuondo with the statement that there had been too much talking, and requested him to conclude his discourse. The debate was again suspended until the 14th. Señor Perojo was also requested to conclude his speech on four successive occasions. Señor Portuondo had finally to give up speaking; on the other hand, the Conservative deputies, Señores Villanueva, Calbeton and Pando spoke at great length and without interruption. The debate was interrupted the third time; on the 17th Señor Portuondo asked to have it again taken up, but President Martos refused.

The Cuban deputies, Señores. Figueroa, Terry and Fernández de Castro, have with difficulty been able to explain some of their interpellations regarding administrative corruption, questions of personal safety, and the administration of justice on this Island.

XIII.

INSECURITY OF PERSON AND PROPERTY.—PRISONERS SLAUGHTERED
UNDER PRETEXT OF PREVENTING THEIR ESCAPE.—COSTLY AND
INEFFICIENT POLICE SERVICE.

No. 92.   COLLEGE OF SANTO
ANGEL.

I am truly sorry that I know not your surname, friend Paco, were it only that I might vary the Andalusian vocative which I am obliged to make use of. I presume you are a Pérez, or Méndez, or López, or Azpeitegurrea; but no matter, the fact remains that after so many letters addressed to you about our affairs, I find myself really growing fond of you, and am sometimes tempted and on the point of calling you " Pancho," which is a diminutive of our native origin, with which I am on more familiar terms.

But let us get to our point, and quickly, for it is time to put an end to these pages, too numerous already,—and of which you have assuredly had a surfeit.

I acknowledge squarely, that the picture drawn by Moreno in his 15th " Conversation," concerning

personal security in our country, is quite true to life. Really,
and without undue exaggeration, we live miraculously.

In the country we have
armed assaults, kidnappings,
abductions, fabulous ransoms,
gangs of robbers led by wretches
as cultured as Dumas' bandit-
hero Luigi Vampa, or as philanthropic as the Diego Corrientes
of our own dramatic legend.

NO. 93.
D. JOSÉ SUÁREZ GARCÍA.

In the cities we have the rapacious land sharks,
the pickpockets, the snatchers of watch chains,—
the terrifying cry of "your money or your life,"
assailing the ear of the defenceless passer-by at
every obscure corner; the stabbings, the shootings,
the cries, the incessant alarms, the rushings to and
fro—everywhere a bloody picture of shameful and
abominable barbarities.

The anxious wife waits in suspense for the return
of the absent husband. The mother watches her
tender babe, fearful lest the precious one may, at any
moment, be snatched from her bosom. But do not
imagine that the Government fails to take all the
steps necessary, or that it fails to receive from the
country even more than is necessary to prevent such
confusion and disturbances.

In the first place it does not fail to afford the country the edifying example of the morality of its ministers, who don't defraud the treasury nor deceive the taxpayers, who do not falsify the public accounts, nor break into the official vaults and steal the Government revenue stamps, and who do not sell justice, and who in like manner endeavor to make those whom they govern follow in the path traced for them by their governors.

In the second place, the government does not fail to suppress and do away with lawful proceedings and to sanction indiscriminate fusilades, such as are known as *Amarillas*; frightful hecatombs like that of Madruga, and such executions as that at Las Puentes and Alquízar. Under pretext of preventing *attempted* escapes, the minions of the law have not failed to redden the roads, the streets, and the public places with the blood of untried prisoners.

In the third place, the authorities have not indeed invented, but only restored the inquisitorial proceeding known as the *componte*, the corporal punishment of those who, whether in the fields, in the barracks, in the villages, or in the towns, are arrested on suspicion. These proceedings do not fail to permit the wicked to remain at large and at their ease, in a land where the military —armed to the teeth—inspires a salutary terror in the hearts of the villagers, and which in its turn does not fail to lower their character by the maintenance of brute force.[1]

In the fourth place, the government does not fail to prevent and prohibit individual defence by keeping up a strict search for arms and imposing a heavy tax on the license to carry them. Our rulers are persuaded that a disarmed people can be more easily attended to by a strong and far seeing government.[2]

[1] The Civil Government of Havana has just issued a circular which amply justifies what has been stated above. The reader will find it in the Appendix. All persons or residents through whose premises a bandit has passed are to be considered as accomplices of bandits, if they do not possess the necessary personal courage or public spirit to notify with electrical promptness the nearest police authority.

The defenceless peasants, in the face of the bandits who menace them with direful vengeance,—and persecuted by a government which considers their fears a crime—find no other escape from their tribulations than by emigration from a country where a Civil Governor arrogates to himself legislative functions, arbitrarily invents new crimes and dictates new processes of law for their punishment.

[2] In the Royal Decree of October 15th 1886, it was ordered that no arms of any kind should be carried, even for the purposes of the chase or fishing, without a license from the proper authorities. Said license to be given by the Governor of the Province, not by the alcaldes, or mayors. The latter can only give permission to go fishing, always notifying the Governors. There are six kinds of licenses. 1st. For the use of all arms not prohibited, which costs $24

And finally, to deliver us from the highwaymen who infest our roads, and the thieves who parade

---

EACH YEAR. 2nd. For the use of firearms for the defense of rural property, $1.50. 3d. Pocket firearms for personal defence in the outskirts of the towns, $6. 4th. Pocket firearms for the same defence in towns, $9. 5th. Arms for the chase, $6. 6th. Implements for fishing in rivers, pools and lakes, $1.50. Those of the first class are given only to Spaniards over 25 years of age, who pay direct tax. The second, third and fourth classes to persons over 20 years of age. The license of the fifth class may be given to minors under 20 and over 15 years. In such cases guardians must send a written guarantee. Anyone may get a license to fish. There appears to be no danger of perturbing the public peace with hooks and harpoons; but still, if you want to go fishing, you must pay $1.50. These licenses are personal and not transferable, and must be applied for through the Courts on official stamped paper (costing 37½ cents), accompanied of course by the fee itself. The permit is recorded in the register, filed in the archives, and signed by the party interested; everything is foreseen —only the photograph is not provided for. Of course the Governors can dispense licenses gratis, on ordinary paper, to the employés of the civil administration, and to the police when they desire it. On the other hand, in case of war or extraordinary contingencies, or when it is deemed convenient, they simply revoke the licenses that have been granted, without returning the money. The police of each locality keep a list of those who enjoy the concession. The infraction of this law is punishable with forfeiture, fine and imprisonment.

This Decree does not concern the Spaniards, the great majority of whom belong to the Volunteer Corps, and are sufficiently armed without the necessity of paying for licenses.

our streets, in order to guarantee the personal safety which we do not get, and which I, being a suspicious Autonomist, have grave doubts of our ever getting, the Government does not fail to impose the following budget of expenditure.

Civil Guards (Police Service)	$2,132,950 38
Public Order . . . . :	579,093 02
" " Supplies	13,275 00
Total	$2,725,318 40

And furthermore :

PRISONS.

Department of Havana	$21,976 80
House of Correction, Puerto Príncipe[1]	2,772 90
Convict Station, Island of Pines	5,341 00
Transportation and Charity	15,260 40
Transportation of Criminals	2,000 00
Total	$47,351 10

Add the costs of the administration of justice, badly organized and worse paid, $495,061.20; also the sums reserved for secret service in the Departments of the Interior and of the Treasury, which amounts to the bagatelle of $25,000, but the ultimate disposition of which no one knows.

And finally, if it please you, take into consideration the cost of the standing army. The maintenance of the troops alone, without counting the chief officials, commissioners, buildings, supplies, etc., amounts to $4,051,702.94, and this will doubtless

---

[1] Recently abandoned.

NO. 94.   RAFAEL MONTORO.

afford you convincing proof that in Cuba the Government does everything possible to insure the individual safety, and that while we suffer enough and pay too much, there is some purpose in it. All this, which does not include the cost of local, municipal and provincial police service, amounts to nothing less than $7,324,433.64.

* * * * * *

During the grievous administration of General Prendergast (in 1882) a form of legalized murder, of frightfully frequent occurrence, was instituted. Prisoners in transit are shot down under the pretense that they intended to escape. Scarcely a month passes when the Liberal press does not record some exhibition of barbarism in the shape of corporal punishment—the so-called *componte*, which is, in the opinion of your friend Moreno, so harshly criticised by the Autonomists. These excesses were not checked even by the circular issued by the Chief of Police, Señor Denis, censuring and prohibiting these scandalous outrages. That document was an official declaration, a partial confession, but not a corrective measure.

El Triunfo, El País, El Diario de Matanzas, La Lucha, La Tarde, El Popular, La Protesta, El Radical, La República Ibérica, El Liberal de Colón, El Cubano, all the periodicals which, in this unhappy land,

16

defend democratic principles as best they can, have cried out against these unheard of assaults on personal liberty, which are a thousand times more alarming than the barbarous depredations of the highwaymen.

But on the other hand, *El Diario de la Marina* and its congeners, especially *La Voz de Cuba*, have sanctioned and extenuated and frequently justified these proceedings.

In May, 1882, *La Voz de Cuba*, in discussing the question and replying to the just censures of the more advanced press, endeavored to give the matter a political coloring; this paper even went to the extreme of endorsing the expressions, as bloodthirsty as they were extravagant, of a correspondent from Alquízar who (under the guise of a wellwisher of the peace) advocated that capital punishment be meted out for all crimes, not by the Courts of Justice but by the police; whose wisdom, patriotism and disinterestedness appeared to the editor and correspondent alike as more efficient than the law.

Do you understand, Paco? Such precepts and examples, such preposterous doctrines give sanction to perverted moral sentiment as the only law of Government. It is a proposition to do away with the Criminal Code and to abolish all responsible government. One periodical, *La Union de Güines*, I quote with pleasure, both because I myself edited it during six years, and because of the two men who are still fully identified with its noble work. I refer to Leopoldo Cancio, a distinguished Cuban, and José Suarez Garcia, a talented and generous Spaniard, who devoted the work of his facile pen to the defense of our rights and of Cuban Autonomy. This paper treated the subject in the following article which I reproduce as a close to the present chapter. You will observe how different are the views which we Autonomists hold from the Conservatives, in regard to the manner in which Cuba is to obtain the boon of safety for the individual.

" THE SLAUGHTER CONTINUES.

"Our editorial of last Sunday had not yet seen the light when we read in the columns of *El Triunfo* the death of another person—victim of the police—in no less public a place than the *Campo de Marte*, in the centre of Havana. We have also heard, and have reason to credit the news, that at Alquizar, in the Province of San Antonio de los Baños, three prisoners have been killed by their escort.

" Were we to examine these actions by the light of constitutional principles and of penal law, it would be easy to prove that the worst delinquents have not been the victims, but their slayers; but that would be a waste of effort. There is no man of sense who does not fully understand it.

"In the meantime our jails and prisons — entirely dependent on the Government — are sinks of corruption where, in a Babel of confusion, men and women of all ages, prisoners awaiting trial, and convicts, clamor for redress. The desire to do what is right, a sense of justice and of morality, would find there a vast unexplored field for action. This work would be truly worthy of noble hearts capable of self-abnegation and self-discipline.   Just men would applaud, and sentimentalism would not dare to oppose them. But what do the lovers of justice do when they palliate the shooting of prisoners under the pretense of intended flight?

" They are probably the most active in agitating general or partial amnesties or commutations of sentence, full of compassion for the delinquents who pass their time of sentence in the brothels which are called penal establishments, but their sense of justice does not prevent them from applauding the death of the criminal.

" It also rests with the State to increase the number of judges, so as to diminish the number of unpunished crimes. There are scarcely forty judges in Cuba, who must perforce exercise their jurisdiction over large districts.   How is it possible for the trial of criminal cases not to suffer from the lack of good judges ?   Generally the initial proceedings are effected by utterly ignorant persons who, because they can *read* the laws, consider themselves capable of understanding and applying them.   Either increase the number of judges or establish a system of district attorneys.   Then we will surely have less frequent occasion to look with indifference on the slaughter of prisoners who *attempted to escape.* Since so many millions are spent here annually they might well employ a modest sum for reform in such a noble cause.

" The defects of our laws of criminal procedure are

much commented upon. In truth these deficiencies are considerable, but they do not justify all that is said against them. The chief defect being the insufficient protection of the culprit, the reform of the laws would consequently not bring about the result hoped for.

"In short, it must be confessed that the wisdom of civilized nations is right. Laws tending to produce the common good, and their honest enforcement should be the aim of all cultured people. In criminal cases then, we must keep to the code, even if its procedure ruffles the temper of the police officers; and when capital punishment must be inflicted the hangman alone should perform the office.

"We conclude by begging those in authority not to shield the negligence of the police, and to insist upon greater zeal in the performance of their functions as custodians of prisoners.

XIV.

INDUSTRIAL AND ECONOMIC DATA.—THE RESOURCES OF THE
COUNTRY DRAINED BY EXTORTIONATE TAXATION.

Is there anything marvellous in the spectacle of misery which Cuban society presents? Have we to agree with your correspondent, Moreno, that the

No. 95.—ASILO DE MENDIGOS.

causes of this state of things are not that God permits and our rulers do not prevent them, but that they are to be found "in the blunders of the people, the hatred by the Cubans of all that is Spanish, the cost of the civil war, and vice, whether manifested as voluptuousness or as a concomitant of luxury; the failure to replace slave labor by mechanical appliances, and the indolence and apathy of the natives, who want yet more leisure for the purpose of electing Montoro and crying for Autonomy?"

You deceive yourself; poverty does not exist here; at least it is not apparent. We are swimming in plenty. We have been, and still are, immensely wealthy.

Notwithstanding the abolition of slavery, which cost the Cubans a hard struggle to wrench from the Conservatives and the Home Government — the harvests of 1885–1886 have been larger than any recorded in the annals of our sugar production.

At this very moment I have at hand a paper which states that the Province of Güines is supplying the markets of the United States with excellent potatoes. It is not crops that we stand in need of. The best tobacco yet smoked in Germany and London, is from the Vuelta Abajo.

So then, this country works and produces;—can it be poor? . . . .

The war? . . . . . the theatre of hostilities was limited to much less than two-thirds of the island.

. Havana and Pinar del Rio did not feel its ravages, and Matanzas but very little. The torch did not devastate the rich and fruitful plains of these extensive provinces—the richest and most thickly populated of the island. Their sugar and coffee plantations, orchards and farms were not destroyed.

Country and city property has now less than half of its former value . . . . but it has not altogether disappeared !

Oh, we are truly rich !

From 1821 to 1826 Cuba, with her own resources, covered the expenditures of the Treasury. Our opulence dates from that period. We had already sufficient negro slaves to cut down our virgin forests, and ample authority to force them to work. . . .

By means of our vices and our luxury, and in spite of the hatred of everything Spanish which Moreno attributes to us, we sent, in 1827, the first little million of hard cash to the treasury of the nation. From that time until 1864, we continued to send yearly to the mother country, two millions and a half of the same stuff.

According to several Spanish statisticians these sums amounted in 1864 to $89,107,287.

We were very rich, don't you see? tremendously rich. We contributed more than five million dollars towards the requirements of the Peninsula ($5,372,-205).

We paid, in great part, the cost of the war in Africa. The individual donations alone amounted to fabulous sums. But, of course, we have never voted for our own imposts;—they have been forced upon us because we are so rich.

In 1862 we had in a state of production the following estates:

2,712 stock farms.
1,521 sugar plantations.
  782 coffee   "
6,175 cattle ranches.

18 cocoa plantations.
35 cotton   "
22,748 produce farms.
11,738 truck farms.
11,541 tobacco plantations.
1,731 apiaries.
153 country resorts.
243 distilleries.
468 tile-works.
504 lime-kilns.
63 charcoal furnaces.
54 casava-bread factories.
61 tanneries.

The valve of this property, together with its appurtenances, was estimated at $380,554,527, with a net income of $38,055,452.70.

To-day I do not know what we possess, because there are no statistics and because the recently organized assessment is a hodge-podge and a new burden; but we have more than at that time; surely, we must have a great deal more.

According to a statement made in the Cortes by a learned Deputy, Don José del Perojo (who by the way is not an Autonomist), Cuba has given to the Spanish Treasury 137 millions of dollars. And does any one dare to speak of our poverty?

For a very long time we have borne the expenses of the convict settlement of Fernando Po.

We paid for the ill-starred Mexican expedition, the costs of the war in San Domingo, and with the republics of the Pacific; how can we possibly be poor?

While England, France and Holland appropriate large sums for the requirements of their Colonies, Spain does not contribute a single cent for hers.

We do not need it, we are wading deep in rivers of gold.

If the fertility of our soil did not come to our rescue, we must perforce have become enriched by the system of protection to the commerce of the Mother Country. . . . The four columns of the Tariff are indeed a sublime invention.

Our agricultural industries require foreign machinery, tools, and utensils, which Spain does not supply, but as she knows that we have gold to spare she may make us pay for them very high. And since our sugar is to be sold to the United States . . . never mind what they cost.

When there are earthquakes in Andalusia and inundations in Murcia, hatred does not prevent us from sending to our afflicted brethren large sums . . . (which sometimes fail to reach their destination.)

We are opulent? Let us see if we are.

From the earliest times down to the present the officials who come to Cuba amass in the briefest space of time fortunes to be dissipated in Madrid, and which appear never to disturb their consciences.

This country is very rich, incalculably rich.

In 1830 we contributed 6,120,934 dollars; in 1840, $9,605,877; in 1850, $10,074,677; in 1860, $29,610,779. During the war we did not merely contribute, we bled. We had to carry a budget of 82 millions.

*   *   *   *   *

Poor indeed! In 1880 we paid 40 millions. In 1882, $35,860,246.77. Just now we are rendered happy by having the total expenditure of the State fixed at the paltry sum of $25,959,734.79; this is without counting the municipal taxes.

We count 1,500,000 inhabitants; that is to say, one million and a half of vicious, voluptuous, pompous spendthrifts, full of hatred and low passions, who contribute to the public charges and never receive a cent in exchange; who have given as much as $92 per capita, and who at the present moment pay to the State what no other taxpayers the world over have ever contributed.

Does any one say that we are not prodigiously, enviably rich? Only a fool would believe that we are starving to death.

XV.

RESUMÉ.—THE YEARNING FOR FREEDOM.—THE LEADERS OF THE
AUTONOMIST MOVEMENT.—THE RELIGIOUS SENTIMENT OF THE
PEOPLE.—MERCENARY SPIRIT OF THE CLERGY.—SOCIAL CONDI-
TIONS REVIEWED.—THE WOMEN OF CUBA.

We have come to Señor Moreno's chapter of re-
sumés, and although I have followed step by
step the plan of his work, I shall not take up
again the hopeless sub-
ject of administrative
corruption, in connec-
tion with the recent
scandalous embezzle-
ments in the Depart-
of Public Works.

My opinion, the pub-
lic opinion, in regard

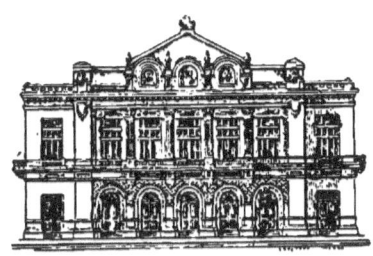

NO 97.—TEATRO TERRY, CIENFUEGOS.

to these matters, has already been stated. The
responsibility for them falls upon the nation which
has founded, maintained and still upholds a frightful system of spoliation, resulting in the consump-
tion of the vital tissues of the social body; a system
which has brought us to the state of prostration in
which we find ourselves and which is dragging us
down an inclined plane to perdition and ruin.

Neither shall I refer to his diatribes regarding our political demoralization. If you have read my preceding letters attentively, you must be persuaded, or rather convinced, that the Cubans present the highest example of disinterestedness, virility, abnegation and patriotism ever offered in the history of a people educated for and subjected to servitude. They have never remained passive under the misfortunes of their country; never given themselves up to indifference or despair. Always ready for sacrifice, indomitable and strong in the face of all afflictions, they have battled in the cause of regeneration and progress, and they still battle without an hour of repose, and without hope of recompense. The political struggle in Cuba has not been a business enterprise in quest of the spoils of office or the plunder of the tax-payers, or of other and nameless mercenary schemes.

NO. 98.
D. JOSÉ MARÍA ZAYAS.

Our country counts for something in the North American hemisphere. We Cubans love the liberty which we have never known, and strive for it because of our sincere longing for freedom. Yesterday the Vardas, Sacos, Pozos Dulces, Azcárates, Morales Lemus, Aguileras, Céspedes, Agramontes, Aldamas,

Cisneros, and so many others, gave the example of endless labor and sacrifice, without other ambition than the good of their country.

And to-day, Gálvez, Govín, Saladrigas, Montoro,[1] Cancio, Hernández Abreu, Bruzón, Millet, Labra, Fernández de Castro, Figueroa, Ortiz, Bernal, Ocejo, Marcos García Spoturno, Santa Lucía, Portuondo, and others; all those who, with zeal, patriotism and intelligence, excluded from all participation in public matters, direct the liberal

NO. 99.
D. RAMÓN ZAMBRANA.

autonomist movement. Not one of them dreams when giving his best days to the defense of his cherished ideals, of reaping any personal benefit in the way of exalted position, the incumbency of office, or the obtainment of ostentatious honors. Rather do they discern in the bitterness of deception and in moments of infinite sadness their dreams of a brighter future swallowed in an ocean of disappointment and borne down into an eternity of hopelessness.

* *
*

But let us now treat of the religious condition of the Cubans. Moreno has given you to understand

---

[1] Montoro was the founder of the Autonomist Party and has never acted with the Conservatives as Moreno supposes.

that our people are accustomed from early youth to meddle in politics, but that they are insensible to

NO. 100.
D. TRISTÁN MEDINA.

the importance of religion. He finds occasion even to quote Voltaire concerning the necessity of a religious life. I have something to say myself regarding our clergy; of the example it gives the Catholic community, and the way in which those of our countrymen, who are ordained for the pulpit, are excluded from ecclesiastical offices.

I will not say that the people are unbelieving, but they are certainly not fanatical. Here, where until recent years (1871) none but the Roman Catholic religion was tolerated; where the clergy was, and is still to a great extent, a power which vies with the military authorities in the exercise of tyranny, it is not strange that indifference predominates. God's ministers are so repellant here that they alienate the devotion of the faithful. It has not been found possible in a land where gold has been amassed with the blood of slaves, to erect those sumptuous cathedrals which, in the home country and in Mexico, are still the admiration of architects —though perhaps from another aspect they do not merit so much esteem. Our churches give but a poor idea of the cult, particularly if their shabby

AVENUE OF PALMS, MATANZAS.

No. 96.—GERTRUDIS GÓMEZ DE AVELLANEDA.

construction be compared to their fabulous incomes. It is not an easy matter to build even a poor hermitage, although the first step taken in projecting the construction is to authorize the popular fêtes, (misnamed fairs) at which illicit games of hazard—monte, roulette, etc., are permitted. It is possible that the church undertakes to cleanse the consciences stained in adding to its prestige. The end is but too frequently made to justify the means, and to an extreme degree.

Our clergy does not trouble itself with dogma nor propaganda. It is a question of lucre—of administering the sacraments, and of collecting the fees thereon, and more than the fees. There is not one parish which supports a free or endowed school.

NO. 101.
PBRO. MIGUEL D. SANTOS.

Just now there is an active crusade against the civil marriage ceremony, recently instituted. The pulpit launches against it the thunderbolts of its wrath. The newspapers give daily instances of this crusade against a legitimate institution.

The division of the dioceses into parishes accord rather with financial exigencies than with spiritual

17

necessities There are rectorships which embrace extensive and thickly populated districts where the

NO. 102.—D. JUAN VILARÓ.

parishioners are neglected, but which are known as of the *1st class* on account of their profits. They are sought and given in this sense as signal favors to such as have sufficient influence. There have been a few chosen ones who have reaped a harvest from three or four of these snug berths.

According to the canon law the parochial livings should be held in the sense of proprietary holdings. In Cuba there are scarcely any proprietary clergy, and the canonical provisions have become a dead letter. The bishops reserve the right to make appointments, and since 1864 there is no pretence of complying with the law. The arbitrary dispensation of favors and benefits is thus greatly facilitated.

The local newspapers have published much in reference to these appointments. What I know as an absolute fact, Paco, is that the natives of the country who have chosen the priesthood as a vocation have never had any share in them. They have always been excluded from all places of importance; these are reserved for the Spaniards. On some occasions they have even been denied the right to preach. I can prove it. The Bishopric of Havana comprises 144 parishes ; only twenty-two of these are attended by Cuban priests. Though many positions are vacant, we ˙ find only two Cuban rectors, three chaplains of institutions, and one assistant. In the cathedral chapter there is but one Cuban, and only two natives of the country have ever obtained canonships . . . . the mitre never! . . .

Many proofs might be given of the general ignorance of the clergy, while at the same time, priests of acknowledged worth and learning, famous pulpit orators, are shut off in obscure villages because they are Cubans.

But this is nothing ; at other periods they were unmercifully persecuted and exiled from the country. The Spanish clergy take active part in the politico-social battles, and offer lamentable examples of forgetfulness of their high calling.

The chaplaincies are considered dainty morsels. The Collector appointed by the Bishop receives ten per cent. The appointments constitute another privilege which the favored ones enjoy. In regard to this, only one fact needs to be commented upon— the faithful, in their wills no longer request Chap-

laincies to be founded. The institution has fallen
into disrepute . . .   or the faith of the faithful
has diminished.

During the rule of Señor Pardo, Vicar General,
the See being vacant, the Cemetery Fund, which
had been accumulating in the Bishopric for years,
suddenly disappeared . .   It was a matter of
a fabulous sum.

Do you want more information, Paco? . . . Oh
no; it is enough for you to be able to refute the
assertions of Moreno regarding the religious cultus
in Cuba.   But in conclusion, and in order that you
may be convinced that this people, even if unbelieving, knows and feels that religion is necessary,—
just see what part the cultus plays according to
general estimate of its current cost.

Fixed charges :

Diocese of Havana . . . . $ 5,481
 "   Cuba   17,133
Pensions   1,200
Ecclesiastical Tribunals   20,430
Supplies for same   400
Cathedral clergy 121,492
Supplies for same   11,000
Parochial clergy 144,632–62
Supplies for same   72,376

General expenses :

Rent of buildings . . . . $ 15,832
Repairs and construction   15,666

Sundry expenses :

Ecclesiastical trips.	$3,000
Assistance to clergy who immigrate from other parts of America	2,000
Seminarians	5,196–40

Expenses incident to religious orders :

Personal	$64,532
Supplies	30,039

War Department, Military Clergy:

Personal	$4,200
Material	300

Military Hospitals:, Personnel

Of the Clergy and Sisters of Charity	$14,488
Chaplain	296

The purification of our consciences costs us a total of $548,694,2.

Little less than what is spent in public improvements.

Let him who accuses us of religious demoralization take heed !

Social Demoralization.

The Cuban woman and family have drawn from Moreno the most bitter taunts and insulting criticism. Each time he has had occasion to deal with the cherished sentiments of this community he has soiled the paper with disgusting calumnies giving vent to his unjustifiable hatred.

" *Together with the home of the family, the temple, of pleasure; in front of the house of God, that of vice . . .* (See page 12) . . . . *the girl or boy before reaching the age of reason has very little to learn in the way of wickedness . . . . The peculiar dances of Cuba are another strong incentive to corruption . . . . in public as well as in private balls, the mode of dancing is indecorous.*" (Pages 142 and 143)

No. 103.—DA LUISA PEREZ DE ZABRANA.

" *Woman if not a slave on that Island is an object of luxury.*"

"*She is not possessed of an idea; she has not a heart to feel, nor a soul that inspires . . . . Everywhere immorality and scandal.*" (Page 195)

The hand which traced those lines never touched the hand of an honest woman; never breathed the atmosphere of virtue and simplicity which pervades the modest hearth of the Cuban family.

It is not I, who, inspired by patriotism and the natural enthusiasm of one who has professed as a supreme cult, love and respect for woman, and especially the Cuban woman, that model of austere virtue, of tender sentiments and of generous impulses, it is not I alone who shall defend her here.

A learned soldier who has aged on the fields of
battle defending the national flag, who fought ten

years against the Cuban
troops, but who, in a spirit
of justice, has advocated
the liberty of this land—
Colonel Francisco Camps
y Feliú—in his most interesting historical memoirs
on the events of the Cuban
Revolution, has made the
defense of the Cuban woman

NO. 104.—DA. AURELIA CASTILLO
DE GONZÁLEZ.

in a concise, positive manner in the following para-
graphs with which I am enabled to brighten this publication ; these expressions have the double merit of
having been written by a sincere and dispassionate
eye-witness, without pretense to niceties of language
or display of rhetoric :

" Before concluding this chapter, we desire to say something of what is, morally and physically, considered most
interesting in the Island of Cuba—woman ! ' Las donas,'
says the celebrated Catalonian writer, Valentin Almirall,
' by the beauty of their complexions, the regularity of their
features, and their luxuriant hair, form one of the most
perfect types of the Caucasian race.'

" This description by the distinguished Catalonian has

reference to the impression which the Castilian populace produced in him, and with a few variations due to the ardent sun of the tropics, it answers faithfully the description of the Cuban woman, who is just as beautiful and just as Castilian as her European sisters. She is also intelligent, impressionable, sympathetic, and above all she idolizes her children.

"Whether living in the greatest opulence, in moderate circumstances, or in humble poverty, she is always dignified and sweet in her behavior and charitable to the poor. She is the ideal wife, of whom history has given us some perfect examples. They are naturally home-bodies, but while, when on pleasure bent, she shows her many charms to advantage and attracts attention by the grace and beauty of her person, she can also attend to her household duties and ply the needle like a finished seamstress.

"The woman who lives in the country and who is called 'guajira,' or 'guajirita' if she is young, has no reason to envy her city sisters. On Sunday, when she lays aside her domestic work and makes her toilet to sit at the cottage door or go to the dance, she does not look like a peasant girl; her rich hair arranged in the latest style, adorned with a rose or some other natural flower, a well-fitting muslin gown and neat slippers — the *guajirita* might well sit in a box at the Tacon theatre ; she would soon lose a certain timidity of expression and shyness of manner caused by a lack of ease in refined society. For the rest, our *guajira* is superior in culture to the peasants of other nations. The delicious freshness of some of them make one think of rosebuds, and if you add to these charms of person the honest coquetry natural to all women, and her many virtues, it is not surprising that many of them have married distinguished Cubans, and officers of our army.

"The Cuban woman, whether she hail from city or country, is good, intelligent and industrious; those who scoffingly say that she neglects domestic work and is only fit to lie in a hammock and fan herself, do not know the Cuban woman. This warm-hearted woman is a chaste spouse and a slave to duty even under the most adverse circumstances; on the battlefields she fulfilled her sad mission, courageously following her father or husband. The noble Cuban girl, in the midst of all dangers, remained as pure and unsullied as the painted Virgin immortalized by Murillo. This just tribute to the ever honorable daughters of Cuba is rightfully due, inasmuch as the falsehoods and calumnies of ignoble writers have confounded the frailty of some unfortunates (who have companions in all lands) with the high morality and purity of the stainless majority. We make these assertions with a thorough knowledge derived from what we have witnessed in Camagüey, in Santiago, and in Las Villas. Our companions in arms who have united in holy wedlock with Cuban ladies, can vouch for the truth of our assertions.

"The virtuous Cuban woman is worthy of love and respect, whether her lot has been cast in splendor, in poverty, in the cities and towns, or lonely and afar in the dangerous battlefields. In thus expressing our admiration for them, we but acquit ourselves of a duty as honorable men."[1]

---

[1] Don Francisco Camps y Feliú was born in Gerona on August 21st, 1825. He came to Cuba for the first time in

1851 with the rank of captain, and remained until 1862. Returned a second time in 1866. His record is here condensed as follows: Knight, with cross and star, of the order of San Hermenegildo, twice decorated with the red cross of the second class of M. M. and with the third of the same order; received the medal of the Cuban war with ten pendants, representing as many years of campaign; three times declared Benefactor of his Country; Lieutenant Governor and defender of Holguin in 1868; first Chief Commander of the Volunteers of Cadiz and Barcelona, also of the " El Rayo " lancers; chief of half brigade with the Spanish battalion of the Lancers of Vergara; Chief of Line in San Miguel of Nuevitas; Commander of the districts of Camarones, Arroyo Blanco, Banas, Santa Gertrudis, Copey, Santa Cruz, Jobabo, Fray Benito, Puerto del Padre; Colonel of the Infantry Regiment of Havana; ex-General Commandant of Holguin and of Victoria de las Tunas, and retired Colonel of Infantry.

NO. 105.
FRANCISCO CAMPS.

Señor Camps, during the last war in Cuba, distinguished himself for his valor and his humane conduct towards the vanquished; although not affiliated with any party, he has disinterestedly taken up the defense of Cuban liberty in many articles signed under the pseudonym of " *Un guajiro practico* " (A practical peasant). Among his magnanimous actions, is quoted that of having offered to accompany General Dulce to the Cabaña fortress when the latter, angered at the insubordination of the volunteers, went alone to free the political prisoner Belisario Alvarez.

He has recently published in a volume of 400 octavo pages his memoirs entitled " Espanoles é Insurrectos," (Spaniards and Insurgents).

If you have honest judgment, Paco, and know how to draw logical conclusions, then consider the dispassionate opinions of the veteran Spaniard, whose veracity is backed by thirty years of faithful service in Cuba in his country's cause, whose accurate criticisms betoken a prolonged and familiar contact with Cuban society,— choose between his testimony and the stupid diatribes of the author of "Cuba y su Gente," who, judging from what he has written, has confined his investigations in the country to the lobbies where the bureaucrats reign supreme, and to the dens of vice where they seek amusement.

NO. 106.
DA. SUSANA BENÍTEZ.

And if you desire further information, let me tell you that in 1826 the celebrated German traveler and philosopher ALEXANDER VON HUMBOLDT, in treating on the Island of Cuba in his "Political Essays," contributes the following testimonial to the Cuban woman: "Our attention was once more attracted to the vivacity and cheerfulness of mind which characterize the women of Cuba, both in the city and country; wondrous gifts of nature to which the culture of European civilization adds a higher charm; they are also pleasing in their primitive simplicity."

This enchanting child of the tropics has the supple figure, sweet voice, bright expression and ardent glance which betoken an intelligent mind and sensitive temperament, and which reveal a natural habitude of purest virtue; she is queen of home by right of her physical charms and the immaculate purity of her soul.

In the humble cottage of the laborer she shares with him the rude tasks of the day, and encourages him with the example of her industry and humility. In the city the working class is employed in trades proper to their sex, and does not throw away their meagre earnings in feasting and dissipation. In towns like Bejucal and Santiago she works in the cigarette factories,—but always and everywhere, be it in the lowly or the affluent home, as mother, wife, or daughter, she mitigates with her many charms, her sweetness, and tender affection, the burden which weighs so heavily on the heart of the Cuban—his eternal proscription in his own country.

At the hour of supreme danger, when the voice of duty and the demands of patriotism called upon her,—her generous spirit kindled with heroic inspiration and her enthusiasm was communicated to the . husband, the lover, and the son; she rushed with him to the battle-field to urge him in the fight, and either followed him in his bitter lot or shared his triumphs. And she has followed him—valiant in adversity, and serene throughout martyrdom,—in the sad and thorny paths of exile and of persecution.

Woman of Cuba! Seal the infamous lips of him who has insulted you, for in you the sweetest and noblest virtues are conbined with the heroic courage of the Spartan!

CONCLUSION.

A book has been answered by another book, because it was necessary to refute with convincing reasons and unquestionable proofs, the iniquitous charges made a g a i n s t a people irresponsible for their many misfortunes; because it was fitting to show in a brief sketch the efforts which this country has made for progress and regeneration; because, in a word, it should be cried from the housetops with all possible strength that the rabid slanderers of Cuba and her people are the very ones who exploit and

No. 107.—GRUPO DE PALMAS.

oppress her; that is why this collection of letters sees the light. They were written for the purpose of publication in a newspaper.

Some are of opinion that an insult launched in the world of letters by an unknown author—without reputation or political importance — should be ignored; the malignity of the work, they maintain, refutes itself.

By so doing, however, we would allow the accusation to stand, to be circulated in libraries and homes; to be read and even consulted as a volume which pretends to describe the moral and social state of a country. It would be to forget that Señor Moreno—obscure and what you will—is but another example of a class of writers who in Spain pride themselves on describing Cuba and the people by stigmatizing them.

May these letters, written without anger or prejudice, serve to silence his calumnies. " Cuba y sus Jueces " is a refutation of " Cuba y su Gente."

Those who have been amused or led astray in reading the lucubrations of Señor Moreno, must not lose sight of the fact that the Cubans are legitimate children of their progenitors, whose vices and virtues they reflect, with all the littleness of the former and all the greatness of the latter.

But, after reading these pages, which describe in broad outline the innumerable trials of a part of the Spanish commonalty — worthy but disinherited — you will observe that among all the virtues which adorn the Cuban is one of unusual brightness: the loyalty and perseverance with which, under diverse forms and at different epochs of history, he has sustained his noble purpose of social and political regeneration.

When the hour of catastrophe approaches; in the

face of a frightful political crisis; threatened with ruin, bankruptcy and misery, without hope of obtaining from the Home Country the needed remedy for all these calamities and misfortunes; the Cuban, full of faith by virtue of his principles, has not even surreptitiously raised another flag nor sought salvation under the protection of foreign influences.

Steadfast in his convictions, with eyes fixed on the mother land which refuses to listen to his clamors, he stands on the brink of the chasm into which traditions, country, hopes of glory and of progress seem to vanish; embracing the flag, he begs for Autonomy as the saving anchor for the Colony and for the Nation.

Let Spain not forget, after the sad experiences and lessons of its history that, as has been pointed out by Leroy Beaulieu, "the formation of Society should not be abandoned to chance. It is due to a colonial people that the new social organism which they create shall be established under new conditions, such as are most appropriate for the evolution of their natural powers; that their way be paved and they be afforded all necessary facilities for development without ever restricting their enterprise. Colonization is an art learned in the school of experience, and perfected through the discarding of methods whose failure has been demonstrated, and by the adoption of such measures as observation and study may suggest."

18

APPENDIX I.

APPENDIX 1.

EXTRAORDINARY POWERS

To be used in unusual emergencies and in cases
which do not admit of delay for consultation,
conceded to the Captain General of Havana,
May 28th, 1825, and again promulgated in the
Royal Decrees of March 21st and 26th, 1834.

His Majesty being firmly persuaded that at no time
and under no circumstances will the principles of rectitude and love to his royal person which characterize Your
Excellency ever be weakened; and H. M. desiring to
obviate any difficulties which might arise *in extraordinary
cases* from a division of authority and the complication of
command and control by the respective officers, and to the
important end of preserving in that precious Island his
legitimate sovereign rule and the public peace, has been
pleased, in accordance with the judgment of his council of
ministers, to invest Y. Ex. with full authority, conferring
all the powers which by royal decree are conceded to the
governors of cities in a state of siege. H. M. consequently
invests Y. Ex. with full and unlimited authority to detach
from that Island and to send to this Peninsula all officials and
persons employed in whatsoever capacity and of whatsoever
rank, class, or condition, whose presence may appear preju-

dicial, or whose public or private conduct may inspire you with suspicion, replacing them in the interim with faithful servants of H. M. who are deserving of the confidence of Y. Ex., and furthermore to suspend the execution of any orders or general regulations issued in whatever branch of the administration to whatever extent Y. Ex. may consider convenient to the royal service; such measures to be always provisional and a report thereof to be sent by Y. Ex. for the sovereign approval of H. M. In dispensing to Y. Ex. this signal proof of his royal favor and of the high confidence which H.M. places in your perfect loyalty, he hopes that, worthily co-operating, you will use the greatest prudence and circumspection, together with indefatigable activity, and trusts that Y. Ex. will, being endowed through this same favor of his royal goodness with a greater responsibility, redouble your vigilance in seeing that the laws are observed, that justice is administered, and that the faithful subjects of H. M. be rewarded ; at the same time punishing without delay or hesitation the misdeeds of those who, forgetting their obligations and what they owe to the best and most · beneficent of sovereigns, violate the laws and give full vent to sinister machinations by the infraction of the said laws and of the administrative ordinances relating thereto. The which, by Royal Order, I communicate to Y. Ex. for your instruction. God keep you, etc. — Madrid, etc. — To Señor, the Captain General of the Island of Cuba.

INVESTITURES

OF THE DEPARTMENTS OF PUBLIC WORKS, SANITATION,
CHARITY, PUBLIC INSTRUCTION AND JUSTICE.

*1854, August 17th.—Royal Decree investing the Governor
Captain General with the executive administration of the
Boards of Public Works, Health, Charity and Public
Instruction, said Boards maintaining the character of con-
sultative agencies for the former.*

Most Excellent Sir : H. M. the Queen has deigned to
issue the following Royal Decree :

In consideration of the reasons laid before me by the
Minister of State, and in compliance with the advice of my
Council of Ministers, I decree the following :

Article 1st.   The Boards and other special corporations
which form part of the public administration of the Island
of Cuba will in future be Consultative Councils of the Governor Captain General in the matters concerning their respective institutions and authority.

Article 2d.   The Governor Captain General will assume
the active functions of administration now relating to the
Boards of Public Works, Health, Charity and Education.

Done in the Palace, on the 17th of August, 1854.,
Signed by the Royal hand.   Minister of State *Joaquin
Francisco Pacheco.*

By Royal Order communicated to Y. E., etc., Madrid
17th of August, 1854.—To Señor, the Governor Captain
General of the Island of Cuba.

CIRCULAR

It having been brought to my notice that certain individual members of this body not only make use of rude expressions and gestures, but that *under pretext of obtaining intelligence of secrets they have recourse to violent measures* against peaceful and honest citizens ; it having transpired that *some of the latter, through fear on the approach of the officers, have abandoned their homes;* and such being contrary to the letter and spirit of the law, I have accordingly to state to you that the captains of the Command in your charge shall be directed at once to promulgate all the ordinances pertaining to this subject, and require their exact fulfillment. By proceeding in the manner therein provided, in accordance with the provisions of Article 8, Chapter 1 of the law, the presence of the police will everywhere inspire confidence; on this basis the force of the organization should always rest, in order to protect the lives and property of honest persons, as well as to pursue relentlessly all those who for various crimes are put under the ban of justice.

The escorting of prisoners being one of the most important and responsible functions which devolve upon the members of the Corps, that service should be rendered with the greatest exactitude. The prisoners should, while under escort, be securely bound, and vigilance redoubled when the surrounding circumstances so require, not only so

as to fulfill the requirement that they be conducted without
delay to the place prescribed by law, but also to preclude
escapes, which would entail a great responsibility upon the
guard.

I have observed with displeasure that in spite of the definite terms of the law, *it very frequently happens that persons
who are being conducted by the forces of the police attempt
escape*, thus *necessitating* their guards *to make use of their
arms*; the repetition of these incidents indicates that guard
duty is not properly discharged nor the service rendered in
the manner prescribed in the ordinance; and although this
same law ordains that they be treated with consideration
and humanity, it must never be understood that in fulfilling
this requirement it is necessary to relax in the slightest degree the precautions of safety.

Be pleased to instruct all the persons in your command
that I am determined to execute the law to its full limit if
another escape of a prisoner should occur. The Captain of
the guard, or even the Chief of the command, may be held
responsible, if it shall appear that due vigilance is not
exercised to assure the proper performance by the individuals of every class of the command of their respective
duties. God keep you many years.

Havana, October 15th, 1883.

DÉNIS, Prime Chief of Command.

PUBLIC INSTRUCTION.

PREAMBLE OF THE DECREE REGARDING REFORMS OF
THE PLAN OF STUDIES, PUBLISHED IN THE OFFI-
CIAL GAZETTE OF HAVANA, NOVEM-
BER 17TH, 1871.

MOST EXCELLENT SIR:

Shortly after Y. Ex. entered upon the exalted station which you occupy, you charged the undersigned to devote himself with especial zeal to the investigation of the existing Plan of Studies, to whose viciousness the origin of the insurrection of Yara has in great part been attributed, in view of the perversion of ideas and the demoralization of sentiments which for some time past had been going on under the influence of a bad system of education. This investigation concluded, he had the honor to transmit to Y. Ex. a report in which were indicated the defects of the system of Public Instruction and the reforms required, so that in future this element of the social organization may serve to educate and espaniolize, as far as possible, the coming generations, to the end that the dominion of Spain in the Antilles may be permanently assured.

So important is this subject and so deserving of profound thought that the undersigned has been impelled to define his ideas in extenso, and with the view to calling the careful attention of Y. Ex. to all the important points, he submits the following:

"One of the first duties," says the sage Balmes, *"which should occupy the attention of rulers, and of all such as have a direct or indirect influence on society and who interest themselves for the good of their fellow-creatures, is, without doubt, elementary instruction. If this is properly regulated and is preceded by religious and moral training, men will become more educated and less vicious, because the generality of men are not fitted for high scientific studies, nor destined to pursue literary callings, but rather to live in humble circumstances, and they preserve to the end of their days that which was taught them in early youth, without having occasion to add to their stock of knowledge other than the lessons of experience."*

This is so obvious to a person of education, who has had occasion to study men, consider the events of history and meditate on the present times, that Y. Ex. will doubtless unhesitatingly assent to these propositions. The influence of the instruction given in early youth is so positively effective because the mind of the child is like soft wax whereon any desired impression can be made, and whereon these impressions become so fixed, that they become like old paintings, which, notwithstanding the new pictures that may be wrought over them, reappear even after a great lapse of time, under the influence of a reactive agency. Man feels throughout his life the influence of the ideas and habits taught him in childhood. It happens sometimes that on leaving the parental roof to enter upon another sphere of life, he seems to change completely, but when the snows of time cool the ardor of his blood and temper the enthusiasm of a thoughtless spirit, the memories of those first inspirations return and he becomes another man, the man corresponding to the child that was, and to this reversion is applicable the saying that the aged become childish.

But for the very reason that this early instruction is of such importance, we should proceed in regard to it with the greatest caution and prudence.   There are two systems that may be followed, either to teach a little of everything, that is to say, to impress on the mind the principal ideas of all the various branches of human knowledge, or to teach a little thoroughly, not cultivating the memory alone, but developing the intelligence, step by step, without fatiguing its faculties.

Formerly, in the times of so-called darkness, the process of education was very slow.   The writer can speak of those times from experience; after spending a long time in learning the primary branches, which consisted only of reading, writing and arithmetic, and more especially Christian doctrine, accompanied by religious practices, the youth proceeded to study Latin, and Latin only; then philosophy, which comprised but three branches, divided into three courses, logic and metaphysics, physics and ethics, and moral philosophy, with which studies he was equipped to enter the professions of law, medicine or theology.   To-day it is just the contrary; one must go hurriedly into everything, learn a great deal in a short space of time, and reach manhood while still a child.   That is the effect and character of the reaction; the intelligence must sparkle with a phosphorescent quickness; man must advance in mental development with locomotive speed; in short, everything must keep step to the same rapid beat.

Under these circumstances it was but natural that the

Plan of Studies projected for this Island should be influenced by this common eagerness for hurry, and hence the defects of the system, defects which, as has been said, are the source of the evils which Public Instructioa has produced. The realization of these objections suggests of itself that this system of vicious influences should be abandoned, and that a method be adopted dictated by prudent foresight, going backward a few steps, since the hurry and anxiety to do much in little time has obviously given such poor results. Moral and intellectual development should accord with the conditions of nature, as in the case of physical development, which proceeds in accordance with the natural laws of material conditions. Thus, it is well to observe what faculties the child possesses, so as to decide how best to cultivate them, and on this subject I yield my pen to that of the profound Catalonian thinker already quoted.

"*One of the facts*," says Balmes, "*which the teacher of primary studies should never forget, is that childhood has two very notable qualities, and according as one proceeds with regard thereto results will be fruitful or barren, very good or very bad. These qualities are: first, the capacity of receiving impressions; second, the difficulty of comprehending many things at one time. The child may be compared to a level table covered with a very soft paste, which need be touched but very lightly to become impressed by the object touching it; it may, furthermore, be compared to a bottle with a very narrow neck, which, if it is attempted to fill it quickly, the liquid is spilled and barely a few drops enter, but if, on the contrary, the operation is slowly proceeded with, it might be filled to the brim, without any of the liquid intended for it being lost.*"

The conclusions which the present writer deduces from the above is that in the existing Plan of Studies for primary instruction, the branches of elementary agriculture, industry and commerce, mentioned in paragraph 5 of article 2, be suppressed, and likewise those of geometry, drawing, surveying, physics and natural history.

This number of studies is too great; it is a labyrinth for the weak understanding of a child; these teachings can, at best, be impressed but very lightly on its understanding; and, easily impressed, they are as easily effaced by others, so that precious time is lost in useless and fatiguing effort, learning things which cannot be long retained.

Another error committed in passing from the past methods to the present, in going at locomotive speed from restraint to liberty, is to make religious instruction secondary to that of the arts and sciences, a fatal error, which has produced disastrous consequences. It was but natural that such should be the case.

Intelligence is not the only attribute of man; he has also a conscience; and both finding expression through the will, they should be united by the link of morality. If the flame of intelligence is fanned to make it brighter, while conscience is left dormant, and both are left to themselves, then the will, having full sway, will be at the mercy of pleasure unbridled by conscience. It follows obviously that individual activity will have no other curb than the law, which will always be eluded and thus the most healthy and robust society will become undermined and weak, and go onward towards dissolution. We have experience of this. France had a veritable furore for extending education, believing it to be the panacea for all evil, and see what have been the results. The criminal statistics afford us light on this subject, and here are the data obtained by Balmes from a work entitled, "*Education practique*," which have been confirmed by the statistics of the succeeding years. In brief, the investigations made lead us to conclude, 1st, that the number of crimes and offences has increased year by year in proportion to the spread of education; 2d, that in these crimes or offences the number of the convicts who could read and write is one-fifth greater in proportion than the number of those who are entirely ignorant, while the proportion of those who had received an advanced education is two-thirds greater; 3d, that the degree of perversity in crime and the likelihood of escape from justice and from the penalty of the law is in direct proportion to the degree of education; 4th, that in the provinces where instruction has been most diffused crime is most abundant; that is to say, morality is, in principle, opposed to education; 5th, that the recurrence of crime is more frequent in the case of those who have received instruction than among those who do not know how to read or write. As intelligence has gradually become disseminated the number of offences against person and property, of criminal assaults, of illegitimate unions, of foundlings, of cases of mental aberration, of suicides, have palpably increased, in proportion not alone to the extension, but also to the higher degree, of education.

"So great an evil, a condition so contrary to the expectation of those who had looked for happy results from the growth of intelligence, attracted the attention of thinking men. But where was the remedy? Who could imagine that learning was a scourge that had to be suppressed? who dared to say that the schools must be closed and the place of the teacher given to the constable? Aimé Martin was the first to divine the truth, becoming convinced that instead of *instructing* it is necessary to *educate*, that while lighting the fire of intelligence the heart must be also well directed; in a word, that religion is indispensable."

But notwithstanding his good intentions, Aimé Martin was also in error. It would have been easy to follow his advice if only one religion — the Catholic religion — had existed in Europe, but since the Christian sects—offsprings of Protestantism—have become sub-divided and multiplied as they are, which religion was to be taught to the children? It was not to be expected that Aimé Martin and his friends should point to the Catholic as the best religion, and they did not. Aimé Martin himself formed a sect that had a little of everything except religious devotion, so it is clear that the evil, far from being remedied, would but thrive in proportion to the growth of this irreligious religion. Consequently the subsequent criminal statistics give evidence only of the increase of the general evil. The sad spectacle which France presents to-day is manifest evidence of what is herein stated.

But the criminal statistics of Europe, examined in another aspect, demonstrate more clearly, if possible, the nature of the vice which contaminates the atmosphere in which it exists. Thus the statistics of suicide, which have recently been made known to us in contributions to the *Diario de la Marina* by Señor Lasagra, who has occupied himself with the analysis

19

of a work exclusively devoted to the study of this important phenomenon. These statistics, leaving aside details which would take too much space, demonstrate the following very significant facts: 1st, that suicides are much more numerous in Protestant than in Catholic countries; 2d, that they are more numerous in the capitals than in the rest of the country. In all France, says Lasagra, there are 110 suicides per million inhabitants; in Paris, 646; in Prussia, 123, and in Berlin, 212. In Denmark, 288, and in Copenhagen, 447. The same proportion of suicides is apparent in other nations. He then adds: "In conclusion, says the author of this interesting work, the principle fact developed is the general and rapid increase of suicides; this sad phenomenon leads us to inquire whether the modifications that have occurred in philosophic and religious opinions, whether the reforms effected in social and economic conditions, from the point of view of the degree of freedom given to individual responsibility and enterprise, whether these have not engendered the decay and depression previously unknown."

The thinker who studies history and reviews the course of philosophic and religious thought during the present century soon perceives where and whence the evil originates. The human conscience was declared free three centuries ago, thus making it at once judge and arbiter, and since then reason wanders desolate. Religions have multiplied, and where man does not adore himself as God, he is an atheist or indifferent. Philosophical sects also have sprouted from this individual self-sufficiency; the multiplicity of these schools has always and everywhere produced doubt and skepticism, which in their turn have engendered a materialism whose only offspring is disbelief in virtue and morality. But how is it possible to avoid the utter depression of some, or the frenzied despair of others? Some are tortured with constant unhappiness, without hope of the future, while others have their hearts filled with the poison of envy and the passion of pride. Aimé Martin's book on education was intended to cultivate mothers, Mme. Campan having assured Napoleon that the best education for women was that which formed the best mothers. But his book is rather calculated to create *free women* than *good mothers;* he proposed to educate religious mothers because he understood that mere instruction was not sufficient to improve mankind, and yet his book is anything but religious.

What are we to deduce from all this with regard to Cuba? Pedro Agüero, a Cuban, who has busied himself with the study of public instruction on the Island, in a work written in 1866 on the basis of data and experience gathered as member of the Board of Higher Education, says: "Everywhere, in schismatic as well as in Catholic countries, in absolute monarchies as well as in democratic republics, law and custom, in other words, the government and the people, have made religion the basis of public instruction, recognizing in it the principle of all science and the origin of all virtue." After presenting statistics showing that in Germany, England, France and the United States elementary instruction is almost exclusively in the hands of the clergy or of religious organizations, he adds: "In Cuba, with the exception of establishments directed by religious orders, in which a truly Christian education is obtained, the moral and religious instruction is generally confined to an imperfect idea of Christian doctrine and of sacred history, without anything adapted to elevate the spirit and which should be held apart from teachings that tend only to cultivate the intelligence.

Our present system of public instruction naturally places religion in the first rank with other learning ; but besides, the right which, according to the ecclesiastical authorities, naturally pertains to them of directing the development of the moral and spiritual faculties of the child, it provides that the supreme civil government is to see that the respective parish priests conduct reviews on moral and Christian doctrine in the primary schools at least once a week.   Notwithstanding this, the priest and the teacher continue to be almost strangers, and from this divorce of the Church and the School result enormous evils for which it is necessary to provide a remedy.

And what is to be this remedy ?   It is very easy to find. As in medical science a knowledge of the cause of the disease renders it easy to cure the malady, so the Latin aphorism, *sublata causa, tollitur efectus* has become almost proverbial.   Avoid, accordingly, this lamentable divorce. Christianize, or rather Catholicize education by putting into effect the provisions of Article II of the Plan; put the Governmental and Municipal machinery of education in the hands of religious teaching orders, and the evil will disappear.

Another important point is the method of education, and in regard to this also, two systems present themselves, that of liberty, and that of restriction.   Which is the better? Agüero says in the work above quoted: " Education in Cuba is not free in the same sense as in the United States, where it is not restricted; nor even as in England where public opinion, if not the law, somewhat controls it, since an official investigation exposed the vices of the old free system, and revealed the existence in the country of more than five hundred primary teachers who did not know how to write; but it is as free as that of Germany and France, not to mention Spain, Italy and other countries which in this respect are about on the same level with us.

"As regards the practice of both public and private instruction, it is a well-known fact that inspection not having heretofore been exercised, nor the authority of the Government enforced in schools and colleges, the most absolute liberty has reigned both in form and spirit, in method as well as in doctrine; it sometimes occurring that in matters of religion the latter has not been altogether orthodox.

"It is not then a want of liberty, but rather, in some particulars, an excess of it that is injuring education in Cuba; a proof of this is the fact that in none of the large centers of Europe and America is the number of primary schools greater in proportion than in Havana, nor is there a proportionately greater number of lawyers, physicians, literateurs and students to be found elsewhere than in our Island.

"Moral and religious education is usually neglected both by the family and by the teacher; nor have the other branches been properly taught, owing to the lack of adequate means and the absence of a proper system of gradation in advancing studies; teacher and pupil appear always eager to boast of precocity and to forestall time, instead of extending their knowledge and giving proof of real learning."

These are grave assertions, Most Ex. Sir, and yet the undersigned, basing himself on the practical knowledge obtained by him in the course of his experience in connection with public instruction, proposes to go beyond the ground taken in Agüero's report. Not only has there been, and still continues to be, exercised in Cuba an excess of liberty in teaching, but this liberty has degenerated into a state of veritable anarchy. Articles 20, 149, 221, 222 and 259 have been interpreted and applied with such latitude that many young men are admitted as a matter of right to courses after the term of matriculation is closed, or examined before the conclusion of the course; they take whatever course of study suits them and change it at pleasure; or they study under private tutors, or at all events present certificates to that effect, while persons lacking the qualifications stated in Article 259 have been priviledged as private teachers; and all because of the inconsiderate eagerness to extend education, of the desire to learn a great deal in a short space of time, and to receive a degree as soon as possible, so as to kill the sick through ignorance, or to lose suits at law through a sacrifice of right to a garrulous loquacity.

What must be the natural, logical consequences of this state of things? Y. Ex. already knows. Physicians without patients and lawyers without briefs, full of ambition and unable to attain their original aspirations, betake themselves to conspiracy, which is an easier business, and perhaps more profitable. Thus, some, being incapable of teaching science, which they have not mastered, have taught evil or concealed ignorance, and others have taken to intrigue and to disturbing the public mind, thriving on the discord and disorder which they have managed to spread. The result of all this has been the insurrection which has so endangered the dominion of Spain in Cuba? and to subdue which has cost the nation so much of money and of blood, and Y. Ex. so much anxiety and labor.

One of the first schools established in Havana, quite re-nowned, was that of Carraguao, and to appreciate the kind of education to be had there it is sufficient to read the fol-lowing, published in one of the principal organs of the traitors to the country: *"El Demócrata,"* in a reference to the execution of Pedro Figueredo. "Don Manuel Fran-cisco Jáuregui, formerly teacher of mathematics in San Fernando, and some of the most learned of the exiles, con-stituted the faculty of the College of Carraguao, where Pedro Figueredo, Francisco Aguilera and many others who have since figured among the foremost of the enemies of Spanish tyranny were educated. *From the lips of their masters, nearly all of whom were themselves victims of despot-ism, they frequently heard maxims which, in their tender years, could not but be deeply graven on their memory, and in time produce their natural fruit."*

Afterwards there was established the College of *El Sal-vador*, directed by José de la Luz Caballero. Not a little has been said of this College as to its education being anti-Catholic and anti-national; its friends and patrons always endeavored to dissipate these imputations as calumnies devised by envious rivals or by exaggerated and prejudiced patriots. *La Revolución*, however, has just published the following: "The Spaniard may say what he pleases of Don José de la Luz, but if the latter can see from the spiritual world what is going on here, he will rejoice at the result of his labors; he will sleep peacefully in his grave because his pupils know their duty, and because those who have not already sacrificed themselves for freedom are in the active field of the Revolution ; one and all gather to rear the edifice whose foundation he, with his own hands, laid by preparing the future generations to vanquish tyranny and make the independence of the country triumphant.''

And finally, when a newspaper has occasion to print the biography of one who has paid with his life the penalty of his treachery on the rebel battlefield, before a file of Spanish muskets, or on the scaffold, especial mention has been made of his having been a teacher; of how he inspired the youthful mind with patriotism and the desire for Cuban liberty; of how the lessons learned in the College of Don José de la Luz Caballero had urged him to the anti-national field. These sentiments have been expressed in the obituary articles inspired by the deaths of Izaguirre in Manzanillo, and Luis Ayestarán in Havana.

What other fruit could be afforded, Most Ex. Sir, by an education so immoral as the one which teaches children to hate the land of their fathers, and the very fathers themselves? Fatal inculcations! To inspire perverse sentiments, to incline the will to evil, to envelop the intelligence in mists of error, and kindle the fire of passion with diabolical ardor; inciting the spirit to rebel in behalf of false rights, conceived without the counterpoise of a sense of duty ; this has been the work of the conspirators for many years! The anxiety to propagate education, crushing and trampling upon the provisions of the law, was the object of the insurrectionaries of Yara.

To teach without educating and to develop the intelligence without imbuing the heart with morality is an incomplete system, conducive to evil; it is to sow good and bad seed in the same furrow. But teaching to read, to write and to count, ignoring conscience, failing to develop in the tender minds of youth the idea of God, of a future life, or of natural law, is still worse; it is to permit them to take poison as nourishment, and deny them the antidote. Journals, novels and tracts are placed in the hands of the pupil, which he devours with avidity; his pride, his self-esteem and his evil passions are flattered by the honeyed doctrines, and he is unable to distinguish the good from the evil which enters into his soul because he has not been taught the rules of good and evil, and thus another soul is lost, another heart is made accessible to perversity. What fruit can be produced by bad seed sown on virgin soil and cultivated by tillers of evil design? Even in text-books of elementary geography have wicked doctrines been inserted. In one of them we read that the greatest event of the present century in America was the revolt of Bolivar. See under what seductive form the minds of children are predisposed to admire the crime of treason! From admiring it to considering it a patriotic duty, to desiring its enactment, there is but a brief step, to which the vivid and ardent imagination leads precipitately. To relate other analogous proceedings which have prepared the way for the insurrection at Yara would be but to tell Y. Ex. what you know full well.

We now beg Y. Ex. to put a check on all this evil,

caused by an excess of liberty in the matter and manner of instruction, by reforming the existing method, beginning with the enforcement of such restrictions as public opinion demands, and the interests of the country require. Give greater scope to religious training by instructors who are sincere, and above all, of great morality; by those whose religious vocation consecrates their lives to teaching for the love of God; do away with the branches which fatigue without benefiting the weak understanding of the child; arrange the methods and the studies in such manner as to do away with the confusion introduced under cloak of simultaneous courses and special examinations; suppress private teaching, and exercise great vigilance in seeing that the Catholic clergy are entrusted with the enforcement of the plan of studies; such are the reforms which should be effected in the methods of public instruction.

Y. Ex. was pleased to accept these considerations and granted to the subscriber the authority prayed for, to reform the plan in accordance therewith. What has thus far been done by virtue of that authority, is the reform of the secondary grade of instruction, which I now submit for the approval of Y. Ex.; the other projects relating to the subject I will transmit hereafter, trusting that Y. Ex. may sanction them with your superior judgment.

Havana, August 25th, 1871.

Rámon María de Araístegui.

1851. April 25th.—Royal Order prohibiting the introduction into the Island of publications which tend to inspire ideas pernicious to the tranquility of the country.

Most Ex. Sir: The Queen has been made acquainted with Y. Ex.'s letter number 66, dated March 10th ultimo, in which you report having prohibited the introduction into that Island of the "*Revista de España y de sus posesiones de Ultramar*" because of its containing pernicious principles and ideas. H. M. is pleased to approve the measure adopted by Y. Ex. and at the same time charges Y. Ex., as I affirm by Royal Order, to subject to like prohibition all publications tending to inspire pernicious ideas, endangering the peace of those dominions or their union with the Home Country. God, etc., Madrid, April 25th, 1851.

To the Governor Captain General of the Island of Cuba.

1856. September 20th.—Royal Order decreeing that neither the Antilles nor Philippine Islands, except the Marianas, be considered as places of confinement, exile or deportation.

Most Ex. Sir : The Minister of Public Affairs charged with the Concerns of the Colonies, hereby declares to the Ministers of War, of Pardons and Justice, and of Government, the following :

In view of various communications from the Governors General of the Colonial Provinces, in which they lament the evil effect on the public spirit of those countries, produced by persons deported thither for political reasons, and considering:

1st. That it is most difficult if not impossible that those so deported should maintain during their confinement a desirable degree of circumspection and moderation in the manifestation of their ideas, whether in the circle of their private life, or in the business intercourse and occupations which they pursue as a means of livelihood.

2d. That the severity of misfortune, to which men are prone to solely ascribe the sad results of their own errors, often sours their temper, embitters their minds, and moves them to wrath and detraction. That when this arises from political disasters, it always engenders, even in the soundest moral natures, an irresistible and fatal tendency to a detestation, or at all events to an invincible aversion, for the principle of authority in all its manifestations, religious, social and political, inasmuch as in its immediate, if not its ultimate representatives, they discern the source of their misfortunes and sorrows.

3d. That the exiles are always imbued with the spirit of restlessness and prone to migrations peculiar to political agitators; they infuse the turbulent spirit of Peninsular agitations and discord into those remote regions, which are under a special system of government, and which require, above all, that public opinion remain undisturbed and as uniform as possible in its estimate of public affairs.

They lower the prestige which Spanish rulers should uniformly enjoy in the Colonial provinces, by manifestations of ill-will and discontent, which defeated politicians cannot but betray in their words and actions. They are always

disposed to stigmatize the victors as unjust and inconsistent,
and to take as a martyrdom that which is but a proper and
merited punishment; and finally the wretchedness of exile
sometimes clouds their understanding to such an extent as
to bring them to sacrifice love of country and national
interests to their political resentment.   They confuse the
due vengeance of those who pass sentence upon partisan
offences with the rancors and hostile designs of those who
are enemies of the country and inimical to everything that
is Spanish.

4th. That those deported beyond the sea for political
reasons are not necessarily or usually the leaders or heads
of the popular revolts but the instruments, and because of
their character and temperament they do not settle down
(not even desiring to do so if they could), to a measured,
orderly, methodical life, under tranquil, pacific, and normal
conditions.

5th. That it is extremely dangerous to inject these disturbing elements into communities from which all sources
of inquietude and alarm should be withheld with the
greatest solicitude ; into countries wherein it is desirable that
not even the slightest echoes of our civil discords should be
heard, and to the inhabitants of which all the members of
the Spanish race should appear as united in one common
sentiment.

6th. That experience fully confirms the accuracy of the
above observations.   Because not only the exiles, but even
those who, owing to political mutations, have voluntarily
left the home country and chosen to reside in the colonial provinces, have at all times been (with some hon-

orable exceptions) an element of moral or material disturbance in those countries. Because, in the rebellion of our former dominions on the American continent, many of the principal promoters, instigators and agents were Spaniards whom political rancor and frenzy converted into infamous criminals capable of the most villainous treachery ; or who, by their ungovernable conduct and unreasoning complaints, by their writings, or by overt rebellion, unruly and reckless, gave more or less directly or more or less openly, substantial aid to the carrying out of projects for separation from the home country. Because, in the conspiracies hatched in the Island of Cuba, there have always figured in more or less important relations, Spaniards who forsook their country for political reasons. Thus it happened during the term of General Tacon ; certain Spaniards were the source of great uneasiness, for whether through imprudence or evil intent, they never lost an opportunity of instilling in the colony the poisonous virus of their extravagant doctrines and partisanship, or rather of the school of irreconcilable prejudice to which they belonged.

From that time dates the origin of the evil spirit which, in a sense hostile to the interests of Spain, begins to spread in the colony where heretofore Spain has been venerated to a degree almost amounting to superstition.

And 7th. That it is imperative that evils so grave and which may be so easily guarded against, be prevented by no longer treating the colonial provinces as colonial prisons, even in cases when, under suspension of constitutional guarantees, the inexorable requirements of public safety render deportations necessary. The Queen has, therefore, been pleased to command that in the future, neither judiciously nor executively shall the Antilles or the Islands of the Philippine Archipelago, except the Marianas, be designated as places of confinement, of exile, or of deportation.

Royal Decree communicated, etc.—Madrid, September 20th, 1856.

To the Governing Captain Generals of Cuba, Porto-Rico and the Philippine Islands.

CIRCULAR

FROM THE CIVIL GOVERNMENT OF HAVANA CONCERNING
THE SUPPRESSION OF HIGHWAY ROBBERY.

In the circular letter, dated August 1st ultimo, which his
Excellency, the Governor General, was pleased to dictate
for the purpose of directing generally a more active and
efficient repression of highway robbery, occasion was taken
to note that one of the causes which contributed to render
difficult the total extirpation of this disturbing and dangerous element of society was the more or less positive protection which the bandits usually receive from the country
people. Many of these, either through culpable complicity,
or from lack of energy and courage, contribute to making
more difficult, when not completely defeating, the action of
the authorities, by maliciously concealing the passage of
bandits through their fields, or reporting it too late, and in
many cases withholding information of important matters
which, on this account, remain ignored or come too late to
the knowledge of the public officers who are charged with
prosecuting and punishing offenders according to law.

The responsibility which thereby devolves upon those
who so conduct themselves cannot be more palpable, nor can
the consequences to the safety of persons and property be
more fatal than to the administration of justice, whose representatives thus see depreciated the muniments of the law,
over whose integrity and sacred ministry it is their duty to
keep watch.

20

Such criminal proceedings cannot and should not receive toleration of any kind, and I therefore consider it absolutely necessary to decree the following:

1st. All persons are under the imperative duty of immediately informing the nearest authorities or police force of the presence of malefactors in the house or property in which they may, either permanently or temporarily, be residing.

2d. Delay in communicating said information, if it exceed the time deemed necessary in the judgment of the authorities, will be considered as shielding the malefactors and be made the subject of a due investigation, the result of which will be made known to the proper authorities, who will thereupon proceed according to law.

3d. The local mayors will bear in mind the various circulars and instructions, public as well as private, which have been addressed to them concerning the adoption of measures in case of the presence of bandits in their respective localities, and more particularly the speedy report of all such matters to this office, to the General of the Island, and to the neighboring authorities and forces, in conformity with the instructions aforesaid.

4th. In order that no one may allege ignorance respecting the responsibility devolving upon his or her actions or omissions in this matter, the mayors are hereby required to give these provisions all possible publicity by means of notices or proclamations, or by personal notification to the owners or administrators of properties if they deem such procedure requisite.

Havana, November 14th, 1887.—*Luis Alonso Martin.*

APPENDIX II.

APPENDIX II.

REFERENCES CONCERNING THE ILLUSTRATIONS INCLUDED IN THE TEXT.

No. 1. RAIMUNDO CABRERA, author of this work.

No. 2. JOSÉ DE LA LUZ CABALLERO.—Born in Havana July 11th, 1800. His education was directed by the Rev. José A. Caballero. Studied in the Seminary of St. Carlos, where he became Professor in 1824. Travelled through the United States and Europe until 1831. Published in Paris a translation, with notes, of Volney's "Travels through Europe and Syria." Was elected member of the Royal Academy of Agrarian Economics of Florence. Published a set of graded reading books. Became President in 1832 of the great College of Carraguao, where he founded a Chair of Chemistry, established a course of philosophy and published his report on the *Instituto Cubano*. In 1834, elected Vice-President of the *Sociedad Patriotica*. Published an "*Index to Philosophical Subjects*" (*Elenco sobre materias filosoficas*) in 1835. Received the degree of Doctor of Laws in 1836. Elected President of the *Sociedad Economica* in 1838, and re-elected in 1840. Held the Chair of Philosophy in the College of San Francisco (Havana) until 1843. In 1840 published his *Impugnación al examen de Cousin* on Locke's Essay on the Understanding. In 1841

was made corresponding member of the *Academia de Buenas
Letras*, of Barcelona.   In 1842 he initiated and effected the
revocation of the action of the Sociedad Economica, expelling
from membership the English writer Turnbull, Consul of
Great Britain, who was disliked because of his anti-slavery
ideas. La Luz formulated a strong protest against this resolution, which latter had been suggested by the local government.   Returned in 1843 from Europe, where he had gone
to recuperate his health, for the courageous purpose of
appearing before the Military Commission, accused of having taken part in the Negro conspiracy.   He was acquitted.
In 1848 he established the famous college *El Salvador*,
over which he presided until his death, June 22d, 1862.
Under his guidance were developed the men who in latter
days have most distinguished themselves in Cuba for their
patriotism and learning.   He was a just man, a good
patriot, a great character, and a perfect educator.   Amid
the oppressive atmosphere of the Colonies, where every
manifestation of thought was a crime, suspected and persecuted, he was always resolute in teaching the doctrines
which redeem the spirit and develop character.   His cog-
nomen, *Don Pepe*, so popular and venerated, signifies in
Cuba not only a philosopher and an ideal, but stands as a
symbol—that of protest against tyranny; that of the peaceful effort which extirpates error and sows the seed of all
that is good, of truth and of justice.

No. 3. MORRO CASTLE AND LIGHT-HOUSE.—Built on
a rock at the entrance of the port of Havana in 1589
(Antonelli, Designer). Finished in 1597, during the reign

of Philip II, while Captain General Juan Tejeda was Governor of Cuba.

No. 4. FRANCISCO ARANGO Y PARREÑO.—Born in Havana, May 22d, 1765. Educated at the Seminary of San Carlos. Studied law at the Pontifical University. In 1787 went to Spain, where, in 1789, he graduated in his chosen profession. Deputy in the Municipal Council of Havana before the age of twenty-five. To him are due the municipal reforms of 1789–94. Improvements in agriculture and commerce and much of the progress and enterprise developed in the subsequent intellectual and material advance of the Island are traceable to his influence, notwithstanding his mistaken support of the African slave trade, which he afterwards rectified by demanding its abolition. He was President of the *Sociedad Patriótica*, which he greatly promoted. In 1792 he published a treatise on Agriculture in Cuba and succeeded in establishing in Havana a Chamber of Commerce and a Mercantile Tribunal. In 1793 he published his brilliant project of a tour of investigation through England, France and their Colonies, which led to his being commissioned by Count Montalvo to make a tour of scientific observation in those countries, with the view to studying their industrial improvements and introducing them into Cuba. He initiated the establishment of the Royal Consulate, and was the first incumbent of the office. He was one of five chosen by the *Sociedad Patriótica* to edit the *Papel Periódico;* became legal adviser of the Court of Appeals. In 1794 he published in England a paper on the evils resulting from the exclusive privileges

granted to the refineries of the Home Country, and on his
return in 1795, a narrative of his travels. He introduced
into Cuba the sugar cane of the Sandwich Islands. In
all his enterprises he had the effective support of General
Luis de las Casas, who confided to him in 1803 a delicate
diplomatic mission in Guarico, of which he gave an account
in a memoir printed in 1832. Appointed supervisor of the
tobacco industry in 1805. He had to combat the abuses
growing out of an odious monopoly ; published a report on
this subject. But his great work, that which afforded the
capstone of his reputation as statesman and as jurist was the
obtainment, in 1815, of free trade for the ports of Cuba,
a result due to his labors and his luminous reports and
dispatches. During various journeys to the Home Country,
he risked his fortune and his health in waging hot battle
against the persistent holders of the monopoly. There was
no enterprise of public interest, no movement conducive
to the good of Cuba with which the name of this eminent
man was not associated. He contributed largely to the
improvement of education. Died March 21st, 1837. His
complete works have recently been published in Havana
in two volumes. Pezuela considers him "the man who has
most influenced the destinies of his country," and Baron
von Humboldt calls him its "most eminent statesman."

No. 5. CALLE DE EL PRADO. An avenue laid out in
1772 under the name of *Paseo del prado;* it began at the
Calle de Neptuno (Neptune St.), where there existed a
fountain of this name, and terminated on the beach ; it is

now longer, beginning at the wall of the arsenal. The view represents the first section.

No. 6. GRAN HOTEL INGLATERRA is situated in the most central and frequented part of Havana, facing the fine *Parque Central*, near the theatres and public offices; was recently reconstructed, tastefully improved, and luxuriantly furnished. The rooms are large, well ventilated and comfortable. Has drawing and reading rooms, elevators, telephone and mail service, and all the conveniences of the best European and American hotels.

No. 7. COUNT OF POZOS DULCES.—Born in Havana, September 24th, 1809. Was educated in Baltimore, and returned to Cuba in 1829. Settled in Paris in 1842, and devoted himself earnestly to scientific studies. Possessed of a store of learning, he returned to devote his energies to his native land, and in 1849 his treatise on the Fisheries of Cuba was adjudged the award of merit by the Lyceum. In 1851, as counselor to the Board of Public Works, he presented an admirable Report on the institution of chemical investigations. In 1854 the government considered his presence in Cuba prejudicial. He was imprisoned in the Morro and exiled to Osuna. He published, in Paris, an account of the agricultural work and population of Cuba, in which he combated colonization with negro immigrants. In 1860 he published a collection of articles on agriculture, industry, science and other branches of interest to Cuba, having previously, in 1859, published *La Cuestion de Cuba*, works written while in exile. On returning to

Cuba, he founded *El Porvenir*, a newspaper devoted to the arts and agriculture. Co-operated with Don José Quintín Suzarte in founding the famous journal *El Siglo*, the noted champion of political reforms, which he managed after Suzarte. In 1865 he was elected by the municipality of Villa Clara, Commissioner on the Committee of Inquiry at Madrid, where he advocated the immigration of whites and other political reforms. The commission was, however, dissolved by the government, and its noble endeavor fell through. The strong protest of the commissioners was drafted by the Count, who returned to Cuba convinced of the utter futility of such efforts. Resumed the management of *El Siglo*, and colaborated in various journals until the revolution of 1868. In 1869 his property was confiscated and he emigrated to Paris, living there in poverty, eking out a subsistence with his pen, in contributions to numerous Spanish publications.

His name figures in all the literary and other associations which have contributed to the intellectual advancement of Cuba. Died in Paris, October 24th, 1877.

No. 8. PAPEL PERIÓDICO. First perodical in the Island of Cuba. Its publication was commenced October 31st, 1790, under the auspices of the *Sociedad Económica*, which put it in charge of a committee consisting of five members. It was edited by the distinguished men of the day—Arango, the priest Caballero, Romay, the poet Zequeira, and others. It was the size of half a sheet of foolscap folded in two, with four leaves, and appeared on Sundays and Thursdays.

No. 9. GASPAR BETANCOURT CISNEROS. (EL LUGA-REÑO.) Born in Puerto Príncipe, April 28th, 1803. Educated in the United States, and there colaborated in the *Mensajero Semanal.* Returned to Cuba in 1832, and both in the *Gaceta,* of Puerto Príncipe, and afterwards in *El Fanal,* published brilliant scientific, literary and critical writings on agriculture, industry, colonization, etc. Promoted public instruction, founded schools for the poor, and also taught in them personally; made a scientific excursion over the Island. Founded an agricultural colony; projected and established the railway from Nuevitas to Puerto Príncipe, and was President of the railway company; established cattle fairs in the Province. In 1846 was imprisoned, exiled, and his property confiscated; lived by teaching in the United States. Afterwards went to Europe, and under amnesty returned to Cuba (1861). Colaborated subsequently in *El Siglo.* On account of ill health did not accept the candidacy for membership of the Colonial Committee of Inquiry. Died in December, 1866.

No. 10. JOSÉ QUINTÍN SUZARTE. Born in Havana, October 31st, 1819. Educated in the Seminary. A distinguished poet, publicist and political economist. Colaborated in all the periodicals of his time. Founded *La Siempreviva;* wrote fiction. Settled in Caracas, where he discharged various public offices. In 1847 returned to Havana; continued his journalistic efforts, and managed *El Faro Industrial.* Founded *El Artista,* and the daily newspaper *El Siglo,* in which he began the valiant defense of the social and political interests of his oppressed country, and which was continued by Pozos Dulces. Director of the Institute of Secondary Education of Matanzas, and editor of the newspaper *La Aurora del Yumurí*. In 1868 emigrated to Mexico, where he continued to practice journalism. After the peace of Zanjon, in 1880, he published a treatise on economic questions and founded the paper *El Amigo del País*. Died in Havana, 1887.

No. 11. RICARDO DEL MONTE. Born in Cimmarones, Cardenas, 1830. Educated in the United States, traveled through Europe and colaborated in various Spanish journals. Colaborated with Suzarte, Pozos Dulces, and other writers of the time in all the periodicals which, from 1847 to 1868, mirrored the intellectual advance of Cuba. After the peace of Zanjon he managed the newspaper *El Triunfo*, now known as *El País*, organ of the Autonomist party, of whose Executive Committee he is a member. Ex-Provincial Deputy. He is a chaste and admirable writer and a distinguished critic.

No. 12. FRANCISNO A. CONTE. Born in Cadiz; a distinguished Spanish writer and economist. Settled in Cuba, where he has practiced the profession of journalism with brilliant success. Since the peace of Zanjon he has devoted his pen to the social, political and economic reforms of the Colony, and to the cause of colonial Autonomy. Member of the Executive Committee of the Autonomist party. Among other works which attest his merits, may be mentioned *Los unos y los otros*, recently published, and *Las aspiraciones del Partido Liberal*, which first appeared in the periodical *Revista Cubana*.

No. 13. José Antonio Cortina. Born March 19th, 1852. Educated in Havana. Studied law, and completed the course in Madrid, 1873. Founded in Havana, in 1877, the well-known *Revista de Cuba*, a literary and scientific magazine, in which the most notable writers of the country colaborated, and which was awarded a gold medal at the Amsterdam Exposition. Member of the Executive Committee of the Autonomist party, 1878. Gained great popularity as a public speaker. Elected Deputy to the Cortes in 1881, but the session being adjourned he did not take his seat. Published various poetical compositions. Died November, 1883; thus unhappily extinguishing the well-founded hopes which the country had centered on this gifted and patriotic young man.

No. 14. José Antonio Saco. Born in Bayamo, May 7th, 1797. Entered the Seminary of Havana at twelve years of age, and afterwards attained the Chair of Philosophy in succession to his former teacher Varela. In 1824 left for the United States, and later on went to Europe where he founded *El Mensajero Semanal*. Translated Heineccius' Roman Law. In 1833 his essays on the roadways of the island of Cuba, and on vagrancy and means for extirpating it, obtained first prizes in the competition opened by the *Sociedad Patriótica*. In 1832 he returned to Cuba and became manager of the *Revista Bimestre Cubana*, which he so distinguished with his important essays on statistics, immigration, abolition of the prescribed system of education, etc., that the publication came to be regarded as the leading periodical in the Spanish dominions. At the same time he directed the College of *Buena Vista*, until, like all eminent Cuban patriots, he was accorded the sad but glorious lot of exile. Migrated to England. Maintained in the journals of Madrid the necessity of reforms in Cuba, and in spite of Tacon's opposition was three times successively elected Deputy to the Cortes. But the Spanish Congress denied the Cubans the right of representation, and Saco, who was not permitted to sit in the Cortes, drafted, and with his companions, published the forceful and famous protest which completed his renown. Afterwards visited Germany, Italy, Austria, Portugal and Switzerland, and fixed his residence in Paris. In 1848 opposed, in a pamphlet, a suggested annexation of Cuba to the United States.

Had permission to return to Cuba under the amnesty of 1854, but did not avail himself of it until 1861, when he did so temporarily for the purpose of promoting the establishment of a journal in Madrid to defend Cuban interests, going back to stay permanently in Paris. In 1866 he was elected by Santiago de Cuba to represent that province on the Committee of Inquiry, in which he took an active and efficient part. Signed with the three Commissioners the protest against the renewed fraud of the Madrid Government. Besides numerous minor works, making up the *Papeles de Saco* and *Colección póstuma*, he published the *Historia de la esclavitud*. In 1879 was again elected Deputy to the Cortes for Santiago de Cuba, but did not occupy the post by reason of his sudden death, September 26th, 1879.

No. 15. JUNTA DE FOMENTO. This cut represents the building occupied by the famous *Junta de Fomento* (Board

of Public Works), a body in which the most distinguished
men of the country have figured, and to whose initiative
are due its most important reforms and improvements;
among these is the construction of the first railway in Cuba,
in 1833, before any had been built in Spain. The terminal
station was called "Villanueva" in memory of the Count
of Villanueva, Superintendent of the Island, who favored
the enterprise.

No. 16. LEOPOLDO CANCIO.   Born in Sancti-Spiritus,
May 30th, 1851.   Educated in the College of San Salvador under the guidance of José M. Zayas.   Graduated in
law at the University of Havana, 1873.   In 1878, elected
member of the Executive Committee of the Autonomist
party, of which he was one of the founders.   Deputy to
the Cortes from the District of Las Villas in 1879, but did
not occupy his place.   Is a distinguished writer, journalist,
and lawyer, and one of the men whose erudition and patriotism reflects credit on the college founded by "Don Pepe"
(de la Luz).

No. 17. JOSÉ SILVEIRO JORRÍN.   Was born in Havana
June 20th, 1816.   Educated in the College of Carraguao
under José de la Luz.   Graduated in law at the University
of Havana in 1841.   Traveled through the United States
and Europe.   Returned to Havana and devoted himself to
the practice of his profession with great success.   Was
appointed Deputy Judge of the Court of Havana, and subsequently Judge of that of Burgos, which latter post he soon
resigned.   Counselor and syndic of the Municipality of

Havana. Discharged many important offices; among others the commission for the establishment of a new Cemetery, on which he made a notable report. A zealous promoter and patron of public instruction. In 1839 he wrote a treatise on free-hand drawing, published by the Board of Public Works. In 1845 his brochure on the establishment of a normal school was awarded a prize. Published numerous articles on pedagogics and popular education and started the project to erect a new University Building. Inspector of Schools and member of the Public Board of Education. Delegated by the government to preside over the examinations of graduates in law; promoted scientific agriculture by distributing publications on the subject freely among the country people. Donated an extensive collection of works on Agriculture to the *Sociedad Económica*. Donated $4,000 towards establishing fellowships of agricultural science in French and Belgian schools. Was made honorary member of the *Sociedades de Amigos del País* of Havana and of Santiago. Colaborated in many of the scientific and literary journals published in Cuba since 1835. Was exiled in 1869. During his exile published anonymously the famous treatise entitled "Ginebra." Translated Tacitus. For his work, *Disquisiciones Columbianas*, he was awarded a bronze medal at the Amsterdam Exposition. Corresponding member of the Historical Society of New York. Elected Deputy to the Cortes by the Autonomist party in 1879; twice elected Senator by the province of Puerto Príncipe, which office he now fills for the University of Havana. A brilliant orator, effective writer and accomplished linguist, a man of wisdom and a persevering patriot, he is justly regarded as one of the most distinguished Cubans, not only in his own land but abroad. His country anxiously awaits the publication of his work on the "Life and Voyages of Christopher Columbus," to which he has devoted long years of labor and investigation.

No. 18. SALA JORRIN. The cut represents one of the galleries in the Library of the *Sociedad Económica*, founded and maintained by private endowments. It bears the name of Jorrín since June, 1880, in memory of the large sums donated by its honorary member, José Silverio Jorrín, whose portrait in oil ornaments the central nave.

No. 19. JUAN BAUTISTA ARMENTEROS. Born in Puentas Grandes, May 8th, 1833. Bachelor of Laws. Founder of the Autonomist party, and member of its Executive Committee, ex-counsellor of the Municipality of Havana, to which post he was elected in 1879. As Librarian of the *Sociedad Económica* he gave most valuable service to that institution, referred to previously in this work, restoring the library, which had been completely abandoned during the revolutionary period.

No. 20. CARLOS NAVARRETE Y ROMAY. Born in Havana, 1837. Lawyer, writer of prose and poetry, whose name figures in many of the publications of the period from 1850 to 1868. Published a volume of lyric poems, highly praised by the critics. President of the Lyceum of Guanabacoa, 1867, and Rector of the *Beneficencia* institute in 1880. Present Librarian of the *Sociedad Económica*.

21

No. 21. ENRIQUE PIÑEIRO. Born December 19th, 1839. Graduated in law 1863, traveled through Europe by means of the legacy left him with this object by his teacher, José de la Luz Caballero, of whose college he was sub-director in 1862; became known as a brilliant orator and as a critic. Contributed largely to the scientific and literary journalism of the country up to 1869, in which year he emigrated to New York and took an active part in the Revolutionary Junta; at this period he published various historical and political brochures. Returned to Cuba after the peace of Zanjon and now resides in Paris, where he published, in 1880, *Estudios y Conferencias* and *Poetas famosos del siglo XIX* (1883), works which alone suffice to justify his high reputation, placing him among the most distinguished of his countrymen.

No. 22. JOSÉ IGNACIO RODRÍGUEZ. Born in Havana. Graduate in law, 1851. Known first to the public by his thesis *Utilidad de la Historia*. Doctor of Philosophy in 1855. Professor of Philosophy in the University of Havana, where he had previously studied. Appraiser of the Board of Public Education; Magistrate; Secretary of the *Sociedad Económica*, in which office he rendered distinguished services. Published a text-book on chemistry in 1856. He occupied a conspicuous place as a writer during the period from 1850 to 1868. Was exiled in 1868 and settled in Washington, where has devoted to Cuba his labors and talents as demonstrated by his articles in the *Monitor Republicano* of Mexico, and in other publications, and by his works *Vida de Don José de la Luz*, 1874, and *Vida de Don Felix Varela*, 1875.

No. 23. JUAN GUALBERTO GÓMEZ. Born in Santa Ana, Matanzas, July 12th. 1854. Educated in Havana under the guidance of the mulatto poet, Antonio Medina. Went to Paris to learn the trade of carriage making, which he abandoned to enter a school of engineering. Poverty obliged him to give up his study and become a journalist. Traveled through the French Antilles, gaining his livelihood by teaching and clerking. In 1878 he settled in Mexico, and after the peace of Zanjon returned to Havana where he colaborated in the periodicals published by the Marquis of Sterling. In 1879 he founded the newspaper *La Fraternidad*, devoted to the interests of the colored race. Deported to Ceuta in 1880, he remained there 20 months. He proceeded to Madrid and acted as substitute for Labra in the management of *La Tribuna*. Published several essays, and acted as correspondent for various journals. Returned to Havana in 1890 and became manager of *La Fraternidad;* is at this writing suffering renewed imprisonment for political offence against the press laws. He is a Cuban of energy and talent who does honor to his country and his race.

No. 24. RAFAEL M. MERCHÁN. Born in Manzanillo, where he began his literary work by colaborating in *La Aurora* and in the *Eco de Cuba*. Edited, together with Pozos Dulces, *El Siglo*, and later *El País*. Author of the famous article *Laboremus*, which was an effective appeal for the revolution. Exiled in 1869, he settled in New York, taking part in the work of the revolutionary Junta. He now resides in Bogota; is a forceful polemic writer and has published, among other interesting works, *Estudios críticos.*

No. 25. ENRIQUE JOSÉ VARONA. Was born in Puerto Príncipe in April, 1849, and was educated in the College of San Francisco in that city. Colaborated in *El Fanal,* and in 1867 his odes on the death of *El Lugareño* received an award from the Lyceum of Puerto Príncipe. In 1868 he published a collection of verses, entitled *Anacreónticas,* and in the two following years two small volumes of " *Poesías y Paisajes cubanos.*" Together with Varela and Sellén he published the volume of *Arpas Amigas.* But his fame rests not alone on his poetic productions. Varona, without academic degrees, without having passed the threshold of the collegiate halls, is not only a fine writer but a linguist, a philsopher and a sage. He contributes largely to local, national and foreign publications, and is now editing *La Revista Cubana,* founded by Cortina, and which still continues to be one of the best magazines of its kind in the Spanish language. A mere enumeration of the works of this gifted writer will suffice as indication of the high place due him, notwithstanding his youth, among Cuban notabilities. *Juicios críticos sobre el Diccionario provincial de Pichardo,* 1876. *Sobre la Filosofía Positiva de Andrés Poey,* 1878. *Sobre las Conferencias de Piñeiro,* 1880. *Observaciones sobre la Gramática é Historia de la Lengua. Ojeada sobre el movimiento intelectual de América.* Study on *El personaje bíblico Caín. Disertaciones* on Victor Hugo, Emerson, Cervantes; Essay on Realism and Idealism; Discourses in the *Sociedad Antropológica,* of which he is

President; and finally his three last works on Psychology, Logic and Ethics, which have extended his reputation to foreign lands, where they have been translated; they serve as text-books in Universities of repute, but not, indeed in those of Cuba, which confine themselves to diffusing the doctrines of Balmes and other Roman Catholic thinkers.

No. 26. PRINCIPAL NEWSPAPERS OF HAVANA. The engraving represents a collection of the newspapers of the Capital of Cuba. *El País*, organ of the Autonomists; *Diario de la Marina*, organ of the Conservatives; *La Lucha*, a republican journal of large circulation; *La Discusión*, Autonomist, very popular; *La Tribuna* and *La Fraternidad*, Independent; *La Habana Elegante*, *El Figaro* and *Gil Blas*, literary, comic and satirical weeklies: *La Unión*, published in Güines; *La Revisto de Derecho*, organ of the legal fraternity, and finally the magazine, *La Revista Cubana*, edited by E. J. Varona.

No. 27. ANTONIO BACHILLER Y MORALES. Born in Havana, June 7th, 1812. Educated in the Seminary of San Carlos. Graduated in law 1837. From 1829 to 1868 he figured as founder and colaborator in the principal publications which characterized that period of our literature. His most important didactic works are *Cultivo de la Caña; Estudio sobre la propiedad; Filosofía del Derecho; Antigüedades Americanas; Tradiciones Americanas; Historia de las letras en Cuba*, and others. He filled some of the most important public offices; was President of the Institute of Higher Education, in which capacity he greatly furthered the advance of the country. Was an exceedingly laborious bibliophile and historian. His most remarkable work is, without doubt, *Cuba Primitiva*, on the origin, languages, traditions. etc., of the aborigines. Was exiled in 1869 and his property confiscated. Colaborated in important foreign magazines. Died in Havana, 1888.

No. 28. José Maria Heredia. Born in Santiago de Cuba, December 31st, 1803. Educated in Caracas and in Mexico. Graduated in law at the University of Havana in 1823. He cultivated poetry from childhood, and translated *Florián*, Alfieri, Ossian, Horace and other writings. In 1824 he was condemned to perpetual exile for the crime of treason. Teacher of languages during his exile. In 1825 he published, in New York, his first volume of poems, which gave him universal fame. His Ode to Niagara is one of the most precious adornments of the Spanish Parnassus. His tragedies, both original and translated, are *Sila*, *Cayo Graco*, *Tiberio*, *Atreo and Triestes*, and *Abufar*, the latter being the most noted. He wrote the *Lecciones de Historia Universal* and many other works of note. Discharged important public offices in Mexico. Died at Toluca, May 7th, 1839, in his 35th year.

No. 29. Cirilo Villaverde. Born in San Diego de Núñez, October 28th, 1802. Educated at the College of San Carlos. Devoted himself to literature and education. Is not only the most notable, but may be regarded as *the* Cuban novelist, *par excellence*. Contributed to all the important journals from 1830 to 1868. Among his many novels, that which especially justifies his reputation is *Cecilia Valdes*, published in 1838. He wrote various didactic works, among others a text-book on the Geography of Cuba, and a school reader. Took part in a political conspiracy in 1848. Was condemned to a wretched death by the garrotte, March 31st, 1849, but escaped from prison and got away in the hold of a coasting schooner. Edited *La Verdad* in New York, 1853, and published *El Independiente* in New Orleans, 1854. Settled in Philadelphia, where he taught Spanish; married there Dona Emelia Casanova, a Cuban heroine whose name will ever be an honor to our history. Repaired to Cuba under the amnesty of 1858, but returned to New York and there edited *La América*, Frank Leslie's *La Illustración Americana* and *El Espejo*. Figured among the revolutionists of 1868. He still resides in the United States, his contributions yet continuing to distinguish our literature.

No. 30. JOSÉ JACINTO MILANÉS. Born in Matanzas, August 16th, 1814, of indigent parents. Mastered the classic writers and the modern languages of Latin Europe, through self-culture. Began a business career as a clerk. Was first known through his lyrical compositions in the newspapers. He gained reputation by his drama *El Conde Alarcos*, 1837, and was, after Heredia, the most popular poet of Cuba. Lost his reason while still young. Died November 14th, 1863.

No. 31. JOAQUÍN LORENZO LUACES. Born in Havana, June 21st, 1826. Studied philosophy and law in the Uni-

versity of Havana. Figured brilliantly among the representatives of Cuban literature from 1845 till 1867, the
date of his death. He was not only a great lyric and epic
poet and translator of the classics, but also a notable
dramatist. His drama *El mendigo rojo* and his tragedy
Aristodemus gained him a place in the foremost ranks of
Spanish-American poets.

No. 32. ANTONIO GUITÉRAS. Born in Matanzas, June
20th, 1819. Educated in the College of *Carraguao*,
Havana. Graduated in law at the University of Seville,
1843. Traveled through Europe, Asia and Africa. On his
return devoted himself to education, and was President of
the College of *La Empresa*, in Matanzas. Translated Virgil
and distinguished himself as a writer. He was, after José
de la Luz, the most noted Cuban educator. He eventually
settled in Barcelona, where he has successfully devoted
himself to literature.

No. 33. JUAN CLEMENTE ZENEA. Born in Bayamo,
1831. Educated in Havana. At 17 years of age he
actively engaged in a conspiracy with Narciso López.
Traveled through the United States. In 1854 he devoted
himself to teaching; was Professor at *El Salvador*, and
Principal of the College of *Humanidades*. In 1867 he
edited *El Diario Oficial* in Mexico. Took part in the
revolution of 1868, identifying himself as Secretary in the
unfortunate expedition of the "Lillian." Began his *Historia de la revolución* and lectured on this subject in New
York. In 1870 he went on a secret mission to confer with
the Cuban insurgents. On his return was captured and

taken to the fortress Cabaña at Havana, where, after eight months of horrible suffering, he was shot.

His original compositions, translations, adaptations and romances accord him the right to a high place in our Parnassus. *El Diario de un mártir*, comprising the poems written in prison while awaiting the hour of death, from a collection of exquisite lyrics.

No. 34. JOSÉ FORNARIS. Born in Bayamo, March 18th, 1827. Educated in the Seminary of Cuba and in the College of *San Fernando*, Havana. Graduated in law in 1852. Went to Bayamo, where he was imprisoned and deported. Settled in Havana in 1855, and contributed from that time to 1868 to all the important periodicals. Was one of the most fruitful writers of his time. Published *Ensayos Dramáticos*, various didactic and several eductional works. Made teaching his profession. Emigrated in 1871. Published four volumes of lyrical composition, his " Legends of the Aborigines" being especially popular. Died in Havana, 1890.

35. FRANCISCO J. BALMASEDA. Born in Remedios, March 31st, 1833. In 1846 published a volume of *Rimas Cubanas;* in 1861 a collection of moral fables. Has written comedies and novels, and contributed until 1868 to the most important periodicals of the country. Founded the Public Library at Remedios. In 1869 he was deported to Fernando Po, whence he escaped with Castillo, Embill and others. In New York he published a history of that memorable and horrible consignment of more than 300 Cubans to a deadly land. A volume of

his complete works has been published in Colombia. Was Minister Plenipotentiary from that republic to Madrid. Resides in Havana where he has published in three volumes his *Tesoro del agricultor cubano*.

No. 36. FRANCISCO CALCAGNO. Born in Güines, June 1st, 1827. Educated in the College of *Carraguao*. Studied philosophy and the classics in the University of Havana. Afterwards visited Europe and the United States. Translated Rachel's repertoir into Spanish and English. Having lost the fortune left him by his parents he returned to Güines in 1860, where he established the first newspaper (*El Album*), the first printing press, the first public library, and the first school of languages in that district. Was principal of an elementary school. Settled in Havana in 1865. Among his many works we may mention the following : *Poesías*; *Mesa revuelta*, a collection of criticism and translations; *Historia de un muerto* and *En busca del eslabón*, scientific fictions; *Mamá Concha* and *Uno de tantos*, political novels. But his most valuable work, which reveals the indefatiguable labor of this Cuban writer, is his *Diccionario biográfico cubano*, the first work of the kind in the country.

No. 37. EUSEBIO GUITÉRAS.[1] Was born on the 5th of March, 1823, in Matanzas, Cuba, of Spanish parents, and was consequently a Creole, in the proper sense of the

---

[1] This biographical sketch is reprinted from a memoir by Miss Laura Guitéras, published in the "Records" of the American Catholic Historical Society, 1894.—*Editor*.

word.[1] The youngest of a family of six, he had the great misfortune to lose his father in 1829, when but six years old, and his mother and oldest brother followed in the terrible cholera epidemic of 1833, thus leaving him an orphan at ten years of age. He always cherished the memory of his parents, and never ceased to lament their loss; and I have heard him remark that had they lived to guide him, he might have served his country and his fellow-men. This was the highest ambition of his life—to better the lamentable condition of his unhappy land and her people. How well he

EUSEBIO GUITÉRAS. 1853.

has accomplished it thousands of grateful Cuban hearts can testify.

He was educated in Havana, at the College of San Cristóbal (better known under the name of Carraguao), where he soon won the love and esteem of his companions and teachers, particularly of San José de la Luz, leading spirit of the College and one of the most illustrious men of Cuba.

---

[1] The word Creole means a person born in America of foreign parents. Popularly, but erroneously, it is used to convey the idea of a mixture with African blood.

Here he devoted himself chiefly to the classics and literature; the latter remaining ever afterwards his favorite study. At fifteen he commenced to write verses, and shortly after to contribute both poetry and prose to the Cuban press.

Even while at school he and his talented brother Antonio had conceived the idea of establishing an institute of learning, of which it stood in such sad need, in their native city of Matanzas. It was with this end in view, and in order to perfect themselves in the modern languages, that they left Cuba in 1842, traveling extensively through France, Italy, Spain, Greece, Turkey, and their possessions in Egypt and Syria; they made the pilgrimage to Jerusalem and visited the pyramids, being the first Cubans to undertake this, at this time, perilous journey. They had always the interests of their loved country at heart, giving special attention to the various systems of education in the principal cities of the continent.

In Paris they took the course of literature at the Sorbonne, where they had the privilege of studying Dante under the great Ozanam, whom Leigh Hunt quotes as an authority on the subject. They also listened frequently to Lacordaire and Michelet. Among the distinguished persons they met on their travels were His Holiness, Pope Gregory XVI, the famous polyglot, Cardinal Mazzofanti, the Spanish statesman Olozaga—ex-President of the Cortes —and Salvá, of dictionary repute.

During their stay in Constantinople, the Spanish Ambassador put his caique with their servants at their command, thus giving them opportunity of visiting many persons and places which would otherwise have been difficult of access. The history of these travels is written in a most delightful style, and full of interesting anecdotes and circumstances. The description of the Cathedral of Seville is particularly noteworthy, the author having had ample time for observation and study, during the three weeks he was obliged to take refuge within its sacred walls while the city was in a state of siege.

Returning to Cuba in 1845, my uncle married, in July of the same year, Miss Josefa Gener, to whom he had been deeply attached from boyhood.

In 1848, the delicate health of his wife necessitated his again leaving Cuba for the United States. While on this trip he had the pleasure of visiting Longfellow several times at his home in Cambridge, and awakening in him a desire to learn something of Cuban literature; the outcome of which was an article on the subject published in the January number of the North American Review, in 1849.

He also corresponded with many men of note, among whom were William Cullen Bryant, Washington Irving, Ticknor, Bancroft and John Greenleaf Whittier.

On his return the following year, he was imprisoned in the Morro Castle of Havana, on the charge of spreading liberal ideas among the inhabitants. The event occurred during the heat of the Summer, while an epidemic of cholera was raging in the city, of which the prison, with its squalid surroundings, was the very hot-bed. But not on this account did any word of murmur cross his lips; nor did his patience and cheerfulness flag at the delays and innumerable steps necessary to take, in order to set an innocent

man free.   This work of love was finally accomplished at
the end of six months through the untiring efforts of his
friends, and principally of his brother Antonio; not, however, before the cruel blow of the sudden death of his
daughter was dealt him; which sorrow was the harder to
bear, because at that time he had not the grace of resignation to the holy Will of God, which in after life sustained
him through so many years of suffering.   During the weary
months of his confinement he read every day the speech of
the Vicar of Wakefield to his fellow prisoners.   This book,
as also I Promesi Sposi, and·Don Quijote, were a source of
infinite enjoyment to him.   The latter he was in the habit
of reading at least every year.   On my once asking him if
he never tired of Cervantes, he answered smiling,—"do the
English ever tire of Shakespeare?   Well, you know this is
our Shakespeare."

Immediately on his release from prison, he set about
founding the college which he and his brother were to make
famous under the name of " La Empresa," and which will
be the wonder and admiration of generations of Cubans to
come; for this was no easy task to undertake, much less to
accomplish, in a country where political disturbances were
of frequent occurrence, and where a wretched local Government made the progress of civilization slow and difficult.

Unfortunately he had been at the head of this Institute
but a very short time, when apprehension for the life of his
only surviving child, John, forced him to leave Cuba in
1854, for a third time, his brother remaining at the head of
La Empresa.   He established himself in Philadelphia, in
which city he now wrote the series of Spanish readers which

has made his name familiar in nearly all Spanish speaking countries. These books have received the highest commendation and praise of reputed scholars, not only for the style in which they are written, but also for the ingenious way in which he has combined pleasure and instruction for the pupil. Among others he had the gratification of receiving a flattering letter from Arjona, a famous Spanish elocutionist, and tutor of the late King Alfonso XII,—in which he expressed his satisfaction at seeing a long needed want filled in such an admirable manner.

The books have been the coveted property of several Cuban publishing houses, which have reaped enormous fortunes from them. Many editions have been issued by Appleton & Co. of New York; the largest in 1886, counting upwards of 18,000 volumes. This is an unprecedented success in the Island of Cuba!

    *   *   *   *   *   *   *   *   *

There was no educational, literary or scientific movement in Matanzas that did not look to him for support. He was one of the founders and for some time president of the *Liceo*, literary centre, of Matanzas. In 1861, on the occasion of the "Juegos Florales" (literary contest), he received the gold medal for his poem entitled "Romance Cubano" from the hands of the distinguished Cuban poetess Gertrudis Gomez de Avelleneda, whom he had previously met in Madrid.

Don José de la Luz repeatedly requested him in the most flattering terms to assume the directorship of El Salvador, at that time the most reputed school of Havana. The inherent qualities of his nature, however, prompted him to decline these tempting offers, not permitting him as a brother, to preside over a rival college in a rival city.

He devoted himself therefore to the duties of teacher in La Empresa. But in 1868 the ill-fated revolution broke out, and put an end to what he has termed the happiest period of his life. La Empresa, the college where upwards of five thousand Cuban boys received a liberal education, and where lessons of truth and morals were inculcated; La Empresa, which prepared so many of them for the high places in the learned professions which they occupy to-day, was denounced by the cultured Colonial Government as a nucleus of revolutionists. Even the series of Spanish readers was prohibited for a time from being circulated.

Any one who had the happiness of knowing my uncle, must be aware how opposed to his views was anything like revolt against the existing authorities, whatever they might be. Ignorance, he thought, was at the root of all evil. Shortly before his death, on speaking of the interests of Cuba, which were ever nearest his heart, he exclaimed: "Educate! Educate! Cuba will not prosper until she has built many schools!"

He has published in late years a text-book for the study of French; "Irene Albar," a novel illustrating Cuban life; the description of a Winter in New York, entitled "Un Invierno en Nueva York," and numerous essays and poems. At the request of Archbishop Wood he corrected a reprint of an old Spanish version of the Bible; rectifying with infinite pains the many errors in the voluminous notes of the original, particularly in regard to references. Unpublished, he leaves a novel, entitled "Gabriel Reyes," a translation of the "Inni Sacri" of Manzoni; a complete account of his travels; a volume of religious poems; another of Reminiscences; Essays on education, and a reader for the study of the English language.

He was a member of the Historical Society of Pennsylvania and of the American Catholic Historical Society.

After having left Cuba for the last time, in 1869, he again fixed his residence in Philadelphia, where (with the exception of four years spent in Charleston, S. C.) he remained until the date of his death, December 24th, 1893.

LAURA GUITÉRAS.

No. 38. NICOLÁS GUTIÉRREZ. Born in Havana, Sept. 10th, 1800. Doctor of Medicine in our University, 1821. Professor of Anatomy and of Pathology in the same institution, and author of notable treatises on chemistry and therapeutics. Elected corresponding member of the Cadiz Medical Academy, 1835, and of the Phrenological Society of Paris, 1837. Was sent on a commission to Paris; on his return opened a course of lectures on Clinical Surgery and another on Obstetrics, the first in Havana, 1840. Founded the periodical *Repertorio Médico*, the first of its kind in the country. Founder and President for life of the Academy of Sciences of New Orleans. Has filled important posts in connection with public instruction, and published numerous scientific works. The reputation of this learned Cuban, ex-Provost of our University, was recognized in his election as Vice-President of the first Pan-American Medical Congress in Washington. Died in Havana, December 31st, 1890.

22

No. 39. PEDRO GUITÉRAS. Born in Matanzas, March 17th, 1814. His work on the education of women was awarded the prize in the literary contest of 1848. Founded an institute with this object. Established himself in Washington, and published in 1856 a history of the conquest of Havana, and later a general history of Cuba, reputed as the best of its kind. Died in Charleston, S. C., 1890.

No. 40. NÉSTOR PONCE DE LÉON. Born in Havana, 1838. Graduated in law, 1858. Founded with Valdés Aguirre the newspaper *Brisas de Cuba*, and in 1868 *La Revista crítica de ciencas, literatura y artes*. Translated Heine. Manager of the Revolutionary organ *La Verdad*, 1869. He was exiled and his property confiscated the same year. Published in New York *El Libro de sangre* (The Bloody Book). Resides in New York, where he is now publishing his monumental work, A Technical English-Spanish Dictionary.

No. 41. ANICETO MENOCAL. Born in Matanzas. Studied Civil Engineering in Troy, N. Y. Entered the United States Navy as Engineer. Consulting Engineer of the U. S. Navy Department. Chief Engineer of the Navy Yard at Washington, where he also superintended the erection of the Washington Monument. Worked successfully on the Panama Canal. Author of the plan for the Nicaragua Interoceanic Canal, which gained for him the cross of the Legion of Honor of the French Republic, and is at present Chief Engineer of that undertaking.

No. 42. Francisco Albear y Lara. Born in Havana, January 11th, 1816. Educated in the College of Buena Vista. Graduated as Civil Engineer at Madrid in 1835. Fought against the Carlists as lieutenant in 1839. Planned the defences of Segura and fortified the hights of San Mateo. Captain in 1842; in the same year professor of mathematics in Guadalajara. Promoted to Commandant in 1843 in recognition of his mastery of fortification and coast defence. Author of several works on Military Engineering. Sub-inspector of military engineers in Cuba, 1844. Was sent as commissioner to Europe to study improvements in this branch, and published important works on the subject; his reports and memoirs are innumerable. Corresponding member of many national and foreign societies. But his most important work, and that on which his fame will re-main permanently based, is the plan and the construction of the Vento Aquaduct, which was awarded a prize at the Paris Exposition, and which to-day bears his name. He died in Havana, 1889.

No. 43. Álvaro Reynoso. Born in Durán (Havana). Studied under the illustrious Casaseca in Carraguao. In 1854 he obtained the prize at the Academy of Sciences. Laureate of the Imperial Institute of France. Fellow in science of the faculty of Paris, where he achieved reputation through various works, especially on the extraction of iodine. Editor of the Records of the *Sociedad Económica* in the *Diario de la Marina*, and of other publications. Invented and constructed an apparatus for manufacturing sugar. Among his more important works are *Estudio sobre*

materia científica (1861); *Ensayo sobre el cultivo de la caña*
(1862); *Notas sobre el cultivo en camellones,* Paris, 1881; a
paper on the presence of sugar in urine, written in French,
and various others. Member of numerous scientific societies,
both Spanish and foreign. Died in Havana, 1889.

No. 44. FELIPE POEY. Born in Havana, May 26th,
1799. Devoted himself from childhood to the study of the
natural sciences, especially ichthyology. In 1826 he took
with him to France a collection of drawings of fishes which
he placed at the disposal of Cuvier and Valenciennes, who
quote him as an authority. Was accorded in France the
degree of Doctor of Laws. He cultivated literature with
success, and was an eminent linguist and philologist. Figured in Paris in the Entomological Society of France. In
1832 he published there two numbers of his *Centuria de
lepidópteros de Cuba.* Was elected corresponding member
of the Zoölogical Society of London in recognition of his
work on the fauna and flora of Cuba. In 1836, published a *Geografia de Cuba,* a *Tratado de mineralogia* and
a *Geografia Universal.* Founded and directed a museum
1839. In 1860 he published his *Memoria sobre historia
natural de Cuba,* in two volumes, and in 1865 *Catálogo
razonado de los peces cubanos.* Colaborated in all the
literary and scientific periodicals up to 1868. Member of
many Spanish and foreign scientific societies. He kept up
a scientific correspondence with the most famous naturalists
of Europe and America. His writings on varied subjects
are exceedingly voluminous. His work on *Ictiologia
Cubana* (bought by the Spanish Government for the miserly

sum of $3000, and which remains unpublished because of the cost of bringing it out) is the result of forty years of study and investigation. If this learned Cuban had conceded it to a foreign government or to a private individual, his work would now be published. He died in Havana, January 28th, 1891.

No. 45. NICOLÁS RUÍZ ESPADERO. Born in Havana, 1833. Distinguished pianist and composer. Associate of Gottschalk and Strakosch. Highly praised in the French and Spanish musical reviews. His biography figures with that of Villate in the *Dictionnaire de biographie universelle des musiciens* as a distinguished composer. Died in 1890.

No. 46. JOSÉ WHITE. A notable violinist, called the Cuban Paganini. Born in Matanzas, January 17th, 1836. His mother was a colored woman. At sixteen years of age he wrote a mass for the Matanzas orchestra and gave his first concert. In 1856 entered the conservatory of Paris, and in the following year obtained the first prize as violinist among thirty-nine contestants. Afterwards substituted Professor Allard in that institute. Soon gained a wide reputation among the great European violinists. Rossini wrote him a letter saying that the French school might well be proud of him. In January, 1875, full of honors, he landed in Havana, and on June 8th of the same year he was driven out by the Government. Like all eminent Cubans, he added that leaf to his crown of laurels. He is now President of the Conservatory of Brazil, in Rio Janeiro, where he resides.

No. 47. RAFAEL DÍAZ ALBERTINI. Born Havana, August 13th, 1857. From childhood he showed great talent for the violin; his teachers were Anselmo Lopez and José Vanderguntch. Went to Europe and was first known in Cadiz; from there he proceeded to Paris, where he played at the Spanish Legation before the Diplomatic Corps. Emigrated to London during the Franco-German war. Studied with the German professor Riez. Entered the Paris Conservatory in 1871 and obtained the first prize in 1875. In 1878 he played in Madrid at the popular concerts of Monasterio and was presented with a laurel wreath. Returned to Havana in 1879 and was warmly received by his countrymen. Since 1881 he resides in Paris, making concerts tours with Saint Saens through the principal cities of Europe. From 1883 to 1887 he was one of the examination judges at the Paris Conservatory, an honor usually reserved for artists of advanced years.

No. 48. JOSÉ M. GÁLVEZ. Born in Matanzas, November 24th, 1835. Educated in the College of "La Empresa" and "El Salvador." Lawyer of great erudition and a famous forensic orator. Journalist; has published anonymously many political articles, and is especially excellent in his satires. During the revolutionary period he was confined in the Isle of Pines. Before and after his imprisonment, and up to 1878, he remained in Havana, exercising his profession and co-operating with the Revolutionary Junta of New York. In recognition of his patriotism and talents he was elected by acclamation as President of the Organizing Committee of the Autonomist party, and in this important office he has displayed the greatest energy and intelligence. Counsellor, and President during three biennial terms, of the *Sociedad de Amigos del País*. He is, furthermore, a noted political orator. Resides in Havana and enjoys great popularity.

No. 49. STATUE AND FOUNTAIN OF THE INDIES. A monument erected through the efforts of the Count of Villanueva. It is situated in the centre of a square, at the southern extremity of the street of the Prado, in Havana.

No. 50. RAMÓN PINTÓ. Born in Cataluña, 1802. Began an ecclesiastical career, but abandoned it during the political revolts of 1820. His liberal ideas drove him from Spain in 1824 and he went to Cuba as tutor to the children of Baron de Kesel. Went into business as general agent. President of the Lyceum of Havana (1853). Colaborated in the *Diario de la Marina*. Organized the corporation which owns that journal. Exercised great ininfluence; took part in the Separatist conspiracy in 1855, was arrested and put to death in Havana with that infamous contrivance, the garotte, May 31st of the above year.

No. 51. CARLOS MANUEL DE CÉSPEDES. Born, April 18th, 1819, in Bayamo. Studied at the University of Havana. Graduated in law at Madrid in 1840. Conspired with his friend Prim and was exiled to France. Returned to Bayamo in 1844, after having traveled through Europe. Cultivated literature. Was imprisoned during the conspiracy of Narciso López and confined in Palma Soriauo. Afterwards practised his profession in Bayamo. On

the 10th of October, 1868, at the head of 140 poorly
armed followers and his 200 slaves, whom he had liberated,
he started the cry for independence on his plantation of
Demajagua (Yara), and on the following day he published
a manifesto.

Two days later he was joined by 4,000 men, and the
entire country gave its sympathy or active aid to the
movement, which lasted throughout ten years and extended
from the extreme east of the Island to the vicinity of
Havana. He presided at the Congress of Guáimaro and
was elected President of the Cuban Republic, as established
by the insurrectionists. But party discords and rivalries,
inherent vices of our race, caused the downfall of this
unconquered chieftain. He died homeless, starving and
abandoned, wounded by an enemy's bullet, March 22d,
1874. His unfading crown of glory is not lacking the
withered leaf of man's ingratitude.

No. 52. JULIÁN GASSIE. Born in Havana, 1850.
Lawyer, 1872. Founder of the Anthropological Society
of Havana and author of its constitution. Was an eru-
dite philologist. Published a remarkable work on *Lin-
güística moderna*. Was the real initiator and founder of
the Liberal Cuban Party after the peace of Zanjon, and
first Secretary of its Executive Committee. Untimely
death (December, 1878) shattered the hopes which his
country had justly founded on him.

No. 53. CARLOS SALADRIGAS. Born in Matanzas. A
distinguished lawyer and brilliant political speaker. Vice-
President of the Executive Committee of the Autonomist

party, of which he was one of the organizers. Ex-President of the Provincial Deputation of Havana, in which city he resides.

No. 54. MANUEL SANGUILÍ. Born in Havana, March 26th, 1849. Pupil and afterward professor in "El Salvador," 1868. In January, 1869, sailed from Nassau, bound for Cuba, in the schooner "Garvani," which was captured, but he escaped in a boat with nine other members of the expedition. The same year he entered the revolutionary ranks as private. Lieutenant-Commander of the Camagüey Cavalry and of the Southern Brigade, 1870. Was twice representative in the Congress of Guáimaro (1869 and 1874). Wounded in the attack at *Torre de Colon*, under Agramonte (1871). Chief of Staff during the invasion of Las Villas by General Maximo Gomez (1874). Proceeded to New York on a commission with his brother, General Julio Sanguilí, to organize a new expedition. After the Peace of Zanjon (September, 1878) he went to Europe and graduated in law at Madrid. Returned to Cuba in in 1879. Distinguished as an orator, publicist, historian, and as an authority on American archæology. Among his literary works are *Los Caribes de la Isla*, *Cristóbal Colón y los caribes*, *Los oradores de Cuba*, numerous critical and political dissertations and scientific essays, and a specially notable work on *José de la Luz y Caballero*. Is resident in Havana.

No. 55. MARTA ABREU DE ESTÉVEZ. Born in Santa Clara. Daughter of industrious parents, and reared in

simple and rigid manners. . Married to a learned professor
of jurisprudence, Dr. Luis Estévez, this wealthy heiress
has maintained the traditions and honored the name of her
family by her virtues, modesty and great philanthropy.
Donated a fine theatre to her native city, applying its
income to the support of public schools. Also constructed
public baths for the benefit of the poor of that city. Together with her two sisters, Doña Rosalía Abreu de Sán-
chez and Doña Rosa Abreu de Grancher, she supports in
the same community an asylum for the poor, a school for
colored children, and a school for boys and another for girls
of the white race, which latter were endowed by the be-
quest of her parents. To the support of the asylum and
the three schools they have devoted the sum of $100,000
and to the theatre and baths $150,000. Señora Abreu de
Estévez devotes special attention to these schools, attending
the examinations and giving unusually large amounts in
prizes to both pupils and teachers.

There is no work of public interest to which this distinguished woman does not contribute munificently. Her
generosity, simplicity and earnestness render her a true
model of Cuban womanhood.

No. 56. TEATRO DE LA CARIDAD (The Charity Theatre), Santa Clara. The illustration represents the building
erected in the city of Santa Clara by Marta Abreu de
Estévez. The structure was designed by the well-known
Cuban architect and publicist, Herminio Leiva.

No. 57. FRANCISCO VICENTE AGUILERA. Born in
Bayamo. Highly educated in Cuba, and afterwards in

America and Europe. A millionaire. At the outbreak of the Cuban revolution of 1868 he was one of its most decided partisans and promoters. Liberated his slaves. Minister of war in 1869; Vice-President of the Cuban Republic; succeeded Céspedes in the Presidency. Proceeded to New York on a diplomatic commission and died there in 1877. The municipality of New York took part in his obsequies, and his body lay in state in the City Hall.

No. 58. SALVADOR ZAPATA. Born at Santa Maria de Guiramo, in Galicia, Spain. Was brought to Cuba while very young; studied pharmacy. Graduated in 1813. Made a fortune in the country, and died April 21st, 1854, bequeathing a large fund for the support of schools, with the income of which the *Amigos del País* are enabled to maintain six schools known by his name. Two of them are for children, two for adults (white and colored), one for girls and the sixth is a normal school. He was one of the few Spaniards who manifested their love and gratitude to country where they acquired their wealth.

No. 59. JOSÉ ALONSO Y DELGADO. Born in Laguna (Canary Islands), in 1812. Came at an early age to Cuba; founded the Lancaster Schools in Regla in 1830. He there established his famous College of *San Francisco de Asís y Real Cubano*, which together with *El Salvador* of Luz Caballero took the lead of all institutes of the kind in Havana for its methods, effective material equipments, its admirable buildings, which were specially erected for that purpose, and above all for the excellence of its corps of teachers. He afforded over fifty pupils gratuitous instruction.   He encountered many difficulties during the Revolution and was finally brought to the necessity of closing the college.   He died in 1890.

No. 60. JUAN BRUNO ZAYAS. Born October 15th, 1825, in Cimarrones, Matanzas.   Studied medicine at the University of Havana.   By dint of his industry and talents he accumulated a fortune, and instituted, exclusively with his own means, a free college, wherein he gave his personal service in teaching until November 27th, 1871, when the Government ordered it to be closed.   Member of the Executive Committee of the Autonomist party.   Provincial Deputy.   Founded an annual prize in the Academy of Sciences.   Enjoyed an immense popularity for the free medical assistance which he dispensed to the poor, for the gentleness of his character and his great philanthropy. Died in 1886.

No. 61. JOSÉ EUGENIO MORÉ.   Born in Santa Marta, U. S. of Columbia, in 1810; son of a Spanish army officer. Emigrated to Cuba at an early age in poverty.   Here he made a large fortune, and realized the idea conceived by the Count of Pozos Dulces and cherished by the *Círculo de Hacendados de la Habana*, the establishment of a school devoted to the theory and practice of Agriculture.   He invested over $200,000 in this philanthropic enterprise. Honorary member of the Sociedad Económica. Died in 1890.

No. 62. JUAN J. D. ESPADA Y LANDA.   Bishop of Havana.   Born in Arrayave, Alava, April 20th, 1756. Studied in Salamanca.   Appointed Bishop of Havana,

January. 1800. The establishment of the Cemetery of Havana, which bore his name, is due to him; it is now closed. He abolished the practice of interment in the churches. During his thirty years of incumbency, he took an active part in all projects and undertakings tending to the improvement of the country. The regeneration of the parochial clergy and of the monks, the dissemination of vaccine, which had been introduced into the country by Dr. Romay, the funds contributed by him to the support of new public schools (his conduct in this regard contrasting strongly with that of his predecessor, Tres Palacios, who opposed their increase), his large charities to the *Beneficencia* and to the Insane Asylum afford evidence of his breadth of character. The draining of the marshes of the Campo de Marte, the reformation of the plan of studies in the University, the institution of new professorships, the introduction of scientific apparatus, the impulse given to the labors of the *Sociedad Económica* over which he presided; the erection of the *Templete*, the establishment of the College *San Francisco de Sales* were among the results effected by this noble man, a model for prelates and for rulers, whose name will remain forever venerated in the hearts of the Cuban people.

No. 63. HOSPITAL DE NUESTRA SEÑORA DE LAS MERCEDES. (Our Lady of Mercies.) Occupies an area of 12,500 square metres, on stony ground twenty-one metres above the level of the sea, isolated and removed from the turmoil of the city, with which it is connected by a wretched roadway, which the Havana Municipality has not learned to improve. It has provision for more than three hundred patients. The corner-stone was laid in November, 1880, and the institution was opened in an unfinished state February 8th, 1886.

Towards its erection was applied a legacy of $37,000, bequeathed by Joaquín Gómez; another of $160,000, left by Doña Josefa Santa Cruz de Oviedo, and another of $20,000, bequeathed by Salvador Samá; these sums were, however, seriously diminished by municipal mismanagement, and reduced to a total of $186,035. Numberless difficulties had to be overcome in the accomplishment of this work— all of them of an official character—brought about by the opposition of the military authorities, and the delay of the Treasury in handing over the deposit of the legacy of Sra. de Oviedo and of others. Out of these legacies the institution was forced to pay for the removal of the old and delapidated Hospital of *San Juan de Dios*, the materials of which were, indeed, sold at auction for the benefit of the new work, but the proceeds were lost in the inscrutable and mysterious abyss of the Colonial offices. The life of this institution is its Manager, Dr. Emiliano Núñes, who, by constant recourse to public charity, through bazaars, collections and all kinds of entertainments, and with the efficient co-operation of various charitable organizations, has succeeded in keeping it afloat.

No. 64. THE REVEREND FATHER FÉLIX VARELA. Born in Havana, November 20th, 1788. Spent his childhood in Florida, and was ordained in 1811 at the Seminary of San Carlos, Havana, where he succeeded his former teachers, O'Gavan and Caballero, in the Chairs of Philosophy and Theology. He introduced into Cuba the true study of philosophy and founded in the Seminary the first laboratory for experimental physics. From 1812 to 1814 he published in Latin, essays and treatises on logic, metaphysics and ethics, which he afterwards translated into Spanish. In 1817 he published his *Apuntes filosóficos* and also *Miscelánea filosófica*; in 1820, *Lecciones de Filosofía*, an elementary text-book on Physics and Chemistry, and another on Anatomy and Physiology. His panegyric on Charles IV, his eulogy of Ferdinand VII for his protection of Spanish-America, and other like orations, prove his mastery as an orator. He established in the Seminary a Chair of Political Economy, the first in the Spanish dominions, and obtained the professorship of Constitutional Law against the competition of Escobedo, Saco and the Rev. Father Echevarría. In 1821 he was elected a deputy to the Cortes. In Madrid he republished some of his works and colaborated in various journals; in the Cortes he moved for a permanent representation for the provinces of Cuba in the interest of the Island. Voted for the overthrow of Ferdinand VII, and was condemned to death at the restoration; escaped and emigrated to the United States. Founded in Philadelphia the newspaper *El Habanero* (1824). Reprinted some of his works and published new ones, among them (1825) *Ocios de los españoles emigrados* (Idle days of Spanish Emigrants), which was forbidden circulation in Cuba. Entered the priesthood in New York. Colaborated in the *Revista Bimestre;* published a little work in English in defense of the Church; kept up diverse religious polemics, and in 1835 began his famous *Cartas á Elpidio*. Founded a church in 1834. Was elected in 1845 Vicar-General of New York, in which city he was venerated for his earnest piety and infinite charity. In 1849 he removed to St. Augustine (Florida) in quest of health, and died there February 18th, 1853.

No. 65. ESTATUA DE COLÓN. (STATUE OF COLUMBUS). Monument erected in the Plaza de Armas of Cárdenas by the Municipality of that city.

No. 66. GUILLERMO BERNAL. Born November 24th, 1847. Educated in the College of Belén. Graduated in civil law at the University of Havana; began the practice of his profession in 1878; has filled important judicial offices in Cuba; City Attorney of Havana, and Special Commissioner; is at present Judge of the Court of first instance for the Western District, with the rank of Justice of the Court of Oyer and Terminer and Supervisor of the Registry of Deeds. He published in 1880 a work on Criminal Law.

He is one of the Cubans whose efficient exercise of magisterial functions has demonstrated that the natives of the country possess ample abilities for the discharge of such important offices.

No. 67. ANTONIO GOVÍN Y TORRES. Born in Matanzas, September 22d, 1849. Educated in Havana, while maintaining himself and defraying the cost of his education by teaching in prominent colleges. Graduated in law 1872. One of the founders of the Autonomist party in 1878.   Elected Secretary of the Executive Committee in 1879, which office he still holds.   Grand Master of the United Masonic Order of Colon and of the Island of Cuba. First editor of the political newspaper *"El Triunfo,"* now known as *"El Pais."*   Managing Director of the *Revista General de Derecho y Administración.*   Colaborated in other literary and scientific journals.   Has published a Treatise on Administrative Law, in three volumes, a volume of Commentaries on the law of Civil Procedure, various pamphlets and collections of political reviews, and treatises on subjects of jurisprudence, some of which have been awarded prizes by the Law Association of Havana.

Orator, jurisconsult, publicist, a man of affairs, public spirited and energetic, this young man figures among those admirable characters whom John Stuart Mill had in mind in his famous work, *Self-help;* he is unquestionably one of the most admirable representative of Cuban manhood. Prominent among his other services to his people is the famous editorial utterance entitled *Nuestra Doctrina* (Our Doctrine), which, at a critical and perilous juncture, defined the platform of the Autonomist party (1881), and allayed a situation of grave anxiety.

No. 68.   PALACE OF THE MUNICIPALITY AND CAPTAINCY GENERAL.   Erected by the Municipality of Havana and occupied by its offices in part.   The Captain-General, the Governor and the officials of the general government occupy the other and principal portion of the building, although the State makes no recompense to the Municipality for this tenancy.
23

No. 69. NICOLÁS ESCOBÉDO. Born in Havana, September 10th, 1795. Educated in the Seminary and pupil of Varela, whose place he took in the Chair of International Law. Professor of Philosophy and Lecturer on Aristotle in our University. Founder of *El Observador* periodical. Lawyer and notable forensic orator. Went to Spain in 1825, became assistant to the Bishop of Michoacán in the Ministry of Justice and Pardons, and while at that post he lost his eyesight. Laboring under this affliction he continued the practice of his profession in Havana and for fourteen years was the leading spirit of the Cuban bar. In 1836 he was elected Deputy to the Cortes, and served until the Cuban representatives were expelled. Leaving Madrid he settled in Paris, where he died May 11th, 1840, bequeathing to his country $6,000 for the education of poor children.

No. 70. RAFAEL M. DE LABRA. Born in Havana, 1841. He was educated in Madrid and became known at an early age as a lawyer, orator and writer, devoting himself to Antillan interests in general and especially to the cause of the abolition of slavery in the Spanish Antilles; with that historic movement the name of this great Cuban will always remain associated. He is an indefatigable agitator, an orator and parliamentarian of European reputation. An eminent publicist; an enumeration of his writings on judicial, historical, political and literary subjects would be very lengthy. Notwithstanding that these publications number over thirty, his literary activity has not prevented his giving personal supervision to the extensive business of his law-office, nor restrained him from taking an assiduous part in the work of the scientific and commercial associations of which he is an officer or member, and still less withheld him from his onerous duties as a Colonial representative.

In 1870 he delivered in the Athenæum at Madrid a course of lectures on the Political Affairs of the Colonies. He was accorded, in the Central University, a professorship of Colonization which was afterwards suppressed; and in the Normal Institute he holds the chairs of International Law and of Contemporary Political History. From 1871 he has figured in the Cortes as Deputy for Infiesto, Porto Rico, or Havana, or as Senator from the Sociedad Económica of Cuba.

This man of extraordinary capacity has been successful in every field of action, and presents one of the most remarkable contemporary examples of great energy, industry and versatility.

No. 71. EL TEMPLETE. Monument erected in 1828 in the Plaza de Armas to commemorate the site where the first mass was said in Havana.

No. 72. TOMÁS GENER. Born in Barcelona, 1787. Came to Cuba in early youth and settled in Matanzas, where his talents and industry enabled him to gain a considerable fortune; afforded eminent services to the municipality of that city and likewise to Governor Terry in his patriotic enterprises. Promoted public instruction. Was elected Deputy to the Cortes in 1820, and voted for the deposition of Ferdinand VII. At the beginning of the reaction he escaped with Varela and emigrated to the United States. Under the amnesty of 1834 he returned to Cuba and died in Matanzas, August 15th, 1835. This noble Catalonian, a liberal and abolitionist, was a good friend to the country. His son, Benigno Gener, followed in his footsteps, and in Cadiz, whither he emigrated during the revolution of 1868, he acted as a generous protector of his exiled countrymen.

No. 73. FRANCISCO DE ARMAS. Born in Puerto Príncipe in 1804. Educated in the Seminary. Graduated in law with distinction in 1822. Publicist and honorary magistrate. Elected Procurator to the Cortes by his native city in 1836, but did not occupy his seat, the Cuban representatives being refused admission. In 1842 he founded in Madrid the newspaper *El Observador de Ultramar* and wrote for other publications in defense of the interests of his country. Died in August, 1844.

No. 74. NARCISO LÓPEZ. Born in Venezuela, 1798. Entered the Spanish army when very young and fought against the Spanish-American rebels. Distinguished himself in the Peninsula during the War of the Succession. For his valor and gallantry he was made General in 1840. Occupied various official posts in Spain. Came to Cuba in 1841 with General Valdes and discharged important functions. Under O'Donnell's rule he was recalled. Devoted himself to business pursuits, and married a native of Cuba. Took part in seditious undertakings, and in 1849 emigrated to the United States, where he identified himself with the Cuban conspirators in New York. In the same year he undertook his first expedition to the Island, landing at Cárdenas, May 19th, 1850, at the head of 610 men. Took possession of the city, but the people did not respond as he expected, so that he was obliged to retire. His second expedition, composed of 600 men, sailed from New Orleans August 1st, 1851; he unfortunately landed at Las Pazas, Vuelto Abajo, where he was defeated after an heroic defense; was captured through the treachery of a certain Castáneda (who afterwards paid for his villainy with his life at the hands of an unknown patriot in a public café); was taken to Havana and there vilely executed by the garrotte, September 1st of the same year. Fifty of his followers were shot in the fortress of Atarés.

No. 75. Francisco Serrano. Spanish Captain-General; President of the Council of Ministers; Regent of the Kingdom, and Count of San Antonio. Governed in Cuba from 1859 to 1862. He left in the country pleasant memories of his fostering care of public instruction; of the honors accorded by him to the Cuban sage José de la Luz on the occasion of the latter's obsequies. He is remembered for the spirit of tolerance and liberality which he infused into the government of the oppressed Colony, and for the comparative freedom which he allowed to the press and to political manifestations generally. The coincidence of this new policy with the triple intervention in Mexico, the Civil War in the United States, the annexation of Santo Domingo, and other disturbances in this hemisphere, has led many to believe that it was these

international influences that reacted markedly on the destinies of the Antilles.   It was feared that the military
forces of the nation being engaged in outside undertakings, Cuba might rebel, for, as Serrano himself said, "if
the condition of the Cubans be not improved they will
have reason to revolt." This idea was strengthened by
the fact that the policy of Serrano and Dulce was succeeded, after the pacification of the continent, by the deplorable administration of General Lersundi.

No. 76. DOMINGO DULCE. Spanish General, born in
Rioja, May, 1808. Discharged important duties and exercised great political influence. In December, 1862, he
was appointed Governor of Cuba. He energetically repressed the slave traffic; caused the city walls of Havana
to be demolished; established free High Schools and continued the tolerant policy of his predecessor. He left the
country calling himself *un Cubano más* (a more than
Cuban) and published in Madrid a report favoring reforms and abolition. Married in Madrid a Cuban lady,
the Countess of Santovenia. On the outbreak of the Cuban Revolution, the provisional government of Spain again
confided to him the government of Cuba (January, 1869);
he published an appeal for peace and an amnesty; decreed the liberty of the press, excepting in regard to religion and slavery, and proposed political and administrative reforms. His efforts were fruitless, the revolutionists
would not yield, and the Spanish and bureaucratic elements
rebelled against him and defeated his plans, compelling
him to return to Spain in June of the same year, notwith-

standing that he combatted the insurrection with energy, instituted the confiscation of the property of the insurgents, organized the military commissions, and decreed the iniquitous deportation of more than 300 Cubans to Fernando Po.

No. 77. JOSE MORALES LEMUS. Born in Gibara, Cuba, 1808. Educated in the convent of San Francisco, Havana. Graduated in law in Puerto Príncipe, 1833, and practised his profession with great success in Havana. As an abolitionist, he liberated the slaves that he inherited. Took part in the conspiracy of López and later in that of Pintó, and was expatriated in 1855. On his return to Havana, he became one of the supporters of *El Siglo*. Was elected commissioner by the city of Remedios on the Committee of Inquiry in 1865. Feigned illness to avoid presence at the Royal levee of Isabel II, and was the first to decree that the commissioners ought to retire and protest. Returned to Cuba; when the revolution broke out he was prosecuted and his property confiscated; fled to the United States, was made President of the *Junta Cubana*, and did his utmost in Washington to obtain for the revolutionists a recognition of belligerency. Died in New York, June 23d, 1870.

No. 78. NICOLÁS AZCÁRATE. Born in Havana, 1828. He is identified with the city of Güines, having spent his childhood there. Graduated in law at Madrid, 1854, and practised his profession in Havana. Edited the *Revista de Jurisprudencia* (1856), and colaborated in *Piñeyro's Revista del Pueblo* (1865); cultivated and fostered literature, his house having been a gathering point for all the noted literateurs. He published the proceedings of these social gatherings in two volumes, under the title of *Noches Litera-rias*. Was elected by the municipality of Güines as member of the Committee of Inquiry in 1865, and distinguished himself by his eloquence and liberalism; when that Committee dissolved, he established himself in Madrid; founded the newspaper *La Voz del Siglo* and managed *La Constitución*, both journals of democratic tendencies. Returned to Havana in 1875, and, notwithstanding his well-known anti-revolutionary opinions and his anti-slavery views, he was exiled by General Valmaseda. Went to Mexico and edited the *Eco de Ambos Mundos*. He now resides in Havana. Founded and was President of the new Lyceum.

No. 79. CALIXTO BERNAL. Born in Puerto Príncipe, October 14th, 1804. Graduated in law at Havana, 1822, and there practised his profession with success. Went to Europe in 1841, and settled in Madrid, where he published various notable books; *Impresiónes de Viaje, Teoría de la Autoridad,* which latter has been translated into several languages, *El Derecho* and several others, besides a work in French, *La Démocratie au XIX Siècle*. Distinguished himself as journalist. Elected by Puerto Príncipe to the Committee of Inquiry (1865). Twice elected Deputy to the Cortes by the Autonomist party for Santa Clara. Died in Madrid, 1885.

No. 80. RAFAEL FERNÁNDEZ DE CASTRO. Born in Havana, 1856. Lawyer and journalist. Professor of History in the University of Havana. Member of the Executive Committee of the Autonomist party. Provincial Deputy from Jaruco, and Deputy to the Cortes from Las Villas. Author of the famous interpellation on administrative corruption. A forcible orator. Is, at present, Commissioner in Madrid for the *Círculo de Hacendados* (Planters' Association) of the Island of Cuba.

No. 81. BERNARDO PORTUONDO. Born in Santiago de Cuba, 1840. Colonel in the Engineer Corps of the Spanish Army. Professor in the Military Engineers' Academy of Guadalajara. Commissioned by the Government in 1864 to follow the operations of the allies in the war with Denmark, and to report on the various military situations. Returned to Cuba in 1865; superintended several military constructions and devised the plans of the Central Railroad. Fought in the Cuban war as Chief Engineer until 1874, when he returned to Spain. Was elected Deputy to the Cortes in 1879 by the Autonomists of Santiago de Cuba and has been re-elected successively to the present time. He is a notable orator and lecturer, Professor of Mathematics, journalist, and political leader, and has published *Un Tratado de Arquitectura, Estudios sobre organizaciones militares extrangeras*, and other literary works.

No. 82. GABRIEL MILLET. Born in Havana, 1823. Educated in San Fernando and in the Seminary. Graduated in law at Barcelona, 1847, and after extensive travels practised his profession successfully in Havana and Pinar del Rio. Through laborious efforts and industry he

amassed a fortune.   He was imprisoned in 1869 as a dis-
loyal subject and subsequently emigrated to Spain.   He
thence aided the revolutionary movement, was prosecuted
for his political writings, and expelled from the country.
He organized a corporation with a capital of $30,000 for
the publication of *La Tribuna*, a periodical devoted to the
interests of the Antilles, published in Madrid and edited by
Labra.   In 1881 he was elected Deputy to the Cortes by
the Autonomists of Santa Clara; published a political
brochure, *Una Pascua en Madruga*.   Contributed generously
to the erection of the mausoleum of José de la Luz in the
cemetery of Havana.   An indefatigable agitator and steadfast patriot.   Is widely reputed for his generous donations
to the philanthropic institutions of his country.

No. 83. JOSÉ GÜELL Y RENTÉ.   Born in Havana, 1815.
Went to Barcelona in '35 and there graduated in law, 1838.
Married, in Valladolid, the sister of King Francis of Asís.
Conspired against Narváez.   Was deputy to the Constituent Assembly and took part in the September revolution.
Poet, writer and journalist.   Elected Senator in the Cortes
by the University of Havana in 1879.   Organized a project
for erecting a new building for the Havana University,
which was, however not realized; he obtained the necessary
concessions from the State, came to Havana in 1884 to lay
the corner-stone, and if death had not overtaken him in
1886 his patriotism and tenacity of purpose would have
accomplished his object.

No. 84. JOSÉ MARÍA CARBONELL.   Born in Matanzas.
Is a distinguished jurist, Professor in the University of

Havana, and Secretary of the Lyceum. Is at present Dean of the Law Association. Was elected Senator of the Kingdom by the University in 1886; delivered in the Senate a notable speech in favor of autonomy for the Spanish West Indies. He is a member of the Executive Committee of the Cuban Autonomist party.

No. 85. EMILIO TERRY. Born in Cienfuegos and educated in *La Empresa*, Matanzas. Lawyer. Son of the wealthy capitalist, Don Tomás Terry, who figured worthily in the Committee of Inquiry (1865). Fulfilled his father's last wish by erecting the Terry Grand Theater in Cienfuegos, the profits of which are devoted to the support of public schools. Member of the Executive Committee of the Autonomist party. Elected Deputy to the Cortes in 1886, and energetically agitated the sugar question. Is now resident in Paris.

No. 86. JOSÉ R. BETANCOURT. Born in Puerto Príncipe, 1823. Lawyer. Published, 1850, a novel, *La Feria de la Caridad*. President of the Lyceum of Havana (1857). Colaborated in many newspapers. In 1869 he settled in Madrid. Was elected Deputy to the Cortes by Porto Rico in 1873. Author of the political brochure *Las dos Banderas*. Elected Deputy to the Cortes for Puerto Príncipe by the Autonomists (1879). Senator of the Kingdom by the same party, 1886. Published a volume entitled *Prosa de mis Versos*, and another, *Campaña Parlamentaria*. Died in Havana, 1890.

No. 87. ANTONIO ZAMBANA. Born in Havana, 1846. Graduated in law, 1867; colaborated in *El Siglo* and *El Pais*. Professor of Jurisprudence at an early age. Distinguished himself as an orator. Took part in the revolutionary movement from the beginning of 1869. Member and Secretary of the Congress of Guáimaro. Went to New York; published there his *Revolución de Cuba* and delivered lectures. Was commissioned to Mexico and Chile. Figured as diplomatist in Central America. Returned to Havana in 1886 and affiliated himself with the Autonomist party, which elected him Deputy in 1887. His election was not officially sanctioned because he was considered a foreigner. Founded, in Havana, the paper *El Cubano*. Resides in Baracoa, where he practises his profession.

No. 88. MIGUEL FIGUEROA. Born in Cárdenas, 1851. Lawyer. Member of the Executive Committee of the Autonomist party. Elected Deputy to the Cortes by Las Villas in 1886. A brilliant orator. Maintained in common with the other representatives of his party the agitation which finally resulted in the complete abolition of slavery.

No. 89. ALBERTO ORTIZ. Born in Matanzas, 1851. A distinguished lawyer. Elected Deputy to the Cortes by the Autonomist party, of whose Executive Committee he is a member. Labored assiduously for the interests of his country in Madrid. Founded and edited in Havana, where he resides, the political journal *El Acicate*.

No. 90. ELISEO GIBERGA. Born in Matanzas, 1855. Lawyer. Elected Deputy to the Cortes by the Autonomist party; Member of the Executive Committee of the latter. He has distinguished himself in the performance of his duties by his intelligence and industry, and by his unsullied patriotism.

No. 91. JOSÉ BRUZÓN. Born in Havana, 1841. Educated in the College of *El Salvador*. A prominent and noted lawyer, who has a large and important clientelle. He was elected for three consecutive terms as Dean of the Law Association of Havana. He is an able forensic orator, and was the founder of the Liberal Autonomist party, in whose Executive Committee he occupies a conspicuous place, taking an active part in its deliberations and decisions. Elected member of the Havana Councils in 1878, when the Zanjon reforms were introduced. He discharged important commissions as member of that body, made a number of lucid reports, and was the energetic leader of the Autonomist minority. He was the unanimous nominee of the Liberals of Havana for the Presidency of the Councils. His firmness of character, unswerving rectitude and uncommon talents would have accorded him a membership of the Cortes, or other important public posts, had not his excessive modesty led him to refuse all honors. He has, however, occupied a place given only to men of the highest character and patriotism—the Presidency during two biennial terms of the *Sociedad de Amigos del País*.

No. 92. COLLEGE OF SANTO ANGEL. An educational institute founded by Doña Susana Benítez during her life and supported since by her testamentary bequests. It gives room for twenty free scholarships, and furthermore affords primary instruction to a large number of day pupils. Its administration is in charge of the admirable educational section of the Sociedad Económica.

No. 93. José Suárez García. Born in Gijón, 1849. Came to Cuba in childhood. During the revolutionary period he distinguished himself in Güines by his moderation and humanity as captain of a company of volunteers. Founder of the Autonomist Committee of Güines and secretary of the same. Co-operated in establishing the weekly liberal journal *La Unión*, which he afterwards edited. He died in Güines, 1888, and the premature death of this Spanish writer, whose nobility of character was manifested by his disinterested love for Cuba, was mourned by the whole country.

No. 94. Rafael Montoro. Born in Havana, 1852. Educated in the College of *El Salvador*, in the United States and in the College of *San Francisco de Asís*. Went to Madrid in 1867 and became known as a critic and litterateur, and through a course of lectures delivered by him in the Athenæum; was Vice-President of the section of Ethical Science and Political Economy of that institution. Editor of *La Revista Contemporánea* (1877). Colaborated in the *Revista Europea;* published an interesting study on Mary, Queen of Scots. Under-Secretary of the Society of Spanish Authors and Artists under the Presidency of Emilio Castelar. Returned to Cuba 1878;

he figures as one of the founders and pillars of the Autonomist party, of whose Executive Committee he is a most active member; prosecuted an active and vigorous campaign for the organization of that party. Editor of the *Revista Cubana*, *El Triunfo* and *El País*. Vice-Secretary of the *Sociedad Económica*. Lawyer. Elected Deputy to the Cortes by Havana and by Puerto Príncipe in three successive Legislatures, and in that capacity he has energetically maintained the rights of the country. Commissioned by the Sociedad Económica (1890) to report to the Government in Madrid on the financial crisis. The exceptional talent and vast erudition of this publicist have gained for him, notwithstanding his youth, an extended reputation. He is unquestionably one of the most brilliant lights of the Spanish bar.

No. 95. ASILO DE MENDIGOS (CHARITY ASYLUM). One of the departments of the Maternity and Charity Hospital, supported, like the others, from the general fund of the institution, which is wholly derived from private endowments and donations. It receives no aid from the State. Through the efforts of Don Tomás Reina, a former President of the institution, a bazaar was organized for the purpose of raising money for the asylum, but the large sum that was thus realized was arbitrarily appropriated by General Concha and eventually became lost. Through subsequent fairs and similar undertakings, and with the aid of private benefactions, the building was finished and opened to its beneficiaries in 1884. Far from lending the institution any aid, the Government has put

endless difficulties in its way. Its present Director, Don
Cornelio Coppinger, one of the learned and industrious
Cubans who reflect honor on their country, has succeeded
after a hard struggle in emancipating the institution from
the crushing weight of official tutelage. The municipality
of Havana, inspired by Don Ramón de Armas, is seeking
to gain control of this institution under the pretext that the
private donations which support it are municipal in character. Should this ingenious scheme succeed, it would do
away with the only almshouse in the country, and the
institution would share the fate of everything of the kind
under bureaucratic financeering.

No. 96. GERTRUDIS GÓMEZ DE AVELLANEDA.—Born
in Puerto Príncipe, March 23d, 1814. A poetess from her
childhood. Went to Spain in 1836, and soon became
known in Seville, Cadiz, and in the Lyceum of Madrid
through her lyrics, dramas and novels. Published a volume
of poems (1841); the novels *Dos Mujeres*, *Espatolino*, *Gu-
atimozin*, *La Baronesa de Joux*, and various biographies and
essays. *Alfonso Munio*, a tragedy, was acted with great
success (1844); *Saúl*, which has been translated into three
languages, *El Príncipe de Viana*, *Egilona*, *Catilina* and
others ; and last of all, *Baltasar*, her masterpiece, which
crowned her reputation and which confirms the opinion of
the eminent critics who regarded her as among the foremost
of the Spanish poets. In 1860 she was laurelled in the
Lyceum of Havana, where she was triumphantly received.
She founded here the periodical, *El Album;* published
various novels and other literary works. Died in Madrid

February 2d, 1873. Her genius has greatly contributed to enhance the standard of Spanish literature.

No. 97. THE TERRY THEATRE. A grand auditorium erected in Cienfuegos by the wealthy banker, Don Tomás Terry, and endowed by his sons and relatives. The net income is devoted to the support of common and industrial public schools.

No. 98. JOSÉ M. ZAYAS. Born in Sabanillas, Matanzas. Educated in the College of *San Cristóbal.* Graduated in law, 1846. Vice-President of the College of *El Salvador* under Luz Caballero, and on the death of the latter, succeeded as President. Author of a Spanish grammar. Colaborated in *El Siglo, El Triunfo* and *El País.* Translated the story of Blue Beard from the French of Eugene Sue. Published, in 1869, the political tractate *Cuba, su Porvenir.* Member of the Executive Committee of the Autonomist party. Died in 1888. Was a man of extensive learning, firm character and unswerving rectitude.

No. 99. RAMÓN ZAMBRANA. Born in Havana, 1817. Was the first graduate in medicine and surgery in our university (1846). Professor in the same and in the seminary. Made important original researches. Discharged many scientific commissions and offices. Inspector of the Institute of Chemistry and of the Botanical Garden. Contributed scientific and philosophical articles to all the principal publications of the Academy of Sciences, of which he was one one of the founders; also aided in the establish-

24

ment of the *Gaceta Médica, Prontuario Médico Quirúrgico,
El Kaleidoscopio* and other notable publications. Published a volume, *Soliloquios,* 1865. Died in 1866. His body was laid in state in the Hall of the University.

No. 100. TRISTÁN MEDINA. Born in Bayamo, 1833. Travelled through the United States and Europe. Was ordained to the priesthood, in 1845, at the Seminary of San Basilio the Greater, where he became professor. Acquired reputation in Havana and in the Peninsula as a writer and ecclesiastic. Was selected by the Spanish Academy to deliver the oration on the anniversary of Cervantes' death in the Church of the *Trinitarios,* Madrid ; his deliverance gaining for him a leading place as a pulpit orator. A poet, novelist, and profound thinker ; he fell away from Catholicism and became a Protestant minister. He died in Madrid.

No. 101. MIGUEL D. SANTOS. Born in New Orleans, 1843, of Cuban parents and brought to Cuba the following year. Was educated in the College of Carraguao and graduated in philosophy. Abandoned the pursuit of law for that of theology. Received holy orders in the Seminary of San Carlos in 1869. Soon distinguished himself as a facile and clear-minded speaker. In 1876 he was deported, together with Arteaga and Fuentes, clergymen who had greatly elevated the pulpit. Was elected in 1888 to the rectorship in Santiago de las Vegas, where he resides. Is beloved by his parishioners for his gentleness, culture, and active charity ; he donates considerable sums yearly to reward the pupils of the charity schools, which he frequently visits and inspects.

No. 102. JUAN VILARÓ Y DÍAZ. Born in Havana, 1838. Graduated in natural sciences and in medicine at the University of Havana. Favorite pupil of the learned naturalist, Felipe Poey. Member of numerous scientific associations at home and abroad. Professor in the University of Havana. Emigrated during the revolutionary period, and acquired reputation abroad through various scientific labors.

Dr. Vilaró's researches and writings, particularly as member of the Fisheries Commission, have gained for him a recognized place as an accomplished naturalist. His specialty is Pisciculture. Although still young he is rich in knowledge and enthusiasm, and with a persevering patriotism he follows in the footsteps of his great master Poey. He is universally popular.

No. 103. LUISA PÉREZ. Born in Cobre (Santiago de Cuba), 1837. Educated herself in the country with the aid of a few books. Became known as a poetess through the newspaper press of Santiago and Havana. Married Ramón Zambrana in 1858. As a poetess she is second only to Avellaneda in merit and in popularity. Published two volumes, 1856 and 1860. Translated several works. Published a treatise, *Educación y Urbanidad*. She ceased writing after the death of her husband. Resides in Havana and devotes her time to the duties of the humble home, which she embellishes with her virtues.

No. 104. AURELIA CASTILLO DE GONZÁLEZ. Born in Puerte Príncipe. Colaborated in the newspapers of that city. Her poems are highly praised by the critics. Has published a narrative of her travels in Europe, chiefly descriptive of the Paris Exposition, highly instructive and written in a charming style.

No. 105. FRANCISCO CAMPS. (Read note on page 265). Has recently published an octavo volume of 400 pages, entitled *Españoles é Insurrectos.*

No. 106. SUSANA BENÍTEZ. Born in Havana. Founded and supported during life the free school of *El Santo Angel;* at her death she endowed the institution with means sufficient to maintain it, placing it in charge of the Society *Amigos del País.*

No. 107. A GROUP OF PALMS. The most beautiful tree of the tropic zone. Its beauty, however, does not exceed its usefulness, both its fruit and its material being applied to many rustic needs.

EDITOR'S SUPPLEMENT.

GENERAL DESCRIPTIVE AND HISTORICAL REVIEW OF THE ISLAND OF CUBA.

EDITOR'S SUPPLEMENT.

Note.—The general condition of Cuban affairs, as it presented itself in its latest political and social developments up to the outbreak of the present insurrection, has been clearly and fully demonstrated by Señor Cabrera in the preceding pages. As already noted, his work proceeded on lines laid out for him by another writer, whose misrepresentations he has taken occasion to correct. These limitations excluded a detailed consideration of the geography and history of Cuba, which to English readers, unfamiliar with the subject, is necessary for its fuller comprehension, and the following has accordingly been added by the editor.

GENERAL DESCRIPTIVE AND HISTORICAL REVIEW OF THE ISLAND OF CUBA.

Cuba, "the Pearl of the Antilles"[1] as it is called by Spanish writers, the "pearl in the mire" as it is termed by Cuban authors, "the most beautiful land that eyes ever

---

[1] The term Antilles is doubtless derived from Antilla, the name of the unknown island in the Western Sea which Aristotle mentions as having once been visited by the Carthegenians, and which, in the uncertainty of geographic knowledge during the Middle Ages, became confused with the mythical island of Atlantis, referred to by Strabo and Plato. Martin Behaim, the noted German cosmographer, who constructed a globe at his home in Nuremberg in 1492, after his return from his explorations for the Portugese Government, marks the island "Antilia" as situated in the Atlantic Ocean on the Tropic of Cancer, midway between the coast of Africa and the great island of "Cipango" or Japan. on the coast of Asia. The appellation as referring to the discoveries of Columbus was first used by the historian Pietro Martire d'Anghiera in 1493. It was soon thereafter applied to the island of Haiti by Amerigo Vespucci in his writings, and subsequently was made to include the entire West Indian archipelago.

beheld" as it was described by Columbus, is an island lying
between the Gulf of Mexico and the Atlantic, extending
from 74° to 85° of west longitude and 19° 50′ to 23° 10′ of
north latitude. It is the largest of the West Indian Islands,
and presents the form of a long, rather irregular crescent,
with its inner curvature to the south. Its greatest length is
760 miles, its greatest width 135 miles, while the average
breadth is 80 miles. Its total area is 43,300 square
miles, exclusive of the surrounding smaller islands. At
its northernmost convexity its coast at Cape Yeacos is but
130 miles from Cape Sable in Florida; its western extremity,
Cape Antonio, is less than that distance from Cape Catoche
in Yucatan, while on the east the still narrower Windward
Passage separates it from the neighboring Island of Haiti.
The coast of Cuba, almost uniformly low and flat, is in-
dented with numerous bays and estuaries, many of which
afford most excellent harbors. The coast is guarded
throughout almost its entire extent by an outlaying chain
of coral reefs, many of which expand into islands of considerable size, and which make the approach to the coast and
its harbors a matter requiring accurate pilotage. Of the
habors, the most important on the north coast are Bahia-
honda, Cabañas, Mariel, Havana, Matánzas, Cárdenas,
Sagua la Grande, Caibarien, Nuevitas, Manati, Puerto
Padre, Gibara, Banes, Nipe, Levisa, Tánamo, and Baracoa,
and on the south Guantánamo, Santiago de Cuba, Manzanillo, Casilda, Trinidad, and Cienfuegos. Of these, the last
named is famous as one of the most magnificent harbors in
the world, containing upwards of fifty square miles of land-
locked water. The northern coast is studded along the

middle of its length with some 570 islands and keys, while the southern coast is dotted along the greater part of its extent with 730 islands, of which the largest is the Isle of Pines (Isla de Pinos), whose area is 1214 square miles.

The surface of the island is traversed in the middle, throughout practically its entire length, by a mountain range which, running from the western end of the island, gradually increases in altitude and extent as it approaches the eastern end. At its western extremity it forms the peak Guajaibon, which attains a height of over 2500 feet; further east, near the middle of the southern coast, just back of the harbor of Trinidad, the summit of Potrerillo is 3000 feet above the sea; still further east the peaks of Yunque and Ajo del Torro rise to a height of 3500 feet, that of Gran Piedra to 5200 feet, and finally in the Cobre Mountains on the southeastern coast the peak of Tarquino rises to nearly 8000 feet, the highest point on the island. The central and western parts of the island consist geologically of two ridges of limestone, one of sandstone, and a smaller one of gypsum. In the limestone formations are found, as usual, numerous caves, some of them of considerable extent. Eastward of the central section the higher mountain ranges show a main formation of limestone with secondary formations of syenitic and serpentine strata, from the latter of which petroleum oozes in many places and gathers into pools in the rocky district toward the eastern extremity of the island.

The fluvial system of the island necessarily consists of streams of inconsiderable length, flowing down the northern and southern watersheds from the mountain range to the sea. But few of the rivers are navigable for any consider-able length, and of these the largest is the Rio Cauto, which flows from the Copper Mountains (Cobre) westerly through the valley of Bayamo into the bay of Buena Esperanza. It is navigable for a length of sixty miles. Next in size are the Sagua la Grande and Sagua la Chica, which empty into the Atlantic on the northern coast, the former being navi-gable for fifteen miles, the latter for a shorter distance. Smaller than these and scarcely navigable at all are the North and South Iatibonica, the Cuyaguateje, the Sasa, and several others. In a huge cavern in the hill of Moa, northeast of Guantanamo, the river Moa forms a magnifi-cent cascade, descending for nearly 300 feet. Throughout the island the fertile valleys between the uplands are drained by a close network of streamlets, which, as they approach the coast, spread into swamps and marshes, some of which, like the Cienaga de Zapata on the southern coast, southeast from Havana, have much the character of the Florida Everglades.

The climate of this mountainous island is, in general, agreeable and salubrious. Situated as it is, just under the line of the northern tropic, the four seasons of the temperate zone are merged into the two which characterize a tropical climate, the wet and the dry season. The former, occurring when the sun is north of the equator, is the hot season, which lasts from April to October, while the cooler dry season takes the place of the autumn, winter and early spring of the more northern latitudes, when the sun is south of the equator.

The temperature on the lowlands along the sea ranges

throughout the year between a minimum of about 60°
and a maximum of 90°. The average temperature of the
year at Havana, which lies on the outer curve of the
island on the north, is 77°. At Santiago, near the south-
ernmost point of Cuba, it is 80½°. The average temperature in July and August at Havana is 82°, at Santiago
85.4°; in January and December the average at Havana
is 72°, at Santiago 74.2°. All along the coast the heat
of the summer is tempered by the sea breeze, which makes
itself felt from noonday to the evening. Away from
the coast, on the uplands of the interior, the climate is at
once more temperate and bracing. The yellow fever,
which during the hot season affects the seaports of the
islands, more, indeed, because of lack of proper sanitation
than for any other reason, is wholly unknown in the interior. There the temperature, in the cooler months of the
year, falls to the freezing point and the winter is charater-
ized by cool north winds which are more especially marked
in the northern and western sections of the island. The
storms which sweep northward from the tropic zone of the
Atlantic, especially at the equinoctial seasons, center east-
wardly of Cuba, and the hurricanes, which so frequently
whirl over the Lesser Antilles and which are so dreaded on
the islands of the Bahama group, are but rarely felt on the
Cuban coasts. These atmospheric disturbances are checked
and their severity tempered by the influence of the continuous mountain chain that traverses the length of the
island and which, in its wider part, splits into separate
ranges in proximity to the coast. Though of recent geo-
logic origin, the island is free from volcanic disturbances.

Earthquakes, which are of frequent occurrence on the volcanic islands of the Lesser Antilles, are comparatively rare
in Cuba and have been recorded only as slight disturbances along the southern coast.

The mineral resources of Cuba have attracted attention
from the time of its discovery, but remain, as yet, only
slightly developed. Alluvial gold deposits in the rivers
Holguin, Escambray, Sagua la Grande, Agabama and
others have been known for centuries, but have never been
worked successfully, though it is probable that with recent
improvements in amalgamating appliances these workings
could be made profitable. Silver ore has also been found,
which, with modern machinery for its reduction, would well
repay for its mining. In the Sierra Cobre (Copper Mountains), on the eastern coast of the island, are extensive lodes
of copper ore, some of it very rich in metal, and a flourishing
mining and smelting industry is carried on in that section,
of which the city of Santiago de Cuba is the centre.
Valuable deposits of a high grade iron ore are found in
various parts of the island, and are being mined successfully. Bituminous coal of excellent quality is also found
in extensive layers, and asphaltum beds and petroleum are
found in the districts between the base of the eastern mountains and the coast. Gypsum, slate, jasper, and marble quar-
ries have been opened at various points on the island, some
of the products proving of extraordinary value and utility.

Excepting where the rock foundation of the mountain
ridges breaks out in the lower levels, the soil of the island
has all of a tropical fertility. Only a fraction of the arable
surface is under cultivation and vast stretches of land are

covered with primeval forests. The dominant growth throughout the island, but especially in its western half, is the royal palm (*Oreodoxa regia*), which is at once the typical, most majestic, and most valuable tree of Cuba. Besides this, the growth consists principally of cedar, mahogany, ebony, and other hard-wood trees, several of which, like the granadilla and sabicci, are peculiar to the island. The forests are thickened with an exuberant undergrowth of tropical plants, which makes it almost impossible to penetrate them except by hewing the way. Tropical fruits flourish in abundance. Besides the orange, lemon, pineapple, and banana, and especially the plantain, there are the sweet and bitter cassava, the former an edible fruit, and the latter, after preparation, baked into a kind of a bread. Coffee, cocoa, and chocolate are also grown ; rice is easily cultivated and indian corn is native to the soil. Cotton has also been planted with success, but the chief agricultural products of the island are sugar and tobacco, which have thus far been the main sources of its wealth, the export of coffee having almost ceased under the competition of the products of Brazil and Java. The sugar, tobacco, and herding industries, forming the main factors in the present economic and political conditions of Cuba, have been fully treated by Señor Cabrera in the course of his work, and there remains only a brief résumé of the general history of the island to be added for the information of the reader.

———

On October 28th, 1492, sixteen days after Columbus had made his first land-fall on the island which he named

St. Salvador, he set foot on what is now known as Cuba. The natives wore gold ornaments, which so greatly excited the interest of the Spanish sailors that the natives were led to interpret the questions, put to them by Columbus, as having reference to gold, and they gave him to understand that it had been gotten from "Cubanacan," in the interior. Columbus named the country Juana, after Prince Juan, the son of Ferdinand and Isabella. After the King's death, Diego Velasquez, who had accompanied Columbus on his second voyage, renamed the island in his honor, Fernandina. Subsequently it was called Santiago, after the patron saint of Spain, but this was again changed to Ave Maria, in honor of the Virgin. The confusion of these various appellations naturally resulted in none of them being retained. "Cubanacan" was well remembered; it was the "place of Cuba" where the gold was found, and thus that native name became generally accepted for the entire country.

The island was twice visited by Columbus after its discovery, in 1494 and in 1502. He appears to have always regarded it as a part of the mainland, as he believed, of Asia, and it was not until 1508 that it was proved to be an island. In 1511 Columbus' son Diego undertook to colonize it and sent out Velasquez with some 300 men for that purpose. They settled at Baracoa, and in 1514 they planted communities at Santiago and at Trinidad. In the following year a settlement called San Cristobal de la Habana was located at what is now known as Batabano, but in 1519 these settlers removed their town and its name to a more inviting spot just across the island on the northern coast, and there the settlement soon grew into importance.

These immigrants found the natives peaceable, happy and contented, spread over the island under the government of nine independent chiefs. They were well on beyond a condition of savagery, cultivated the soil and led a settled life, and appear to have had ideas of an invisible and beneficent Supreme Being, and a religion without a priesthood or ceremonial rites. They were quickly subjugated by Velasquez, who, however, treated them humanely, as did also his immediate successors. Negro slaves were imported to work in the fields and the natives were left unmolested. In 1538 a French privateer attacked Havana and set fire to the town, and it was thereupon determined to guard against a repetition of such a disaster by erecting defences. Hernando de Soto, who, as an impecunious adventurer, had followed Pizarro to Peru and had returned enriched with the plunder of that unfortunate country, was commissioned by the Emperor Charles V as governor of Cuba and Florida. He was to build a fortress at Havana, and began the erection of the Castillo de la Fuerza, which was finished under De Soto's lieutenants, while he was searching for the El Dorado supposed to exist in Florida and finding in its stead a watery grave in the Mississippi. Under these lieutenants and their successors the Cuban natives were enslaved and notwithstanding that like all the American aborigines they could not live in slavery and rapidly pined to death, the fatal policy was persisted in with the result that in a few generations the semi-civilized aborigines were practically extinct, and only remnants of the more barbarous mountain tribes remained. In 1551 the residence of the governor was transferred from Santiago to

Havana and the latter rapidly gained in importance. In 1554 Havana was again attacked by the French, and partially destroyed, and in the following year it was plundered by pirates. But the commanding situation of Havana and its exceptionally fine harbor overcame all obstacles to its progress, and the fertility of the soil attracted increasing numbers of immigrants. The colonists devoted themselves to cultivating sugar and tobacco in addition to that first resource of new settlers, the raising of cattle. Negro slavery became an important element of the colonial organization, and together with its superficial economic advantages the system duly developed all the deep-seated evils inevitably resulting from it. The colony became more and more an object of attack by the enemies of Spain in the course of the successive wars that marked the reigns of Charles I (Emperor Charles V) and his son Philip II. Havana having been seriously menaced by the English under Drake in 1585, it was determined to protect the port with additional defences. Two fortresses, the Bateria de la Punta and the castle of the Morro were accordingly begun in 1589 and completed in 1597, and these defences served their purposes until the development of naval armament rendered them inadequate. Havana became the commercial center of the Spanish-American dominions and the calling place of the Spanish treasure-ships bearing silver from Mexico and gold from Honduras. The expulsion of the Moriscoes from Spain by Philip III in 1609, a complement of the equally idiotic crime against the Jews in 1492, brought about, among other results, the practical extinction of the sugar and tobacco culture in Spain and its correspondingly increased development in Cuba. But the wars in which Spain was almost incessantly involved throughout the seventeenth century reacted severely on the prosperity of Cuba and greatly hindered its progress. The maritime power of Spain, which had been shattered by the destruction of the Armada in 1588, had declined to the lowest point during the Thirty Years' War, and after the capture of the Spanish treasure fleet with its three million dollars by the Dutch in 1628, and the subsequent destruction of the Spanish naval fleet in the Downs, the West Indian waters were left almost bare of protection. The Spanish government under Philip IV and Charles II, while unable to properly protect its colonial commerce under the Spanish flag, made it illegal to trade under any other, and furthermore hampered the colonists by restricting their legitimate commerce with the home country to the port of Seville and selling the monopoly of that. The natural result of these trade restrictions was the rapid growth of an extensive smuggling trade between the colonists and all sorts of foreign maritime adventurers. At first the latter found it convenient to make their headquarters in the bays of the neighboring island of Hispaniola (St. Domingo), which, through the repressive measures of its governors and by reason of the greater attraction of Cuba, had gradually been abandoned by its settlers. The few people remaining lived mainly from the herds of cattle which had multiplied and roamed wild over the island; they prepared the meat of these animals by a peculiar process of smoking called "bucanning," from the smoke-houses which were called "bucans," and the smugglers, adopting this method of preserving

25

meat for their ships, came to be known as "Buccaneers."
From being merely smugglers, in constant conflict with the
Spanish officials on land and water, they soon grew to
be a powerful body of freebooters who preyed mainly on
Spanish commerce. They gradually attained to the position of a hireling navy, and aided the French at Tortuga
in 1641 and 1660, and the English in the occupation of
Jamaica by Cromwell's fleet in 1665. Recruited from
the Dutch, French and English privateers, they became
the terror of the Spanish colonies; the town of New
Segovia in Honduras was sacked by them in 1654, and
shortly thereafter the towns of Maracaibo and Gibraltar in
the Gulf of Venezuela were plundered and several boat's
crews of Spanish sailors put to death by them. After the
taking of Jamaica by the English the Buccaneers threatened even Havana, and this, together with the increasing
danger of invasion by the English and Dutch, led to the
erection of a defensive wall across the projecting neck of
land on which Havana is laid out. This was begun in
1665 and completed in 1670. The depredations of the
Buccaneers continued until long after the treaty of 1670
between Spain and England proclaimed peace in the West
Indian colonies, and began to decline only when the war of
1689 between France and England caused antagonism between the English and French Buccaneers. Towards the
end of the century, with the partial abatement of these freebooters, the Cuban settlements revived materially, and after
the treaty of Ryswick in 1697 set the seal of general condemnation on the Buccaneers, the colony grew rapidly in
importance,

The eighteenth century opened with the War of the Spanish Succession, but the complicated relations of the conflicting powers left Cuba comparatively free from the strife. The treaty of Utrecht in 1713, by which the Hapsburg rule in Spain was finally ended and the succession of the Bourbon dynasty established under Philip V, opened a new era in Spain and incidentally in Cuba as well. By this time a considerable number of settlements had been successfully planted in the interior of the island and the agricultural wealth of Cuba began to make a large showing by the side of the bullion products of the other Spanish-American colonies. Up to this period Cuba's contribution to the Spanish exchequer was obtained mainly through commercial monopolies centered in Seville or Cadiz. In 1717 a new policy was adopted ; the tobacco trade was made a royal monopoly and out of that measure grew the first serious clashing between the colonists and the mother country. The enforcement of the monopoly was violently resisted and a number of sanguinary collisions between the people and the military took place. This monopoly, together with the restrictions imposed on foreign trade with the Spanish colonies, again gave rise to systematic smuggling, mainly by British traders in Jamaica. The constant friction and frequent bloody encounters thus engendered brought on another Anglo-Spanish war in 1739, which afterwards (1741) merged into the general European war that ended in 1748. In the thirteen years of peace that followed, the smuggling trade with Cuba grew so completely out of control that the tobacco monopoly was given up and a system of farming out its revenues to private monopolists was undertaken in its stead. But this only resulted in further trouble. The extension of the English colonies and the growth of British commercial influence in America constantly excited the jealousy of France and Spain, and after the accession of Charles III the third "Family Compact" was made in 1759 between the two Bourbon houses to put a check on this expansion. War began in 1762, and in June of that year Havana was taken by an English fleet consisting of 44 men-of-war and about 150 other vessels under Admiral Pocock, carrying an army of some 15,000 men under Lord Albemarle. The Spanish garrison numbered 27,000 men under Governor Porto-Carrero. The siege began June 3d, and after a stubborn resistance Morro Castle surrendered on July 30th, and the city on August 13th. An enormous booty fell into the hands of the English, the prize money divided among them amounting to over three and a half millions of dollars. The English held the city and surrounding districts until early in the following year, when, in accordance with the treaty of Paris (February 1763), Spain regained possession of the colony in return for the cession of Florida to England. During their occupation of Havana the English opened the port to free commerce, and their brief stay proved to be of permanent importance, inasmuch as the Spanish government found it practically impossible to re-establish the old restrictions. In 1765 the commerce of the island with the home country was freed from its former limitations and the colony rapidly advanced in its development. In 1777 Cuba was given an independent colonial administration under a captain-general. At this time England was fighting to prevent the independence of its American colonies and the two Bourbon monarchies availed themselves of the opportunity to get even with their enemy. In 1778 France joined the colonists in their war against the British and in the following year Spain took a hand in her own behalf, recaptured the island of Minorca, laid siege to Gibraltar, and drove the English from a number of the smaller West India Islands, which they had occupied. The northern powers of Europe, all jealous of England's maritime supremacy, assumed an armed neutrality, in readiness to join in the fray when there was anything to be gained by it, and this, together with England's Irish troubles, hastened the treaty of Versailles, whereby Spain, besides retaining Minorca, regained Florida from England. After the establishment of American independence the ports of Havana and Santiago were opened to free commerce with foreign nations, excepting a few minor productions and the slave trade. Havana became the center of this iniquitous but lucrative traffic, and by the end of the century had grown to be the most important city in America.

In 1790 Luis de las Casas was made Captain-General. He furthered the commerce of Havana by removing the restrictions on the slave trade, promoted the agricultural development of the entire island by introducing the culture of indigo and other foreign products, inaugurated a series of important public works and labored earnestly to effect the emancipation of the enslaved remnant of the native Indians. He succeeded in maintaining the tranquility of the negro population of Cuba under the trying conditions brought about by the Revolution in St. Domingo, and aided the immigration of French Royalists from that island.

The administration of Las Casas marks a Renaissance period in Cuban history. The material growth of the colony now began to manifest itself in a degree of individuality and to be reflected in its intellectual life. Semi-political associations under the name of *Sociedades Económicas de Amigos del País* were formed for the advancement of culture, and these organizations continued thereafter to exert an important influence on the current of Cuban affairs. The establishment of the American Union gave an impulse to progress in the neighboring Spanish colony, and Las Casas, in earnest co-operation with the leading men of the community, gave effect to the general liberalizing tendency. His administration ended in December 1796, and its close was signalized by the transfer of the remains of Columbus from San Domingo to Havana, where they were interred in the Cathedral.

Las Casas was succeeded by the Count of Santa Clara, who exerted himself energetically to place the various towns of the island in a condition of defense against the constantly threatened attacks of the English fleet. He strengthened the fortifications of Havana by a fosse and covered way within the city and by a battery outside the town, the latter named after him the redoubt of Santa Clara. He did much to further the material interests of the colony, opening the ports of the island to free entry by neutrals during the blockade of the Spanish ports, and was otherwise active in promoting its development. He resigned in May 1799, and was succeeded by the Marquis of Someruelos.

The rehabilitation of Spain during the 18th century, after its deep depression under the Hapsburg rule, had proceeded largely under the influence of the French alliance. But the "Family Compact" was broken by the Revolution; the Sans-Culottes did away with Louis XVI, the Republic replaced the Monarchy and ended for a generation the support of Bourbon Spain by Bourbon France. The Spanish armies of the first coalition that sought to re-establish the French monarchy suffered overwhelming defeat, and by the treaty of Basel in 1794 Spain gave up to France her remaining share of San Domingo and became a servant of the Republic. Liberal reforms in church and state, otherwise undreamed of in Spanish policy, were forced on Charles IV and his ministers by the Directory, and these reforms were introduced into Cuba and became emphasized in their western environment. In 1796, by the treaty of San Ildefonso, Spain was forced into a new alliance with France, but this time to the advantage of the latter exclusively. Dragged into a war with England, the Spanish naval power was broken at the battle of Cape St. Vincent (1797), communication with the colonies almost completely broken off, and for a number of years Cuba was left practically to its own devices.

The opening of the 19th century found Spain prostrate at the feet of Napoleon. Its Bourbon government was left in place by the First Consul, but he used it as a cat's paw for the furtherance of French interests. So completely was Spain dominated by France that it was coerced in 1800 into giving up its remaining possessions in "Louisiana," to be afterwards marketed by Napoleon to the United States for sixty million francs. The Spanish government had no alternative but to leave the colonies to defend themselves against the British fleets as best they could. Porto Rico was attacked, Cuba threatened, and Trinidad was taken by the English, and only the failure of the British attack on Porto Rico and the increased defenses of the Cuban seaports saved the island from the invasion which the English were planning to undertake when the treaty of Amiens, 1802, put an end to the war. In this same year a serious calamity befell Havana in the destruction by fire of the suburb Jesu Maria, whereby some 12,000 people were rendered homeless, and the resources of the capital largely effected by the loss. During the barely three years of peace that followed the treaty of Amiens, Cuban commerce with the home country was resuscitated, and the colony replenished the Peninsular treasury with the taxes which had remained uncollected during the preceding war. At the same time the slave population of the island was rapidly augmented by large importations of African negroes, the increased difficulties attending the slave trade during the preceding wars being for the time removed. Meantime a bitter contest was going on between the French and the negroes in the neighboring island of San Domingo, the rancor of this race war becoming intensified by the treacherous deportation of the leader of the blacks, Toussaint L'Overture, to Paris, where he died in prison. In 1803 the British came to the aid of the Dominicans, the remnant of the French army surrendered, and the blacks organized themselves into a Republic. These developments caused a ferment of excitement among the negro population of Cuba, and only the prudent measures and liberal policy which had been originated by Las Casas and continued by his successors prevented serious disturbances from taking

CUBA AND THE CUBANS. 393

place. This tranquility was, however, maintained with difficulty, and subsequently gave way to frequent bloody risings.

Towards the end of 1804 Spain was again dragooned by Napoleon into his war with England, and in the following year saw the remnant of its naval forces swept away at Finestere and Trafalgar, and one of its South American colonies, Buenos Ayres, seized by the English. Cuba was again threatened by an English fleet, commerce was much restricted, various minor ports on the island were plundered by freebooters; but while the material growth of the colony was thus in a measure arrested on the one hand, other developments of the course of events tended greatly towards its advancement. The cession of San Domingo, the French occupation of that island and the race war which followed, benefited Cuba through the large immigration of the white settlers who were driven out of San Domingo. The number of these who took refuge in Cuba during the decade ending with 1808 has been calculated at fully thirty thousand; they settled mainly in the eastern districts of the island and contributed greatly to the development of that section. These immigrants introduced the culture of the coffee plant, which rapidly grew into an important industry and soon became a large element of the colonial commerce. The cession of Louisiana had a like effect on a smaller scale, several thousands of Spanish settlers in that territory emigrating to Cuba after Spain relinquished its possession.

Napoleon having conquered peace and quieted the continental powers by the treaty of Tilsit (1807), now turned to carry out his long planned purpose of absorbing the Spanish monarchy, incidentally that of Portugal, and crip-

pling England by barring out its commerce from Europe
and the Peninsular colonies in America. The Spanish
king, Charles IV, was utterly incompetent; the government
was utterly disorganized; the queen carried on a demoralizing intrigue with the prime minister, Godoy, her creature,
who was utterly corrupt; the crown prince was intriguing
to supplant the king, and all turned to Paris to further their
individual ends. Godoy made a treaty with Napoleon for
the avowed purpose of partitioning Portugal, and quickly a
French army crossed Spain and occupied that kingdom.
The crown prince made a bid for Napoleon's support, his
scheme was discovered, he was put under arrest, and Napoleon availed himself of the occasion to send an army to support the prince. The king and his ministers prepared to
flee; Madrid rose against the government, and the king was
forced to abdicate in favor of his son. This step, however,
was premature for Napoleon; his army under Murat occupied Madrid (March 1808), the king was induced to retract
his abdication; the crown prince was forced to step aside
and the king was then coerced into abdicating without a
successor. Napoleon now put his brother Joseph on the
Spanish throne and his larger policy was then revealed.

The Spanish people, who, through the rising in Madrid,
had obtained the abdication of Charles IV in favor of his
son Ferdinand, saw themselves cheated and humiliated by
the French Emperor. The country, thrown into confusion
by the storm of events, now became wrought into a frenzy
of passion against the French invaders; the populace rose
on every side; a provisional government was organized at
Madrid in the name of Ferdinand VII; this was soon driven

to take refuge in Seville, and then began the struggle against the French autocrat which marked the beginning of his downfall.

In the new condition of affairs England turned from being an enemy of Spain to becoming its ally and protector. An English army under Wellington in Portugal became the nucleus of resistance against the French, and eventually, after a bloody and protracted struggle, the independence of the country was preserved. In place of English fleets threatening the Cuban coasts, English ships now aided in extending the commerce of the colony, and thus an influence that had long opposed the development of Cuba became a factor of its progress.

When the news of the detention of Ferdinand VII in captivity by Napoleon was officially brought to Havana in July 1808, the colonists, without distinction of party, refused to recognize the government of Joseph Bonaparte, and determined to maintain the island under the sovereignty of the deposed king and to support the Captain-General, Somerue-los, in defending it against the usurper. The Spanish provisional government of the Junta of Seville was recognized as representing the royal authority, and war was declared against Napoleon. The divisions and distinctions between the Cubans and Peninsulars, which at various periods, especially before the administration of Las Casas, had become more or less manifest, were lost sight of at this time, and the colonists strove by every means, through contributions of men, material, and money, to aid their struggling countrymen in the Peninsula.

The Junta of Seville proclaimed equal rights for all

Spaniards, both at home and in the colonies, and the expectations of the latter, of obtaining the benefits of the freedom which they saw so effectively exemplified in the new confederation of the United States, were raised to the highest pitch. But, unfortunately, the majority of the thirty-four members of the Junta represented commercial interests which were too closely identified with colonial monopolies to permit of a just consideration being given to colonial rights, and the hopes of the Spanish-American colonies were sorely disappointed. In Cuba, the crisis was passed by the authorities assuming the responsibility of modifying the orders of the home government and of freeing the colony from the restrictions put upon its commerce under foreign flags. But the result on the continent was that the standard of rebellion was raised in Buenos Ayres in 1809, carried northward to Peru the same year, taken up by Bolivar in Venezuela in 1810, and thus began a war of independence which eventually, after twelve years of spasmodic resistance by the Spanish government, ended in the loss by Spain of all its continental American colonies. During these years the Spanish adherents whom the various revolutions forced out from South America and Mexico took refuge in Cuba, thus considerably augmenting the white population of the colonies. The concentration in Cuba of these Spanish loyalists had naturally a positive influence on its subsequent political development, and contributed to the success of the reaction which finally, in Cuba as well as in Spain, followed the Bourbon restoration after Napoleon's fall.

Coincident with the outbreak of the South American revolutions came the capture of Seville by the French in

1810, and the Junta, before retiring to Cadiz, convoked a Constituent Assembly to frame a new constitution for the Spanish monarchy. To this assembly the colonies were invited to send representatives, but the reduced proportion of the representation conceded to them caused general dissatisfaction and additional discord. Three Cuban deputies were sent to the assembly, which met on the island of Leon, at Cadiz, September 1810, and after long deliberations in the midst of the turbulence of war a new constitution was formulated in 1812. This constitution was framed on the French model of 1793, but it was the expression of only a part of the Spanish people, the liberal and radical elements which were temporarily in the ascendent. Lacking the support of the peasantry and bitterly opposed by the nobles and the priests, whose influence was curtailed by its provisions, the constitution of 1812, far from bringing order out of the political chaos of Spanish affairs, became only another factor in the prevailing disorganization.

In the discussions of the assembly which framed this constitution it was proposed by some of the Spanish leaders that slavery should be abolished in Cuba after a term of ten years, but the earnest remonstrances against the measure as being premature, made by the Cuban deputies and especially urged by Francisco Arango y Parreño, prevented the measure from being adopted. Rumors of the proposed abolition became circulated among the Cuban slave population, and when the defeat of the measure became known among them their disappointment found expression in a serious rising led by a free negro, José Aponto, which was, however, vigorously put down and its leaders executed.

The promulgation in Cuba of the constitution of 1812, which was made in Havana with great public ceremony in July of that year, marks a highly important epoch in the political history of the island. The subsequent events of that history have been traced in full detail by Señor Cabrera, particularly in his twelfth chapter (page 197 *seq.*), and need not here be further considered. A consideration of some of the more important developments preceding the insurrection of Yara (1878) will complete this cursory outline of Cuban history and carry us to a review of the Ten Years' War, which Cabrera, through the exigencies of his subject, has omitted.

Under the governorship of Someruelos, whose administration ended April 1812, the colony made important gains in population, partly, indeed, it has been noted, in consequence of the political changes that took place during his term. The census of 1810 figured a population of 600,000, a gain of about 328,000 over the census of 1791. The number had accordingly more than doubled in twenty years. Of the total, 274,000 were whites, 114,000 free blacks, and 212,000 were slaves. The proportions of the increase were 45½, 19, and 35½ per cent. respectively.

Someruelos was succeeded by Juan Ruiz de Apodaca; he inaugurated the new constitution in Cuba, under which the military executive was divested of civil power and the latter vested in three intendants responsible to a civil governor resident in Havana. The war of 1812 between the United States and Great Britain caused much friction between the American and Spanish governments, and Apodaca devoted himself to gathering a naval force in Cuba for

possible emergencies.   The British, who were preparing
for the southern campaign that ended at New Orleans in
January 1815, were availing themselves of their alliance
with Spain to utilize the ports of Pensacola and Mobile
for their preparations and as harbors for their fleets.
Tecumseh, who had been sent from Michigan to stir up the
southern Indians to take part in the war, had succeeded in
his errand, and at Pensacola the Indians were supplied with
arms and munitions.   The United States claimed Mobile as
belonging to its newly acquired territory of Louisiana, and
fearing lest that point, which was being held by a Spanish
garrison, might also become a base of supply for the Indians,
a force of Americans under General Wilkinson moved upon
it and captured the town and garrison in April 1813.   The
garrison was allowed to retire to Pensacola, and the incident
might well have led to further hostilities but for the disorganization of the Spanish government, the defeat of the
English at New Orleans, and the end of the war.

The Peninsular struggle was ended through the crushing
defeat of the French at Leipsic, October 1813; Napoleon
was compelled to release the Spanish King, and in March
1814, Ferdinand VII returned to Madrid and to his throne.
He was a typical Bourbon; in his four years of luxurious
captivity, while his country was being racked with convulsions, he had learned nothing but a more refined hypocrisy
and forgotten nothing but his promises to his people.   His
first act was to abrogate the Constitution; his next to dissolve
the Cortes, and his further efforts were given to restoring
the old absolutism in all its mediæval rigor.   The liberal
party was ruthlessly suppressed, its leaders imprisoned or

driven out of the country, and soon the new despotism was translated to Cuba. In July 1814, Apodaca received orders to reinaugurate the *ancien régime* in the colony, and although the formality of turning back the hand on the dial of time was duly and publicly performed, the momentum of liberal progress in the colony was not so easily arrested. The reaction was official and superficial; the old order of things could not possibly be completely restored, and many of the reforms effected under the constitution remained practically in force after its abrogation.

The administration of José Cienfuegos, who succeeded Apodaca in July 1816, was signalized by the agitation for the suppression of the Spanish slave trade in 1817, the concession to the colony of unrestricted foreign trade in 1818, and the cession of Florida to the United States in 1819.

The deportation of African negroes into slavery, which had been interdicted to their respective subjects by Denmark in 1792, by England and the United States in 1807, by Sweden in 1813, and by Holland and France in 1814, was still being carried on by Spain and Portugal when the Restoration was accomplished. England having been the main factor in saving Spain and Portugal from Napoleon's grasp, the English government utilized its sway in the Iberian peninsular to bring about the suppression of the Spanish and Portugese slave trade; to this end the negotiations, which had been going on since 1814, were concluded by a treaty at Madrid in 1817, by which the importation of negro slaves into the Spanish West Indies was made illegal after 1820. Spain received £400,000 from England in compensation for the loss of revenue from this trade and a few years later the English paid Portugal £300,000 for a like concession. This measure was violently opposed in Cuba, not so much by the people generally nor even by the planters, whose human chattels seemed likely to appreciate in value through it, but by the trading interests involved, and for many years after the interdiction of the traffic cargoes of African negroes continued to be smuggled into the colony.

To compensate Cuba for such loss of commerce as would result from the suppression of the slave trade, and as a measure of policy with regard to the proposed recovery of the revolted colonies on the continent, the Spanish government in 1818 opened the ports of Cuba to unrestricted foreign commerce. This concession was obtained largely through the persistent efforts of the eminent Cuban statesman, Francisco Arango, who had succeeded in gaining the confidence of Ferdinand VII and whose representations were strengthened by the influence of the English government. At the same time the former policy of restricting emigration to the island was reversed, and special inducements in the way of free passage and homestead possessions were offered to Spanish emigrants with a view to increasing the white population of the island. In general, the Bourbon Restoration, which in Spain manifested itself in a most violent reaction, was in the West Indies greatly tempered by foreign influences, and especially by the successful revolutions on the Continent.

The progress of the latter became a factor in the cession of Florida to the United States. The hold of Spain on that territory had always been but slight, and after the departure of the English in 1815 revolutionary refugees from Mexico

26

and Venezuela, together with a number of foreign adventurers, gained a foothold in the province. On the other
hand, the Florida Indians, under the protection of the
Spaniards, afforded an asylum to the fugitive slaves of the
Georgia and Carolina planters. The latter, in common with
all the slave-holding interests of the Union, were clamorous
for the occupation of the Spanish territory, and Spain, recognizing the futility of attempting to hold the province,
ceded it to the United States by treaty in February 1819,
in consideration of the American government settling with
its citizens their sundry claims for damages in Cuba and
other Spanish jurisdictions up to that date.

In August 1819, Juan Manuel Cajigal succeeded Cienfuegos as Captain-General of the island. The latter had
successfully exerted himself to further the general interests
of the colony, and had effectively utilized the naval forces,
organized by his predecessor and strengthened by himself,
in an active pursuit and repression of the corsairs who
preyed on the colonial commerce. These freebooters carried
on their depredations under commissions from the new South
American and Mexican republics, which Spain was still
fighting to subdue, and it was only after the opening of the
Cuban ports to foreign commerce that these semi-piratical
privateers were generally suppressed.

Cajigal was sent to Cuba commissioned to direct a renewal
of the struggle against the continental republics, and to that
end a considerable reinforcement of troops was gathered at
Cadiz for shipment to Cuba and thence to the continent.
The soldiers were ill-content with their mission, the people
were ill-content with the government, and the general dis-

content had given rise to secret societies, in which both elements of the population were combined. On January 1, 1820, the standard of revolt was raised among the troops by two of their officers, Riego and Quiroga, the constitution of 1812 was proclaimed, and the movement quickly spread over the country. The king and his ministers attempted to suppress the revolt, but their troops gave way before the insurgents, and in March the king accepted the constitution. The nobles and the priests were again set back, the liberals took the reigns of power, the Cortes assembled in July, but unfortunately the country was yet far from ready for self-government, and the liberals could not agree on a permanent constitution. The discord was fomented by the king and his party, the bigoted peasantry was incited to insurrection; but notwithstanding all this, by 1822 the liberal ministry, with Riego as president of the Cortes, was gradually making headway towards order.

The re-establishment in Cuba of the constitution of 1812 was not so unanimously effected as had been its first proclamation. When the news of the acceptance of the constitution by the king reached Havana, the new Captain-General, Cajigal, attempted to delay action, but was overborne by the garrison of the city, a part of which at once pronounced for the changed order of affairs. The citizens joined with these troops and proclaimed the constitution; another portion of the garrison held out for absolutism, but the conflict thus threatened was happily averted through the discretion of the General, who gave way to the popular impulse (April 16, 1820). The political prisoners in the Cabana fortress were liberated, the civil organization as it had stood under the former régime of the constitution was re-established throughout the colony, and deputies to the Cortes were elected by the various municipalities.

In March 1821 Nicolas de Mahy was sent out as successor to Cajigal. He was a man of advanced years and though of a liberal temperament was unprepared for the tumultuous conditions which now prevailed in Cuba, a result of the disturbances in Spain on the one hand and the successful revolutions in Spanish-America on the other. The liberal movement in Cuba was taking a form which led him to mistrust the consequences and he strove to restrain its progress. His efforts were, however, cut short by his death, July 1822, a year after his accession ; but his policy of restriction was continued with increasing rigor by his subordinate, Sebastian Kindelan, who retained the command until May 1823. Both Mahy and he strove to reunite the military and civil power in the hands of the Captain-General, in contravention of the liberal constitution, and aroused intense antagonism between the Spanish troops, which were under their immediate command, and the local militia which, in the main, supported the municipalities.

Secret societies, some of them under the form of Freemasonry, others like the Italian Carbonari, which were being made the instruments of social reorganization in Western Europe after the Napoleonic period, had rapidly taken root in Cuba. The two elements of the population, the zealous supporters of the liberal constitution, mostly native Cubans, on the one hand, and the adherents of absolutism and the church on the other, were gathering in opposing organizations. The latter joined with the commercial interests which

had been injuriously affected by the free opening of the
Cuban ports in a movement for the repeal of that measure,
and from this time dates the division of the people into two
bitterly contending parties, the Cubans and the Spaniards.
The former included in its ranks all the more radical as well
as the moderate liberal members of the community, while
the latter comprised the beneficiaries of the former monopolies and the conservative and reactionary elements which,
under the policy of the Governor Generals, naturally crys-
tallized around the officials of the government and their
coadjutors in the church.

While the Captain-Generals, who were governing Cuba
under the re-established Spanish constitution, were busy in
preventing the colony from following the example of the
continental provinces, the constitution itself was broken down
in Spain by a French army under behest of the Holy Alliance.   That pious compact had been made in Paris, after
Waterloo, (September 1815,) between Russia, Austria and
Prussia for the promotion of religion, the establishment of
peace and the maintenance of the existing dynasties, and its
main object was now found to be threatened by the success
of a popular movement in Spain.   So a Congress was called
together at Verona (October 1822) and there it was determined, in spite of the protest of England, to suppress the constitutional government in Spain by force of arms.   France
was now the servant of the northern autocrats and was
called upon to do their bidding.   Bourbon though he was,
Louis XVIII was a moderate ruler, himself reigning under
a constitution, but he had to take up the task of re-estab-
lishing absolutism in Spain.   The French armies were sent

on the errand (April 1823) and the work was effectively
done.   The Spanish constitution was abrogated, Ferdinand
VII ruled absolutely and soon Cuba felt the weight of the
renewed despotism.

While the French armies were on their way to Madrid to
put an end to the constitutional régime in Spain, Marshal
Francisco Dionisio Vives was on his way to Havana intent
on saving Cuba from all possible dangers of a liberal government.   He began his work May 1823 and soon succeeded
in reproducing in Cuba the discord that was then prevalent
in Spain.   Resistence to the new absolutism was attempted
by a secret association known as the ''Soles de Bolivar,'' but
the project of this rebellion was discovered and the plans of
its leaders, which had in view the establishment of a Cuban
republic, were frustrated.   The rising was to take place
simultaneously in several cities of the island on August
16, 1823, but on that day its principal leader, José Francisco Lemus, and a number of his lieutenants were arrested
and imprisoned.   Others of the conspirators escaped from
the island, while of those who were taken some were deported and others found means of escaping from prison and
reaching the main land.

The formal proclamation of the restored absolutism in
Cuba followed close upon the final crushing out of popular
resistance in Spain, October 1823.   The King now set about
to carry out the plan of the Holy Alliance, which was to
make an arsenal of Cuba whence to resubjugate the newly
established Spanish-American republics.   This project, however, was broken up by the intervention of the United States,
whose opposition to the undertaking was formulated by

President Monroe in his famous message to Congress, December 1823. This opposition was furthermore strengthened by England, which now proceeded to back up its protest against the work of the Holy Alliance in Spain by recognizing, in 1824, the independence of the Spanish-American republics as had already been done by the United States.

These general commotions had their natural reaction in Cuba. The antagonism between the Cuban people and the government became embittered to an extreme and the discord extended to the military. Various risings were attempted during 1824, but they were insufficiently organized and all of them failed to spread. They sufficed, however, to place the Spaniards on their guard; the troops intended for the renewal of the struggle on the Continent were kept in Cuba, especially in view of the possible outcome of a Congress of the American Republics which the South American states had now proposed. This Congress, which was projected on the basis of Monroe's declaration of 1823, was to meet at Panama in 1826 to confer regarding the mutual interests of the American Republics in view of a possible European aggression. The United States had naturally been invited to participate in the proposed conference and President John Quincy Adams in his first message (December 1825) informed Congress that the invitation had been accepted and that commissioners would be appointed. But the representatives of the slave states saw in this convocation a danger to the peculiar institution which they so zealously cherished. The Spanish-American republics had each of them abolished slavery on attaining independence and the Panama Congress was believed to be a stepping-stone to a like independence and abolition in Cuba. The debate in the Senate made it clear that between independent Cuba without slavery and Spanish Cuba with slavery the slave holding States would prefer the latter, while on the other hand the annexation of the island with slavery would arouse antagonism at the North. The nomination of the commissioners was finally confirmed, but with closely restricted functions, and the attitude of the United States resulted in depriving the Congress of all influence or result. On this account furthermore, a proposed invasion of Cuba by Mexico and Columbia, under the lead of Simon Bolivar, planned and organized by fugitive Cubans in those countries (1826) was also given up, and by tacit understanding generally, Cuba and Porto Rico were abandoned by the American continental governments to the undisputed possession of Spain. The latter took advantage of the situation to consolidate its power in the islands and with a view to repressing the liberal elements of the population, as well as to proceed more effectively against the opponents of the government, there was created, March 1825, a Permanent Military Executive Commission which was empowered to try political prisoners according to the articles of war, and finally, by royal decree of May 28 of the same year, the Captain-General of Cuba was clothed with all the powers and authority of martial law.*

The failure of repeated attempts at resistance to the dominant absolutism did not deter a number of zealous patriots from concerting further movements of a like character. The

---

* See author's appendix I, page 277.

exiles in Columbia and Mexico formed in 1827–29 a secret society called the "Black Eagle," which was organized to start another revolution on the island. The headquarters of the conspiracy were in Mexico and its ramifications extended through many of the Cuban towns and cities. But the anti-slavery agitation had now become an element of discord and complication in every movement of this kind, and the opposition of the slave-holding interests in Cuba and in the United States rendered this extensive conspiracy abortive from the start. The Spanish government had no difficulty in ferreting out the conspirators, and the military commissions made short work of their trials. Numbers of them were comdemned to death and others to deportation (1830–31), but Vives was far-sighted enough to refrain from consummating the martyrdom of these unsuccessful patriots and their sentences were mitigated in every instance.

After the fiasco of the Panama Congress Vives organized a military expedition against Mexico with a view to a possible overturn of its government and the eventful recovery of the country for the Spanish crown. She Spanish forces, which consisted of 3,500 men, landed at Tampico, August 1828, expecting to be augmented by accessions from the Mexicans. This, however, proved a fallacious hope. The Spanish forces were hemmed in by the Mexican troops and what was left of them surrendered their arms on condition of being permitted to return to Havana, where the remnant arrived in March 1829.

The collapse of this undertaking on the one hand and the suppression of the Black Eagle conspiracy on the other left Vives to turn his attention to a reorganization of the colo-

nial government and to its civil administration. He displayed unusual capacity in both directions and used his absolute authority with commendable discretion. His ability
and moderation had the effect of biding the fatal defects of
the system itself and the apparent success of his administration resulted in riveting the system on the Cuban people.

The delegation of absolute power to the Govenor of Cuba,
originally accorded to Vives under the extraordinary circumstances of his time, was continued to his successors
regardless of the fact that similar contingencies no longer
existed. The dictatorship of the Captain-General accordingly became the fundamental basis of the colonial government, and notwithstanding that the home government
thereafter underwent numerous vicissitudes of absolute and
constitutional government, those changes were no longer to
have their due effect on the island. From 1825 practically
to the present time the Captain-General of Cuba has continued to be a military dictator, enacting a despotism harsh-
er or milder according as it has been tempered by the fear
of consequences or by the character, capacity and temperament of the despot. Vives, the first of the line, used his
powers with marked discretion and with an inclination to
govern according to the common law. But many of his successors were far less wise and temperate and they stretched
their powers to the extreme, frequently causing by their irresponsible misrule the very ebullitions of popular unrest
which they were commissioned to repress.

Under Mariano Ricafort, who succeeded Vives in May
1832, a definite beginning was made of the policy of utilizing
the Cuban colonial administration as a feeding-ground for

Spanish politicians. The absolutism which Vives had sedulously retained in his own hands was permitted by Ricafort to percolate to the minor officials of the government, and the venality and corruption which are inseperable from such a system now became grossly manifest.

In 1833 the wretched reign of Ferdinand VII was terminated by his death; his infant daughter, Isabella, was proclaimed queen under the regency of her mother, Cristina; the king's brothers, Carlos and Francisco, who had protested against the abolition of the Salic law by the "Pragmatic Saction" of 1829, took up arms against the regency and began the Carlist wars. The queen regent turned to the Spanish liberals for help; they demanded and obtained a constitutional government under a decree known as the *Estatuo Real*, which revived the Cortes and put an end to absolutism in Spain. But this did not avail for Cuba; there absolutism was continued; the constitution was indeed proclaimed and elections to the Cortes were ordered, but the absolute power of the Captain-General was confirmed and the military commissions were reinforced.

In June 1834 Ricafort was succeeded by General Miguel Tacon, a survivor of the colonial wars in South America. The application in Cuba of a liberal régime, such as was now dominant in Spain, might have closed the gap between the Cubans and the Spaniards, but instead of bridging the cleft by a policy of conciliation, Tacon widened it into a chasm by the most arbitrary exercise of his unlimited powers and a ruthless proscription of all who opposed his will.

In 1836 the Spanish liberals succeeded in extorting from the Queen Regent the re-establishment of the constitution of

1812, but so far from extending its benefits to Cuba the Spanish Cortes in 1837 resolved, notwithstanding the protest of the Cuban deputies, to no longer accord parliamentary representation to the colonies. Tacon used his absolute authority to reverse the action of his subordinate, General Lorenzo, who had proclaimed the renewed constitution in Santiago de Cuba, and to deport him to Spain, whence he had but a few months before been commissioned to his post by the liberal ministry. The latter, notwithstanding the absurd inconsistency of their position, confirmed Tacon's arbitrary proceeding and the Cortes ignored the far-reaching import of the occasion. Thus the hopes of the Cubans of sharing in the political amelioration of the Peninsula were ruthlessly dashed to the ground.

Tacon was left for four years to enact his unbridled despotism in the island and only after his excesses became generally notorious did Spanish public opinion force his recall in 1838. He had extended the exercise of dictatorial authority into the remotest branches of the colonial administration; under his assiduous cultivation absolutism flowered into the fullest bloom and the field of Cuban politics was sown broadcast with the seed that subsequently ripened into repeated harvests of disaster.

The political developments following the time of Tacon have been fully treated by Señor Cabrera; the lamentable effects of the autocratic system and the baneful influences that have grown around it form the theme of his work in general, and the present appendix may accordingly be completed by a cursory review of the extraneous influences which have affected Cuba in the meantime and a brief sum-

mary of the several revolutionary uprisings which have pre-
ceeded the struggle now in progress.

The "period of conspiracies" that began in Cuba with
Tacon's administration reflected more or less definitely similar conditions in the home country. Political disorganization was rife both in Spain and in its colonies, and in both
the modern liberalizing tendency was attempted to be restrained by reactionary expedients. In Cuba these conditions were accentuated by the rapid progress of its material
development and largely influenced by the proximity of the
United States and the increasing intercourse of the colony
with the republic.

The tentative considerations regarding the annexation of
Cuba to the United States, which had been incident to the
discussion of the proposed Congress of Panama in 1825,
gradually became defined as the pro-slavery party in the
United States became more aggressive. In the political
agitation which led to the annexation of Texas (1845), the
proposition to acquire Cuba by purchase or otherwise was
widely discussed in the United States, and during the Mexican war in 1846 a popular movement was started in the
Southern States to the same end. In 1848, after the conclusion of the war with Mexico and in view of the possible
complications resulting from the wide-spread revolutionary
movements in Europe during that year, President Polk proposed negotiations to the Spanish government through the
American minister in Madrid for the acquisition of Cuba
by purchase. The growth of the anti-slavery sentiment in
the United States put an end to that project, apart from
the refusal of Spain to enter into the proposed negotiations·

Meanwhile the Cuban liberals had turned to the United States whence to organize a revolutionary movement in the island. In May 1847 Narciso Lopez and others, who had formed a conspiracy for a rising in central Cuba, were detected and they fled to the United States. In the following year an association of Cuban fugitives was formed in New York under the leadership of Lopez, and in 1849 a military expedition was organized which was prevented from sailing by the United States government. This, however, was renewed the following year (1850) and, mustering his forces outside the United States, Lopez succeeded in landing (May 19) at Cardenas with 600 men. After taking the town Lopez found that the preparations for the extension of the uprising had been frustrated and he re-embarked for the purpose of landing at another point on the island. On leaving the harbor his vessel grounded, and was floated only after throwing overboard the major portion of the military equipment. At this juncture a Spanish war vessel was sighted and only the greater speed of the lighter steamer saved the expedition from capture. Lopez and his men landed at Key West and there disbanded.

The risings concerted in the interior in connection with this expedition took place and continued sporadically into the following year. To strengthen this movement and to extend the insurrection Lopez undertook another expedition, and proceeding from New Orleans he landed near Bahia Honda, some 30 miles west of Havana, August 12, 1851, with about 450 men. But he was at once opposed by a large force of his enemies; his lieutenant, Col. Crittenden of Kentucky, with 150 men, was cut off from the main body of the invaders and after a sanguinary fight was compelled to surrender. Lopez's remaining force was surrounded and cut off from their supplies and from all aid by the islanders; they held their ground until a tropical storm swept away their remaining ammunition, when they scattered into the woods and all of them were either killed or captured. Lopez and some 50 others were taken to Havana; the latter were shot and Lopez was garroted.

The disastrous failure of this expedition did not prevent another being undertaken two years later. This was concerted in Cuba in conjunction with a movement headed by General Quitman, of Mississippi; extensive enlistments of men, collections of money and equipment of vessels were undertaken, but the United States government interfered and the leaders of the movement in Cuba were discovered, imprisoned and several of them eventually shot.

In 1854 certain regulations decreed by Captain-General Pezuela for the manumission of slaves of advanced years caused a general agitation in the Southern States of the Union as being a menace to the institution of slavery. The strain resulting from this political antagonism was increased by the detention in Havana of the steamer "Black Warrior" under a charge of violating the Cuban custom regulations, by the search of several American vessels on the high seas by Spanish cruisers and by the arrest of American citizens in Cuba on various formal charges. These occurrences threatened for a time to lead to a war between the United States and Spain, the contention going so far as to elicit the so-called "Ostend Manifesto" from the American ministers to England, France and

Spain.   Therein it was declared that the possession of Cuba by a foreign power was a menace to the peace of the United States, and it was proposed that Spain be offered the alternative of taking 200 million dollars for her sovereignty over the island or having it taken from her by force.   The removal of Pezuela and the reappointment of José Concha to the post of Captain-General of Cuba served to allay the excitement and to maintain peace.   When James Buchanan, who as American minister to England had signed the Ostend Manifesto in 1854, was elected President of the United States in 1856, the project loomed into renewed importance, but was lost sight of in the political agitations that culminated in the Civil War.

These various events had their inevitable echoes in Cuba; the colonists naturally hung upon them their hopes of a release from the oppressive régime of the home country, and each successive disappointment was marked by another impotent struggle to throw off their yoke.   Concha was succeeded in 1857 by Francisco Lersundi, but the latter's rule was so immoderate that he was again replaced by Concha in 1858.

For a time Cuba became quiescent, but with repeated additions to the burden of taxation imposed by the Spanish government the discontent of the people constantly increased.   The colonial commerce with the home country was subjected to a domestic tariff regulation, and that with foreign countries, especially with the United States, was greatly restricted by almost prohibitory duties.   The material development of the island was hampered by taxing its agricultural products a tithe of their value, by the imposition of burdensome restrictions and taxes on the transfer of landed property, and still further by a systematic restraint of white immigration. The effects of these ill-advised measures were minimized during the period of the American civil war by the moderating sway of two able and liberal minded governors, Francisco Serrano and Domingo Dulce, who ruled successively from 1860 to 1865. The tact and discretion of the former did much to allay the irritation caused in the Northern States by the recognition of belligerency which was accorded by Spain to the Southern forces over a month before the first battle of the war. This irritation was increased by the allied expedition against Mexico in 1861, in which Spain took part with England and France, but the withdrawal of the two former powers in 1862 concentrated American opposition against Napoleon III, who continued the plans of conquest and imperialism which ended with the death of Maximilian in 1867.

The close of the American Civil War, the complete abolition of slavery in the United States and the re-establishment of the power of the Republic strengthened the liberal sentiment in Cuba and gave rise to new movements for its expression. The contention of the Cubans was so far effective that one of the liberal Spanish cabinets that alternated with their opponents in carrying on the government of Isabella II accepted a project for a Commission of Inquiry to consider and devise reforms in the Cuban administration. The project was duly formulated under royal decree, November 25, 1865, but had already been

27

emasculated by its opponents. Spanish statesmen seemed
incapable of recognizing the needs of the occasion, and the
influences controlling the government were strong enough
to render the entire movement abortive from its start. The
Commissioners were elected under regulations calculated
to give the opponents of reform a majority of their number, and the Commission was furthermore packed by the
appointment of half its membership by the government
itself. Instead of a general plan of colonial reform being
considered, the Commission restricted itself to the proposal
of some comparatively unimportant regulations of slave
labor, and declined to entertain the propositions of the
Cuban delegates. The latter demanded a constitutional
system in place of the autocracy of the Captain-General,
freedom of the press, the right of petition, cessation of the
exclusion of Cubans from public office, unrestricted industrial liberty, abolition of restrictions on the transfer of
landed property, the right of assembly and of association,
representation in the Cortes and local self-government.
But the home-government refused to consider any of
these proposals, least of all the restriction of the absolute
power of the Captain-General and colonial representation in
the Cortes.

Not even the moderate demands of the Cuban deputies
for a gradual abolition of slavery were more than considered
and temporized with. Nothing indeed was done, except to
permit Lersundi, who had meanwhile succeeded Dulce, to
tighten the screws on the Reformists in Cuba, and finally,
in June 1868, to impose an additional 10 per cent. on the
direct taxes of the island.

The disappointment that had resulted from the failure of the Commission of Inquiry had sufficed to start anew a secret movement towards insurrection, and this, promoted by Lersundi's purblind policy and by the increase of the direct taxes, had spread extensively, especially in the central and southern provinces. There the movement was fast ripening to fruition, when, in September 1868, the news of the revolution in Spain and the expulsion of Isabella II was received. But the change at home brought none on the island. Lersundi continued in his place and the Cubans were left hopeless of relief. In the eastern provinces of the island plans for an insurrection were matured by Francisco V. Aguilera, Manuel A. Aguilera and Francisco M. Osorio at Bayamo, Carlos M. Céspedes in Manzanillo, Belisario Alvarez in Holguin, Vicente Garcia at Las Tunas, Donato Marmol in Jiguani and Manuel Fernandez in Santiago.

These leaders concerted a simultaneous rising for October 14, but the plan being discovered, the insurrection was started October 10 on the plantation of Yara by Céspedes at the head of 140 men. A Cuban republic was proclaimed and Cespedes was quickly supported by his confederates from the surrounding districts. In a few weeks the leaders had about them over 10,000 men, resolute indeed, but inadequately armed and equipped. A Declaration of Independence was promulgated and a convention called to frame a constitution. The troops which the government sent against the rebels were repulsed, and in the winter 1868–69 the struggle centered along the railway between Nuevitas and Puerto Principe, the Cubans remaining masters of the country. Under the lead of Manuel Quesada, a guerilla

campaign followed, which resulted in the capture by the
Cubans of one after another of the important towns of the
interior. In this campaign the Spanish forces, stated by
the Spanish colonial minister Becerra as including 40,000
regulars and 70,000 volunteers, were checked and beaten
off by a Cuban force of not over 26,000 men, and only the
Spanish fleet prevented the insurgents from capturing and
holding the seaports. The Spanish ministry now hastened
to supersede Lersundi with the former Captain-General
Dulce, upon whose good standing with the Cuban people
they counted to bring about a cessation of hostilities. Dulce
issued a proclamation in 1869, offering general amnesty and
promising consideration of grievances on the restoration of
order, but the Cuban leaders were now bent on independence and refused to entertain the proposals. On February
26 the republican assembly of Las Villas declared for the
immediate abolition of slavery and this was followed by a
rising in that district. Here the Cubans were led by a
Polander, named Roloff, who succeeded in clearing the
province of the Spanish forces and holding them in check.

On April 10 a Constituent Assembly of Cuban representatives, mainly from the Eastern and Middle provinces, met
at Guaimaro in Central Cuba; this convention framed a
constitution and elected Céspedes as President and Manuel
Quesada as Military Commander. At this time the successive encounters between the Cubans and the Spaniards
invariably resulted in the worsting of the latter.

In May two expeditions from the United States, one under Rafael Quesada and the other under Col. Thomas
Jordan, formerly of the Confederate army, landed supplies

of arms and ammunition. But these continued to be entirely inadequate for the occasion. The Spanish navy, reinforced by some 30 light draft vessels purchased in the United States and converted into gunboats, patrolled the coast behind the barrier of coral islands, and made the landing of "filibustering" expeditions hazardous in the extreme. The summer of 1870 was utilized by both combatants to reorganize their forces, but the yellow fever made great havoc in the ranks of the new troops sent out from Spain. In the fall the general movements were renewed, and the insurgents continued to gain ground. Jordan, now acting as a general officer, succeeded, January 1, 1870, in inflicting a severe defeat on a strong Spanish column near Guaimaro, and the spring months passed with a continuation of the Cuban guerilla tactics and the gradual strengthening of their hold on the eastern half of the island.

Meanwhile the western provinces were being terrorized by the Spanish volunteers. These organizations were composed for the most part of the Spanish adherents among the Cuban population, their ranks filled out by enlistments in Spain for that purpose, and consisted generally of a battalion, more or less considerable in numbers, under command of a Colonel, the latter frequently of the wealthy slave trading aristocracy. Some 20,000 of these troops were concentrated in Havana and about twice as many more in the other towns of the island, all of them acting as "home guards." The Havana volunteers became dissatisfied with the conduct of the war in the field and manifested their discontent by repeated acts of insubordination. They made and unmade their commanding officers according to their whim, and practically made themselves masters in the cities, and especially in Havana. There, in May 1870, they fired repeated volleys into the entrance of a theatre, killing and wounding a large number of the people who were leaving it after a performance which, it had been rumored, was given for the benefit of the insurgent cause. Next, while on a street parade, they gutted a café and killed a number of people, and finally, June 2, they took it upon themselves to arrest Captain-General Dulce as being too lenient in his warfare and expedited him away to Spain.

The Spanish government meekly submitted to this unparalleled outrage, and permitted it to be followed by a similar deposition of General Lopez-Pinto, who commanded at Matanzas, and by untold excesses of malignant cruelty throughout the country. The successor of Dulce, Cabellero de Rodas, was a man after their own heart, and he ordered the shooting of prisoners of war without stint. He called for and obtained extensive reinforcements, assured the Spanish cabinet that the insurrection was coming to an end, but was invariably worsted in his movements in the field and six months after his appointment he urged his resignation. He was succeeded, December 1870, by the Count of Balmaseda. But the latter likewise failed to turn back the tide of the insurrection. The Cubans carried on their guerilla warfare, generally with the purpose of capturing war material, and they were largely successful.

The more the war extended in the field, the more gruesome became the work of the home guards in the cities. In November 1871, 43 boy students in the University of Havana were arrested under dictation of the volunteers and tried by court-martial on the charge of having scratched the glass plate on a cemetery vault containing the remains of a volunteer. Through the vigorous defense made by a Spanish officer before the Court, the boys were acquitted, but the volunteers demanded of Balmeseda a new trial before a court composed of their own officers. The Captain-General complied so far as to order a new trial before a court composed of 9 volunteer and 5 regular army captains and a major, with a colonel as judge-advocate. The court condemned eight of the students to death; thirty-one were sentenced to imprisonment and four were acquitted. The next day 15,000 volunteers paraded to the scene of the execution and the condemned boys were shot to death. This terrible outrage was execrated throughout the civilized world, but the Madrid government supinely cowered under the domination of the Havana volunteers.

The campaign of 1871 had helped the insurgents to large stores of ammunition, and that of 1872 was practically a repetition of its predecessor. No engagements of moment were fought; the Cubans held the interior of the eastern half of the island and made excursions towards the coast to receive expeditions that succeeded in landing from time to time and incursions into the western provinces beyond their portion of the territory. The tactics of the insurgents, which consisted mainly in harrassing their enemies, eluding the larger forces and beating the lesser ones, resulted in causing the Spanish troops to suffer terrible losses, not so much by the bullet or the machete, as through exposure and disease. The war grew more and more rancorous, and each side charged the other with the most unheard of cruelties. The details of these have never been fully told, but that the bitterness of the struggle was directly due to the so-called volunteers has been abundantly brought to light.

Not all the cruelties directed or permitted by Balmeseda sufficed to atone in the eyes of his janissaries for his want of success in the field. In September 1872 he was compelled to provisionally relinquish his command to Ceballos, and afterwards in 1873, definitely to General Pieltan. The latter took the command with the view to bringing the war to a close by negotiation, quite despairing of quelling the rebellion by force of arms, and in the summer of 1873 he made repeated but unsuccessful efforts to induce the Cuban leaders to accept peace without independence.

The campaign of 1873 was the climax of the war. In the spring the commands of Agramonte in Camagüey, Calixto Garcia in the eastern provinces and Maximo Gomez in Central Cuba, gained important successes. Through the summer the insurgents not only held their ground but succeeded in extending their sway, notwithstanding the heavy odds against which they were contending.

On October 31st a Spanish gunboat overhauled and captured off the island of Jamaica a steamer named the Virginius, which claimed American registry. The Spaniards regarded the vessel as a "filibuster" and their suspicions were apparently justified by the number and character of the crew. The Virginius was taken to Santiago de Cuba where the crew was landed November 1st. On the 4th, three Cubans and one American were shot by order of the local commander; on the 7th, thirty-seven more men, including

Captain Fry, were likewise executed, and on the 8th, twelve more shared the same fate. The 102 survivors were in a way to being similarly disposed of when the proceedings were interrupted by Commander Lorrain, of the British sloop-of-war Niobe, and the bloody work was stopped. The summary condemnation of the vessel and its crew caused an explosion of wrath in the United States, and for a time the incident seemed certain to lead to war, but this was averted by diplomatic action which resulted in the Virginius and the remainder of her crew being surrendered at Bahia Honda, December 16, to the United States steamship Juniata. The latter started to tow her charge to New York, but while off Frying Pan Shoals, December 26, the Virginius sprung aleak and foundered.

Pending the negotiations which ended in the surrender of the Virginius, Pieltan was succeeded by General Jovellar. A man of force and discretion was required to hold down the mutinous spirit of the volunteers, and Jovellar proved himself the ablest and most competent of the men who had thus far had the direction of the war. This change of commanders on the Spanish side was soon followed by a change of leaders on the part of the Cubans. The Cuban Congress that met at Bijagual, December 1873, brought to the surface a discord that had for some time been brewing among the leaders. A majority of these combined against Céspedes and succeeded in deposing him from the Presidency. They could not, however, agree on a successor and the presiding officer of the Congress, Salvador Cisneros, Marquis of Santa Lucia, became acting President of the Republic. Céspedes retired to San Lorenzo, in Eastern

Cuba, and there, a few months later, he was suprised by a detachment of Spaniards ; he succeeded in escaping mortally wounded, and died March 22, 1874. Céspedes was a man of exceptional ability, unselfishly devoted to the cause he had at heart and possessed in a large measure the confidence of his countrymen. His deposition caused wide-spread dissension in the Cuban ranks and for a time brought the insurrection practically to a standstill. The discord that was manifesting itself among the Cubans was, however, equally rife among their enemies. The campaign in the field was indecisive and Jovellar proceeded to take energetic measures to compass the rebellion. He declared the entire island in a state of seige, conscripted every able-bodied man into the militia and drafted 10 per cent. of the latter for field service. But he thereby encountered the angry protests of the citizens, and raised a storm of opposition among the home guards. Utterly disgusted with his task, Jovellar asked to be relieved and was succeeded, August 1874, by one of his predecessors, General Concha. The latter brought much needed reinforcements and started in for a vigorous campaign. In September, at Yarayaba, he defeated a large band of the insurgents, but his own forces were so crippled in that engagement that he was unable to utilize his victory and the campaign remained practically fruitless.

The war had now lasted six years and the insurrection seemed as far from being quelled as at any time during its progress. It was clearly demonstrated that the insurgents could not, in the absence of a navy, drive the Spaniards from the island, but on the other hand the latter were seemingly unable to do more than hold their enemies at arm's length. The cost in life and treasure had been enormous, but the end was not yet.

The Carlist war in Spain during 1874–75 diminished the number of recruits that could be spared for Cuba, and in the spring of 1875 the decimated Spanish forces were compelled to fall back before the advance of the insurgents. The western provinces of the island were now for the first time seriously threatened with invasion, but the weakened position of the Spaniards was relieved through fatal dissensions among the Cuban leaders. Had they at this juncture been able to act in unison the outcome of the war might have been decided at this time, but the year passed without other result than to leave both the Spaniards and the Cubans perceptibly weakened by the strife.

This condition continued to prevail until the autumn of 1876. The Carlist uprising in Spain had meanwhile been subdued and now General Martinez de Campos was sent over to end the war in Cuba. Campos had won distinction through his having ended the Spanish republic and restored the Bourbon dynasty by his proclamation of Alfonso XII (December 1874), and also in the campaigns against the Carlists in the Basque provinces of the Peninsula and he had had experience of Cuban warfare in the earlier years of the insurrection. He came with 25,000 veterans of the Carlist wars to renew the onset, and started at once to deploy his forces for a decisive campaign. But the winter of 1876–77 passed without apparent result; the insurgents, though now in diminished numbers, succeeded with their guerilla tactics in constantly eluding the larger forces and in defeating the minor ones. The spring of the year was passing, the hot season was at hand, the Spanish troops were again faltering under the inflictions of the climate, and Campos sought to end the war by negotiations. In 1877 Jovellar again took the post of Captain-General, Campos devoting himself exclusively to the military operations in the field; these were now mainly determined for strategic ends, the fighting having largely ceased through general exhaustion. Campos steadfastly kept in view an ending of all hostilities through some measure of compromise, and early in 1878 an armistice was agreed upon. The insurgent headquarters were then in Camagüey, and there the Cuban leaders met to consider overtures of peace from General Campos. That meeting appointed a Commission of nine members, which, with General Vicente Garcia, who had recently succeeded Cisneros as President, met General Campos and a number of his officers at the camp of St. Augustin, near Zanjon, in the district of Camagüey. The conference resulted in the compact known as the peace of Zanjon, February 10, 1878. This was virtually a compromise by which the Cubans gave up their contention for independence and the Spaniards conceded, in form at least, most of the demands made by the Cubans before the Commission of Inquiry in 1867, and which had meanwhile been conceded to Porto Rico.*

After the pacification of the island Campos returned to Madrid and laid before the cabinet of Canovas de Castillo his plans for effectuating by legislative action the reforms in the government of Cuba which had been accepted by the insurgents as a condition of their laying down their arms.

---

* See pages 218, 219.

But Canovas was unwilling to lay these proposals before the Cortes with his recommendation, and accordingly resigned the ministry March 3, 1879. Campos took his place, organized a new cabinet, dissolved the Cortes and appealed to the country, obtaining a majority of the new legislature. His proposals, however, were only partially supported by his colleagues in the cabinet, and this caused a split which resulted in Campos resigning his task. Canovas again took the reins of government (December 9, 1879) and the promises made at Zanjon were practically ignored.

The war, like all wars, had cost enormously in life and treasure, but as in all wars, the untold misery and ruin of the ten years' struggle was greater than that which was recorded. On the side of the Spaniards, as registered in the war office at Madrid, over 8,000 officers and more than 200,000 privates died in battle or in the hospitals in the course of the fearful ordeal, while on the part of the Cubans the loss of life has been computed to have been fully 50,000 men. The cost in money aggregated over 300 million dollars expended by Spain, and not less than as much more lost to Cuba by destruction. The worst feature of the contest was its intense bitterness; no quarter was given on either side, and prisoners were taken only to be slaughtered, the Spanish government refusing throughout to agree to an exchange.

During several stages of the conflict the question of recognizing the belligerency of the insurgents engaged the attention of the United States Congress. President Grant, as indicated in his messages of December 1869 and 1875, repeatedly offered the good offices of our government for the re-establishment of peace on the island, and January 1876 he proposed to the European powers a joint intervention in the conflict. No action was, however, finally taken by our government, the problems growing out of the reconstruction of the Southern States crowding foreign affairs from the public mind. Several of the South American republics recognized the Cubans as belligerents and Peru recognized their independence.

One of the results of the insurrection was the hastening of the final abolition of slavery. In 1870, under the so-called Moret law, freedom was decreed to every child born of a slave mother after July 4th of that year, and furthermore to such slaves as had helped or would help the Spanish troops against the insurgents. Under the same law freedom was given to every slave who was 60 years old on the above date, and to all who reached that age thereafter. In January 1880, as a partial concession of the proposals by Campos as noted above, a further measure was enacted by the Cortes providing for the more rapid extinction of slavery in Cuba, by virtue of which the institution of negro slavery became finally extinct in 1887.

The current of Cuban affairs following the peace of Zanjon, and the failure of the Spanish government to fulfil the spirit of that compact, have been graphically narrated by our author in the body of this work. The efforts of the cultured and patriotic Cubans to maintain their country as an integral part of the Spanish monarchy under a form of home-rule government have been eloquently set forth by Señor Cabrera and the anachronism of the conditions that existed when he wrote has been forcibly indicated in his work.

It was the continuance of these conditions that brought on the armed conflict which began February 24, 1895, and which has now grown to greater proportions than any which has preceded it. ·It is manifest to every student of modern history that this conflict can have no final ending but in Autonomy or Independence, and that Cuban independence can have no future; it means simply annexation to the American Union.

L. E. L.

PHILADELPHIA, March 1896.

INDEX.

28